THE MONSTER ON HOLD

SECRETS OF THE NINE
THE MONSTER ON HOLD

PHILIP JOSÉ FARMER
AND
WIN SCOTT ECKERT

Meteor House

THE MONSTER ON HOLD
by Philip José Farmer and Win Scott Eckert

Meteor House
ISBN 978-1-945427-24-4
First Trade Paperback Edition

DEDICATION

For Christopher Paul Carey
The Gold-Flecked Eyes Have It . . .

And for Philip José Farmer

ACKNOWLEDGMENTS

With gratitude to Atom Mudman Bezecny, Christopher Paul Carey, Michael Croteau, Keith Howell, Doug Klauba, Rick Lai, Chuck Loridans, Sean Levin, Frank Schildiner, John Small, T. L. Owen, Art Sippo, Paul Spiteri, Michael Toman, Mark Wheatley, Chuck Welch, and of course Bette Farmer and Philip José Farmer.

A Note From Philip José Farmer and Win Scott Eckert

As with *The Mad Goblin*, the prior volume of journals recounting Doc Caliban's battle against the Nine, the editors have insisted upon publishing this work as a novel rather than as a memoir under Caliban's own byline. But it is the work of James Caliban, M.D. He has once again documented his story in the third person singular, but it is nonetheless autobiographical.

Doc Caliban still insists that he does not like to get personal.

And yet in the telling of this tale he has willingly stripped away several layers of bronze armor.

TABLE OF CONTENTS

A tentacle slid around his throat, ropelike, soft and yet strong. He endeavored to kick out, sought to use his arms. "I'm caught, helpless," he thought. "My God, what are these things? Can this really be Hell?"

Up from Earth's Center
Lester Dent (writing as "Kenneth Robeson")

A thick, black cloud swirled before my eyes, and my mind told me that within this cloud, unseen as yet, but about to spring out upon my appalled senses, lurked all that was vaguely horrible, all that was monstrous and inconceivably wicked in the universe. Vague shapes swirled and swam amid the dark cloud-bank, each a menace and a warning of something coming, the advent of some unspeakable dweller upon the threshold, whose very shadow would blast my soul.

"The Adventure of the Devil's Foot" by Dr. John H. Watson,
    M.D., London, Spring 1897
His Last Bow, Sir Arthur Conan Doyle, ed.

There was a Door to which I found no Key:
There was a Veil past which I could not see:
Some little Talk awhile of ME and THEE
There seemed—and then no more of THEE and ME.

Rubáiyát of Omar Khayyám, translated by Edward FitzGerald

What seems Up may be Down.

Escape from Loki
Philip José Farmer

So Many Unanswered Questions

Chuck Welch

As a long-time fan of both, I have the honor of writing a foreword to a book by my friend Win Scott Eckert based on work originally proposed by Philip José Farmer.

Farmer started his Secrets of the Nine series with *A Feast Unknown* and continued it with *The Mad Goblin* and *Lord of the Trees*. In 1983, he spoke about his ideas for the fourth book in the series, *The Monster on Hold*. Though he never had the chance to write that novel, he left behind notes and concepts he intended to explore. A decade after Farmer's passing, Meteor House knew there is no one better suited to bring alive *The Monster on Hold* than Win Scott Eckert. In addition to his own fiction, Win's *The Evil in Pemberley House* had superbly completed another work Farmer left unfinished.

There are many other reasons Win is uniquely suited to working with Farmer. For years he has been immersed in the characters and themes that inspired and entertained pulp and new pulp readers and authors. His non-fiction work has explored the past and helped map out the future of some of our most important pulp characters. But he hasn't stuck to non-fiction. Win is an accomplished novelist in his own right.

Win's novels are interesting, exciting, perfectly paced, entertaining, and, most importantly, satisfying. Not because they answer every question posed, but because they do not. They treat the reader as a partner. One who can use their own imagination. That's especially important for this novel. There were so many unanswered questions in the Secrets of the Nine series . . . and the works that inspired it.

Oh, to be sure, Win answers a lot of those questions in this book. Not just from Farmer's works, but also a few from the final Doc Savage pulp novel, *Up from Earth's Center*. That wasn't easy as the man of bronze you discovered as a teen isn't the star of this novel.

A love and respect for Doc Savage is something I share with Win. That's one reason why I was honored when Win and Meteor House graciously asked me to contribute this small foreword. I have decades of experience in the Savage world. First as a reader, but in addition to that, for over twenty-five years now I've maintained a forum, edited fanzines, and discussed Doc Savage daily with other fans.

First, I'd like to speak to those Doc Savage fans who have made the wonderful choice to purchase this book. If you're at FarmerCon reading this foreword trying to decide if you want to buy this book . . . I'll give you the gist: you'll love it. Hand over your money, find a comfy chair, and turn to page one.

For those still wondering, one question that comes up often by one Doc Savage newcomer or another is "Were *A Feast Unknown* and *The Mad Goblin* Doc Savage novels?" My answer is always the same: they were not. They were pastiches. They, like *Lord of the Trees*, were Farmer's take on Doc Savage and Tarzan novels. They used imagery and concepts better suited to the adults of the 1960s and 70s that were his audience. Farmer also loved and respected Doc Savage. His research was actually responsible for sparking my interest in the character. But sadly, Farmer wrote only one Doc Savage novel, *Escape from Loki*.

That said, the "Doc" of this series, Doc Caliban, and our Doc Savage share so much DNA. They reflect each other as they reflect their readers. We're so much more mature now than when we discovered those Bantam reprints. The Doc in the novel you're holding will speak to you today and yet remind you of the character you discovered as a teen. And as we coexist in time with our teen selves, these Docs serve as aspects of each other. Win has expertly, and entertainingly, woven them together.

Lastly, I'm here to tell that still unsure Doc Savage fan, you will enjoy this book even if you haven't read the first three novels in the series. Win has taken Farmer's ideas and fleshed out a novel that is accessible, and enjoyable, to the reader just stepping into this world. Not only that, but the Doc in this novel will also help you see deeper into the pulp Doc. Given the opportunity, Win would write one hell of a Doc Savage novel.

That's a hope for "someday" though. Right now, in your hands is one hell of a Doc Caliban novel. I'm glad Win wrote it and I bet you'll enjoy it.

Chuck Welch
Sherbrooke, Québec
Fall 2021

What Has Gone Before

(From Philip José Farmer's introduction to the
1983 World Fantasy Convention Program)

The Monster on Hold (prior working titles are *The Unspeakable Threshold, Some Unspeakable Dweller, The Leaser of Two Evils,* and *Down to Earth's Centre*), is a Doc Caliban novel and the latest in the series beginning with *A Feast Unknown* and continued in the *Lord of the Trees* and *The Mad Goblin. Feast* started in east Africa and is told in first person by John Cloamby, Viscount Grandrith (pronounced Grunith), an Englishman raised by a subhuman species (a variant of *Australopithecus*) in west Africa. Grandrith, while still a youth, became one of the high-echelon agents of the Council of Nine. The Nine are the secret rulers of earth, most of whom were born circa 30,000–20,000 B.C. though they looked as if their age is only a hundred.

The Nine have considerably slowed their aging with a longevity "elixir" which they share with certain agents who have earned it. Grandrith is one of the very few so privileged. Though eighty-one in 1969, he looks and feels like a twenty-five-year-old man.

In *A Feast Unknown,* Grandrith is suffering unforeseen side effects of the elixir. These make it impossible for him to get an erection unless, and to avoid one if, violence is involved. He finds this out when he is attacked by Jomo Kenyatta's forces. Then he discovers that an American agent for the Nine is out to kill him. Doc Caliban believes (wrongly) that Grandrith has killed Caliban's cousin, Patricia Wilde, also an agent of the Nine. Caliban is suffering from the same side effects of the elixir.

Just as the two have what should be a final confrontation, they are summoned to a meeting of the Nine in a subterranean area in east Africa. The oldest man of the Council, XauXaz, has died, and Caliban and Grandrith are the top two candidates to replace him. One must kill the other to get a seat on the Council. In the end of *A Feast Unknown*, after many adventures, the two almost kill each other, but they then unite to fight against the Nine.

In *Lord of the Trees*, Grandrith manages to kill Mubaniga, the proto-Bantu member of the Nine. In *The Mad Goblin*, Jiinfan, a proto-Mongolian member, and Iwaldi, an ancient Germanic member, are killed during a battle at Stonehenge. Four of the Nine are dead, leaving as head of the Council Anana, the withered hag born about thirty thousand years ago in the area which would become Sumeria. Other living members are Tilatoc (an ancient Amerindian), Ing (the patronymic leader of the early English tribes when they were living in Denmark), Yeshua (a Hebrew born circa 3 B.C.), and Shaumbim (a proto-Mongolian).

The three novels above took place in the late 1960s.

PART I

SOME UNSPEAKABLE DWELLER

1977

The things flapped their leathery wings all around Doc Caliban's head, pointed beaks packed with cutting teeth snapping at his exposed, bronzed cheeks, talons clawing and ripping the upper sleeves of his parka.

One cabled hand shot out and caught one of the things by the neck. He squeezed and wrung the thing back and forth, finally snapping its scaly neck as one of its companions repeatedly pecked its sharp beak at his reinforced protective eyewear, seeking the moist, gold-flecked eyeflesh behind it.

Caliban swept the thing away, kicked at another that clawed at the thighs of his thick, winter-weight trousers, and attempted to pull the flame-throwing gun from the clasped holster at his hip while the creatures whirled and flapped around his face, constantly harrying him.

"Doc, Doc!" came a call far behind him in the ice-encrusted tunnel.

"Stay back, brothers!" Caliban, the flame gun loosed, squeezed the trigger and a jet of hot, blue fire shot out at the nearest predator, vaporizing it. Another clamped its hellish jaws about Caliban's lower left arm, tearing his jacket and puncturing bronze flesh. The ice-packed ground was stained crimson as blood pumped out of the gaping wound.

Doc's right fist clamped about the thing's neck and tore it from his left arm, shredding more of his flesh and muscle in the process. He flung the creature, hard, against the ice-walled tunnel and its skull made a sickening crunch at the impact.

The three remaining flew about Caliban, more warily now that their numbers were halved.

"Doc, what is it?" The deep, grunting voice of Pauncho van Veelar echoed weirdly through the ice tunnel.

"Some kind of pterosaurs," Caliban replied. His voice was calm and even, evoking the gentle yet powerful strains of a fine cello. "Wingspan about three feet, talons, jaws lined with needlelike teeth, off-white scaly hides. Three left, they're holding off further attack at the moment."

"Pterosaurs!" The voice was that of Trish Wilde, Doc's cousin. "So now the Nine are dabbling in reviving long-extinct species?"

The pterosaurs flew upward and disappeared into the Stygian heights of the frozen tunnel.

"Not only that," Caliban said, "but also clearly experimenting with bio-engineering. These are acclimated to a sub-Arctic climate. Extraordinary."

"Doc," Barney Banks called, "can we come forward?"

"Slowly, and with your flamethrowers drawn and primed. There may be more of them."

"We weren't born yesterday, Doc." This was another's feminine voice, not Trish.

Their spiked-soled boots echoed up the icy passageway, and this resulted in an odd rustling in the darkness in front of and above Caliban.

He called out sharply to his crew behind him, "Stop!" The group's forward motion halted, and the rustling ceased.

Caliban commanded, "Forward," and again in response to his crew's footfalls, there came the ominous rustling above.

Barney, Trish, Pauncho, and Barbara Villiers, the latest addition to Caliban's crew, crept up behind him. All were dressed in cold weather gear: hooded parkas, thick gloves, and heavy snow pants.

Pauncho was six feet tall with unnaturally long arms and equally unnaturally short legs. Small eyes squinted out from under a slanting forehead and massive brow ridge and hung like tiny obsidian dots above the thrusting jaw and receding chin. He was of that particular type of sociable-looking homely that brought women out of the woodwork—to the constant dismay of his classically handsome buddy, Barney.

Barney was equally tall, trim but not skinny, and perfectly proportioned. His nose was straight and symmetrical, as were his mouth, dark eyes, and eyebrows. His black hair was flawlessly swept back.

Trish Wilde was a knockout, bronze of skin tone and strongly resembling her cousin. She was curvy in all the right places, six feet tall, and, with wavy bronze hair perhaps a shade darker than that of Doc Caliban, was the perfect embodiment of the ultimate in feminine pulchritude.

Barbara Villiers, as Pauncho had once indiscreetly remarked, gave Trish a run for her money in the beauty and brains department. Her hair was deep red, her skin was fresh and clear, and her violet eyes were big and wide. Her figure, like Trish's, was splendid.

Caliban, a bronze Hercules, raised a forefinger to his lips and motioned upward with his eyes. These were gray-green and curiously speckled with bright yellow or gold, and were startling to those who met him for the first time.

The five slowly turned their gaze away from the six-foot-seven inch giant and toward the ceiling, directing their flashlights upward.

The circular tunnel opened in front of them into an ice cavern perhaps twenty-five feet high.

Perched, and hanging upside-down from the frost encrusted roof of the cave as if they were giant whitish bats, were hundreds of the pterosaurs, eyes glinting balefully in the beams of battery-driven light thrown by the party's torches.

"Lights out," Doc breathed. Each member of his group complied, and they crouched in darkness and silence.

Then, Barney whispered, "Doc, I saw a gap, I think the continuation of this tunnel, at the far end of the hollow. Did you see any other exits?"

"No, Barney, you're correct," Caliban said. "The only way out is through the cavern, past and under the pterosaurs. Surely they won't let us pass unhindered."

Caliban partially unzipped his parka and took from a vest pocket underneath three small glass blisters, which he in turn tucked into three metal spheres that evoked smooth grenades. He stepped forward away from the others and tossed each sphere, one at a time, at the roof of the cavern. As each metal ball left Doc's grasp, they heard a mild whirring which faded as each sphere neared the ceiling, followed by three *chunks* of each embedding in the frost above.

"Hold your breath. One minute."

Pauncho, Barney, Trish, and Barbara did as Doc instructed.

After the passage of more than sixty seconds, the party did not hear the hoped-for *thunking* of unconscious pterosaur bodies hitting the ground. The bronze-skinned man flicked on his torch.

Reptilian eyes gazed back at them unblinkingly.

"Knockout gas didn't work. Any other ideas?" Barbara asked.

"Only one," Caliban said. "Make a run for it full bore for the opposite end, flamethrower guns on full and aimed at the roof." He paused. "Anyone who considers this too foolhardy of a move is welcome to go back and regroup at camp, no questions asked."

"No way, Doc—!" Pauncho boomed and was promptly kicked in the shin by Barney.

"Keep it down, you excuse for a baboon!"

Abashed, Pauncho grimaced, gray gristle eyes disappearing under the massive ridge of bone above them, and didn't even think to hurl an insult back at his "dumb-dumb-buddy," Barney.

"Geez," Pauncho whispered, "I'm sorry, Doc. But no way are we leaving you, we're in it for the long haul." Then instinct reasserted itself and he jerked a hairy thumb at Barney. "Except this guy, he may want to go back, and make sure he don't get any hair out of place, haw, haw!"

"Get that thumb—which by the way is only one evolutionary step away from being non-opposable—out of my face you hairy—"

"Cut it," Doc said. He was accustomed to their perpetual bickering and insult-hurling—just as he had been to that of their fathers—but now was not the time. Almost ten years ago, he had brought the sons of two of his most trusted aides, Porky Rivers and Jocko Simmons, into the fold. The sons, Banks and van Veelar, had their stepfathers' surnames but their biological fathers' thirst for excitement, and had eagerly taken up their "Uncle Doc's" offer of adventure and intrigue—despite the risks of going up against the Nine. That Doc might finally succeed in concocting an immortality elixir that was more effective than the Nine's—and that Doc would share it with them—was mere icing on the cake.

Pauncho van Veelar and Barney Banks were born to adventure with Doc Caliban, elixir or no elixir.

"What these two schoolboys are trying to say, Doc," Trish said, "is that we're all in it together. No going back."

Barbara Villiers added, "I'm in, too."

Doc nodded. "I should have known better than to waste time asking."

No more words were exchanged, and scant seconds later the five were running full tilt across the ice, the metal spikes in the soles of their boots providing some traction.

The pterosaurs swooped and were engulfed in five streams of blue flame. Some of the leathery wings caught fire and the creatures plunged to the ground, bones cracking on impact. Others were vaporized upon direct contact with the blazing lines of fire.

Nonetheless, too many teeth and claws tore at exposed faces and ripped at cold weather gear—gear that might prove to be precious if they succeeded and escaped from Tilatoc's Arctic fortress.

"Aim for the roof!" Doc yelled. By example, he turned his flame-thrower gun away from a swarm of pterosaurs and guided the spouting flame directly at the ceiling of the ice cave. His four teammates followed suit, all the while sprinting for the opposite end.

Halfway across the ice-encrusted cavern, cracks appeared in the ceiling, from which melted water began to pour in disturbing quantities.

Caliban realized they would not attain their goal. "Stop!"

As the others skidded to a halt beside Doc, he motioned them to crouch in a circle. Chunks of ice and snow slushed down upon them in a sea of white at an exponentially increasing rate.

Caliban tossed a compact sphere of cloth in the middle of the circle they formed. It popped open when it hit the ground and formed a hollow sphere with a round opening on one side. The sphere's fabric was of Caliban's invention, forming an extraordinarily strong bubble in which to take shelter against burial under the falling tons of snow and ice.

The five piled in without hesitation and Doc closed the opening with a watertight seal.

The half-slush piled on the bubble tent, buffeting it and the five within. They felt as if they were bobbing on the sea in a violent storm, or were in a hollow ball being pounded back and forth by giant pinball flippers. They were knocked against each other's bodies and limbs, and Doc's blood, from the untreated forearm wound, got over everyone.

Pterosaur talons sliced open one side of the bubble tent and, as the sphere collapsed and was pulled this direction and that, Barbara Villiers was sucked out of it.

"Barbara!" Pauncho van Veelar scrambled through the tangle of bodies and went through the slit after her.

"Damn it, you big ape!" Barney yelled as he scrambled after his friend.

Doc shot out an arm to grab Banks by the ankle and haul him back inside the protection of the sphere, but missed and Barney was gone.

The melted slush-ice roared down upon them in a final wave of whiteness, burying Caliban and Trish in the collapsed bubble—and also burying the flying creatures, which had been Caliban's intent.

As they struggled to move and breathe under the crushing heaviness of slush, the last warmth being sucked from their aching muscles, Doc and the others heard a gruesome and mindless cry emanating in unison from the masses of buried and dying pterosaurs—*"Tekeli-li! Tekeli-li! Tekeli-li! Tekeli-li!"*

Caliban dreamt. He felt he was ensnared in some unspeakable liminal space, neither here, nor there, nor anywhere.

A veil of white, forward, behind. Above. Below.

He pierced the veil and was seated in a cockpit, at the controls, clad in cold weather gear and boots of another time and place, a radio headset clasped to one ear.

Caliban's late comrade, Williams, he of the Peruvian digs, Antarctic expeditions, and big words—*"Brobdingnagian linguistic components"*—sat in the copilot's seat.

Then, Caliban was Professor Williams himself, seeing through the expedition leader's eyes, desperately fleeing an impossible and ancient—and *alien*—city in the Antarctic wastes. Copiloting the fragile aircraft through jutting peaks, anxiously trying to wipe from his mind the nightmarish revelation of the grotesque intelligences who had ruled the planet fifty million years before the ancestors of humanity had crawled from the muck. The ancient whiteish bloblike things encircled by tentacles and topped with star-shaped heads that appeared, from what Caliban and his fellow explorers had gleaned from the history told by gargantuan underground frescos and engravings that wrapped around the bases of gleaming circular towers, to be able to mimic the shapes and patterns of other objects and creatures. The heartpounding fear they felt as they fled the awakened thing that pursued them through misshapen corridors and over arching bridgeways, the pulsating pustulelike mass that glowed faintly with some inner greenish-whiteish luminescence, and was composed, if that was the correct word for something that by its very nature refused to hold some definite shape, of rapidly forming and melting smaller pustules encasing yellow-rimmed bloodshot eyeballs oozing some ochre substance. The dread they felt as they realized that the thing that pursued, and its brethren, had rebelled against the bloblike star-headed masters of the ancient city and driven them to other far reaches or to extinction.

Several surviving star-headed blobs, inadvertently revived from millennia-long suspended animation, had slaughtered their fellow expedition members who had preceded them to the incomprehensible city—and then themselves had been slaughtered by the thing, now shrieking "Tekeli-li! Tekeli-li!" that was newly awakened from its eons-long frost-shrouded sleep and relentlessly pursued Caliban and his fellow explorers.

Caliban and Williams, steering the airplane through the icy vapors toward the vast whiteness of the Antarctic horizon, had trembled with relief at their escape—only to be hauled back down to the depths of despair by the mad, gibbering shrieks of Williams' graduate assistant in the cabin behind them.

"Tekeli-li! Tekeli-li!"

And then Caliban was Williams' grandfather, Jeorling, aboard the trading brig *Halbrane*, who, along with Captain Len Guy and Dirk Peters, sought the answers to the mystery of the disappearance of Arthur Gordon Pym and the crew of the *Grampus* some eleven years before, in 1828.

The dream shifted and fluttered once more, and now Caliban was Pym himself on the far southern island of Taalal, stranded along with the crew of the schooner *Jane Guy*, and he heard once again the cry of strange white birds, echoed in terror by the island's natives at the merest sight of any white object.

"Tekeli-li! Tekeli-li!"

Doc Caliban awoke. He struggled for oxygen, caught it in a pocket of air. He dribbled, spit, and powered through the ice and snow in the direction he felt must be up, opposite the falling saliva. He was frighteningly aware of the disorientation common in snow burials, and that what he thought was up might well be down. He could be powering his way straight toward Death itself.

He realized he was not pressing against snow and ice, not directly anyway, but against the supertough fabric of the deflated bubble tent. He managed, against rising pressure of the piled snow, to maneuver one cabled hand to his hip, felt for the sheath, and drew a massive hunting knife gifted to him by his half-brother.

"Your inventions are ingenious," Grandrith had said, "but some time you may find your gadgets are too clever by half. You might be in a situation calling for brute force, of which you have plenty, aided by the tools of our ancestors."

The knife was steel, not flint, but Caliban had understood and accepted the sentiment, and the knife.

Doc, working blindly, slashed at the tent's fabric and swept away the sliced ribbons, going slowly and feeling his way to ensure he did not cut Trish. He felt around, located hard objects—Trish's ankles—grabbed them, and pulled them along with him. He struggled under the weight of the snow, and the ice biting at his ears, nose, and cheeks.

Caliban pierced the surface and gasped, filling his strong lungs with cold air. Disoriented, he shook his head, flinging water and ice crystals from his dark bronze hair. He tugged at Trish's ankles and legs, pulling her toward the surface. Her mouth reached the air, coughs and gasps indicating life. He rapidly rubbed her arms, legs, hands, and cheeks to warm them and encourage the flow of blood.

Then Caliban collapsed on his back and the cavern spun as he struggled to regain his perspective. The dream visions he had experienced were real, more real than any dream he had ever had. He felt that he had been back in that time and place, some forty-eight years ago, experiencing those events again, just as if they had occurred a few moments ago. After which, he felt that he had literally been present in the others' bodies and minds, seeing through their eyes.

He focused on the here and now. He was not Arthur Gordon Pym, or archaeologist Jonathan Williams, or Benedict Jeorling, mineralogical and geological researcher. He was James Caliban, M.D. Righter of wrongs. Nemesis of evildoers—except when the Nine had had him perform certain horrific deeds in their service, in exchange for their elixir of immortality.

But those schizophrenic days were past.

Caliban, and his half-brother, Lord Grandrith, had turned against the Nine, and shortly thereafter Caliban had reproduced and perfected—with the help of fellow Nine candidate-cum-turncoat Barbara Villiers—an elixir that topped that of the Nine.

The Nine's elixir was a concoction administered to "candidates" annually at ceremonies held in the caverns of the Nine, deep in the heart of central Africa. The ceremonies involved the quite agonizing removal of certain extremely sensitive body parts, which then rapidly regrew due to the elixir's effects. Caliban never knew if the painful removals were truly necessary for the elixir to function, or if they were only part of the Nine exacting control over their subordinates. He also was not sure if the elixir was actually the liquid itself, or if that was misdirection. It could have been something else entirely.

Regardless, the elixir drastically slowed the aging process. For example, the Nine's leader, the ancient crone Anana, was perhaps thirty thousand years old, but appeared to be somewhat over the age of one hundred. Caliban and Grandrith's grandfather, the late XauXaz, was possibly twenty- or twenty-five thousand years old at the time of his death nine years ago (the old man had presumably died of old age), and, like Anana, had looked about a hundred.

The elixir also regenerated lost organs and limbs, but did not restore one to a younger biological age; thus, it was best that one began taking it when relatively young.

By contrast, the rejuvenation elixir developed by the renegade member of the Nine, Iwaldi, stopped aging and actually restored lost youth. To be fair, Iwaldi had developed his elixir based on research stolen from Caliban, who had long been conducting his own experiments into independently creating the Nine's elixir—or an elixir superior to that of the Nine. After Iwaldi's death in a three-way battle against the Nine, and against Grandrith and Caliban's forces, at Stonehenge, Iwaldi's companion, the Duchess of Cleveland, Countess Castlemaine—Barbara Villiers—had thrown in with Caliban's crew and had provided a few key pieces of information that enabled Doc to recreate Iwaldi's more desirable elixir.

And Countess Cleveland had also provided to Caliban and Grandrith the maps of the caves of the Nine, including all the traps she knew about, as well as some addresses of the Nine around the world—locations where members of the Nine were hiding in plain sight, as well as bolt holes and stronghold headquarters, such as the one, here, that they were presently attempting to penetrate.

Here?

Again, Caliban focused, trying to compartmentalize the dream-visions he had had, in order to minimize their effect on him in the here and now. Why was he here?

Tilatoc. The Nine.

They were at Tilatoc's supposedly impregnable fortress hideout in northern Canada. Tilatoc, the wrinkled and ancient member of the Nine, was of Native American ancestry. When had he been born? Ten thousand years ago? Fifteen thousand? No one knew, perhaps not even Tilatoc himself.

The Nine's forces had attacked Doc's crime sanatorium in upstate New York and were using the scientific secrets they had learned there against Caliban and his crew. In the 1930s, Caliban had discovered that a certain brain operation performed on criminals would eliminate their compulsive anti-social attitudes and actions. The Nine, interested in his scientific discoveries, had allowed Doc to carry out his battle against crime as he wished, including the surgeries.

Now, using Caliban's own science against him, the Nine were turning out super criminals, soldiers who had been "graduates" of Doc's crime sanatorium. Their brain operations had been undone, the microcircuits removed and the deep hypnosis reversed, and thus they had been "liberated" by the Nine.

In fact, the Nine had been sending out so many "un-graduates" from the sanatorium that Doc was now playing defense. He could not focus on his offensive battle plans against the Nine. These liberated un-graduates had severe and dangerous criminal tendencies. They also, thanks to Doc performing these surgeries on them, and wiping clean their former lives, now had deep and personal reasons for wanting Caliban dead. The great rewards that would undoubtedly be bestowed by the Nine were a bonus.

Doc wondered if Lestski, the Vienna-based surgeon with exceptional skills, and the only other person who understood the critical steps and secrets of Doc's brain surgery and hypnosis techniques, had perhaps given the Nine the information necessary to reverse the operations and produce super criminals.

Had the Nine somehow gotten to Lestski?

Then there was the matter of the sanatorium itself, and the graduates all over the world who had served as his eyes and ears. When Caliban had first rebelled, the Nine's forces had attacked and taken over his headquarters in the Empire State Building and his estate near Lake George, in upstate New York. Doc had anticipated this and moved out as much important and sensitive material as possible. This did not prevent the Nine from gaining a good deal of his research, as his revolt was sudden. If he had had time to plan, he could have secreted away even more of his research and inventions.

Caliban had, however, had time to evacuate the sanatorium graduates to a location he was sure the Nine didn't know about. It would not have been safe to use any prior headquarters or research laboratories of which the Nine were aware, including his Canadian hideaway up near the Arctic Circle (perhaps coincidentally somewhat near Tilatoc's fortress). But he was sure the Nine were not aware of the extensive subterranean fortress he had constructed deep under Lake George itself. While the Nine's forces had busied themselves ransacking the estate, offices, laboratories, armory, and living quarters of the graduates who helped run the aboveground facility, Doc and his crew and graduates had hunkered underground and waited them out. After the Nine's soldiers had finally departed, the decimated and deserted estate was the perfect cover for the bustling headquarters under the lake, from which Doc continued to prosecute his revolt against the secret masters of the world.

A short time ago, the Nine had apparently discovered the extensive facility below the lake and attacked it, reversing the operations on the remaining sanatorium graduates who had been stationed there helping Doc run his operations.

The Nine had also, somehow, gotten to Caliban's graduate agents all over the world.

So many unanswered questions.

Caliban had decided to take the battle to the source.

Coming by the information that Tilatoc was the member of the Nine who was primarily behind the un-graduates, after capturing one of his own former agents, Sargent, and using a truth serum, Doc and his crew outlined a plan to attack Tilatoc's sub-Arctic headquarters and cut off the campaign at its head. Barbara Villiers had helpfully supplied the location of Tilatoc's fortress in the frozen wastes of northern Canada, as well as several mousetraps to be avoided.

Villiers hadn't mentioned the pterosaurs.

Doc patted Trish on the cheek, gently, then a bit more forcefully. His cousin's eyelids fluttered, and she sat up, sucking in deep breaths. All around them, crushed and broken pterosaur wings and beaks and talons poked up through the snowpack. Snow and ice still fell from the huge cavern's ceiling, as if they were outside in a swirling blizzard.

"We need to get out of this cave before there's another collapse and we're buried for good."

Caliban pulled Trish to her feet, and they trudged in the direction they had been going before the winged reptiles had attacked—or at least, in the disorienting sea of white, what he judged to be in that direction.

"What about the others?" Trish asked.

"We'll hope for the best."

Trish frowned. "Someone once told me hope is not a strategy."

Doc kept marching. "Do you have any recommendations?" he asked dryly.

"You're the one always planning three steps ahead."

He shook his head. "Not this time. Pauncho and Barney and Barbara are innovative, with a will to survive. We don't have the time or equipment to locate them in this whiteout."

Long minutes passed during which the two silently tramped across the snow and icepack, occasionally slipping and catching themselves, miniature crystalized fogbanks puffing from their mouths with each exhaled breath.

Finally, the two came upon the far end of the cavern, a wall of ice barely visible through the churning whiteness. The opening Barney had previously identified was no longer visible.

"Stay here," Doc ordered.

"Damn it," Trish said, but Caliban was already edging away from her, walking sideways to her right, feeling the uneven surface of the ice wall.

He came back, slipped past Trish, and continued on to her left, bending low and stretching high as he felt his way, in case an egress might not be at the height of his arms and hands.

Caliban stopped, pressed against the icy wall in a way that described a circle, and went back for Trish. Then both returned to the spot he had found.

Doc withdrew the steel knife and hacked at the ice, eventually revealing a circular doorway that resembled nothing so much as a space station airlock in a science-fiction film. He sheathed the knife, doffed a glove, and punched at the keypad's glowing numbers and letters.

The round door rolled aside, revealing a long, straight circular walkway of white plastic, or metal painted white, brightly lit by light panels affixed to the corridor's sides at regular intervals, to the left and right at three and nine o'clock.

Caliban and Trish entered, and the door rolled shut behind them.

"How did you know the code?"

"I wasn't certain. An educated guess," the bronze man replied. No trace of emotion crossed his regular and handsome features. His voice was steady, deep and mellifluous. "Someone wants us to come this way."

Trish pulled back the hood of her parka, and shook bronzed hair just a shade darker than Doc's. "Then let's go."

35

The two walked, and walked. The corridor seemed to stretch on for miles, unchanging. The tunnel was perfect and smooth, with no joints or seams indicating connected panels, broken only by the repetitive light fixtures. It was as if a giant, mile-long worm had bored a pencil-straight tube directly into pure white rock. The entryway quickly receded from their vision, invisible in the distance they had covered when they looked backward.

They plowed on, step by step, left foot, right foot, left foot, right foot. Left foot, right foot, left foot, right foot.

The effect of the tunnel was hypnotic, disorienting. No one before had ever succeeded in hypnotizing Doc, a fact of which he was privately quite proud. He valued self-control, both mental and physical, above all else.

Now he was in danger of losing this, and was inwardly shaken, though he effectively concealed it from his cousin.

Doc noticed Trish's steps were sluggish, her eyelids heavy. She lumbered forward, each footstep indicative of massive effort expended, as if she were struggling to raise and lower great weights attached to her feet.

She stumbled, and he caught her in his massive arms. The tunnel seemed to rotate like a giant kaleidoscope. Now they were walking on the light panels. And now the ceiling, with the floor above them. Round and round.

Doc felt wobbly, as if he had spun in place for several minutes and could no longer maintain his balance. Trish's knees buckled and she collapsed to the floor in a heap.

Caliban crumpled next to her as the kaleidoscope continued to spin.

Doc and Trish were in the caverns of the Nine, naked.

This was all wrong and both knew it. They had never been together in the caves of the Nine during the annual elixir ceremonies. Too, they had been in northern Canada, at the edge of the Arctic Circle, and the Nine's caves were hidden somewhere in central Africa.

Doc looked at Trish, her magnificent, dark bronzed skin glowing in the torchlight emanating from the center of the cave, and raised a forefinger to his lips.

The two stood at the top of the slope in a circular grotto, the subterranean cavity in which the annual ceremonies were held, where the Nine's age-delaying elixir was dispensed to the candidates. At the center of the circle, below them, was a pool of blackish water encircling a conical island constructed of rough beams of oak. This was topped by a ring-shaped table about which were stationed nine elaborately carved thrones of oak and ash, all of which bore engravings of various creatures both real and mythical—or were the "mythical" beings once real in a very different time and place?

Nine huge torches positioned behind and to the side of each throne were lit, and it was these that cast orange firelight upon Doc and Trish's bronzed hides, and upon the nine crystalline stalactites which depended from the shadows in the cavern ceiling above the chairs of the Nine.

Through a trapdoor, set in the middle of the oaken platform upon which sat the ringlike table, came a man more massively built than Caliban. The hulk of a man carried a staff that looked like a swizzle stick in his massive paw. The staff was nine feet long, topped with an ankh, the ancient Egyptian symbol of life, and had carved upon it three feet from the top a *hannunvaakuna*, a square with loops at each corner, used by the ancients as a symbol or charm against evil.

Caliban took in all these details in a split second, for the man himself was dressed in the blue toga that denoted his status as the current Speaker of the Nine, the majordomo charged, for a certain time period, with organizing the Nine's activities, and with communicating and enforcing their will.

But that was not what surprised Caliban, a man who was rarely caught off guard.

It was the man wearing the Speaker's robes.

"Krotonides!" Caliban mouthed the name.

Trish, her exceptionally fine hearing almost matching Doc's, heard her cousin breathe the name, but even if she hadn't, she too recognized the mountain of a man facing them.

Krotonides. One of Caliban's greatest successes. Was he now one of Tilatoc's un-graduates, returned to service as one of the Nine's most valued candidates?

After the epic battle at Stonehenge eight years ago, Caliban had captured the injured and unconscious Krotonides. Doc had thought his days of performing rehabilitation—the brain operations involving the implantation of a microcircuit, wiping of memories, and retraining via deep hypnosis—were over, after he had had to conduct the operation twice on his faithful graduate, Sargent.

But once Doc had captured Krotonides, he found he could not resist the temptation of attempting to convert a candidate of the Nine into an ally. He had succeeded and the Greek had been a faithful and trusted agent for almost eight years, helping run operations at Caliban's subterranean headquarters, and coordinating the secret actions of a worldwide network of agents and fellow insurgents against the Nine.

Now, here, was Krotonides, standing to one side of the Nine's chairs, almost naked save the thin material of the toga, six foot nine and a mass of muscle, with no neck, gray beard, and a bullet-shaped, shaven head. Krotonides, the ultimate un-graduate, a trusted ally and friend of Caliban for eight years, and now with Caliban's brain operation undone, the ultimate enemy out for revenge—or so Caliban presumed, for Krotonides had had no love at all for Caliban even before the battle at Stonehenge.

As if in response to Doc's thoughts, the Speaker motioned him and Trish to step forward. Krotonides glared at them both from beneath bushy eyebrows. The huge scar that cut diagonally across his bulbous nose, where Doc had almost severed it at Stonehenge, flared red in the torchlight.

As Doc and Trish approached the dark waters circling the island containing the table and thrones of the Nine, Doc reminded himself that this couldn't be happening. Could it? Had Caliban and Trish been drugged at Tilatoc's fortress, captured and flown to Africa, and only awakened once they arrived? It was possible, but didn't seem likely.

Doc had an almost infallible internal clock, and this told him that little time had passed since the disorienting trek through the seemingly endless kaleidoscopic tunnel. Too, Doc's and Lord Grandrith's intelligence sources, and others who had joined the revolt, such as former candidate Langston Dumont, had informed them that the Nine had suspended choosing new candidates for the time being. The immortals had been avoiding the African caverns because Barbara Villiers had given Caliban, and thus Grandrith, the maps of the caves of the Nine, including all the traps. This had halted the annual meetings for the elixir ceremonies, and had also postponed replacement of deceased Council members with new candidates.

If they were not in central Africa, in the caverns of the Nine, then what was this? An elaborate recreation? Or an illusion, a vision of some kind?

Had their bodies crossed beyond a terrible border into a realm in which time was immaterial, therefore rendering Caliban's internal clock useless? Or was something casting illusions directly into their minds?

Caliban recalled that Grandrith's mother, Alexandra Applethwaite, was also subject to visions and premonitions. She had reportedly been able to sense the location of Grandrith and Caliban's father, James Cloamby, Sr.

If Caliban and Trish were currently under the influence of a vision, perhaps inflicted upon them by some sophisticated mechanism, or perhaps even some transcendent entity, he wondered if this also could have been responsible for Alexandra's reputed abilities.

Caliban's speculations were interrupted as, one following the other, the members of the Nine silently emerged from the trapdoor through which Krotonides had surfaced moments ago.

The ancient beings moved to their thrones, the last, as always, being the ancient crone Anana, reputedly the oldest of the Nine—even before four of their kind had died or been killed over the last nine years—and certainly the most influential.

Five of the Nine were here. This, at least, reflected reality as Caliban knew it. Perhaps it was not a vision or an illusion. Or, the illusion-maker was very clever, or was drawing all the information from his mind.

The five surviving Council members were dressed in hooded monks' robes, with the hoods hanging about the backs of the necks and shoulders. They each wore elaborate headpieces: Anana, the head of a wild sow, symbolizing ferocity and courage; Tilatoc, that of a jaguar, so prominent in Native American mythology; Yeshua, that of a ram, representing the cycle of birth, leadership, death and rebirth; Ing, that of a bear, expressing the warrior's strength; and Shaumbim, the ancient proto-Mongolian, that of a wolf's head, for ancient Mongolians had believed they sprang from the wolf.

These beings, despite the recent deaths of four of their number—XauXaz, Jiizfan, Mubaniga, and Iwaldi—were impressive and intimidating. Most had lived since the Stone Age, with greater strength and endurance than humans of the twentieth century. Even the younger Council members, such as two-thousand-year-old Yeshua, were likely the descendants of other Nine members many times over, and thus also inheritors of immense physical strength and health.

The five took their seats and locked eyes with Doc Caliban and Trish Wilde. All had the skin of wrinkled parchment, save youngish-looking Yeshua who appeared to be about the age of fifty. Not much was known of Shaumbim, other than he had likely been the originator of the myths of Yama, the god of death, and of King Yan, ruler of Diyu, the "Ten Kings of Hell"—and that fellow renegade Dupont had confided to Caliban and Grandrith that Shaumbim was his real father.

Tilatoc had perhaps been the real man behind the Aztec god Tlāloc, also called Chaak by the Mayans, responsible for rain and fertility, but also, when displeased, lightning, storms, and drought. Tilatoc, with long, white hair, had the appearance of a North American Indian; but he also had slight Mongolian features.

Anana was the most terrifying, the inspiration for goddesses of love, manipulation, war, and above all else, survival. If it were true that those who took the Nine's elixir aged at a rate of one biological year for every one hundred years that passed, then she could still have, astoundingly, a biological age of as much as three hundred to five hundred years.

She was small, shriveled, wrinkled. Her dark blue eyes shone brightly and were the only sign of life in what otherwise appeared to be a desiccated husk. She was uncannily still, yet paradoxically radiated limitless power and energy. To have this effect, Caliban thought, at this age, Anana must have been a fearsome force of nature when she was young.

Caliban remembered that Grandrith had speculated that Anana might not even be human.

"Caliban. Approach." The old woman's voice was like crumpled metal in a junkyard compacter.

The bronzed man went forward, his cousin trailing his steps, until both stood at the edge of the water and looked up at the Nine.

"You," she said, "have a different elixir, Iwaldi's elixir. One that restores lost youth."

Caliban nodded. There was no point in disputing what was already known, though he kept to himself his own role in the development of the rejuvenation brew.

"Rejoin us," the crone said. "Convince Grandrith to rejoin us. You, your cousin, Grandrith, and his wife will fill the four vacant Council seats. Give us the new elixir, and what has transpired between us over the past decade will be disregarded."

Caliban appeared to consider it. "A clean slate?"

The old woman smiled horribly, showing cracked and blackened teeth. "What is a decade among immortals?"

Anana raised a withered arm, pointed a crooked finger at him. "You have no idea, youngling. Your arrogance. The nine of us have forgotten more battles, more wars, than your infant's mind can conceive. Do not fool yourself that you are our equal. Once you have lived ten thousand years, then, *then*, you will have forgotten all this. You will have transmogrified. You will have become someone else.

"And after another ten thousand years pass, you will, again, be someone else. And so on."

"The new elixir," Caliban said. "The annual doses, the yearly ceremonies, will not be necessary."

"The ceremonies," Anana stated, "will continue nonetheless."

"I see," Caliban said. And he did.

"I must add," the bronze man said, "that Iwaldi failed to eliminate certain side effects when he developed his formula."

The beldame spread her tree branch arms expansively in a gesture to continue.

"Your elixir caused an unhealthy relationship between violence and sexual satisfaction."

"No. It only revealed, enhanced, what was already there."

Caliban acceded the point. "Iwaldi's elixir can have adverse effects that can make the battle you engineered between Grandrith and me look like a kindergarten playground dustup."

"*Good.*" Anana's mouth gaped even wider in what passed for a smile, and even Caliban, the model of self-control, struggled to conceal his revulsion.

"Then we are agreed," the old woman said. "You will join the fold of the Nine once more, end your revolt. And then convince Grandrith to do so as well."

"That may be difficult," Caliban said. "He will not join us without his wife, and she has been missing for several years."

Anana waved away the objection. "That situation is easily dealt with."

Caliban rubbed his chin with one cabled hand, appeared to consider the offer. Perhaps, he thought to himself, the Nine could be destroyed from within. But if they rejoined, they would be constantly watched. Their chances remained better on the outside.

He turned to his cousin.

"No?"

"Definitely not," Trish responded.

He turned his head back to the Nine. Or rather, he thought to himself, the five.

"I'm afraid we must decline."

Anana's withered body remained stone still, as if she has been frozen in place by Medusa's glare. But her face contorted in a grimace of evil.

"Then we shall extract the information directly from your mind and concoct it ourselves."

Doc shook his head. "I doubt it."

Krotonides spoke up. "He's put himself under post-hypnotic control. I've seen him do this. I doubt he'll ever break under torture—nor under threats of torture and death directed at his cousin or his other aides and agents. He'll never reveal the formula for the elixir."

Doc remained silent and motionless.

"However"—and here, Krotonides smiled cruelly—"I suspect Caliban did not subject himself to post-hypnotic commands regarding his experiments and researches into brain transplants."

Anana nodded thoughtfully.

Pauncho van Veelar and Barney Banks stood in the vestibule of Doc Caliban's Empire State Building headquarters. There was a slight buzzing and the door unlatched and swung open automatically.

The two men stepped in, and the door closed behind them. The lock clicked.

Barney strode over to the big pane glass window and looked down at the antlike people and cars some eighty stories below.

Pauncho pressed two apelike fists, knuckles down, against the exquisitely inlaid table that was the centerpiece of the reception room. "This ain't right," he said.

Barney glanced back at his companion and did a double take. "You said a mouthful, brother. You're about ten inches shorter than me, now. And those hairy arms are just as freakishly long, but now you're so short they practically drag on the floor!"

Pauncho scowled. "Well, you look like your pa, too, but you did anyway, foxy face and slicked back thirties playboy hair. But that getup, that's somethin' else! How much did the white tie and tails set you back?"

Barney looked down at himself, then back at Pauncho. Normally he would have some witty put down in response, but he was momentarily rendered speechless. Then: "Yeah, I got style, but never like dear old Dad. And you, you got your dad's apish face and rusty hair and swinging arms, and his stubby chimp legs, but almost a full foot of your torso is gone. What the hell is going on here?"

The telephone, an old-fashioned 1930s model, rang, and Pauncho, closest to the huge oak desk, picked up the receiver.

"Yeah?"

"Pauncho? Pauncho, is that you?"

"Barbara? Where are you?"

The line went dead and van Veelar put the receiver in the cradle.

"Again," Barney asked, "what the hell? Doc abandoned this place right before we joined his outfit, right after he and Grandrith went at it."

"Yeah, but the place looks like it did in the thirties and forties and fifties before everything went to hell. I mean, look at the phone."

"And look at you. By which I mean that getup. They haven't made suits that loud and checked for forty years."

"Someone," Pauncho said, "is trying to get in our heads. Make us think we're our fathers, Jocko and Porky."

"But," Barney said, "in some strange way I feel I *am* him right now."

"Hogwash!" Pauncho shot back. "Haw, haw! Get it? Porky? Hogwash?"

Barney Banks shook his head, still uncharacteristically not in the mood to trade verbal barbs. He and Pauncho were in a weird spot. They were lifelong friends, despite the endless rounds of insults, and had served in the Korean War together and were now part of Doc's war. But they had never been in as wild a spot as this. It was unsettling.

"You're right," Barney said, "about someone pulling some trip on us. Let's get to the armory."

Pauncho grinned, showing a huge mouth of blocklike teeth. "Best idea you had all day, shyster!"

"I'm not a lawyer," Barney shot back as they entered a corridor that snaked around the perimeter of the massive scientific laboratory.

"That's even worse—practicin' bein' a shyster without a license!"

Barney grabbed a rapidfire pistol, tossed it to Pauncho, and removed a second pistol and several clips from a hidden rack.

"Best place for a defensive position?"

"The library, far corner," Pauncho said. "No windows."

Barney agreed and they edged their way there. Although they had not been part of Caliban's outfit when this headquarters had been in its prime, they had visited it, and their "Uncle Doc," with their fathers quite often as teenagers and young adults. They knew their way around.

Pauncho and Barney stopped at blind corners to cover each other. They both felt considerably more at ease now that they were armed, though they still didn't understand what they were up against.

The two made it to the library and headed toward a nook they felt would be easily defended.

Sitting in a leather club chair, reading an old hardbound volume, was Barbara Villiers. She was wearing an elaborate gown of the Restoration era. She closed the book carefully and set it on a side table. Gilmour's *The Great Lady: A Biography of Barbara Villiers, Mistress of Charles II.*

Pauncho looked at her questioningly.

Barbara shrugged and smiled ravishingly. "I was curious. Gilmour got quite a bit wrong."

As always, Pauncho and Barney were dazzled by Barbara's grin. Though rendered in 1600s portraits as a brunette, Barbara's hair was a deep red, framing an aristocratic face with large violet eyes and clear, pale skin. The two men could never decide if Barbara was more entrancingly beautiful than Trish Wilde, or the reverse.

These were private conversations, of course—or so they thought.

Here, in the library of Doc Caliban's defunct skyscraper headquarters, they knew she was out of place, just as they were, but in a dreamlike way it didn't matter. One part of their brains knew this was all wrong; another part was deeply inclined, or perhaps influenced, to accept it and roll with whatever came next.

Barney took an oversized volume from an upper shelf, flipped it open to reveal a hollow core containing a rapidfire pistol and a few more clips. Barbara took the pistol and handled it expertly.

"Gonna be hard to maneuver in that dress, your ladyship," Pauncho said. "How'd you get it on anyway?"

"No idea, I was just here and was wearing it," Barbara said. "But you're right. Undo those clasps.

Pauncho did so, while Barney watched, his dark eyes wide. Then Barney turned, slid more books out of the way, and tripped a large switch, killing the lights and plunging the entire headquarters into semidarkness, the only light coming from the reinforced glass panels fitted into the exterior walls.

Barbara stepped out of the gown and hefted her pistol. As she did so, a concealed wall panel near them slid open, revealing three heavily armed men, two of whom Barney and Pauncho recognized from Doc's sanitorium.

"Shit!" Pauncho raised his pistol and let loose, mowing down the intruders.

"Split up," Barbara yelled. She took off between two tall bookshelves and the two men followed suit, scattering to different areas of the book-lined chamber.

Pauncho clambered on top of an eight-foot-tall bookcase and commando crawled along its thirty-foot length, using the high vantage point to his benefit, scanning the aisles to either side for interlopers.

He saw five shapes hugging the shelf in one aisle, facing away from him and heading toward Barbara. He scrambled down, crept up behind the five, and smashed together the skulls of the two in the rear. He took off, leading the remaining three away from Barbara and on a chase up and down the aisles. He vaulted a lower bookcase that served to mark off the foyer to the library, the three un-graduates hot on his heels.

Pauncho cut right, ran to the far end of the shelf and spun around it, and tilted a certain book on the lower shelf.

A glass barrier dropped from the ceiling, cutting Pauncho off from the three men. He stood up and waved, and the three began blasting with their submachine guns. Webbed cracks appeared in the glass, spidering out from where each of the three streams of bullets centered on the transparent barrier. Bullets ricocheted off both the glass Pauncho had dropped, and from the glass panel behind the men that overlooked the great New York skyline. This glass was also bulletproof, and it didn't take long for the pinballing bullets to strike the three men, two kill shots in the chest and head, while the third took a bullet in the upper thigh. Pauncho figured he would bleed out before too long.

He turned to go when four more un-graduates piled into the section of the library that was cordoned off from Pauncho. They had entered from the front reception room that Pauncho and Barney had quitted not fifteen minutes ago. Upon spying Pauncho, they raised their weapons when one, a shade brighter than the others, raised a hand and pointed out what had happened to their three predecessors.

Pauncho flipped a switch on the underside of the shelf which locked and sealed the door between reception and the library. He flicked a finger against another switch and a brown-yellowish gas began pouring from the ceiling vents in the un-graduates' airtight chamber.

The gas, Pauncho knew, was non-lethal. Doc would have been proud. As for the two killed by machine gun fire, they had done it to themselves.

The apelike man headed back to the main section of the library, rapidfirer at the ready. He heard the signature hum of another stream of rapidfire bullets and made for the giant laboratory. In his haste and the dark, he tripped over something soft. One overlong arm shot out, preventing him from falling flat on his face.

Pauncho turned, examined the corpses of two more un-graduates. Both had had their throats slit and blood pooled beneath them. "Callagan. Damn." Callagan and Pauncho had become friendly at Caliban's subterranean Lake George headquarters. There would be no more congenial dart games over a pint.

Pauncho silently cursed the Nine.

Then he remembered the gunfire in the lab. He paled at the thought of Barney or Barbara in danger and hurled forward at a sprint, or what passed for a sprint in someone who could almost run on all fours, on the knuckles of his hands.

Pauncho slammed against the lab doors, bounced back, and put his massive shoulder into it again. The huge oak doors gave, but didn't break.

What he needed was his uncle Kidfast's giant fists to crash through the door panels. But Kidfast, and the others, were long gone. Pauncho grabbed a fire axe from a glass case that also held an extinguisher and chopped at the thick wood panels. He punched, widening the breach he had made, reached through, slipped the latch, and tumbled into the lab.

The light from the open doorway drew fire from above and he threw himself to the ground.

A torrent of rapidfire bullets spewed toward a spot above Pauncho, and three men fell from the false ceiling, dead before they hit the floor.

He made to get up and Barney yelled, "Stay down!"

"What—?"

"They have you pinned, brother!"

Barney let loose another blast from his rapidfire pistol in a bull-fiddle roar and then it clicked. Out of ammo.

Pauncho heard his buddy curse and toss the weapon aside. Shortly thereafter, a hose of fire streamed at the ceiling and through breaks in the panels that comprised the false ceiling. While the panels were fire resistant, the men poking their faces and guns through the breaks in the panels were not.

Four men, on fire and shrieking in agony, fell from the ceiling and desperately rolled on the lab floor, striving in vain to extinguish the flames that crisped their clothing and exposed skin.

"That it?" Pauncho called.

"All clear," Barney replied.

Pauncho peeked up over a lab counter; he didn't detect any further threats. He walked calmly over to the burning men and quickly put a bullet in each of their heads.

Barney strode over, disentangling himself from a belt apparatus connected to the flame-spewing gun, an invention of Doc's which was essentially a smaller and more portable version of an industrial strength flamethrower.

"That was brutal," Pauncho said. "Remind me not to cross you."

"I would, but that monkey brain of yours would only hold the concept of not crossing me for about three seconds. Besides, where do you have room to talk?" Barney asked, pointing at the corpses.

"That was mercy, brother, mercy."

Then: "Jesus! Where's Barbara?"

"Right here, you big ape." Barbara Villiers climbed through the shattered lab doors, holding a bloody dagger. "Took you long enough to ask. And here I thought you cared!"

"I do—"

Pauncho caught himself and Barney gave him the side eye.

"Look," Pauncho said, "what the hell happened here? None of this can be real."

"Of course not," Barney said, "you look like your daddy, Jocko, and he was better looking than you, so we know this has got to be a bit of high-tech fakery—"

Everything wavered and faded to a blinding whiteout.

Doc Caliban still did not speak.

The caverns of the Nine were eerily silent.

One by one, the cones of torchlight illuminating the immortals faded out, until only Tilatoc remained.

"We are still in northern Canada," Doc said.

He watched the Native American carefully. Looking at him, no one could have imagined Tilatoc was twelve, or fifteen, or perhaps even twenty thousand years old—though if he were really that old, then he had somehow managed to regularly travel back and forth between the Old World and the New, for the annual ceremonies, at a time when it took the better part of a year to traverse a small part of a small continent, to say nothing of vast, uncharted oceans.

Now, *there* was a mystery that needed unpacking—another time, Caliban thought.

Tilatoc's brown hand extruded from the folds of his monk's robe, and waved Krotonides over to him. The giant bent over and the ancient Native American whispered. Even Doc's superior hearing could not make out the words.

Then Krotonides stood straight and spoke to Doc and Trish.

"These are the words of Tilatoc, known as Misquaneqes, Tlāloc, Tezcatlipoca, Otsheemonetou, Chaak, and Mantoec, god of war, death, and the night. 'I am also the god of rebirth, rebirth of those whose natures you suppressed, whose free will you stripped, including that of the man who stands before you, Krotonides. This man, the Greek, Krotonides, once served Ing, but I, Tilatoc, discovered the means of releasing those whose free will you eradicated, and as a reward and by decree of Anana, the Greek now serves me. Your revolt is at an end, Doctor Caliban. I have instructed Krotonides to extract the information that Anana wants and then to kill you.'"

Krotonides' dark eyes locked with Caliban's golden-flecked orbs. "I now speak for myself, Caliban. Anana has decreed that whoever kills you and Grandrith will become Council members—even if they are not candidates. I was a candidate, you son of a bitch, until you fucked with my mind. Even after Tilatoc rescued me from your sanitorium, they didn't restore my candidacy. No, I was 'tainted.' You tainted me.

"So, I'm going to kill you, Caliban. I was always better than you. I intend to make this as painful as possible. And once I've torn you limb from limb, I'll do the same to your girlfriend."

Krotonides tossed aside the Speaker's staff, took a running start, and dove headlong into the black pool.

Caliban steeled himself for the attack and grasped at the Greek's arm as the latter lunged from the dark waters. Krotonides' skin was slick, and Doc's grip slipped.

Hard as it was to credit, Krotonides had two inches of height, and probably forty pounds, on Doc. If Doc had the body of a bronzed Heracles, the Greek's was that of the monstrous Minotaur.

His head was as tough, and skull bones as thick, as those of the ferocious creature of Greek myth. All he lacked were the bull's horns.

Krotonides bent, wrapped one thigh-sized arm around Doc's own sizable thigh, and heaved. The bronze man was flipped backward, but rolled into the landing with a backward somersault and came up in a crouch. He dropped, pivoted on his right arm, and swept his legs around like the speeding hands of a clock, taking the Greek's legs out from under him.

Caliban was on him in an instant, pummeling his former aide repeatedly in the face, smashing the already disfigured nose in a plume of crimson and mucus. Krotonides wrapped his arms around Doc's massive chest and squeezed, forcing the air from his lungs. One, and then two, sinewy bronze arms snaked around the Greek's head, attempting to constrict his throat and suffocate him.

Krotonides' neck, such as it was, was too thick and heavily muscled, and Doc couldn't get proper purchase to apply enough pressure to faze his opponent. Caliban had only met one other human who quite literally had, like Krotonides, no neck: his own late aide, Jocko Simmons, or as Porky Rivers had laughingly called him, Jocko "Simians."

Krotonides' wide mouth gaped, and he bit at Caliban's face, tearing out a chunk of cheek flesh. Doc managed to slip an arm up and got a bronze thumb in the other's eye, but not hard enough to cause the Greek to release his hold.

Focus, Caliban, focus. He was beginning to see stars. Krotonides' iron grip was implacable. It seemed impossible, but the Greek's strength matched his own and that of his half-brother, Grandrith. Was Krotonides also a direct descendant of some members of the Nine, a direct inheritor of massive Stone Age bone structure and musculature?

Caliban's vision swam.

Trish Wilde, for her part, was not one to stand on the sidelines. She performed an Olympic-caliber dive into the dark, frigid waters and front-stroked rapidly to the center island, smooth muscles rippling under her bronzed skin. No one seeing her could ever have imagined she was sixty-six years old. She looked eighteen, the age at which she first began taking the Nine's elixir.

Trish launched herself at Tilatoc, who, with agility belying his apparent age—biologically speaking, perhaps ninety or one hundred years old—grabbed the Speaker's staff, and held it before him in a defensive position. She launched a right hook at his head, which he blocked with the staff, followed by a quick left jab, also blocked. Tilatoc was strong, agile, and had stamina.

Trish hammered at the ancient's head once more, and when he swung the staff to block her yet again, she grabbed it in one bronze fist and yanked it from his grasp. She twirled it like a baton at a dizzying rate.

Caliban, close to blacking out, raised his heel and brought it down hard on the top of the Greek's foot, smashing bones and shredding cartilage. Krotonides' grip loosened and Caliban head-butted him. Both their skulls rattled. The Stone Age thickness of the Greek's cranial bones was all that saved him from a fractured skull. Of course, the same held true for Doc. But the senses-shattering blow caused Krotonides to release the bronze man and they broke apart.

Doc's former aide limped as they circled each other warily, and fresh blood flowing from his shattered nose continued to paint his gray beard with shots of crimson, but he otherwise gave no sign of pain or discomfort.

As they sized each other up, preparing for the next engagement, Doc wondered why Tilatoc didn't have his men just come in and slaughter them with machine guns. Were his forces, and the rest of the un-graduates that Caliban had not disposed of yet, deployed elsewhere? Had Tilatoc not expected a frontal assault on his headquarters?

On the small island, Trish Wilde swung the staff and the ankh slammed against the jaguar headpiece, sending it soaring into the dark waters. Tilatoc's eyes automatically followed the flying head for a split second, and Trish caved in his skull. The ancient crumpled to the ground and she repeatedly slammed the staff down on his body in an orgy of crunching bones and pink-gray brain gore.

Krotonides was momentarily distracted by Trish's ferocity and Caliban lunged, grabbed the other's beard, and smashed a hard knee into his mouth, knocking out several teeth. The Greek tore Caliban's left hand away from his face and squeezed the bronze man's fingers in his massive paw, breaking several bones.

Doc got his right hand into the other's left armpit and took hold, jabbing his straightened fingers into a sensitive bundle of nerves. Krotonides doubled over and Caliban grabbed him by the beard with his right hand. His left thumb—the only unbroken digit on that hand—poked into the Greek's eye socket and the orb popped out with a sucking noise and spew of blood and dangling nerves and gore.

Krotonides screamed and Caliban fast walked him over to the waters surrounding the thrones of the Nine, kicked his knees out from under him, and shoved the bullet head under the black, black liquid.

While Caliban, with his good right arm and hand, twisted the Greek's right arm and held it fast behind his back, he kept a foot on his opponent's head below the water's surface. The Greek's body and left arm flailed in an attempt to free himself. Caliban maintained the pressure as the flailings devolved into spasms and twitches.

Still, Caliban did not let up. If Krotonides had half of the skills and stamina that he, Caliban, had, then the Greek might be able to hold his breath for up to four minutes.

"Doc. Doc!"

Caliban ignored his cousin and held the Greek's head under water until the body went limp.

Five minutes. Six.

Caliban let loose and the huge, dark body slipped quietly into the water.

He had drowned Krotonides, the un-graduate, his former friend and ally. He had almost lost his life gaining the information regarding Anana's decree, that anyone who killed him would automatically be elevated to membership in the Council of the Nine. And one of his trusted aides, a friend, had lost his life.

Caliban went into himself, plunging into the dark place deep inside, the place where he had put the guilt he felt over other killings, such as Big Eyes, and men who had murdered his father, and Li—

"Doc! C'mon, Doc!" Trish Wilde had him by the shoulders, shaking him. "Snap out of it!"

Doc and Trish were in a stark white, featureless cube. The bodies of Tilatoc and Krotonides were sprawled on the clean, white floor, staining it with their blood and gore. Dark brownish water spilled from the Greek's dead mouth.

Crouched in the opposite corner of the blank white cube were Pauncho, Barney, and Barbara, and a pile of dead bodies. Seeing their companions, the three rushed over.

"Holy smokes, Doc," van Veelar asked, "what happened to Zeus?" This was Pauncho's nickname for the big Greek.

"He was an un-graduate."

"Damn," Barbara said. "And you killed Tilatoc, too."

"That was Trish," Doc said, causing Barney and Pauncho to look at Doc's cousin with newfound respect. Not that they hadn't respected her abilities before, but doing away with a member of the Nine . . .

Trish changed the subject by asking the others what had transpired with them, and Pauncho brought them up to speed, with color commentary from Barbara and Barney.

"Then," Caliban said, "Tilatoc sent his cadre of un-graduates after you three. The hubris of the Nine. He figured he and Krotonides could take care of me and Trish by themselves."

"So," Trish said, "different visions or illusions which seemed incredibly real. It truly seemed we were in the caves of the Nine, which, really, is impossible."

"Just as impossible," Barney added, "as us being in Doc's old headquarters in the Empire State Building, in our fathers' bodies."

"Then we weren't transported somewhere else, somewhere completely different," Pauncho said. "We were here all the time."

"How'd Tilatoc pull it off?" Barbara asked.

"It was a magnificent illusion," Trish said. "We felt we were actually speaking to Anana, that we were truly present in the caves of the Nine. Events unfolded in a way that was incredibly realistic, as if we were really there with those five members of the Nine after all these years. And Anana—or the illusion of Anana—knew about the revitalization elixir. Did the Nine, in some way, manage to read our minds, to insert those images and conversations into our brains?"

"Or," Doc said, "was there some other, external force at work?"

"Like what?" Pauncho asked.

"Unknown. But . . . the water." Doc pointed at the dirty water from the caverns of the Nine, still dripping from the drowned Greek's gaping mouth. "And the men you killed with weapons from our old headquarters. How can that be possible, if the whole experience took place only in our minds? If the illusion is over . . . why is the water still here? Why are the corpses here?"

Doc realized their victory was pyrrhic. There was much more going on, unplumbed depths, that he did not understand.

Perhaps he would have gotten answers if Tilatoc or Krotonides had lived, but it was unavoidable.

One week later, in a safe bolt hole in Calgary, Doc Caliban sent a message to John Cloamby, Lord Grandrith, surreptitiously attached to and hidden within an otherwise unremarkable satellite transmission.

Caliban's transmission conveyed Krotonides' message that any-one—candidate or not—who killed them would automatically get a seat on the Council of the Nine. Caliban was sure this message would reach his half-brother, but was not sure when. For the past eight years, Grandrith had been devoting all his energy to locating his wife, Clio Jeanne de Carriol, rather than pursuing a pitched battle against the Nine. This did not, of course, save Grandrith from having to play a defensive game against the Nine's forces, which diverted precious time from the jungle lord's search. On the other hand, perhaps these attackers might have a lead or information on Clio. When engaging and defending himself against the agents of the Nine, Grandrith was always careful to spare a likely contender for interrogation—spare, at least, until it became clear that no information about his beloved wife was forthcoming.

Doc switched off the transmission.

Trish came up and put a hand on his shoulder. He placed his right hand on hers. The fingers of his left hand and his torn cheek were already healing at an accelerated rate, due to the rejuvenation elixir which Barbara had helped him to complete.

Less visible wounds would take longer to heal, if ever.

"You're feeling guilty about Krotonides."

Doc was quiet for a moment, then ran a hand through his dark, reddish-bronze hair. "Yes. And all of them." This was new for Doc. In the wake of the monumental battle with his half-brother, years ago, when they had both been under the influence of the Nine's elixir and manipulated into fighting each other, Caliban had had an awakening, of sorts. He would never be highly emotionally expressive. But those golden-green eyes could now shed tears. He could now admit emotions: sadness, love, anger . . . and guilt.

Trish said, "Jesus, Doc, maybe it's time to stop messing around with those goddamned brain operations. I can't believe I'm even saying this, but maybe Krotonides had a point about his own free will?"

"Or maybe," Caliban said, "my operations uncovered the goodness within Krotonides and the others. Maybe it unleashed their real free will to be good, and do good things, which had been entrapped all their lives in a web of criminality and evil?"

Trish Wilde looked at her cousin and shook her head. "Then why do you feel guilty?" She walked away.

Doc sat motionless, by himself, staring at the blank walls. "Because I couldn't save them."

Caliban and the others went their separate ways and into hiding. The five of them together were too distinctive, too easily identified, and the subterranean headquarters under Lake George was certainly no longer safe.

As Caliban bid his friends adieu, he couldn't shake the image of what he had seen, that no one else had noticed, as they climbed their way out through the stark white tunnels and ice caverns of Tilatoc's sub-Arctic fortress.

Writhing and squirming on the icy floor, Doc had seen a worm, a long whitish *thing* that was horrifying. Twelve tentacles protruded from one tip of the worm, the bases of which were surrounded by tiny blue eyes with vertical pupils like those of a cat. Each tentacle was tipped with wicked-looking needlelike points.

He had certainly never seen the like in all his years of scientific research.

Doc, shaken, had turned away in momentary disgust, and when he had looked back, the thing seemed to be melting, merging, chameleonlike, into the ice along which it had been crawling, until it faded from his view altogether.

Part II

The Guardian at the Threshold

1984

The old wino drew his army surplus coat tighter about him. He pulled his bent knees closer to his chest in an effort to disappear even further into the shadowed alcove in which he hunched in the darkened alleyway. He took a swig from a green bottle and gave a small belch.

He wiped a hand across grizzled whiskers and pulled the hood of his jacket further down, close to but not quite covering his dark eyes. Patches of longish, stringy gray hair poked out from the hood. He wore dirty pants of some tough denim and black boots that had seen better days.

The wino shifted position slightly as the setting sun cast a slowly moving shadow on the garish canary yellow mansion across the street. The pile looked about to collapse in on itself, paint peeling, paneling sagging, and stones coming loose from the mortar in the high surrounding wall.

From his vantage, looking between a large blue garbage dumpster and the brick wall against which he was propped, he could just keep the front door in his line of sight.

The old-timer kept watching the yellow house, an aging Victorian that was destined to be demolished if it didn't get some care soon. That might be for the best; this was no longer the neighborhood of a century ago. The financial barons and mining millionaires had been replaced by dope peddlers, prostitutes, and dropouts from society.

Most of the people shambling by didn't even look down the alleyway. They looked down at the crumbling and decrepit sidewalks as they walked, minding their own business, or thinking about their next score.

Every once in a while, a passerby ducked into the alley to take a piss or inject their drug of choice. They ignored the old wino, which was his intent. The homeless were invisible, unseen, even to those who were one small step away from living on the streets themselves, those beset by alcoholism and addiction. Once or twice, in the hours that he crouched there, a passerby using the alley as a shortcut did stop to wordlessly drop a dollar or two, though the wino was not actively begging for money.

Shortly after sundown, a gang of juveniles, scraggly and smelly, came through the alley, laughing and cursing. Upon seeing the wino crouched behind the dumpster, they stopped.

One of them, a youth with greasy blond hair and a smattering of whiskers, said to the others in a slow voice that apparently was supposed to be menacing: "Predator and prey, man, predator and prey."

They flipped out switchblades and came at the old man for the little money they thought he might have—as well as whatever remained of his booze.

The old wino shot to his feet. One of the gang members swung his blade, unskilled and uncontrolled, at the old man's torso. A large hand appeared from the sleeve of the army jacket. Sinewy fingers grabbed the attacker's wrist and snapped it easily. The knife clattered to the pavement amid the youth's screams of pain.

Another delinquent slashed from the left and cut the old wino's hand which had been raised in defense. Rubbery looking skin flapped around but there was no blood. The old man hammered a boot into his stomach and a fist into his teeth. The youth fell to the pavement, writhing and spitting blood, and didn't get up.

The third juvenile, the one who had called the wino prey, launched forward with brass knuckles. The old-timer stopped the metal-wrapped fist in his own giant hand. He grabbed the blond's wrist and lifted. The youth was held dangling, his feet flailing uselessly in the air, for the wino had risen to his full height of six foot seven. With his other hand, the old man pulled the brass knuckles from the youth's bony fingers. He dropped the gang member, took the metal knuckles in both hands, and bent them in half before the other's unbelieving eyes. He tossed the ruined knuckles in the dumpster and kicked the youth in the chest, slamming him into the bricks. The young man slid down to the pavement and didn't move.

Doc Caliban had disposed of his young attackers quite easily, if bloodily, but his cover was ruined.

He edged out of the alley and noticed a shadow in a back lane abutting the yellow mansion on the opposite side of the street. Caliban stepped further out of the alley, stumbling as if he were a drunk wino. The shadowy figure exited his or her own passageway and turned in the opposite direction from Caliban. Caliban moved away as if he had not seen the figure, and shambled off in the opposite direction of the spy.

Caliban shuffled down broken sidewalks and glass-strewn dirt pathways where the concrete had crumbled away. He stopped at trashcans and rummaged through them. Once, while stopped, he was able to see, in the angled recessed bay window of an abandoned dry cleaners, the reflection of a man shadowing him. Certainly, this was the one who had observed Caliban's fight with the youths, or else was a compatriot of similar height and weight.

Caliban led his shadow on a crisscrossing path of darkened streets and alleyways. The sun had now set completely, and the last oranges and purples of dusk had faded. There were no streetlights, and only a few slivers of yellow lamplight escaped pulled down shades and curtains from the few occupied tenements. Caliban leisurely turned a corner into a pitch-black passageway next to a three-story apartment building. Once he was sure he was out of sight of his follower, he leaped straight up, caught a metal railing in one cabled hand, and easily pulled himself up. He silently darted up a fire escape, climbing it monkey-like as if he were his half-brother.

Caliban's shadowy tail cautiously entered the alley and took slow, careful steps into the brick-lined maw. Caliban dropped silently behind him. The other must have somehow sensed the bronze man's presence, despite Caliban's unnatural silence, because he whirled, but far too late to save himself. Caliban took two strides, caught his adversary by the shoulder, and pressed certain nerves at the base of the shoulder in the neck, inducing instantaneous unconsciousness. This state would last until Caliban worked those nerve clusters again; if he failed to do so, the man would never awaken and would eventually die of dehydration and starvation.

Caliban hefted the spying man over his shoulder and strode through the darkness of the night to a large, beat up blue Ford LTD that was about ten years old.

He tossed the man in the back seat, got in, started the engine, and drove.

Caliban turned the car toward a coastal highway, and as he steered the Ford along the bay, an acrid stench soon drifted in through the vents and open windows. This was the noxious result of a permanent oil slick, the consequence of the notorious "Glory Hole" oil drilling disaster in Los Angeles Bay, the after-effects of which would continue to plague the city of angels for decades, or even centuries, to come.

Caliban recalled his own extrapolations, his report to the Nine back in the mid-forties, in which he had predicted the fouling of the atmosphere; the rising and deoxygenation of the oceans, leading to the extinction of whole species at an alarming rate; and the catastrophic effects of unchecked deforestation. Caliban had posited all this, and more, and over the decades his projections had been shown to be frighteningly correct. Add in large scale technological disasters such as the Cal-Pax oil spill, and it was clear humanity was on a precipice, and that it would not take much more to tip it over the edge.

The issue had actually divided the Council of the Nine, to such a degree that the evil gnome, Iwaldi, had revolted, favoring the course of letting humanity destroy itself so that they—the Nine— could rebuild better the next time around. Anana, for all her vile manipulativeness, had opposed this course as too risky: the Nine themselves might not survive the ecological and societal destruction. Anana had decreed that the Nine would intervene, that measures would be taken to address overpopulation and pollution.

Caliban, perhaps a cynic, privately believed that Iwaldi's revolt had more to do with his discovery of his own rejuvenation elixir; having no more need of the Nine's elixir, he had gone his own way in a mad grab for complete power.

As Caliban drove on the dark highway, breathing in the sea air as he finally left the oil slick behind, he allowed himself to briefly think of his friends, and of Trish. He had been on the run for years, staying at hideouts all over the world, sometimes for weeks, and one time for almost a year. He had been to Buenos Aires, Saigon, the Aleutian Islands in Alaska, a small fishing village at the heart of the Amazon rainforest, Denmark, and Tredannick Wollas, near Poldhu Bay in Cornwall, among many other locations. It was at the latter locale where he had researched the singular properties of a peculiar root whose origins lay in deepest west Africa. He had seen his cousin Trish twice, when she insisted on visits after claiming to not be able to take the separation.

He had not seen his pals Pauncho van Veelar and Barney Banks since the assault on Tilatoc's fortress, although he knew how to contact them. But it had not been safe to do so. Of Barbara Villiers, he had had no word, and he had not been in touch with Grandrith in over a year.

Doc was alone.

Except for the dreams—dreams that, over the years, had become more vivid, more real, just as the experiences he and the others had had in Tilatoc's fortress had appeared to be so real.

Finally, he had received some intelligence from his tattered network, his few remaining agents, that the decrepit canary-colored mansion in Los Angeles might have some sort of tie to the Nine. Tired of hiding and running, he had decided to attack. But, first, he needed a lead. Caliban had decided it was time to surveil it, and see if there was a reaction.

Now, Caliban arrived, after following a long and meandering drive through a narrow and low tunnel of forestry, at what had been a late Victorian house of the Queen Anne style located in northern Beverly Hills. The mansion, or rather the fire-scorched remains, was sprawling. One section of it, the side facing the driveway with a turret over bay windows and a wraparound porch and steeply pitched roof, was still extant, having mostly survived the blaze that had destroyed the remainder, although it was still not safely habitable. Doc knew that the original house at the heart of the mansion had been built a century before, in the early 1800s, and had been, in keeping with the period, a hacienda built by a wealthy Spanish landowner and rancher, Don Pedro del Osorojo.

The ruins of the mansion, Trolling House, were surrounded by heavily forested land, firs and oaks, which in turn was bordered by a brick security wall, in which iron spikes were set with white mortar, through which barbed wire was thickly strung.

Trolling House had been the site of some very strange goings-on years ago. It had been abandoned for over a decade, never repaired after the destructive blaze, when Caliban, through an impenetrable chain of intermediaries, had purchased the property and set it up as another bolt hole.

Doc had first come to the place hoping to research the private library, which was reported to have one of the few remaining copies of Michel Le Garrault's works, particularly *Les Murs ecroules* (*The Collapsed Walls*). Le Garrault was a nineteenth-century Belgian scholar and occultist and the first to propose the existence of parallel or alternate dimensions occupying the same space as our own—not just worlds that were very much like our own, with subtle divergences, but other planets occupying the same physical space as Earth did, existing in dimensions that had wildly different laws of physics. Le Garrault also proposed that the walls between the universes could be broached, and had, in fact, already been broached, and that there were gates— perhaps accidental breaks or flaws, or perhaps created purposefully— via which a dweller of one dimension might travel to another.

Although the mansion had been mostly ruined by the fire, Caliban did locate the research volumes for which he searched in the ruined library. The extensive complex of rooms and cells below ground level was much more well preserved, and Caliban had outfitted these chambers with a laboratory with the latest scientific equipment, a medical bay, a communications hub, mainframe computer and several access stations, as well as standalone personal computers, and a frugal but serviceable living quarters. The bolt hole was also equipped with a small armory, and large closet—really a room—packed with clothing and sophisticated makeup for disguises.

It was in this room that he quickly shed the plastiskin, wig, beard, and other trappings of the old wino who had staked out the canary-colored mansion.

In the medical bay, Doc Caliban deposited his captive on an examination table and secured the man with straps. He placed his fingers upon nerve centers, releasing the prisoner from his unconscious state, and then administered a highly effective truth drug he had invented in the 1930s. After detailed questioning, Caliban learned the man was indeed an agent of the Nine, and also that he was a religious nut, a member of the Soldiers of Jehovah, a cult involved in multiple counts of terrorist activities related to the L.A. oil disaster.

Caliban sometimes wondered if Iwaldi, in his own way, had been correct. Humankind seemed determined to destroy itself. Was it worth all of his, and his friends', monumental efforts to save it? He knew his brother, Lord Grandrith, also often expressed these feelings, though in the end he, like Caliban, never failed to step into the breach once more.

Caliban was intrigued that the man sent to spy on him was a member of the Soldiers of Jehovah—the SOJ—*and* an agent of the Nine. Had the Nine been the puppet masters behind the oil catastrophe and the subsequent terrorist activities, pulling the SOJ's strings? But that went against Anana's position that the world (and therefore humanity) needed to be saved from ecological disasters, in order for the Nine to retain its power and control.

Unless Anana had changed her mind in the last fifteen years. It was certainly possible. She was a canny old bitch.

Curious, Caliban questioned the SOJ man about the Cal-Pax oil disaster, but learned nothing. He gave the man a drug that would knock him out for an hour, injected him with a subcutaneous micro transmitter, and carried him up out of the hidden headquarters. He tossed him in the back seat of the Ford, drove for forty-five minutes to a secluded ocean cove, and dumped him on the sandy beach.

Caliban backed out of the pull-off by the beach, put the car in forward gear, and drove up a road with hairpin turns for about ten minutes, finally parking at a high bluff overlooking the beach and ocean below. He killed the engine. The moon had set hours ago, and the stars glittered brightly. He opened the glove box and pressed a button with a soft click. A screen lit and cast a faint bluish light, giving his bronzed features a weird tinge.

Doc sat, and waited for the SOJ man to wake up, and a moment later was lost in infinite seas of blinding whiteness.

Doc saw the knife glinting in the gaslight as it stabbed down again and again, red and bloody. Up, down, slash, cut.

The knife, the steel, the handle, the blood, crimson, spattering, the organs cut out. The steel flashing. The knife, the knife, the knife.

The steel hunting knife Grandrith had given him.

The knife swelled, got larger, growing and expanding until it consumed his entire field of vision, as if he were in a theater and seated far too close to the screen, or his face was smashed up against a television screen that had gone blank with silver static.

The silver wavered and shimmered and was replaced, almost as if someone had changed the channel.

Los Angeles.

Doc Caliban pulled up to the curb, set the handbrake, and climbed out of the Model-T. He tugged his raincoat tighter around the collar and pulled his fedora low on his forehead.

He ambled over to a corner and lit a cigarette, and loitered, taking in the street and sidewalk and brick tenements to the north and south of him.

Thirty minutes passed, in which he saw several shady characters drive up and exit yellow taxicabs in front of one particular low-rise apartment building. Like Caliban, these men wore raincoats or light overcoats, although the weather didn't call for them, and cloth caps pulled low over their heads to conceal their features.

This was the building, Doc decided. Letting five minutes pass after the last group entered the edifice, he strolled over, opened the wrought iron gate, and went down the concrete steps to the be-low ground entrance. The door appeared to be of a thick, heavy fibered-wood, and had a small box inset at head level—or what would've been his head level if Caliban had not been six foot seven. He rapped heavily on the door with one bronzed, cabled fist.

A moment later, a panel in the barred inset slid open, revealing no more than a shadowed face with a hint of whiskers and a puff of cheap bourbon.

"Password?"

Doc bent down so that his face was level with the other man's and said, "Big eyes." He could feel the other's orbs peering at him, attempting to make out his features under the brim of the fedora, scanning for any hint of recognition.

Finally, the panel slid closed with a sharp crack and Doc heard the clicking of the latch being unlocked. The door swung inward. Caliban ducked and entered quickly. The doorman cum guard slammed the door behind him and rapidly relocked it.

Caliban scanned the low-ceilinged room, taking in cheap wooden tables and chairs, around which men sat playing cards or other games of chance, smoking cigars and cigarettes and marijuana. Low-light table lamps were arranged haphazardly, casting inconsistent cones of yellow-orange in crannies and nooks, projecting weird shadows. The walls were of Chicago brick. Tapestries hung from two of these, while the third was covered by a massive painting, bordered by an ornate two-inch-wide gilt-edged frame.

The painting was bizarre, a conglomeration of iridescent spheres surrounded by a circular arrangement of curious black patches. Waves of purple iridescence streamed and faded into each patch of darkness from the central aggregation of globes. The blobs of darkness were impossibly black, as if they were irregular windows into worlds that were not only lightless, but were planes in which light had never existed.

Caliban found it hard to look away, as if he were spilling into the painting, and at the same time the iridescent streams were spilling into the blackness that existed elsewhere. He mentally chastised himself, and his awareness focused on his surroundings rather than the oddly compelling painting.

The other men in the room had gone silent. They had stopped whatever they had been doing and had turned to face him, much like when, in the stereotypical Old West, the stranger pushed open the saloon's batwing doors and all the townsfolk, insular and suspicious, turned and stopped and stared at the newcomer.

Caliban feigned a slight smile and took a chair at an empty table. He raised a hand at the speakeasy's barmaid and ordered a gin fizz. The rest of the room turned back to their card games and gambling, and the sounds of the room went from utter silence to a low murmur of conversation.

"This ain't the Roosevelt, fella. We got it straight. Gin, whisky, vodka."

"Sorry, I, uh, ain't from around here. Gimma a gin."

"Prohibition's everywhere, pal." She squinted at him. The girl was probably nineteen, maybe twenty, had a hard face and was already developing crow's wrinkles at the corners of her eyes. Her eyes widened as if she really saw him for the first time. "Jeez, you're a big one. You a snooper?"

"Nah, I'm just in from Chicago and heard this was the best drum in town. I was movin' a lot of goods there and things got hot. Had to blow. Lookin' for work. You know anything?"

The girl squinted at him again, shook her head, and walked away.

She returned in a minute with his drink, and had appeared to rethink his question. "I may have somethin' for ya." He nursed his drink and waited. Caliban was not a drinker, but he had taken a tincture of his own devising before entering the speakeasy. The concoction would lessen the effects of the alcohol, since he knew he would be forced to drink in order to fit in with the group of thieves, knife men, and other low-ranking gangsters.

If the barmaid was communicating with anyone about Caliban and his question, he couldn't discern it. Maybe there was a button, or some other device mounted under the bar, out of his sight. Or maybe she was just playing him for a sap.

A few minutes later, the giant painting swung away from the brick wall on what must have been concealed hinges on the left side. A tall, tuxedoed man, straight blond hair parted in a knife's edge, stepped through the large, hidden doorway, and gestured for Caliban to follow him. Doc glanced at the barmaid, and she jerked her head in the man's direction.

Caliban stood as the man stepped through the hole that had been concealed by the painting. He followed the man in the penguin suit and the painting-door swung closed and clicked behind him.

The man said, "Sit," gestured at a large, overstuffed chair uphol-
stered in wine-red velvet, and disappeared into a corner draped in
similar material. In fact, the entirety of the small chamber was done
in wine-red, with gold accents. Even the bulbs in the small table lamps
were red, giving the place a peculiarly intimate atmosphere. It made
him uncomfortable, as if he were rifling through some unknown
woman's lacy underthings, committing a deep violation, and all the
while knowing he was soon to meet the lady in question.

And meet her he did.

She came in, wearing nothing but a floor-length dressing gown
trimmed in lace at the plunging neckline. White fur ringed the
sleeves, from which extended slender pale hands with nails painted
wine-red.

Her blonde hair was waved and curled in the current fashion, her
face was pleasantly rounded, and her red-painted lips were generous
but not overly plump.

Caliban, if he had ever been inclined to drop his repressed
nature, to put aside his self-control, would likely have joined many
other men in agreeing she was easy on the eyes, that is, very pleasant
to look at, although not startlingly beautiful—with one exception
that was startling.

The woman's chestnut brown eyes were extraordinarily large.
They were just on the edge of being too large for her face, of almost
constituting some sort of congenital deformity. The orbs did not
quite bulge, but to Caliban's eye if they had been perhaps one-
sixteenth of an inch larger, had distended just the tiniest amount
more, they would have crossed a subtle threshold that separated the
attractive from the grotesque.

"Jeezus!" she said. "Lookit those peepers! You've got some kind
of gold specks dancing in your eyes, pal!"

She shifted a tommy gun from her right to left hand and stuck
out the former.

"Big-Eyes Llewellyn, pleased to meetcha." She gestured for him
to sit back down. "I hear you're lookin' for a job. I'll getcha another
drink and we'll talk it over."

Big-Eyes went over to a small bar and poured. She turned back
around and saw Doc was still standing. She came about halfway to
him, set down the drink, and backed up.

"I said, siddown. Get your drink and siddown." She raised the tommy gun slightly.

Caliban did as he had been instructed.

She put one foot on an ottoman and rested the tommy gun lightly on her naked upper thigh. "Now, let's start at the beginning. You're a dope runner, huh? What's your name, big boy?"

Caliban was back on the bluff overlooking the beach, scanning for signs of the SOJ man on the sands, and the surrounding areas from his high vantage point.

Doc tried to banish any further thoughts of what had happened back in 1928, when he had been drugged by the drink forced upon him by Big-Eyes, and then had been taken to a house up Topanga Canyon, and bound with strong leather straps that even his corded muscles could not snap. His attempt to infiltrate and break up the drug-smuggling ring had certainly gone sideways.

Caliban was repressed, the product of his bizarre upbringing and his father's obsessive training program. Every waking moment, from the time he left the cradle, had been filled with physical exercises or mental challenges designed to result in the height of human perfection, with a tunnel-vision focus on stamping out evil, the biggest criminal organizations and gangsters, all over the world. There had been no room for girls (when he was an adolescent), nor young women in college and medical school, and no room for close friends or confidants (he was careful to not get too close to his Great War buddies). And Doc had known he was repressed, had known that his ultimate control over his emotions was unnatural, and that his repression was an extension of his father's. He had often wondered what had caused his father to be this way, to be so scarred and wounded, and he had been afraid—if he had ever been honest enough with himself to acknowledge that tiny black dot of fear tying knots deep in his gut—that his father had somehow also passed on that scarring in addition to the repression and control.

Doc Caliban had learned, in that house in Topanga Canyon in 1928, the unspeakable consequences of that repression and control and fear.

Big-Eyes Llewellyn, the gang leader's moll, had had her way with him, and something terrifying had been loosed within him.

Doc had stumbled away from the house in the aftermath, covered in jetting blood, still feeling the crunch of neck bones in his sinewy fingers. The killing rage, the ultimate loss of self-control, had been followed by a long period of almost-insanity, a deep and suicidal depression. His wartime pals knew only that he had withdrawn for almost a year to pursue important scientific research and experiments. When he returned, it was with a renewed dedication to wiping out evildoers—with a new caveat for his five compatriots: there would be no killing of their adversaries, or at least not direct killing. If their foes were hoist by their own petard, that was another matter.

Caliban had responded to the loss of self-control, the killing rage, with *more* self-control. He also accepted, when he returned from his yearlong sojourn at his Arctic hideaway, the invitation of the Nine to join their ranks. When embarking on missions and assignments for the Nine, he was often required to lift his self-imposed embargo on killing. (His five team members, of course, knew nothing of this at the time.) This led to even more internal conflict and disturbance and cognitive dissonance, which he also repressed. Of course, the no-killing mandate had gone out the window when he and Grandrith began their war against the Nine. Doc had few alternatives anyway, since his sanatorium was shuttered, his brain operations had proven to be problematic, and he had no place to send captured enemies.

Pay attention, Caliban. Focus on the SOJ man.

Caliban was disturbed.

He had been having these lapses, these interludes, such as the very real-seeming vision of Big-Eyes' speakeasy and the later events at the house in Topanga Canyon, ever since the assault on Tilatoc's fortress seven years ago. The pauses, or breaks, in reality, varied in frequency, sometimes occurring almost monthly. Once, almost a year had gone by between the visions and reenactments of his life events—or of other weird and peculiar visions he did not recognize, that were not a part of his life history—at least not that he knew of.

He worried the interludes could become more debilitating, or strike at a critical, inopportune moment, and that he, senseless in the throes of the vision, could be captured or even killed.

Doc also wondered at the source of the images. "Images" was not quite the right word; they were not imagery cast upon a metaphorical movie screen. He was in them, experiencing them, living them. How and why did they intrude upon his consciousness?

He had very little data, and no answers, and had made not much progress at cracking the nut, at deciphering the mystery, and determining how to put a stop to the interludes. His best lead so far had been Le Garrault's theories and speculations, which was one of the reasons he had set up a hidden headquarters at Trolling House.

Caliban put these thoughts aside for the moment. The dim blue screen in the car's glove box blinked and a dot moved across it. The SOJ man was on the go. He was on foot, so Caliban did not have to start trailing him immediately. After the SOJ man had covered several miles, the moving white dot on the screen picked up speed. The man had either found his own vehicle, or, more likely, had stolen one.

Doc turned on the ignition and started after the other. The signal from the subcutaneous micro transmitter he had implanted in the man removed the necessity of trailing him too closely.

After winding their way through the asphalt tangle of highways and turnabouts, it was clear to Doc that the man was deliberately attempting to throw off any pursuers. The man's vehicle headed inland from the beach, wound its way around several residential neighborhoods, turning left from S. San Vicente onto Hauser, then a hard right onto Edgewood Place, and a left again onto S. Burnside. He followed this all the way to Wilshire, hung a left, and then appeared to head straight back for the coast. Doc surmised the man felt he had been wily enough, had done enough to shake off any unwanted followers, and was now headed directly for his intended destination.

Soon they were once again driving on the Pacific Coast Highway, and then the man turned right and wound his way up the depths of Topanga Canyon.

Caliban waited and idled at the base of the canyon for ten minutes, to allow his prey to park and go inside what was presumably a SOJ hideout. He put the LTD in gear and drove slowly. The moon was setting, casting a dim but crystalline light which would soon be replaced by pitch blackness. He maneuvered the big car up and around hairpin turns, and as he went up the canyon, the density of habitations decreased. The forest thickened as he passed a dirt driveway and the panel in the glovebox brightened slightly, indicating this was his destination.

Doc wondered where the house was in which he had been held prisoner back in 1928, and so he kept on driving. About two more miles up the narrow dirt road, he saw a scarred hillside, and he realized the old house must have been destroyed in massive mudslides that had occurred during the abnormally torrential rain season in L.A. about a decade or so ago. He was not so self-controlled that he did not feel a small sense of satisfaction the place had been wiped away, leaving behind only rubble and wood debris, embedded in thick mud, which had never been cleared. Of course, he would never admit this satisfaction to anyone else, and he could barely admit it to himself.

Caliban went back to the SOJ hideout, parked about an eighth of a mile down the main road, and made his way back up on foot, and then down the dirt driveway another eighth of a mile, winding through thick forest like a rattler tunnelling through the earth. The moon was gone, and a black curtain had descended. His approach was that of a bronze wraith, his exceptional nighttime vision allowing him to navigate broken branches and dried leaves and brush without the faintest sound. One element of his father's training program had emphasized woodcraft and the art of moving noiselessly through a variety of natural and manmade environments. He had additionally worked on this with Grandrith and was probably only second to the jungle lord in this area.

Caliban sighted the house the SOJ man had gone to and noted that the trees were cleared thirty feet from the structure on all sides, likely to prevent the approach of interlopers such as himself. The forest, however, was dense in all directions, and so it was impossible to see the house from any angle until reaching the cleared area.

The open space surrounding the house would have presented a problem for other intruders, but it fit in with Doc's plans perfectly. He approached the home, again without making the faintest sound. The windows were all heavily curtained and no light leaked from the edges and sills, but he knew there must be some nocturnal activity within due to the arrival of the SOJ man. He picked a likely window, applied to the pane a small rubber suction cup from which issued a tiny wire, and then circumnavigated the house, bending over in some activity at each of the four sides. He then retreated back to the tree line.

Doc tucked a small wireless earpiece of his own devising into his left ear and touched a button on his belt. He foresaw a day when such technology was ubiquitous. He increased the volume slightly and listened.

A woman's voice spoke into his ear, and he could hear as clearly as if he was standing in the room with her.

"—your report. Are you positive you weren't followed?"

"I'm sure!"

Doc recognized the latter's voice as that of the man he had captured and interrogated. But he was most interested and intrigued by the woman's voice, which he identified as that of a Nine candidate he knew, Victoria Lundgren. She had come to the caverns of the Nine for the annual elixir ceremonies at the same time of the year he had. Lundgren had used to tell stories about the ghost of her husband's great-grandfather, but she was such an inveterate liar that Caliban was never sure she wasn't really speaking about her own great-grandfather, or whether she even had a husband or not. He knew for a fact the woman she passed off as her daughter, Barbara—also a candidate—was actually her younger sister. No one knew exactly how old they were. And Victoria's lurid descriptions of the "ghost" of her husband's great-grandfather, the Norwegian sea captain Tors Lundgren, were suspiciously reminiscent of old XauXaz, the huge Stone Age man who was almost as ancient as Anana, and who had been the second oldest on the Council of the Nine at the time of his death. He, in life, had been one-eyed, with a patch over the right eye socket, and white-haired, with a long white beard that fell down and covered his chest all the way to his navel. Caliban and Grandrith had learned, after XauXaz's death, that he had actually been their biological grandfather, having paid regular midnight visits to their grandmother under the guise of an old Norwegian gentlemen calling himself Mister Bileyg. Bileyg—meaning "One-Whose-Eye-Deceives-Him" in Old Norse—had had a strangely strong and compelling personality, so that even though he appeared to be ninety years of age, he had had no problem seducing the maids, as well as the mistress, of Castle Grandrith.

XauXaz was dead now, and thinking back on the connections that Victoria Lundgren implied she had to him, Caliban reflected that it was odd that she had not been present for the old man's funeral ceremony at Stonehenge. Or perhaps she had been, and he had not seen her; the battle there had certainly been violent, tumultuous, and chaotic.

Victoria was continuing to speak. "Caliban is wily, much smarter than you. How can you be sure he didn't trail you here?"

"Mrs. Lundgren, I promise, I had him staked out at Virgil Sol's old dump, just like you said, he was staking the place out himself, pretending to be an old drunk sleeping in the alley. Later, I tailed him around the city, then he ended up at the beach, so then . . ."

"Yes," Veronica prompted, "then?"

"I—I can't quite remember. I found a car, hotwired it, gave anyone following me the runaround, and came here . . ."

"You *fool!*"

This was followed by a gunshot, the report of which Caliban recognized as coming from a .32 revolver, followed by several loud voices and shouts.

Caliban was disappointed. He had hoped to capture and interrogate someone higher up than the man he had questioned earlier, looking for clues, leads, to point him toward the Nine, or for information regarding weaknesses that could be exploited.

Instead, he had reached another dead end.

Doc pressed against a button on his belt in a particular pattern, and the house went up in a ball of fire, set off by the four explosives he had planted. These were combustibles he had invented in the '60s, designed so that the resulting conflagration would consume the object inside their circumference, but leave unscathed anything surrounding it—in this case, the surrounding forest's trees, brushes, pine needles, and scrub. The last thing he wanted was to start a forest fire.

The blue-orange blaze subsided somewhat, and then convulsed in Caliban's brain in fiery sheets of all-white flame.

Caliban dreamed again, the waking nightmare, the infinite blinding white.

He saw himself, or somebody like himself. But there were differences, changes that he could not immediately pinpoint. This man, the other him, seemed to be some sort of shadow of himself. No, that was wrong. The man was not insubstantial, shadowlike. He was big, like Caliban, a substantial presence, both of body and of mind. Caliban did not know how he knew this, because he could not see the man. Rather, he was seeing through the other man's eyes. Then he realized that this man, this Other, was undergoing the same thing that he, Caliban, seemed to be experiencing. That is, this Other felt himself to be looking through Caliban's eyes, and also, in Caliban's dreams and visions, The Other seemed to be dreaming of Caliban, while Caliban dreamed of The Other.

The Other strode across the Johns Hopkins campus, making his way to biomedical research class. In truth, he could have taught the class, as well as have brought an intriguing discovery or two to the professor's attention. But his intent was to get the degree in the shortest amount of time possible, without making waves and drawing too much attention to himself. This was difficult, as he already, at age twenty-four, had a multitude of undergraduate and graduate degrees under his belt. One more year of medical school and he would be a very young neurosurgeon indeed.

The Other turned the corner of a large, stone building housing various classrooms and laboratories and stopped in his tracks.

Strolling across the campus green, perhaps a football field and a half away, were two people he had been unsure he would ever encounter again. They were facing him, walking in his direction, casually arm in arm as if out for a Sunday stroll in the park.

The man was broad-shouldered and handsome. His eyes were green, in this light, and he had a Roman nose. He affected a monocle in his left eye socket. A great cigar was fitted between his lips. When they had first met, this man, who had styled himself a baron, had been an inch taller than The Other, who had not yet been fully grown. Now The Other, at six foot seven, had the height advantage. The Other had not been sure he would ever meet the baron again. There had been times he had felt the baron's presence, but looking about, The Other had seen no sign of him. This was not necessarily dispositive, as The Other was sure the baron had great powers of disguise.

Now, here he was in the guise in which The Other had known him.

The Other was more surprised to see the baron's companion, the countess. He had been positive she had been paralyzed from the waist down, her back broken in the massive train collision that had marked his escape from the notorious Loki prison camp. Yet here she was, walking about as if without a care in the world.

The Other recalled her great beauty. It was impossible not to, even for one such as he, who was so proud of his self-control. Her hair was ash-blonde, her skin was impossibly pale, almost white. Not the pink that was so often called "white," but a true milk-white, ethereal and almost otherworldly. He could only see hints of red-rouged lips under the mass of hair, which was styled differently than when he had last seen her, and now covered most of her face in undulating blonde waves. One thing that had not changed was the bizarrely long cigarette holder. This she held in one white-gloved hand and raised to her lips.

The Other began running toward them.

Seventy-five yards away, they saw him, waved cheerily as if greeting an old friend, and turned a corner, disappearing behind a building and out of his view.

It took The Other, a bronze blur, mere seconds to cover the space, but when he turned the corner the two were nowhere in sight. There were no doorways, no crannies, nor nooks, in which they could have concealed themselves. Just more expansive green grass and shady trees. There was nowhere they could have hidden.

They were just . . . gone.

The Other shook his head, as if trying to clear a fog. It must have been an illusion, a hallucination of some sort. He had heard the baron and the countess both still lived . . . but the countess' back had been broken in the crushing and crumpling of the train cars, and she had been paralyzed from the waist down.

It was impossible that she was up and walking around.

Wasn't it?

The blanket of blinding whiteness withered away.

When Caliban dreamed, or rather when he came out of it, he

could tell that no time had passed, or perhaps only a few seconds. And yet he had experienced a whole incident, and had absorbed much information from The Other in his dream.

Caliban suffered. The dreaming was getting worse, more frequent, becoming debilitating; it was an aberration, becoming more and more of a liability. When was he going to fade into a dream at an inopportune moment?

Then the full import of what he had just experienced through The Other's eyes impacted him.

The man whom The Other thought of as the baron was XauXaz. There could be no denying it: the eyes, the nose, the stance. But he was *young*, so very young. And he had both eyes. Caliban had always wondered why the Nine's elixir, so effective at regenerating lost organs, had failed to restore XauXaz's lost eye. He had even wondered if the old man's lost eye was truly gone, or if the eyepatch was an affectation—just as The Other considered the baron's monocle an affectation.

But how could this baron be XauXaz? XauXaz had died before Iwaldi's rejuvenation elixir had come to light, and even that could not restore the dead.

And who was this Other? He could feel, and he knew, by dreaming that he was occupying this other man's brain, living in his consciousness, seeing through his eyes, that in some way he *was* this other man, or that he was the essence of this other—Other— man, anyway. And in other ways, they were different: different life experiences, different parents, different friends.

But it was the likenesses that captured his thoughts: the births off the Bahamian island, the premature deaths of their mothers, their fathers' obsession with hunting down criminals, and the bizarre and fanatical training programs through which they had been put.

Caliban thought of the woman, whom The Other thought of as a countess. He had known one similar to her, when he and Rivers and Simmons and Shorthans and Williams and Kidfast had escaped the German prison camp. That camp's commandant, Colonel Arnold Etzel von Bissell, had also been a baron. But he had not resembled The Other's baron. That is, von Bissell had not resembled a young (or old, for that matter) XauXaz.

Or had he? The Other was positive that his commandant, his baron, had great powers of disguise. Caliban saw, in The Other's baron, a young version of XauXaz.

Could the ancient XauXaz whom Caliban had known have disguised himself as von Bissell? If so, what for?

It was too confusing of a mystery, even for Doc Caliban's phenomenal intellect. Too confusing, at least, without more data.

Besides, he needed to deal with the little devil who was standing before him, smiling up at him and chuckling in the waning firelight of the burning house.

The Soldiers of Jehovah hideout had burned almost to the ground, with no risk to the surrounding forestry due to Caliban's unique explosives.

Yet the little rotund man, who had seemingly appeared out of nowhere, stood there in a three-piece suit in the dead of night, smirking at Caliban as if this were all the most normal, run-of-the-mill thing in the world.

Caliban recognized him as a man he had last seen in 1948. Like Caliban, the man had not aged—but only candidates of the Nine received the immortality elixir, and Doc never had the idea that this man was a candidate.

So how had he not aged a day?

The flames and dying embers of the burning house cast uncanny shadows and lights across the man's features, making him look like a cherubic devil in the firelight, almost as if he had come up from Hell itself to deliver some important, or unimportant, epistle to Doc.

The little man chuckled again, and his face and body distorted into sinister and impossible positions, as if Doc was trapped in a maze of funhouse mirrors.

Caliban was drowned in an ocean of blinding white, and once again he was thrust into an even deeper vision of The Other. Now Caliban dreamed that he was in The Other's body, in The Other's head and brain and consciousness.

He quite literally *was* The Other.

A man had entered a shop on Hollywood Boulevard a few blocks from Vine. The man was close to seven feet tall, white-haired, white-bearded, and wrinkle-faced. His eyes were blue, but someone standing close beside him might have noticed that he wore contact lenses. The man looked around the large store, which dealt mainly in comic books and science-fiction. He walked over to a counter behind which sat an enormously fat man with spectacles so thick they looked like the bottoms of Coca-Cola bottles.

"Lacewing," the old man said softly.

The fat man rubbed his unshaven jowls. "Follow me."

He rose ponderously from his chair and went through a door. When the big old man had entered, the fat man closed and locked the door. He waddled down a short hall and into a slovenly bedroom, the door of which he locked also. He sat down by a table. The other accepted his curt invitation to take a chair opposite him. He refused the offer of a cigar and a beer.

The fat man drank, then said, "This place isn't bugged. I made sure of that."

The old man pointed at a small steel safe, covered with dust, in a corner. "They're in there?"

"Maybe. First I got to make sure who you are. *They* told me to take all precautions. You know what happens if you don't obey *their* orders."

"I'm not under *their* orders," Lacewing said. "They did a job for me, for which *they* were well paid. But, very well."

He removed the contact lenses. The fat man looked closely into his eyes. "Yeah. Okay. I wondered why you were using the name of Lacewing. Sounds like some fairy. So I looked it up in the dictionary. A lacewing's an insect with golden eyes."

The fat man shook his head, his jowls swinging like half-reefed sails in a breeze, water bags on the side of a walking camel. He put a pudgy paw on the old man's arm, caught a fold of skin in his fingers, and pulled. The big veined pale wrinkled material tore loose, revealing smooth deeply tanned skin beneath. Lacewing's hand came down and squeezed on the offending arm. The fat man's face twisted, and he turned white. Lacewing released the arm. The fat man groaned and held his arm. "You must have bent them together. Jesus! Man! I didn't mean nothing!"

Lacewing said, "Now you know." He patted the pseudoskin down flat. "Get them out of the safe."

The fat man got up unsteadily, his right arm dangling, and went to the safe. His body blocked the view of Lacewing, who, purposefully, showed no interest in the combination numbers.

The fat man brought over a small steel box in one hand, put it on the table, and unlocked it. He opened the lid and said, "I was told you was to check them out. Don't worry, I wouldn't cross *them* . . . or you either."

Lacewing chose the larger object to unwrap first. The cords and paper off, a transparent plastic envelope containing a roughly rectangular and ragged-edged sheet of some yellowed parchment material was revealed. The side to the fat man was blank. Lacewing looked at the writing, which was of an alphabet only a few scholars could read. And they wouldn't admit it.

He rewrapped it, and untied the cords of the second package and removed the paper. He held in his hands a nine-sided greenish stone, flat on both sides, a word in the same alphabet or syllabary incised on one side. A hole had been drilled at one end, ostensibly for a cord to be worn around the neck.

The fat man leaned over the table to look closely at it. But he straightened up and backed away. "There's something coming from it! It's . . . cold . . . evil!"

Lacewing could feel the emanations too, but he said nothing. After rewrapping it, he put both objects in the box, locked it, and slipped the box into a capacious pocket inside his huge overcoat.

The fat man asked, "They're okay?"

Lacewing nodded.

The fat man said, "What are . . . ?"

Lacewing raised a hand and said, "Don't ask." He rose, and a minute later walked out of the store. He wondered what the fat man was thinking; he could guess what questions burned in the fat man as the stone did in his pocket. The fat man would have liked to ask him what he'd been doing since he retired from public view in 1949. Here was a very rich man, a surgeon, an inventor, a philanthropist, a crime-fighter. One of New York's biggest newspapers had called him "a combination of Leonardo da Vinci, Sherlock Holmes, Croesus, and Tarzan. The last of the Renaissance men." And suddenly he'd dropped out of sight. Lacewing knew about the rumors because he'd heard them while in hiding. The one which everybody knew was that the Mafia had finally disposed of him. But the tales told in certain criminal circles was that he'd been engaged, in partnership with a certain Englishman, in fighting an underground battle against the nine persons who secretly ruled the world. The criminals in the know, very few, actually, had word that he was to be killed on sight and a tremendous sum would be paid to the person who would bring his hands and head as proof that the deed had been done.

Then, all of a sudden, the word was that the Nine had been wiped out, but the two nemeses had been killed in the final conflict. The first part of this was true. The second was based on information which Lacewing and his partner had released. Organized crime and many high governmental officials throughout the world had rejoiced. They would not have to share their spoils any longer with the nine controllers.

And then a rumor had followed this. The two had discovered that the Nine had been themselves controlled by even more powerful things. Not persons but things.

That had been scoffed at as sheer fantasy. The cognoscenti were aware that they had been governed by some shadowy and all-powerful organization. That control was gone overnight. But that there were beings, not even human, who had dictated to the Nine, that was unbelievable.

The few very well-informed among the criminal world had their doubts about the falseness of this report. But they kept their silence. There was no way of proving their suspicions. Besides, since the over-rulers were gone, and no one had replaced them, why worry about it?

The man now calling himself Lacewing had heard other rumors, however. There was a story that he had been to Antarctica to investigate the story of one of his most trusted aides about a hidden city there. And there was the tale that he had encountered some terrifying things deep in a cave in New England. Both, as he knew, were essentially true, though the details of the bruited-about stories were mostly incorrect.

He'd heard variations of these tales in Manhattan, Brooklyn, Chicago, Los Angeles, Bristol, Marseilles, Athens, Budapest, Tel Aviv, Istanbul, Saigon, Lhasa, New Delhi, Brisbane, Tokyo, Hawaii,

Buenos Aires, Nairobi, Johannesburg, Cairo, a village in New Guinea, Easter Island, and Guatemala. They were told in soft voices in circles high and low. Nor did the tellers know whom they were talking to.

Lacewing had always been a rationalist, a skeptic, a scientist. But in 1948, when he had trailed a man, or what he believed to be a man, into a subterranean complex, he had found things that he couldn't explain. He could have stumbled into the inferno described by Dante, but he refused to believe that. The weird forms of life could not be the souls of the dead. There was no such thing as Hell, not, at least, that which some Christians postulated.

After his terrifying experiences there, he had blocked up the entrance. Not to keep the things from getting out, since that seemed impossible, but to keep humans from going into it. For the first time in his life he'd encountered beings whom he dared not combat.

However, though he intended to leave them alone, they, who- ever they were, would not let him go his own way. After a series of "accidents" and attacks, in which twice he was badly injured, he decided to go underground.

Had he and the Englishman somehow missed killing one of the Nine, or one of their candidates who was now bent on revenge? Or were the "things" of unspeakable power that had allegedly ruled the Nine responsible? Or, both, working together?

Shortly thereafter, in early 1972, his English partner informed him that XauXaz had indeed survived their recent purge of the Nine. The old man could come after him and his partner, as well as other members of their families. And of course, with the Nine obliterated, XauXaz would want an elixir and he would also likely harass them just for amusement. A thirty-thousand-year-old was easily bored, and XauXaz had been known to be particularly mercurial.

Knowing that if he tried to run his financial empire from a secret headquarters, he could be traced, Lacewing withdrew a large amount of money, hid portions here and there, and in late 1972 faked his and his wife's deaths in an Arctic air crash. It hurt him not to let his daughter, and the men closest to him, his best friends and aides, be privy to his plan. But they could be seized and information wrested from them. He heard through various sources that they had looked for him for a long while, not believing that he was truly dead. Failing, they had retired, since they were already somewhat elderly, and he was the one who'd held them together. He'd finally sent them notes then, telling them that he was still alive but couldn't reveal his whereabouts. If he succeeded some day, perhaps, he would reemerge, and they would hold a reunion. He imagined that they had been deeply hurt, but he had to stay away from them for their sake and his.

He did, however, finally succumb to his wife's pressure, and almost a year after he disappeared, through highly secure and secret channels, he informed his daughter that he and his wife still lived. But not their location, or their next move.

As it was, he was being shadowed and a number of times barely escaped being killed. He safely hid his wife way, and kept moving on until he had felt he had shaken his pursuers. During his travels, he did considerable research into a field which he would once have dismissed as being too irrational to deserve more than a surface study: the occult.

Nine years later, he had determined what he needed to reopen the war. But he had to have a large organization to look for, locate, and get the two items he needed. His own worldwide agency had been dissolved shortly after his disappearance. So, he had made contact with the chiefs of an organization that had once been his bitterest enemy. They were evil, but they were human. Moreover, he was sure that they were not under the control of the forces that were after him.

The meetings had taken some delicate arrangements. The chiefs were surprised that he was still alive. Naturally, they were suspicious. Was he setting a trap for them? But finally, the conferences were held under circumstances which ensured that neither he nor they could harm the other.

It had been difficult for him to convince them that he was not insane. But he had done so, and they, who had committed the most horrifying of crimes in cold blood, were horrified and their blood frozen. They were also frightened. But he did not ask them to get involved. He only required that they obtain for him the two items he desired.

The chief of chiefs, the *capo di capi*, had said yes. They would attempt to get the items, provided, of course, that he pay the price.

Business as usual, even if Armageddon threatened. In spring 1984 he got the word to go to the store in Hollywood. During the two years of waiting, he had planned the attack. Then he'd gotten the two items, and he'd taken six months experimenting with them. He'd also pursued researches ranging from geological through psychic. And he'd resisted the temptation, most often occurring late at night, to call in his former aides to help him.

Much of his life, he'd been alone but not lonely. Now, however, as he considered what he hoped to do, he felt a loneliness that sometimes made him throw himself on the floor and beat his fists against it while he wept. Until a few years ago he had not believed in a soul, since there was no scientific evidence for its existence. Now he knew that when he went down into the depths, he was placing his soul in jeopardy. Using the two items, pitting evil against evil, he was in direst peril. Even if they were weapons for good, they would not thereby be changed in nature. And, unless handled with a steady mastery, they would be as dangerous as the foe against which they would be opposed.

Caliban was shaken.

The Other, Lacewing, was gone.

Caliban saw a steel knife sheathed in blood and gore, making deceptively soft and silky slurping noises as it effortlessly jack-hammered deep slices into flesh and muscle and organs.

Then, Caliban's senses fully returned. He struggled to push the knife out of his thoughts as he evaluated the cherubic man standing in front of him. He was short, round-faced—like a youngish, beardless Santa—and was smiling smugly as if he could barely contain his laughter at some joke that Doc didn't understand but was clearly at his expense.

The man, who had called himself Scott Free, had figured prominently in an adventure which Caliban recalled with horror and much puzzlement. That is, when he did think about it, which was as seldom as he could help.

Caliban and his aides and some others had ventured deep into a labyrinthine cavern complex in New England. There they had encountered things which Mr. Free (one of the party) had said were the metamorphosed spirits of the dead. "Devils." Free claimed to be a lower-echelon devil who had escaped from Hades. Caliban, a rationalist and agnostic, did not believe Free's explanation. Yet, some of the events had no acceptable explanations. Whatever the truth, Caliban had escaped something very horrible. He had had no desire to explore the caverns again. At the same time his scientific curiosity about them had tormented him from time to time.

The adventure had been thirty-six years ago, and here was Mr. Free looking as young as then.

The little cherub grinned devilishly in the waning orange fire-light. "What's up, Doc?"

Scott Free laughed uproariously at his own joke. "Get it? Get it? God, I've been waiting *years* for that one!"

"How did you get here, Free?" Caliban's features were like those of a bronze statue. "What do you want?"

Free was still laughing, much too amused with himself. This finally died down to a chuckle, and the little man was able to gasp out a response. "Can't you guess?"

"There were enough guessing games, enough tricks, the last time we met. Are you with the Nine?"

"Well . . ."

"The last time I saw you was outside the caverns in Maine. Now you're here in California. Why haven't you aged?"

"Why haven't *you* aged?"

Doc took a deep breath, stifled an annoyed sigh.

"If you're here, then you know I'm trailing the Nine, which means you're connected to them. You might be with them, or against them."

Free had a sly look on his face. "Why not come with me? All your questions can be cleared up."

"You'll have to do better than that."

"Hmm. What if I said you have no choice?"

"So, you mean to make me your prisoner?"

Free's round face lit up. "Yes! You've got it!"

"Who gives you your orders?"

Now Free looked hurt.

"Come on, give," Doc said. "Are you taking orders from 'Satan,' or whatever you implied, all those years ago, was Satan? Or the Nine? Or are you working on your own?"

Free clamped his mouth shut.

Remembering his prior reactions, Caliban pulled a lighter from a pocket, thumbed the flint, and waved the small flame in Free's face.

The plump little man's eyes widened in terror, and he emitted a strangled yelp of fear. "Now, stop it! You damned—knock it off, I said! I can't take it!"

Doc, waving the lighter in this direction and that, maneuvered Free into backing up against a semicircle of thick trees. The chubby man turned to run, but couldn't fit between the trunks and turned back to Doc, cornered, his eyes round and the whites blazing in the fading firelight. Doc punched him in the mouth, rattling teeth and eliciting an ear-piercing wail from the back of Free's throat. He pulled his punch significantly because he didn't want to kill the little man. On the other hand, he wasn't quite sure exactly what Free was, and whether or not a full-strength punch could actually seriously damage Free.

Doc hit him a second time, and the little man's eyes rolled up in his skull. He fell forward and landed hard in the dirt.

Doc scooped Free up easily in one cabled arm and in short order deposited him in the back seat of the LTD. He started the car and drove it slowly and carefully downhill and out of the canyon, headlights out in case the fire department and police had been summoned in response to the house explosion.

Back at Trolling House, Caliban deposited the still unconscious Free in a cell and barred the door.

Doc had thumped at the nest often enough and hard enough, and now the wasps were buzzing. He got in contact with his two aides, Pauncho van Veelar and Barney Banks. They had been living under assumed names in upper New York, but were prepared to come at once when Doc summoned them.

Caliban then prepared a medical table with straps, measured out a dose of a truth drug and loaded it into a syringe, and prepared a recorder with a cassette tape.

He went back to the cell and peered through the window box set about a foot below his eye level.

Doc saw a black-winged leathery thing fluttering around in the cell, like a small bird trapped indoors. He couldn't see Free anywhere. The leathery thing, indistinct, flittered to the floor below his field of vision. He pressed his face against the bars of the window box and looked down. Scott Free was sitting with his back leaning against the heavy cell door, and tilting his head upward and smirking at Doc.

"Is something wrong?"

"Was something, a bird, in here with you?"

"Nobody here but us chickens," Free replied amiably.

Caliban's mouth tightened, though no one would have noticed it except, perhaps, his cousin Trish.

He unlocked the cell door and took Free by the arm. In the medical bay, he placed the plump little man on an examination table, strapped him down, and rolled up the man's sleeve. He prepared to inject the man with the truth serum.

"That won't work, you know."

Doc produced a lighter, flicked it on, and held the yellow flame close to Free's eyes.

"Will this work?"

"God! You don't have to resort to torture! Or drugs! I'll talk, I have no reason not to."

"That's fine," Doc said. "Let's try the drug anyway." He held the man's arm in an implacable grip with his left hand and worked the needle with his other. Then he flipped the record button on the cassette player. He also placed two electrodes on Free's forehead, which were in turn connected to an instrument panel on the far wall. The purpose of these was to monitor certain brain emanations and help Caliban determine the veracity of Free's answers.

Doc waited a few minutes for the truth drug to take effect, and then began.

"When we met in 1948, you claimed that the deep caverns in Maine led down to Hades, and that the weird creatures we encountered there were the inhabitants, the doomed souls consigned to Hell. True or false?"

Free hesitated. Then, he confessed: "Hades, true. Doomed souls . . . sort of."

"You claimed to be an emissary from Tophet, a minor devil, sent to take back an unfortunate explorer, a geologist who went too far down into the caverns and discovered Hell. True or false?"

"Yes."

"Explain. Tell me about yourself. Who or what are you?"

"Where I am from may as well be Hell," Free said. "And it's easiest to put it in those terms, religious terms and perspectives that are familiar to you. It gives you a frame of reference for understanding us."

"I am an agnostic," Caliban said. "Try framing it for me in non-religious terms. I'll try to keep up."

Free smiled and shrugged.

"Go ahead," Doc said. "You said you were an emissary?"

"Sure, if you like that word. Or a bounty hunter. That works too."

Caliban sighed. Free was testing even his iron-willed patience. He checked the monitor that was supposed to help him determine if Free was being honest or not. Caliban was inwardly surprised to note that the device indicated that Free was being truthful—truthful as he knew it, and at least not being actively deceptive.

"Let's try a different tack," Doc said. "How are you involved with the Nine? I know you are since you showed up at a hideout of their underlings."

"I don't know," Free said, "the Nine are pretty rough."

Caliban flicked the lighter and held it up to Free's face.

"All right! You don't have to be a tough guy!"

"Just talk."

"Okay! I was born in the middle of the eighteenth century. I had worked for the Nine. I got too ambitious. There was a vast fortune to be had, and I went against the Nine. Stupid me! They caught up with me, and I expected to be tortured and killed. Instead, I was condemned to be one of the guards at the cavern complex in New England.

"When I got to the caves in Maine, I discovered that I was to help guard something that the Nine only described to me as 'the monster in abeyance' or 'the monster on hold.' But it did have a name, Shrassk, meaning 'She-Who-Eats-Her-Children.'"

"A monster," Doc said. "Have you ever seen it?"

Free shuddered. "No, and I hope never to." Then he amended his answer and said quietly, "At least, I don't remember ever seeing it."

"Continue. Are you against the Nine now? Or still working for them?"

"Back then, in the eighteenth century, the Nine were faced with a situation similar to that of your and Grandrith's revolt. Three candidates tried to overthrow the Nine."

"Just answer my question."

Free looked hurt. "I'm getting to it! The three rebelling candidates had so disrupted the Nine's organization, slain so many agents and other candidates, come so close to killing some of the Nine, that the Council, in desperation, had summoned a thing from another dimension, or perhaps from a parallel universe."

"Not too parallel," Free added.

"Things," Caliban said, "are either parallel or they're not."

"All right. The other universe is, then, asymptotic. Which is why the area in which the monster is contained in the cave is partly in this world, partly out of it. Or, from what I understand, it may be suspended between two universes, acting as a sort of bridge.

"That thing," Free said, "was the monster, Shrassk."

"Go on," Doc said.

"Shrassk has the power, perhaps uncontrolled by it, a wild talent, to touch the subconscious of some sensitive human receptors and cause nightmares. God only knows what else."

Caliban's mind started to reel at this revelation, though his bronzed features remained as expressionless as ever. He began to put together what had been happening to him—and what had affected his aides back in Tilatoc's fortress, and perhaps even Grandrith's mother, Alexandra Applethwaite. Shrassk's "touching" may have been what caused Lovecraft to form the so-called Cthulhu Mythos, a dimly perceived and mostly fictional concept but based on the real horror.

"In any event," Free continued, "Shrassk was not to be released directly upon the world in an effort to get the three rebels of the eighteenth century. While Shrassk was held in abeyance, it would reproduce after some mysterious mating and conception. It was said that the 'Children' were born out of flame by Shrassk. And the

Children would be loosed to seek out and destroy the three without fail. Some Children, that is.

"Before that happened, the three rebels were caught, tortured, and then fed to Shrassk."

Caliban thought about the three rebels and questioned if the story was true, given its similarity to the story of the three murderers of Freemasonry, who in turn had been referenced in an alleged clue to the Ripper murders. He wondered if Free—Freemason?—knew that his and Grandrith's father was Jack the Ripper, and if the plump little man was trying to tell him something. If so, what? A quick glance at the veracity indicator showed Caliban that the other man was telling the truth about the three traitors.

Caliban decided to let Free continue on the topic of the monster. He'd come back to the Ripper if there was time.

"Shrassk," Free said, "would not go back to where it had come from. The Nine had to maintain the guards for the Children and the forces that held it back from entering this world. Meanwhile, Shrassk was breeding, though very slowly, more of the Children."

Free added, "Shrassk is imprisoned by geometry but, if it escapes, will do so by algebra."

"What does that mean?" Doc asked.

Free smiled amiably but was unable, or unwilling, to clarify this enigmatic remark.

"Up until now," Caliban said, "you've provided useful information. But you haven't answered a question: what are you? What is your nature, your true nature? Don't lie to me, I've already deduced that you are not human, or at least not fully human. No other explanation fits the observable facts."

"Well," Free said, "back in '48, I had escaped from the cavern, but you and your gang had forced me to reenter it. After we all got out of the cave, and you had me thrown in jail, I teleported myself out."

"Really."

"Yes!"

"Then, back then, why didn't you just teleport yourself out of the caverns and leave us hanging there? Or, for that matter, out of the car on the drive up to the caves—unless you can't teleport when you're inside a moving object. Or, why didn't you just teleport away when we had you captive in the schooner off the Maine coast?"

"The teleportation is a power not always on tap. After a few 'discharges,' I have to recharge my battery."

"So, you teleported onto the schooner just before we found you there, and that used up all your energy, temporarily at least?"

"Yes, that's it exactly!"

Caliban shook his head, checked the monitor.

"You're lying."

Free had the good grace to appear embarrassed at being caught in the untruth.

"Come on," Doc said, "give. What are you?"

Free's expression morphed from embarrassment to mirth. "Okay, but you're not going to like it!"

Scott Free shimmered on the medical table. In the place of the little Santa-shaped man was a whiteish-grayish, vaguely humanoid-blob, covered in numerous writhing needle-pointed tentacles. Unblinking, pale blue cat's eyes with black pupils formed from and melted back into the whiteish skin, or whatever the surface of the thing was that passed for skin, at random spots all over its body, with some clustering at the bases of the extruding tentacles. Tiny leathery wings sprouted at random from the thing's skin and were just as quickly reabsorbed.

Then the blob wavered and the human visage of Free was back, grinning.

"Believe it or not," he said, "I don't know where we come from. We've been around for millennia, and some of our ancient ancestors escaped to other planets. Some of their descendants evolved on different paths and have even ended up back on Earth in different times and places."

"All right. Tell me everything you can about your species."

"We are shapeshifters."

"Obviously," Caliban said dryly. "I believe I encountered a thing similar to you in the Antarctic once, and then, a few years later on another Antarctic expedition, we found evidence of your kind, or a related species, dating back at least fifty million years. But the first encounter was definitely of the extraterrestrial kind, and we were able to date that thing to approximately twenty million years old. It had been frozen for that long, and we accidentally awakened it when we discovered its vessel."

"Yes," Free replied, "we've been around a long time. Like I said, some of our forebears left Earth at various times. Many of these undoubtedly developed in different directions and some succeeding generations have clearly explored the cosmos . . . they may have 'discovered' Earth, not even understanding that they were originally seeded from here."

"The first one of you I encountered killed, or caused the deaths of, fifteen men, and some huskies. It could also absorb the memories and persona of whatever it mimicked."

Free laughed. "Sounds bad. I hope you killed it!"

"You do?"

"Of course! I'm a shapeshifter, not a killer!"

Caliban prompted Free for more details. "That thing reproduced itself at will, splitting into different parts and replacing many of our men. How does your race reproduce? And for that matter, what do you call yourselves?"

"We're called Ssk'eth," Free said. "We reproduce asexually, with an approximately once-a-century reproduction cycle during which we produce a huge quantity of eggs. Pretty things, really, look a bit like little star sapphires."

"Can you mate with humans?" Doc asked suddenly.

Free stared back at Doc with a shrewd expression. "Yes."

Caliban once again consulted the veracity monitor.

"You're telling the truth," he said, "as you know it, and I don't think it's the truth serum. Why are you cooperating now?"

Free now evinced an odd expression, a combination of sly and sincere.

"Because I think we can help each other," he replied. "Now, the Nine are so desperate that they are considering letting loose a 'Child' of Shrassk to destroy you, Grandrith, and your cousin and your aides. If that Child doesn't succeed, another will be released. And another."

"Why the business about Hades and the Devil?" Caliban asked.

"Like I said, I was framing it in terms and concepts most people—at least those who hold the prevalent religious beliefs of this time and place—could relate to. Besides . . . that asymptotic space may as well be Hell, and Shrassk and her Children may as well be the Devil and her minions. It's really all the same result in the end.

"Now," Free added, "as long as Shrassk and her Children have awakened, the Nine plan to use them to end your revolt."

"Why have Shrassk and her Children awakened?" Caliban asked.

Free shrugged. "I've told you everything I know."

Doc wondered if, despite Free telling the truth, or at least mostly being truthful, the little round man hadn't been planted by the Nine to lure Caliban to go back to the caves in Maine.

Nevertheless, Doc decided that he would attack.

Caliban would take the fight to the New England caverns.

PART III

DOWN TO EARTH'S CENTRE

1984

Doc Caliban gave the signal. He and three others—Trish Wilde, Barney Banks, and Pauncho van Veelar—approached the small stone and concrete fortress from two sides.

The structure was built into the side of a steep mountain. Doc and Pauncho approached from below, while Trish and Barney had circled around and now were hidden amid the pine trees on the slope above the building, awaiting Caliban's signal.

All four were outfitted in heavy-duty all-weather apparel: tough pants, jackets, and sturdy boots. All wore, under this, a lightweight mesh body armor that Doc had first developed in the 1930s and had refined over the ensuing decades. They also wore hoods of the same material under heavier alloyed helmets which were equipped with small but powerful flashlights controlled by a small set of control switches mounted on their belts. These switches also activated lights mounted on the upper straps of their backpacks and which, when turned on, shot two piercing beams over the wearer's shoulders. The small bulbs held a gas mixture, again developed by Doc, which emitted a high intensity beam, and which were more durable than normal bulbs. This, combined with the tough metallic casing and the lens of transparent steel, would help preserve the critically needed lamps on what was sure to be an arduous expedition—if they even made it through the guardhouse and into the Stygian depths below.

They were also armed—some might have said over-armed, but they would have been wrong—with rapidfire guns, gas-powered pistols that shot drug-coated hypodermics and other projectiles, and flamethrowers.

Caliban also carried, wrapped in a protective waterproof pouch tucked safely underneath his armor, a length of root known to grow only in the Ubangi country of west Africa. This had been sent to him from Cornwall by his good friend, Lord Clanbrasil.

Following Doc's plan, they all moved as close as possible to the bunkerlike structure while still remaining out of sight of any guards within. Then, Pauncho sauntered up and knocked on the huge metal door. Metal louvers in a side window swiveled partially open and a long gun barrel appeared between the slats.

"Whoa!" Pauncho said. "Don't fire! I'm just a lost hiker!"

"Beat it!" came a voice from within.

"Aw, come on, have a heart," Pauncho said. "Just gimme some directions and I'll get out of here."

Then he sprang to the window, grabbed the barrel in his simian paws, yanked it toward him, and with his gorillalike strength bent the metal at a forty-five-degree angle, using the window as a fulcrum. Simultaneously, Trish's rapidfire pistol sprayed the thick door's heavy lock with bullets, pulverizing it.

Cries of alarm came from within the bunker and the front door flew open—the inhabitants apparently opting for offense rather than defense. Anesthetic bullets spat from Doc's rapidfire pistol and the man who had been exiting the door fell forward on his face. Pauncho sprang around the open doorway and liberally sprayed the interior with sedative bullets from his own pistol. He flattened then rolled out of the way in case he missed anyone. Giving it thirty seconds, he inched back to the edge of the door, peeked around the frame carefully and quickly, and noted three forms crumpled on the concrete floor. He scanned the interior and saw nothing else.

Pauncho spoke into the microphone taped under his jaw. "Pongo." He had attempted to whisper but the word still came through the others' speakers as a low rumble.

Doc Caliban approached and turned over the man whom he had shot. "Collins!"

"Who?" Trish asked. She and Barney had just climbed down from behind the fortress, in response to Pauncho's all clear.

"Collins," Caliban replied, "was on board the schooner *Megas Too*. He was a friend of the psychiatrist who had chartered the yacht. They're the ones that found the geologist, Philmore, who thought he had escaped from Hell, and got me and Jocko and Porky into this mess back in '48.

"Scott Free," Doc added, "claimed that Collins was a fellow 'devil,' sent after him after he failed to capture Philmore and retrieve him back down under." He gestured to the unconscious Collins. "Just like Free, he hasn't aged since then."

"Doc," Barney said, "it's all a bit much. I mean, Hell? The actual fires below, with Lucifer and demons and little horned devils?"

"I never said I believed it, Barney," Caliban said. "I'm telling you what Free claimed at the time. He's since stated that whatever awaits us below is not exactly as you've stated, and yet is still a hellish place—a place that may as well be Hell, as far as he and others are concerned."

"Yes, but even so—"

Pauncho thrust his already prognathous jaw in Barney's face. "Can it, shyster!"

"Shyster! That was my dad, not me—I mean—"

"Haw, haw!" Pauncho poked his friend in the chest. "But I mean it. My pa told me all about what he saw up here—he made it down there into the caves with Doc. Your dad didn't get that far, he didn't see everything. It was weird, unexplained stuff. Not like all those other adventures where they found the guys and the gadgets behind what was happening. Now, friend, are you callin' my pa Jocko Simmons a liar?"

"Oh, for God's sake, of course not, Pauncho." Barney, seeing how deadly serious his pal was, refrained from his usual cutting retort. "I'm just saying, these guys Collins and Free were somehow associated with the Nine, or at least Free was, so maybe they have the elixir? Why are we suddenly talking about all this supernatural stuff?"

"It's not so sudden," Trish interrupted, "or have you forgotten what happened to us all at Tilatoc's fortress?"

Caliban said, "And I—"

Hell broke loose.

A gray tentacle was coiling around Pauncho's ankle and making its way rapidly up his calf and tree trunk thigh. He gave a startled cry. The tentacle was extruding from Collins' foot. The rest of Collins melted into the ground and spread out into a puddle of white-gray gelatin. Several more tentacles projected from the mass and shot toward Pauncho's arms and throat. Before he or the others could effectively react, his short legs and long torso were completely encircled. The puddle coalesced into a blob-sphere and started rolling. Pauncho was yanked off his feet like a lassoed calf and dragged through the dirt by the rolling sphere toward the open doorway. Another tentacle flattened into a large flap and covered his face like a rubber death mask.

"Formation L!" Caliban yelled.

He, Trish, and Barney ran a few steps away from the doorway, turned, but remained clustered together. They drew guns that were connected to narrow strong hoses attached to backpack apparatuses which they all wore. Doc had equipped them for this mission with the flame guns he had invented, in anticipation of the difficulties they might face. The guns were powered by highly compressed fuel in the backpack tanks, so that there would be a large supply for their underground expedition.

Very narrow, highly concentrated torrents of flame shot from three muzzles, precisely targeting the thing—Collins—that had Pauncho wrapped up.

The thing gave forth an earsplitting shriek as the flames torched and crisped its skin. The burning skin also gave off an odor that was so acrid, Doc wondered if it might be toxic.

The blob's tentacles loosened, and the rubber flaplike appendage came loose from Pauncho's nose and mouth, and he rolled away from the flaming mass, gasping for breath.

More writhing appendages shot through the open doorway, seeking likely targets.

Trish directed a spray of fire toward them. "Looks like the sedatives have worn off of the other guards!"

"Frankly," Doc said, "I'm a little surprised the anesthetic bullets worked at all on their physiology—though I did have a little time to study Free's makeup and make some adjustments to the formula." He joined his cousin in dowsing the probing limbs with a stream of fire from the flamethrower gun. Their defense was successful mostly because the questing tentacles were bunched, by necessity, in the doorway and therefore could not come at Doc and Trish and Barney from all sides. In short order, no more tentacular appendages ventured forth from the guardhouse.

"Doc!" Barney called. "We've got trouble!"

Banks had turned, back-to-back with Doc and Trish, and was sweeping his flamethrower left and right and back to the left in wide arcs at the menace that approached.

The trees, pines and balsam firs, had uprooted and were shuffling toward them on multi-tentacled "feet," converging on the trio in a steadily shrinking half circle.

One of the pine trees raised a branch toward Barney and there was a great puff.

"Ouch! Dammit!" A clump of needles protruded from Barney's cheek; blood was welling from the pinlike puncture wounds. Several other clumps had stuck in his jacket and trousers, and another bunch had bounced off his helmet.

A purplish blotch appeared on Barney's cheek where the needles were embedded.

"Uh, Doc, I don't feel so good." Barney collapsed in a heap.

"Barney!" Pauncho, recovered from his near-suffocation by the Collins-thing, came running up as more clusters of the pine needles flew through the air. Despite their endless bickering, which sometimes threatened to erupt into physical violence, the two Korean War buddies were devoted pals, either of whom would lay down his life for the other.

"Pauncho, face shield!" Doc ordered. He and Trish had already lowered theirs. The plastic face coverings extended from their helmets and were not airtight, but could provide a defense against the hurling barbs.

Pauncho did as Doc instructed and knelt by his buddy. Doc crouched bedside him.

"It's some kind of venom" the bronze man said. "I'll take care of Barney. You and Trish deal with the trees."

Pauncho grinned a mouthful of blocklike teeth. "You got it, Doc!"

The gorilloid man jumped to his feet and bounded headlong into the battle, firing his flame gun seemingly in all directions at once.

"C'mon, Red!" he called to Trish, and then plunged deeper into the melee. Robbed of their ability to poison their prey with the venomous needles, the shapeshifting trees contorted and extended their branches, like ectoplasm.

"For every limb I fry," Trish yelled, "I miss five more! There're too many of them for just two of us with guns to corral. And the tree trunks are managing to stay out of the way of our flamethrowers while they keep us occupied with their limbs and tentacles."

Doc called from off the side of the battle, where he was ministering to Banks. "Keep on holding them off and covering them for just another few minutes, Trish! Barney will be okay!"

Pauncho gave a whooping war cry at this news and redoubled his efforts, shooting hot blue flame in ever widening and unpredictable arcs, trying to keep the shapeshifters off balance and buy Caliban the time he needed.

Trish also sprang forward, and after dodging several grasping tree branches, managed to set aflame the trunks of two particularly tall Eastern white pines. These screeched in evident pain and fury as they went up in flames and reverted to their true forms, bloblike flesh crisping and boiling under the intense heat.

"Fall back!" Doc yelled.

Pauncho and Trish turned and saw Caliban running uphill on the left side of the concrete guard box, Barney cradled in his powerful arms and being carried as easily as if he were a baby. In seconds, they had joined Doc and Barney, and were crouching on the slope above and behind the guard box.

"Running a little low on fuel, Doc," Pauncho said. "Wasn't planning on using so much up this early in the game . . ."

"Well," Trish said, "the way you were indiscriminately firing without letting up on the trigger . . ."

Pauncho chuckled. "What, you fillin' in for Barney now, Red?"

Doc said, "We've used up more fuel than anticipated in this battle. But it was necessary. When we're out of this, though, we will spend a little more time training on the flamethrower settings which can make them more fuel efficient as well as more precise. Meantime . . ."

Four silver machines flew overhead in a square formation. They hovered over the thicket of mobile trees. In unison they dowsed the moving grove with sheets of orange and blue flame.

"Whirleys!" Pauncho said.

Caliban had the group of shapeshifters, the Ssk'eth guards that had been disguised as various species of Maine pine and fir trees, pinned down with hovering "whirleys." The name was a misnomer because the hovering and flying devices did not have any moving parts. Lift and directional maneuvering were accomplished with small anti-gravity generators that Doc had invented. The whirleys carried the same compacted fuel that was in their backpacks. Facial and body recognitional algorithms had been fed into the navigational and firing computers of the whirleys, and so Doc, Pauncho, Barney, and Trish were not targeted. Anything else moving was a potential target, although if Caliban observed an innocent or unidentified actor come into the field of battle, he could quickly override the whirley's programming, or take manual control.

The trees, or rather now the burning piles of gelatinous flesh, were no longer moving.

A whiteish blob rolled out of the guardhouse below them, extruded a plethora of tentacles, and skittered up the building's walls and across the roof toward them. Several pale blue eyes appeared in the surface of the thing, and these appeared to be blazing in fury. Tiny, deadly looking white needles popped out of the tips of the waving appendages.

One of the whirleys broke formation, darted above the approaching Ssk'eth guard, and spat firestream. The shapeshifter screamed and went up in flames.

The whirley retreated, lowered, directed sensors through the doorway, and rose again. A green light blipped on its surface.

"All clear," Caliban said.

Doc had gotten into contact, after interrogating Scott Free, with van Veelar and Banks and, after some difficulty, with his cousin, Trish.

Preparatory to the assault on the fortress maintained by the Nine and staffed by Ssk'eth shapeshifters, they had converged on the old log cabin far down the hill, the cabin that had been home to the wayward geologist, Philmore, and his sister, Ilona, back in the late '40s.

The cabin was musty, deserted, but serviceable for a few nights' stay and to plan their battle strategy.

"So, Doc," Pauncho said, "the last time you were up here, you suspected just about everyone of not being who they said they were. Scott Free, and the psychologist, as well as his pal who rescued Philmore. Was Philmore really a geologist or was he another one like Free?"

"I believe he was what he said he was," Doc said. "He and his sister cleared out of here pretty quickly after we escaped from the caves."

"What about the shrink?" Barney asked.

Caliban paused for a moment before answering. "There was something off about him. But my perspective at the time, my rational and scientific thought processes, would not allow me to accept that, to explore it further. If it was not based on clearly demonstrable evidence and data, then it was not worth pursuing."

"It seems that your approach has changed somewhat?" Trish asked.

"I had, as you know," her cousin replied, "an awakening of sorts in the aftermath of my battle with Grandrith. I've studied Asian philosophies and meditation, and pursued other modalities of thought, of processing and evaluating information. And since our experiences at Tilatoc's headquarters, my perspective has continued to evolve."

"Well then, what was off about the psychologist?" Trish asked.

"I had the sense, the perception, of the familiar. As if . . . if I could only catch him at the right moment, out of the corner of my eye, I might have recognized him." Caliban shook his head. "It was ridiculous, of course. He resembled no one I had ever known, not in appearance, speech, mannerisms. The sense that he, nonetheless, was known to me, was fanciful, at the time."

"And now?" Trish prompted.

Doc shrugged. "Who knows?"

"Speaking of who knows," Barney said, "what happened to Free? I figured you'd drag him along with us like you did last time. And where's Barbara?"

"I thought about bringing Free with us, but in the end decided it would be more trouble to keep tabs on him than it was worth. And although the information I extracted from him is, I believe, trustworthy, he himself is far from reliable and trustworthy, and I still wasn't positive he's not an agent of the Nine. So, I left him in an escape-proof cell, or what I think is escape proof for one of his kind. There are remote systems to provide for his sustenance and other physical needs, though I didn't have time to make a thorough evaluation of all of his bodily functions.

"As for Barbara, she's completely dropped out of sight, and I couldn't locate her."

"Couldn't locate her!" Barney chortled. "Did you ask Kong here? I figured they'd both be keeping tabs on each other even if we were in hiding and living under assumed names."

"Yeah, yeah," Pauncho said, grumbling. "She took a powder, but good."

"I wonder if she rejoined the Nine," Trish said.

"The Nine," Doc said, "would hardly take Barbara back into the fold after she's battled against them."

Trish, playing devil's advocate, said, "What if she took the improved elixir to them?"

Barney had now recovered, thanks to Doc's superlative medical skills and the unique contents of his first aid kit. Caliban also gave Barney a stimulant since, even though his life was saved from the deadly venom excreted by the shapeshifter's needles, he would take longer to recover without the drug, and they needed to get moving. After all, it was unlikely that, when taking the small fortress at the opening of the cave, they had prevented at least one of the guards from getting a warning message off to someone—whoever or whatever resided in the cavern's black depths.

Doc, Trish, Barney, and Pauncho recovered the whirleys and brought them into the stone fortress. There, the machines were dismantled and the four replenished their backpack tanks with fuel from the whirleys, for the remote flying devices would not be effective or functional in the deep cave system.

Caliban and the others began their descent into the many-leveled subterranean complex. They were equipped with climbing and caving gear: ropes, hiking boots, and all-weather clothing which would retain body heat in areas of great cold, and was made of material that was breathable in the event they encountered heat pockets. They also carried canteens filled with water, water-purification tablets invented by Doc for use in case they came across underground streams, and food packs and tablets for sustenance. Each wore helmet- and shoulder-mounted lights, and also packed first aid kits, as well as their rapidfire guns and flame guns connected to the backpack fuel tanks. The first aid kits carried oxygen pills in case they encountered airless pockets, as well as other medicinal and medical advances developed by Doc. They also carried breathers connected to short term oxygen supplies. Hooked to their belts were several small but highly powerful grenades. Each had a set of night vision binoculars, the batteries of which, developed by Caliban, would power the optical devices for months, if necessary.

Like the last time he had descended, back in 1948, Caliban had applied to the soles of his boots, and those of his party, a fluorescent substance. When light of a particular wavelength was shined upon the ground, it would highlight their footprints, thus creating a suitable trail by which they could backtrack their way out of the cavern system, either as a group or singly, in the event they became separated. Doc once again applied the substance to his companions' boots.

As Caliban shut the reinforced door to the fortress and barred it on the inside, the beam of moonlight shining in diminished to a last sliver, then evaporated. It was not lost on the four that they were now cut off from the last vestiges of what they knew as the normal world, the simple sight of sunlight reflecting from Earth's moon and bathing the secluded New England valley in its silvery rays. The closing of the fortress door was their first step across the threshold, the opening move in a journey into the whispering unknown.

Doc lifted the hatch in the stone floor that sealed off the cave entrance, and descended an iron ladder, the rungs of which had been bolted into the living granite. The ladder went straight down, about fifty feet. The vertical descent through what was essentially a narrow cylinder or tube of rock was claustrophobic. Doc went first, with a little difficulty due to his great size, the backpack, and equipment. He planted his feet on the ground at the dank bottom and shined a light upward, clicking it off and on once. They had agreed to utilize their lights for simple communication and avoid speech whenever possible. They did have radio comms, but if they became separated it was unlikely the devices would function through thousands of feet of rock.

Trish came down next, followed quickly by Barney. Pauncho brought up the rear and closed the hatch above him. The landing at the bottom of the ladder was tiny, and the path forward very narrow. Again, Doc took the lead, and the four, all connected by a stout rope, traversed about forty feet of tight and low-ceilinged rock tunnel. The tunnel widened slightly and the four came to a halt. There were no sounds, and the dry air was slightly cooler. There was a distinct air-flow which carried upon it a weird, flowery scent.

Doc whispered, "The psychologist who tagged along last time, Carlos, speculated that the source of the odor is some subterranean plant life. I recall that Scott Free seemed to find this very amusing. Though they could have been putting on an act for my benefit; I was never really sure if they had been known to each other or not. We've learned about Free's true nature, or at least I think we have, but that doctor, Carlos, is still a mystery. Anyway, we'll be going in much deeper this time, so watch out for that scent, or other strange things, that might affect us. Keep your breathers handy."

The others gave tugs on the rope in response and the group moved slowly forward, and then very rapidly downward. Doc and the others noted that the geological cave formation was typical, at this point, of other more well-known subterranean systems such as Cave of the Winds in Colorado Springs and Mammoth Cave in Kentucky, extending at least four hundred miles, and perhaps as much as six hundred, in a labyrinthine underground complex.

They continued the downward descent, at times having to use their equipment to avoid out-of-control slides to the next ledges. They came to a large cavern and paused, shining their lights toward the ceiling and the far ends. The grotto was large, though not as voluminous as Carlsbad. They kept moving, through narrow tunnels, steep declines, and widening and tightening passages.

Caliban, remembering his last time down here, knew that it should get hotter and hotter below a certain level, but the walls of the caves and tunnels seemed to be lined with something which kept the heat out. Ironic, if they really were descending into Hell below.

The blackness, when they stopped to rest and turned off their electric torches, clung to them like a heavy blanket. The flowery odor was long gone, but stuck in their nostrils like an olfactory afterimage.

Barney checked the luminescent dial on his watch. "Over eight hours in."

"Who are you kidding, pretty boy," Pauncho said. "It's been two hours, tops!"

Barney shoved his wristwatch in the other's simian face. "Here, monkey-man. Didn't mamma van Veelar teach you how to tell time? The big hand here shows the hours, and the little hand—"

Pauncho slapped his pal's hand away, harder than necessary. "Watch it!"

"'Watch' it yourself, Fancy Dan! You and your Rolex are both off your rockers!"

"Knock it off," Caliban said. He pointed to his own timepiece. "Barney is right. We experienced this strange distortion in the perception of the passage of time the last time we were down here."

"No way!" Pauncho said.

"Maybe," Barney said, a snide tone clear in his voice, "if you spent more effort on the basics—telling time, personal grooming, simple addition and subtraction—you wouldn't have made Barbara pull a disappearing act."

"Why you—!"

"Cut it," Trish said, "both of you juvenile delinquents. Doc puts up with it, but I won't. I'm sick of it. It's a wonder any woman has ever gone to bed with either of you. So would you kindly *shut up*."

Both men, chastened, did as Trish demanded.

Eventually, as they continued their miles-long descent below the surface, the nature of the tunnels changed, becoming somewhat wider and easier to navigate, although the downward pitches, when these were encountered, became even steeper and required repeated rather than occasional use of their safety equipment.

Along the more level stretches, stalactites and stalagmites became increasingly prominent, the latter posing a minor hazard as they trudged along. If the stalagmites became more numerous, it could make it difficult to navigate around them without tripping in the darkness.

At the same time, the aroma that evoked flowers or vegetation returned, in force. Caliban had attempted to analyze this during his prior sojourn in the caves, and had determined that it was harmless to breathe, though he had failed to identify it. This time, in the interests of keeping moving, he decided against performing the same testing, but once again warned his comrades to keep their breathers handy in case of emergency.

Caliban, Pauncho, Trish, and Barney marched on, taking short breaks for snacks and water, and other necessities. About sixteen hours in they stopped and made camp, consumed a more substantial meal, and slept for several hours. Doc did not sleep, maintaining a constant guard.

They packed up and continued at least another two miles deep into the labyrinthine complex. Eventually, they arrived at a narrowing path which was cut into a vertical wall. The trail descended at a forty-five-degree angle and continued to decrease in width the closer they came to the bottom. Doc called a halt, shined his light below, and then made a great leap.

Trish aimed her own torch downward, realized her breath was held, and released it in a burst of relief. The path ended in a drop-off half a foot in front of her. Twenty feet below, Caliban stood looking up at her, arms wide.

"You'll each need to jump," the bronze man called. "I'll catch you."

Trish went first and found herself cradled in Caliban's powerful arms. He put her down, to the side, and warned her to watch the ledge.

Barney was next, and again Doc caught his comrade easily and set him down.

"Are you sure about this, Doc?" Pauncho called. "I can just use my equipment, put some spikes in the rock face and climb down."

"Jump for it, please, Pauncho."

The big man sighed and leaped into the abyss.

Caliban, again, caught his friend, for all his size and 280-pound bulk.

He then aimed his flashlight at the ground. They were all standing on a ledge only seven inches wide. The narrow shelf faded into the darkness twenty feet beyond the cone of Doc's light at a gentle but steady declination.

"Geez, Doc," Barney said, "you know we trust you with our lives, but you took a big risk having us jump down to this narrow ledge! We could've just used our equipment. What was the rush?"

Caliban drew a metal piton from his equipment belt and stabbed it into the rock face. The piton sank all the way in as if the "rock" were some sort of thick, gelatinous substance. He pulled downward and a deep, oozing gash appeared in the "rock" face.

"Holy shit!" Pauncho said.

Barney was pale, the blood having drained from his face. "I second the motion," he said weakly.

"How did you know?" Trish asked.

"I've been this way before," Doc said, "when I was chasing Scott Free down here. I recalled that this deep down, things began to get strange—including these fleshlike 'rock' faces. We'll need to take it even slower, more carefully, going forward."

The group moved cautiously down the ledge, Caliban once again in the lead.

Soon they reached a huge cavern, and this seemed to glow with an odd greenish-purple phosphorescence, an unholy luminosity which Doc admitted was inexplicable, because there was nothing living—no underground vegetation, moss, or phosphorescent algae, not even any bioluminescent bacteria—which would account for the radiance, never mind the increasingly pungent flower smell. Caliban also explained that radioactive minerals, or an underground mining operation involving atomic fission materials, had been ruled out.

The weird glow only enabled them to see ten feet in any direction, but their flashlights were little better than that, so they switched off the torches for the time being to conserve power. "This is about as deep as I made it with Free back in '48. Have your flame guns and grenades ready," he instructed.

They pressed forward into the green-purple gloom. Was their destination really Hell? Not the literal Hell as some churchgoers might describe it, but nonetheless a hellish place that might have given rise to hellish beings.

Caliban warned his friends what he thought was coming next. He could be wrong, of course. It had been thirty-six years, and there was nothing dictating that the denizens of this place had to stay put, that what he encountered before would be exactly what they would face this time. But relying on his prior experience was better than nothing, which was what they'd have when they made it past where he had turned back the last time. He instructed them to unhook and prime some grenades, and to be prepared to set timers on the explosives.

Caliban was not wrong.

In the next chamber they could dimly see a field of large things, vaguely spherical but otherwise shapeless, of a sickening whiteish-gray color that had a cast, in the purple-greenish glow, of human bone freshly shorn of flesh. The things were visible as far as they could see in the murky light, and Caliban suggested they not use their flashlights, as these would make instant targets out of the group.

Not that, Doc admitted, he knew whether the things, which resembled nothing so much as boulders, could actually see them or not, or perhaps sense them in a different way.

One "boulder" started rolling toward them, lurching this way and that, and they felt a fear, a reaction programmed deeply in their primate evolution, a response encoded and reinforced and handed down from their Old Stone Age ancestors. Their bowels tightened, their bladders filled, and the cold chill of fear of the unknown, the incomprehensible, shot through their spines and up through their shoulders and down their arms and fingers, and up into their hind-brains, and down through their legs, cementing their feet in place like the roots of thousand-year-old redwoods.

Even Doc Caliban, who had seen these things before, who had faced them and lived, stood entrenched in place as one boulder, then the next, and then the next rolled inexorably toward them, and started rolling faster.

And then Doc Caliban moved.

In one fluid motion, he pulled the pin from and tossed a grenade, launching it almost like a miniature bowling ball, so that it intersected the path and went under the nearest approaching boulder-thing. The grenade exploded, the force mainly directed upward at the stonelike thing above it, and leathery fragments of the shattered "boulder" bloomed up and out, showering Doc and his crew. The pieces were tough, skinlike, and at the same time with the hardness and heaviness of rocks, but the four were well protected by their lightweight armor and helmets.

"Roll your grenades, on timers," Doc yelled, "under the boulder creatures, just as I did. Quickly, before they overwhelm us!"

Trish and Barney and Pauncho touched buttons on their helmets, automatically inserting earplugs, and then rapidly followed suit, and soon were thinning the ranks of the stone things.

"Don't let them come too near," Caliban warned. "I've had one of these things slam into me, and they're just as tough and heavy as they look. They'll steamroll us if they get too close."

Pauncho had a grenade pin clenched between his blocklike teeth as he bowled an explosive toward an approaching stone. It hit its mark with a satisfying boom and the ensuing blast of leather-rock pieces rained down on them. He spit out the pin and his wide mouth broadened in an apelike grin. "Hey Doc, it's just like that arcade game, *Solar Raiders*! They're all coming toward us from the same direction, at different speeds, and we just take 'em out before they reach us!"

"Grow up, you bristly-haired baboon," Barney called.

"Both of you, stuff it," Trish said, tossing a grenade of her own. "While you're yammering, Doc and I are taking out twice as many as you two. And don't assume they'll come from only one direction."

After several minutes of repeated and deafening explosions, they had cleared most of the living boulders they could see and had moved forward through about three quarters of the chamber. Barney, following Trish's advice, had turned and covered their backs as they pressed forward. It was good that he had done so, as several stones had unmoored from the surrounding rock of the cavern and were attempting to close a pincer around and behind the four. Barney tossed a few grenades and Doc also turned to assist him.

Then the group made it through a small opening at the far end of the chamber, wide enough for them to enter one at a time, and were running down the narrow tunnel. Behind them, a massive leathery boulder slammed into the opening, to little effect, as it was much too large to pursue them, though it did block their way should they need to retreat.

The four went downhill for another mile through twisting and turning tunnels, once again using their lights as the bizarre luminescence had faded.

"Doc," Barney said as they trudged along, "what the hell were those things? How can they even be alive?"

Caliban, normally uncommunicative in the face of such questioning, responded. "I'm not sure they are alive, or life as we know it. I don't know what they are. I believe they are in some way related to whatever Free is. Variations on a theme, if you will. But I'm not positive."

That, in itself, was a startling admission by the bronze man.

The next cavern glowed a putrid yellowish brown. Again, the source of light was not identifiable. Ahead was what looked like a forest of densely packed trees. These had thick torsos and were barrel shaped, though also conical, so that the barrel tapered in more toward the top than the bottom. From the bottom extended what appeared to be trunks or boles, while the slightly pointed tops were capped with star-shaped "tree toppers."

"Look like Christmas trees to me," Pauncho said. "Do we grab our axes and chop 'em down?"

"Look again," Doc said, "and get your flamethrower guns ready. These things have tentacles at the trunklike base, but can also extend tentacles from their bodies."

"More variations on the theme of whatever Scott Free is?" Trish asked. "Free told you that his kind had evolved on different paths over the eons. Is this some kind of distant relation?"

"Yes," Doc answered grimly. "This is as far into the caverns as I made it last time. These are the things that sent me and Free fleeing for our lives."

"What do we do, Doc?" Barney asked.

"As I said," the bronze man replied, "they can move, to a point, on tiny tentacles at the bases of their trunks. But they did not move to attack me and Free until we forced our way through the dense 'forest' of them. At the time we were fleeing the boulder things and had no choice but to move forward. Here, we also have no choice; the path back is blocked. These creatures have a spongey texture and can extrude tentacles from their bodies which can grasp at your arms, your throats, your mouths. The appendages are tough, ropelike, and coated in some sticky substance. They resemble beings who appeared in historical and artistic depictions in an ancient city that I explored with Williams—some of whom were inadvertently awakened from their frozen slumber and killed the rest of the expedition members."

"Doc," Trish breathed, "you've been holding out on us."

"Later," he said. "Flamethrowers. One commonality among all these creatures, we've discovered they can't stand fire."

Doc primed his flame gun. The other three held theirs at the ready and formed a triangle behind him while he took point. Doc's gun shot a torrent of blue flame, and he swept it back and forth like a firehose. There arose a great screeching and the cone-shaped creatures at the edge of the "forest" began to move forward, albeit slowly. These were not agile creatures—unless one got too close— and Doc believed the flame guns were up to the task of clearing a path through the cavern.

The four moved forward in formation, Caliban clearing the path and sending the creatures up in flames. An incredible stench arose and filled the space, the odor of burnt and crisped flesh, and some-thing else unidentifiable. The three behind Caliban covered their noses and mouths, finally donning their breathers, while the bronze man marched inexorably forward. The reek was compounded by the relentless and piercing cries of the dying creatures, and the latter filled and echoed within the chamber so horribly that it had a lulling, hypnotic effect on Trish, Pauncho, and Barney.

Trish turned and saw Barney standing immobilized, the spongy tentacles wrapping around his ankles, and torso, and one snaking toward his throat and mouth. This appendage extended from its tip five smaller tentacles which worked in concert to deftly remove Barney's breather.

Trish shook off the rising lethargy that had already overtaken

Barney, and ran back toward Banks, yelling to get Doc and Pauncho's attention. She primed her flamethrower gun, set it for the narrowest stream of flame, and shot a torrent at the tentacles tightening around Barney's ankles.

The creature wailed in pain and the lower appendages loosened, but the five smaller ones entered Barney's mouth and slithered down his throat, choking him.

Pauncho rushed by her, whooping at the top of his lungs, and tackled Barney and the spongy things entangling him. Straddling his friend, Pauncho's gorilla paws, covered in rusty fur, tore at the slimy, sticky tentacle in his friend's mouth, that was attached to the five smaller offshoots that were already far down his throat.

Trish stood over them, alternately aiming her flame at the appendage squeezing Barney's torso and fending off the approach of any more of the cone-trees. She risked a look in Doc's direction, and saw that he was providing a larger field of cover by swinging his flamethrower in wide arcs.

Pauncho tugged at the ropelike appendage, and it gave half an inch. Barney's eyes were dull and glassy in the yellowish glow of the cave. Van Veelar tugged again as Trish once more directed her flame toward the tentacle around Barney's torso, and the cone-tree near them from which all the spongy ropes extended. She increased the flame's intensity and it jetted white-blue at the star-headed thing, which finally burst into flames, howling in agonized death-throes.

The appendage squeezing Barney's abdomen and chest loosened, but the sticky part down his gullet stubbornly refused to come loose despite Pauncho's herculean efforts. Trish directed the smallest jet she could set, in order to avoid burning Barney, at the piece of tentacle hanging from his mouth. That part burned, and the rest of it writhed, and finally came loose. Pauncho tossed it away in disgust as Trish turned her attention back to holding off the surrounding "Christmas trees."

"He ain't breathing!" Pauncho said.

"Mouth to mouth," Trish replied. She darted a look sideways and saw that Doc was close to rejoining them, slowly but relentlessly clearing a path with his flame gun.

"Are you kidding?" Pauncho asked. "I ain't—"

"For God's sake, take over." Trish knelt by Barney while Pauncho gleefully sprayed the next wave of approaching creatures with hot fire from his own flame gun.

Barney revived, coughing and sputtering, to see the knockout redhead leaning over his face and wiping her mouth. He hacked some more and looked dazedly at her. "Trish! You mean . . . ?"

"Don't get used to it, wiseguy!" She stood, pulled Barney to his feet, and the three took positions back-to-back like the corners of a triangle, shooting flames outward from their center.

Momentarily, Doc joined them, and the triangle formation shifted to the four corners of a compass. They were surrounded by the cone-shaped trees, but the four methodically sprayed the hot jets of blue flame outward while simultaneously walking in lockstep through the cavern, trying to avoid frying each other.

They finally made the far end of the chamber, and a dark opening small enough for them to enter one at a time. Barney stepped in first and discharged a startled cry, which was followed within seconds by an alarming *thunk*.

Pauncho called, "Barney!"

"I'm okay! It's not a tunnel, it's a drop-off!"

Trish, duly warned, jumped through the black maw, followed in short order by Pauncho and Caliban, leaving behind the chamber full of dead, or almost dead, star-headed tree-things, and the pungent odor of their roasted flesh.

Caliban and the others took stock of their surroundings, deemed it safe to sit and rest, and made a temporary camp.

Doc took the nutrient-energy supplement and eight ounces of water Trish handed to him, and everything shuddered and swam in white seas of infinity.

Caliban dreamed of The Other, the man calling himself Lacewing. He knew now that the dream, or the vision, was caused by Shrassk "touching" his mind.

Caliban saw through The Other's gold-flecked eyes.

He *was* Lacewing.

The Other, similarly outfitted and equipped like Caliban, was climbing through the mazelike cavern system. He turned and gestured to his companions as they approached a widening in the rock tunnel through which they hiked. The widening tunnel became an opening to a large cavern that glowed with an eerie yellow-brown light, the source of which was not clear. Lacewing primed his flamethrower and watched as his companions did the same.

One was beautiful, dark-bronze haired, and six feet tall—almost the spitting image of Trish Wilde. But Caliban knew, seeing through The Other's eyes, that this was Lacewing's daughter. The other person, a man, a gray-eyed, sun-brown-skinned giant, was not the Englishman with whom Lacewing had defeated the Nine. But the man, Gordon, an Australian by birth, was a very able substitute for Lacewing's friend and partner, since the latter has gone to ground under a new, assumed identity, along with his family—although he and they might resurface one day.

The vision shimmered, and now Lacewing trudged through the cavernous complex by himself, separated from his companions. It was not clear what had happened to them.

The images shifted again, and Caliban was deep in Lacewing's memory, past life events flashing unbidden across the screen of the latter's mind. His birth off the coast of the small island in the Bahamas, the death of his mother, the mysterious and somewhat conspiratorial meetings his father had had, throughout Lacewing's childhood, with his great-grandfather, Land, and other men of power and influence . . .

These visons were followed by those of Lacewing's underage service in the Great War and meeting his five greatest friends, receiving his medical degree and countless other academic honors, and the murder of his father, followed on the heels by the murder of a beloved professor, one of his greatest mentors. Years of adventure, of traveling the world righting wrongs and punishing evildoers, followed, all the while taking up the mantle of his father's secret battle against the Nine. Golden treasure hoards, lost cities, power-mad supervillains, undersea mysteries, and Arctic—and Antarctic—adventures. The giant ape, wrongly torn from its hidden island home, loose in New York and tragically falling to its death from the iconic Manhattan skyscraper where Lacewing's headquarters were located . . . and arriving too late to save the beast.

The second World War and the birth of the Cold War had changed the nature of Lacewing's saga-like battles against the forces of evil; the world was smaller, yet more complex. A black-haired beauty, reformed daughter of a notorious thief with a worldwide reputation, captured his heart, and his adventures, if not entirely curtailed, certainly decreased in frequency—except for his and the Englishman's secret battle against the Nine.

When the immortal puppet masters had finally been defeated, Lacewing had planned to retire and focus all his energies on scientific studies—until the things from the New England caves had reared their ugly heads.

A shimmering veil of blinding white fell over Lacewing as he marched relentlessly downward through the caverns. He gasped and found himself looking out through someone else's eyes. He was embedded in another man's mind, seeing and experiencing what the other man saw and experienced.

This man called himself Caliban.

Doc Caliban looked down at the bloody knife gripped in his cable-muscled, bronzed fist.

The soft yellow-orange light cast by the gas lamps, positioned at intervals too far apart to do much but toss weird, flickering shadows, barely illuminated the blade. Yet it seemed, under the dripping crimson lifeblood, to shimmer with some silvery inner light.

Footsteps clattered lightly on the cobblestones. In the distance, a police whistle urgently piped its music of alarm and peril.

Caliban looked up.

Alexandra Applethwaite, Grandrith's mother, ran down the alley to him, white dress and raven hair whipping behind her. She tripped, caught herself, and extended her arms beseechingly.

Now they were in a cavern. There were torches of pitch and wood in iron baskets atop poles mounted in the rock floor, and arranged in a circle.

Within the circle of cressets was an operating table, around which were crowded men and women in surgical gowns and masks. Medical equipment on stainless steel trays, and the bed, were brightly illuminated by portable hospital lights. To one side, also on wheeled trays, were banks of monitors and other sophisticated hospital apparatus.

"We are not really here," Alexandra told Caliban. "We are as spirits to them. The vibrations allow us to see this time, this place."

This place, Caliban knew, was in the caverns of the Nine in central Africa.

Alexandra brought them closer.

Standing to one side of the hospital bed, looking down at the patient, was Anana, stooped and wizened. Her white hair was wispy and sparse. Her dark blue eyes were watery and shined with an inner light of anticipation.

Caliban saw himself standing on the opposite side of the operating bed, gowned and masked preparatory to a medical procedure.

Caliban's—that is the Caliban watching the scene unfold with Alexandra Applethwaite—attention shifted to the operating table.

On it, unconscious, lay a gorgeous woman who looked to be in her mid-twenties. Lustrous and long ash-blonde hair was swept behind her and fell from the table in cascading waves. The figure under the operating sheet was splendid.

The woman was the missing wife of his half-brother, John Cloamby, Lord Grandrith.

Clio Jeanne de Carriol.

"Doc. Doc!"

Trish's insistent voice tugged him out of the visions.

"Doc, what's happening with you?" Trish whispered. "You were . . . somewhere else for a few seconds."

He shook his head. "Yes, I know. I have a few ideas. But I don't really know."

Refusing to discuss it further, Caliban instructed them to pack up and resume moving.

Over the next twelve hours, the group covered several more miles, traveling through and down tunnels that twisted, corkscrewed, and cut back and forth in hairpin turns. They traversed several more large grottos, and did not encounter any resistance. This was good, since they had expended a large amount of their stored fuel in fighting off the star-headed creatures.

In time they came to a crevasse which was too wide to bridge with their equipment. Doc looked down at the sheer cliff face.

"Looks like we go down," Pauncho said.

"Maybe," Caliban said.

"Maybe?" Barney asked. "What do you have in mind, Doc?"

Caliban knelt, leaned over the edge, and easily sunk a piton into the "rock" wall. "It's more of that fleshy substance," he said. "Our spelunking equipment won't hold fast in this stuff."

Trish peered over the edge. "It's a long way down, not sure I can even see the bottom. What do you propose?"

Doc said, "I'm going. This is as far as you three come."

Overriding a chorus of objections, he continued. "I'm the only one who can make it down. None of you has the strength—"

"Try me!" Pauncho interjected.

Caliban shook his head. "I'm sorry, I can't risk you any further. It's not safe. You have all been of vital assistance thus far. Go back to the cabin. It won't be an easy return journey, so watch each other's backs. Wait for me at the cabin."

"Then . . . you are planning on coming back?" Trish asked.

"Yes," Doc said dryly.

He turned, one steel piton in each fist, took a step backward over the edge, and shot downward. As he fell, he jammed both spikes into the vertical cliff face. His descent slowed slightly as he gripped the pitons, muscles straining, and then he let himself drop so that he hung from them as they cut downward, leaving parallel gouges of ooze in the pinkish, fleshlike wall.

The strain on his wrists was tremendous. If he didn't continue to hold the spikes at the correct angle, pointed ends downward and digging into the sheer cliff, they would slip right out, and he would tumble in free fall into the deep, dark chasm. The open gashes he cut in the spongy and slippery cliff face exuded a horrid stench.

Caliban thought it was just possible that Pauncho could have duplicated his feat thus far, but when his strong legs hit the ground, thick bones and tendons and muscles absorbing the shock of the rapid fall, he knew he had been right in forbidding his friend to accompany him. Pauncho's legs would have been shattered by the impact. And Trish and Barney would have suffered broken wrists on the descent and would have fallen to their deaths.

Doc rolled to further disperse the energy of the impact, sprang to his feet, and took his bearings. His shoulder lamps showed nothing but more caves ahead, and tunnels from which to choose.

"Doc to Trish." He tapped a button on his wrist and spoke into his helmet comm.

"Doc! You made it!" Joy was evident in her voice.

"Yes," he said. "I'm going forward. We'll only be able to maintain contact for a short while. Soon, the thick rock will block our signals. As you return to the surface, watch out for Nine agents—or other things—pursuing us. If you run into any, try to avoid them and just get out alive. That's the best way you three can help me now."

There was a long pause on the other end. Then: "I understand, Doc. Good luck."

"Good luck."

Caliban cut the channel and strode into the next tunnel. He was separated from his companions, Pauncho, Barney, and Trish. He would go on alone, marking his location with yellow chalk at regular intervals—a backup to the fluorescent substance applied to the soles of his boots—and the marks would glow brightly when he applied a special lens filter to his goggles, enabling him to find his way out.

And his friends would backtrack their path to the surface, he hoped, unharmed.

The hours passed as he worked his way downward, a stifling monotony while his shoulder headlamps seemingly illuminated the same rock strata or stalagmites over and over again.

He was utterly alone, and had the loneliest job in the world. He knew the danger was not only physical, but psychic. Due to Shrassk's "touching," he might encounter terrors drawn from his own mind, but he also knew there were objective terrors here. The solution would be to separate which was which, but he would have to act swiftly and make no errors in judgement. If he failed, he might provoke the forces of Hell—or whatever this was—itself.

Eventually Caliban came to another large cavern. The opening of his tunnel was twenty feet above the floor of this cave, giving him ample opportunity to reconnoiter the chamber with his flashlight.

There was a large, pyramidal dais-like structure in the middle of the grotto.

Perched atop this was an entity. It did not move in response to his sweeping flashlight beams, and Caliban wondered if it was a statue rather than alive. However, he had encountered so many things in the cave complex that, at first blush, appeared to be lifeless objects, and then proved to be otherwise, that he took no chances, made no assumptions.

It occurred to him that his flashlight might cause the thing to activate, to awaken, and he switched it off. He continued to observe, letting his eyes adjust, and as they did so he saw the cavern gave off a deep purplish luminesce.

The thing in the center remained motionless.

Caliban cautiously climbed down and approached it. The creature had a spherical center some ten feet in diameter. Set within the sphere was a giant, unblinking eye. On the surface of the sphere's skin were countless other eyes. Leathery bat wings sprouted from all angles of the sphere, the forearms of which wings were lined with yet more eyeballs. The sphere itself rested upon a tangled nest of tentacles, which, though as immobile as the rest of it, gave a vague impression of movement, a gentle writhing.

The creature, or statue, somewhat resembled a larger, more monstrous Ssk'eth. Doc wondered if this was their "true" form rather than the somewhat less horrific visage Free had shown him when he had claimed to reveal his true form.

He wondered, could this be Shrassk herself? Had he attained his goal? Was this it?

The thing stared back at him.

Caliban realized this couldn't be Shrassk. Could it? No. That would be too easy.

He moved to the other side of the statuelike creature, and behind it was a brownish cone, which previously had been blocked from his vision, He attempted to pass this, and the cone melted into a dirty pool of mud which completely filled the width of the tunnel, blocking his way forward. Caliban looked backward; the statue, still locked into the stone base, had extruded from its circumference a bevy of snakelike limbs, at the tips of which were knifelike claws whirling like propellors. While he could have turned back, faced the creature and the whirling and whipping talons, it was clear he was being "encouraged" to maintain his forward path.

Naturally suspicious, Doc produced a coin from an inner pocket and tossed it in the middle of the brown pool of gunk in his path. The coin sizzled, and from where it had settled, there emanated a luminescent greenish vapor.

Then the pool coalesced back into a cone, from the top of which popped tiny waving and twirling tendrils. The tips of these gaped open, revealing horrendous little mouths brimming with needlelike teeth, and tiny red two-pointed tongues which darted out as if lapping at the air. From the points of these shot fluorescent green streams of some vile liquid, which cut hissing gouges in the surrounding rock as it sprayed and geysered in all directions.

A shot of the greenish acid caught Caliban on the cheek, and he fell back, wincing. But not too far back, for in that rearward path were the whirling knifelike talons of the giant eye creature.

He turned back to the cone-thing spitting acid everywhere and aimed the flamethrower at the top from which the hissing shoots radiated.

The top of the cone caught fire and burned like sparklers atop a chocolate covered sundae. The cone-thing gave forth a great screech, and emitted a horrendous stench, and it oozed into the ground slowly, a dark pile of melting gunk, and seemed to be absorbed into a crack in the earth.

Caliban couldn't help but think of the thing, the brown stuff, as the living excrement of the other underworld beings he had encountered so far. Thinking he killed it (and at the same time wondering if that were possible), he took two steps forward, and another crack in his path widened. The dark goo oozed out of it and reformed back into a cone, the shape of the thing he thought he had just killed. Tiny tendrils once again popped out of the top of the cone, and Doc fired as it started spewing the green acid.

This cone, like the last, melted upon being torched, and Doc started to run, hoping to avoid any more of the dreadful creatures.

Other cracks in the ground opened up slowly and new cones of the chocolate-brown goo oozed from them, discharging a rotten-onion stench. Whatever the stuff was, it seemed to have both vegetable and animal properties. It might be edible by other denizens of this underground world. Regardless, if he "killed" one, others formed in its place and in his path; other monsters, like the one he had just disposed of, were forming. More and more of the things appeared, and he knew he might become rapidly outnumbered and overcome.

Caliban sprayed scorching blue fire from his flame gun once more, sweeping it back and forth in wide arcs, hoping to kill or temporarily disable—melt?—a large number of them so he could forge a path forward.

He started running more quickly, as fast as possible in the narrow confines of the tunnel that led from the eerie chamber containing the large eyeball. He heard the brown gunky things making ominous slurping noises behind him as they reformed, and ran even faster than was safe, given the limited light and treacherous footing. He could easily pitch off a dark crevasse or knock himself out on a suddenly appearing low-hanging shelf of rock. But the acid-spewing cone creatures had shaken him, and he hoped he'd left the chocolate gooey things behind once and for all.

Doc entered the next chamber, the walls and ground and ceiling of which gave off an inexplicable greenish-gray light, very dim. As he ran, an albescent shroud fell over him.

Shrassk touched him once again.

He stumbled and fell.

The door opened with a bang and closed with a whimper.

The man with the code name of Lacewing was startled, though he expected the unexpected. So, the nightmare was beginning. His descent into this cave had been the prelude to the nightmare. It aroused vivid memories of the last time he'd been here, November 1948. Thirty-six years ago, almost to the day.

Lights from the top of his beryllium-alloy helmet and from atop each shoulder showed him the narrow gap and the cavern beyond. When he'd been here before, there had been no door. And now, when the lights were off, he could see by a faint grisly, purplish glow which the walls seemed to exude.

His body was covered with a pale yellow suit of flexible metallic material. The face was hidden by a gas mask. A holster in a belt carried a .55-caliber automatic with a ten-round clip of explosive bullets. Attached to the belt were ten hand grenades. A metal cylinder was attached to the back of one shoulder. From it ran a metal hose, its other end held by a clip on the belt. A cylinder on the back of the other shoulder held water and food.

If the gun, grenades, and flamethrower were not enough, and he thought they wouldn't be, he carried in a large pocket on his chest two items which he hoped would be more than enough. Somewhere in the darkness ahead and below, something tittered. Did they know he was here? Or was that sound just one of the many that had echoed for God knew how many centuries, or millennia, in this underground complex?

He sighed, and he edged sidewise along the stone narrowness and then emerged into the great cave. His lights struck something that ran behind a stalagmite. It was so fast that he saw only a blur of a naked body that resembled a human being. But its skin was gray, its head was misshapen, its arms and legs very long, the hands and feet enormous. Was it his imagination or had the overlong fingers and toes seemed webbed?

It was too early to start using his weapons. He had a long way to go on his journey down towards earth's centre. He was alone because the men he could trust were too old. His daughter and Gordon had come as far as they could, and he had sent them back to guard the entrance to the cavern complex.

He bent his head back and played the helmet's beam on the roof. Gray stone oozed water and a light like that at the bottom of a shallow sea. Something clung to one of the many stalactites hanging down from the ceiling, like teeth in a giant's mouth. When the light struck it, it moved quickly around to the other side. It wasn't a bat, since there were none here. But it had batlike wings.

The man now calling himself Lacewing, after the insect with golden eyes, moved forward. He bent his head down so the light would play on a large round instrument banded to the wrist of his left hand. Its face was covered with tiny dials. The humidity was 86; the temperature, 73° F. He expected these to remain about the same, though he could not be sure. Long ago he'd figured out that the labyrinthine passages downward were covered by something which insulated them against the rising heat of the earth's depths.

The floor sloped at more-or-less sixty degrees to the horizontal.

Once, he halted. By the base of a stalagmite lay a body, face downward. It was a woman with a hairless head, her skin bone-gray. He approached her carefully and prodded her with the toe of his boot. She did not react. He turned her over, fully expecting her to explode into a screaming harpy.

But she remained inert, the eyes glazed, the mouth hanging open. The dead playing dead.

Lacewing wore gloves as thin as a surgeon's but more durable. He removed a cigarette lighter from a pocket and rotated its flint. He held the flame an inch from the open eyes, and the thing shrieked and rose up and fled, wailing.

He said, "God!" and though he was agnostic, he hoped in that moment that that spirit was with him. But here was a place in which He possibly did not venture. It was territory staked out by another.

What especially shook him was that the thing had the face of a woman who'd hated him, had tried to kill him, and had instead been grievously injured, though he had not been directly responsible for her fate.

He resumed walking. The slope steepened, then eased again. The chronometer showed that two hours had passed. The temperature had not changed, but the humidity was steadily decreasing. Now and then he turned to look behind him. The lights never struck any moving beings, but always there were shadows that suggested these. He was sure he was being followed, and every half mile meant more dogging him.

There was a sonic amplifier inserted in one ear. He turned up its power and heard shufflings, as of dragging feet, twitterings, and once a voice mutter something in an unknown language. He kept glancing at the chronometer to reassure himself that time still existed. In this dark place, buried under millions of tons of rock, it was difficult to believe that time had not stopped forever. In a sense it had ceased. Those creatures gathering behind him, and perhaps ahead of him, existed outside of time as known on the surface.

At the end of three hours he had to fight the impulse to turn and throw a grenade. Its blast, the fire within the sound and the smoke, would dispel the horde. But they would come back, and he would have one less weapon.

Finally, after four hours, he stopped behind a grotesquely shaped stalagmite. After urinating, he unstrapped the container on his left shoulder, drank, and ate some of the pemmican he had prepared himself. The shadows grew thicker behind the formations rising from the floor. Once, just for a second, the silhouette of something monstrous, a snouted head with a tall crest rising from the skull, flashed and was gone.

He estimated that he was at least four miles beneath the surface. The air should have been thick and unbearably hot. But a slight breeze moved, bringing a hint of water. It also carried the stench of rotten flesh.

His ears sang with the music of utter silence.

And then a screech filled the cavern, a high-pitched yell from hundreds of throats, some of them surely not human. Out into the lights ran, bounded, and rolled hundreds of things, the eyes of some flashing red.

The things rushed forward into the three lights. There were hundreds of them, closely packed, of many strange shapes. But whatever they looked like, they seemed to him to have been human once. He already had taken the cigarette lighter out, and when the nearest, a creature that looked more like a kangaroo with an elephantine trunk than a man, was about forty feet away, he rolled the flint. The flame was feeble, but the kangaroo-thing screamed and bounded to one side and was lost in the shadows. Those just behind it yelled also; some fell; others piled up on it; for a moment, there was before him a mass from which thrashing legs and arms and eyes big with horror protruded. Then the creatures had disentangled themselves and run, leaped, and rolled after their fellows.

Lacewing stood unmoving, holding the lighter above his head. The echoing screams had died out; the thud of splayed feet had vanished. The only noise was the nonsound of silence hissing in his ears.

He turned off the lighter and wheeled and strode down the slope. After an hour he came through an arch beyond which was a cavern as wide as ten Grand Central Stations side by side and as high as ten and as long as twenty. It too held stalagmites and stalactites and had many openings off the floor and in the walls. From these faces stuck out, some of them more gargoyleish than human.

He walked on, though he had to turn every twenty yards or so. The shadows were gathering behind him again, and now he could hear, when he stood still, a breathing. It was the collective breath of hundreds amplified by the acoustic properties of this vast hollow. Now and then twittering flitted through the air. He looked up but could see no flying creatures.

What were these things following him? Long ago, when he had followed the trail of the strange man who'd led him here, and had caught him, the man had told him that this was Hell, and the things were the souls of the dead. He hadn't believed that. But the man claimed to have died centuries ago, to have been a doomed soul who had managed to escape from Hell. Lacewing had disbelieved this, too. Nevertheless, the weird little fellow, Mr. Cri, had vanished from a room in which Lacewing had locked him and which was watched by a policeman.

But the man was no wraith. He was solid and warm to the touch, and these things here were solid, though cold. And they breathed. Which meant they had blood, or something like blood, and, therefore, could be killed. But what did they eat? Was their source of food further down? If they ate, and they must, why, since hundreds of them resided here, had he seen no excreta?

He had a queasy feeling that they ate it. But if that were so, they were not human. They'd be poisoned by their own waste matter.

To get answers, one must submit questions. And the thing at the end of the trail—if indeed it was there—was not noted for giving answers.

Thirteen hours had passed. He had eaten and drunk three times. Then he came to one more in a series of caves, great and small. This was the largest, and its stones were many-colored, throwing jewels of light back in the beams. There were strange formations scattered everywhere, more like massive branches of coral than anything. Their upper extremities seemed to sway slightly, though it could be imagination deceiving him. Once he thought he saw a boulder, which looked like a scarlet-and-green-streaked giant human brain, move a few inches.

He came to a river, a dark sullen stream sliding slowly along. It was about half a mile wide here, and on the other side a smooth wall of stone, spotted with patches of green-blue, like lichen, or a leprosy of mineral, prevented any passage in that direction.

The surface of the water was smooth except for an occasional large bubble or swirling, as if its depths concealed living creatures.

Suddenly, a great scream arose, and hundreds of feet slapped against the smooth stone floor behind. He whirled, bringing out the lighter at the same time. Its flame guttered up, but by the lights of his beams shining from his helmet and suit he saw that the things had their eyes closed. They were shutting out the flame, their hands or semblances thereof outstretched, blindly charging. They hoped to sweep him into the river by their sheer mass. Or perhaps they thought he would not dare to leap into the cold dark stream, and they would seize him and tear him apart.

His left hand grabbed a small metal ring on the left side of his suit. He yanked, a cord came out, and the suit around his chest and back, under his arms, swelled. He could not hear the hissing of air inflating the section, but he didn't need that for verification. He released the thumb activating the lighter but still held it up above him. He turned and leaped out into the water. For a moment his face was below the surface, but the suit was waterproof. Nevertheless he felt the cold penetrate it; it was like the chill of approaching death.

The sluggish current bore him slowly away. He had expected, for no good reason, that the things would not follow him. Perhaps he was attributing his dread of the river to them. But they spilled into the stream, and they began swimming towards him.

He ignited the lighter again. They screamed when the fire flared in their eyes, but then they closed their eyes and thrashed sightlessly towards him.

Lacewing flailed momentarily as he was pulled under. Then he relaxed and let the current carry him, and the things that crawled all over him, along; the suit was airtight, and he had at least twenty minutes of breathable air. The water was filthy, and he could see nothing forward or behind, nor above or below him.

But he felt the creatures picking at him through his suit, biting, tearing with double-jointed limbs and digits, plucking at the hoses and clasps and buckles. Two clawed at his boots and crawled up his legs towards his waist. He squeezed powerful legs together and felt the crunching of bones. The grasping sensation fell away as the crippled creatures let go, only to be replaced by twice as many—or more—clasping fingers. He continued to fracture and snap their limbs with his legs, and arms, and to brush away the clawing extremities that sought his helmet, and air hose.

Lacewing and the massed creatures were borne downstream by the implacable underground current, a glob of broken bones and torn flesh, and blood and gore which flared behind them in the river like the plumes of some great, prehistoric bird-reptile. Every creature he killed or disabled was replaced by two more as the clump of grayish bodies swept along underwater in a seemingly perpetual repetition of cracked bones and torn limbs.

Finally, as his air supply began to dwindle, the frequency of the crawling things picking and cutting at his suit diminished, until, it seemed, he had killed or disabled the last of the hundreds that had swarmed him.

He pulled himself roughly to shore and dragged his body onto the ground, undid his helmet and took in what felt, in comparison to some of the atmosphere he had experienced in the caves, like relatively fresh air. He rolled on his back and sucked in deep breaths, taking in the gray-green cast of the ceiling and the cavern walls.

A gray-limbed creature exploded from the water, landed on his chest, and shoved a webbed hand in his open mouth. The thing's blood-spidered eyeballs bulged in their sockets, and it screamed as Lacewing bit down hard and severed the hand at the wrist, ochrelike blood spewing all over his nose and chin.

Lacewing's bronzed hand flew to the thing's throat, squeezed, and the ghoulish head lolled unnaturally to the side as neck bones crackled and splintered.

He tossed it in the river and the current bore the corpse away as he spit out the webbed fingers and thick blood. He took a large gulp from his canteen, swirled, and spit in the river, almost sick at his stomach.

He sat down heavily to gather his wits and summon the energy to keep going.

Then he felt the "touch" of the thing he sought, and was overwhelmed with past fears and humiliations and auras of lost loves—or those he had never allowed himself to love—and also evocations of the deepest creatures from the abyss of human consciousness. He saw things peculiar to himself and those belonging to every human being. The knowledge that the universe was basically meaningless, death was forever, and everything was futile pressed against his chest like a physical weight crushing him, suffocating him.

He was shown people he had known, people who would claim there is a Hell, and they were in it. He saw his mother, his father, his old aides, appealing to him. The abyss opened before his feet, and before him was nothing, the face of nothingness, which no man had ever seen before. He quaked with true abysmal terror. What did nothing look like? It was not black. There was no color, nor absence of color.

He was conscious of the heaviness of hundreds of miles of rock above him, the overbearing consciousness of all this weight, and he was alone as no man before him, since even astronauts had each other's company and communication with Earth and could see their home planet and the stars.

A hot white flash pierced his brain, and he saw through another's eyes.

Caliban was in the Antarctic, his first expedition there, serving as the group's meteorologist, when calamity struck.

The extraterrestrial vessel, twenty million years old. The thing that had traveled to Earth in it, the thing that had slept the frozen sleep . . . until it had been awakened by the explorers. Fifteen men slaughtered by the thing that could mimic them, not just their physical form, but their thoughts and feelings—and yet retained, deep down, its own alienness, its drive to reproduce and infect others.

Caliban, in the face of disaster, of men suspecting and turning against other men, became the group's natural leader, in a terrifying struggle to prevent the creature from escaping its Antarctic isolation and reaching the outer world, and to save their own lives . . .

The dream, the reliving of the doomed Antarctic expedition, and the extraterrestrial thing that could read their minds, reproduce, and perfectly imitate them both physically and mentally, faded.

Caliban was deep in the caverns. He refocused his mind on the mission.

Free had said that the "Children" were born out of flame by Shrassk.

Why then, as Caliban had proved so many times in the past twelve hours, were they terrified by fire? Was it fire itself, the reality, or the idea of fire that panicked them? Or both? Or something else?

Unless none of the things he had encountered thus far were the "Children."

He crouched behind the seven-foot-high cone of dark brown stuff oozing from the wide crack in the rock floor. Its rotten-onion stink and his knowledge of its origin sickened him. That the cone was building up at the rate of a quart every five minutes meant that monsters like the one he had just killed were in the neighborhood. Unless, that is, the dead thing was excreting after death and its wastes were flowing through the undersurface fissure complex. No. This cone was too far from the carcass.

Others of its kind must be nearby.

Soft noises came from the other side of the cone. Whisperings, chitterings. Nonhuman. He moved slowly along the edge of the cone. The gray-green light seemed to be dimming somewhat. Was the chocolate-brown goo absorbing the light? Nonsense. Or was it? He could not know here what was or was not nonsense. Anyway, calling something nonsense meant only that you did not understand it.

He looked around the cone. In the half-light he could see the rear of a creature he had not encountered so far. It had a tail two feet long, about an inch in diameter, hairless, studded with dark warts, and exuding slime. The tail was switching back and forth much like that of a cat thinking whatever sphinxlike thoughts a cat thought.

He moved slowly further around the edge of the cone, prepared to duck back if the thing should turn its eyes—if it had any— toward him. Then he saw that he had been wrong in assuming that the creature had a posterior part. It was two feet in diameter and a foot high. There was no head, hence, no rear, just an armored dome from which four tails—some kind of flexible members, anyway— extended. If the tail he had first seen came from the south of the round body, the others extended from the north, west, and east. The end of the west tail was stuck into the brown cone and was, since it was twice as large in diameter as the others, swollen with the sucking-in of the excrement.

Because the thing seemed to be eyeless, Caliban stepped forward two paces. Beyond the creature were four others, all feeding with the tail-like "west" organs.

Beyond them, its back to him—he supposed it was the back—was a bipedal creature. It was almost as tall as he and was unclothed. Though human in form, its skin was a dull blue. Black ridges ran both vertically and horizontally over its legs and body and hairless head. The ridges formed squares in the center of which was a livid red circle the size of a silver dollar. One hand, quite human, held a shepherd's staff.

The whisperings and chitterings came from the "shepherd."

The creature began to turn around. Caliban backed away around the cone. He looked around. No living thing in sight—as far as he knew. Here, he could not be sure what was or was not living. The rock floor slanted upwards at a ten-degree angle to the horizontal. At least, what he thought was the horizontal. The only relief to the smoothness and emptiness were some tall rock spirals, huge boulders, and brown cones here and there. The warm thick air passed slowly over his sweating skin.

He walked in the opposite direction so that he could watch the shepherd while it was facing the other way. And then the flickerings began again—flickerings he knew now were not phenomena outside him—and he saw The Other, his near-double.

For a moment he was frightened. Shrassk was touching his mind again. But, he reassured himself, that did not mean that Shrassk knew where he was. On the other hand . . .

He slid that possibility into a drawer in his mind and watched the vision with inner eyes while the outer watched the cone. For the first time, the stark white curtain of transition to The Other's viewpoint, of either-or, was now absent, replaced with a dissociative liminality in which he experienced two pathways simultaneously, without conflict, without contradiction.

If that shepherd strolled around the cone, it would have him at a disadvantage. He should go ahead with his plan. But he could not move.

The man who looked so much like him was walking through a rock tunnel filled with the same light as this cavern, the gray-green of an old bone spotted with lichen. He, too, wore a backpack and a harness to which was attached many containers for instruments and weapons. Suddenly, The Other stopped. His expression shifted from intense wariness to fright. That quickly passed and he stared straight ahead as if he were seeing something puzzling.

Caliban relaxed a trifle. The other man was probably also touched by Shrassk. He was seeing Caliban as Caliban was seeing him.

Caliban anticipated that they might soon do more than just see one another. It seemed to him that The Other was not perhaps in the same universe as Caliban's. Not yet. Perhaps never. But Shrassk was in the third universe which was a bridge between Caliban's and The Other's. A crossroads. And Caliban and The Other could leave their two worlds to meet in the third, Shrassk's.

This anticipation was based on Free's explanation, which meant that neither was grounded in reality, though he had attempted to test Free's truthfulness. But Free could have fooled him and his instruments.

Doc forced himself to move. With the first step, the little glowing stage and its single performer vanished. It was as if his connection with the vision had been switched off by muscular action. By the time that he came to the other side of the cone, he was running and his mind was completely wrapped around his intent. A big knife was in one hand and the gas-powered pistol was in the other.

The shepherd had his back to him. It was turning one of the round things with its staff so that the tail on the south side could be inserted into the cone. Caliban slowed down just a little because he was astonished. The crook at the end of the shepherd's staff was straight now. Its end had split into two, and these were clamped around the lower edge of the dome-shaped cone-eater. Using these, the shepherd was turning the thing so that it could insert another tail into the goo.

The checkerboard-skinned thing must have heard him or have felt the vibrations of Caliban's boots through the rock floor and its bare soles. It yanked the staff from the edge of the round tailed thing and whirled. The ends of the staff merged together.

Caliban noted this and also the sex of the shepherd. It had no testicles, but a thin orange-prepuced penis reached to its knees.

The shepherd grinned, exposing four beaverlike teeth. Its face was human except for the black squares and red spots. It raised the staff as if it were going to throw it at Doc. The end nearest Doc swelled, the shaft shrinking in length and diameter as substance flowed into the end, and the end became a thin pointed two-edged blade.

Doc raised the gas-pistol and squeezed the trigger. There was a hiss. The projectile appeared, its needle point buried in the blue chest. The thing staggered back two steps. It should have been unconscious in four seconds, but, screaming, it ran at Doc, the staff held as if it were a spear. Which it now was. The thing's arm came down; the spear flashed at Doc. He ducked. The spear missed, but the lower back end sagged, became supple, and whipped around Doc's arm.

Still holding the pistol, Doc sawed with his knife at the creature squeezing on his arm. Its body seemed to be as hard as hickory though it was as flexible as rubber.

By then the shepherd was upon him. Doc brought the knife up from the snake-shaft and down into the shepherd's thigh. The blade sank halfway into the flesh, but Doc was knocked down by the impact of its body. He rolled away and started to get up. The snake-shaft coiled the rest of its body around Doc's neck. He fell on his back, dropped the knife and pistol, and, while the thing cut his breath off, got his fingers between it and his neck, though not without cutting his skin with his fingernails, and, with a mighty yank, uncoiled it and cast it away.

Few men would have had the power to do that, but Doc had no time to congratulate himself on that. The shaft was writhing on the floor in an effort to reach him. Lacking the belly plates of the true snake, it was making little progress. The shepherd, however, screaming, blood gushing from its wound, was hobbling towards him. Doc rolled away until his right hand was within reach of the snake-shaft. His fingers closed around it just back of the head, which was swelling—toward what shape?—and he rose to his feet and threw the thing at the shepherd in one fluid movement. He had taken the chance that the staff might be so quick that it would whip itself around his wrist or even, perhaps, around his neck again.

But, cracking it like a whip, he had avoided that. Now the shaft fell around the shepherd's head, chittered something, and the shaft fell off it.

Doc had hurled himself against the shepherd then, and he had knocked it down. It started to get up, but Doc's boot caught it under its rounded and cleft chin. It fell back, unconscious.

Panting, Doc bent over the shepherd. Since he wanted no witness left behind, no one to tell—whom?—that he had been this way, he intended to drag the shepherd to a nearby deep fissure and drop it in. He screamed and straightened up and grabbed at his crotch. Something had wrapped itself around his penis and was squeezing it. For a few seconds, he was so taken by shock and surprise that he did not recognize what it was that had seized him. Now he saw that the proboscislike sex organ of the shepherd—if it was a sex organ—had coiled itself around his penis. It was yanking at it as if it was trying to tear his organ off. Fortunately, the cloth of Doc's pants was interfering with the effort.

The shepherd seemed to be still knocked out. The drug from the hypodermic and its wound had surely done their work. But they should also have made its sex organ, or whatever it was, flaccid. Knocked it out, too. Unless it was partially independent of the blood supply of the main body.

No time to think. Gritting his teeth, Doc backed away, the shepherd's body dragging behind, pulled by the proboscis attached to Doc's penis. The pain became worse. He had a vision of his organ being torn out by the roots, but he kept backing until he was by the knife. He fell to his knees, grabbed it, and sliced away the blue length and orange prepuce with one motion. Blood, almost black in the dim light, geysered out from the shepherd.

"God Almighty!"

Doc staggered to the gas-gun, picked it up, sheathed it and the knife, and ran. The pain faded away but not the memory. After a few yards, he slowed to a walk. A glance showed him the shepherd's still body, the shaft writhing, and the five round things. What next? When he reached the far wall of the cavern, he went along it for perhaps a quarter of a mile and found in the shadows the entrance of a smooth downslanting tunnel. With both arms outspread, he could touch its walls. The top was a foot higher than his six feet and seven inches.

The tunnel, after a half a mile, ended with a flaring out as if it were a trumpet. Before him was silence and the biggest cavern yet. This he knew from a series of clicks he uttered and listened for, the result of years of training himself in human echolocation. The walls opposite him were draped in blackness which, for a second, he thought moved. The ceiling soared into darkness. The floor, far below, was bathed in a brighter light than that which he had gone through and was now green-yellow. Its source, however, was still unknown.

A ledge extended from the tunnel exit. Two feet wide, it ran more or less horizontally from both sides of the tunnel mouth as far as he could see. The straight drop from the ledge to the floor was, he estimated, about a mile. From here, the floor seemed to be smooth among the ridges, hillocks, and curious shapes, some of which looked human. Vaguely. They could not be, however. For one thing, they did not move. For another, they would have to be far larger than elephants for him to make out their shapes at this distance and in this twilight.

He saw water in an even larger quantity. A river wound through a rock channel, its surface dark, smooth, and oily. Perhaps it wasn't water.

Something darker than the river and the stone banks moved slowly on the surface. Doc removed his backpack and took out the night-vision subsonic-transmitter. He lay down on the ledge, his elbows propped near the edge, put the viewscreen to his eyes, swept the area that had attracted his attention, adjusted the dials, moved the instrument back and forth, and held it steady.

The slowly floating mass was a rowboat with an unmoving figure seated in it. The figure seemed to have its back to him. But something extended from its front out over the water. A fishing rod? What kind of creatures could live in the barren river? There was no food for them. Unless . . . there were cracks in the river bottom and the chocolatey onion-stinking stuff oozed up from them. Maybe the "fish" ate that stuff.

Doc moved the line of sight over the boat. It was white, though that may not have been its color. Objects on which the instrument focused looked white; objects near the edge of the screen and in the background were dark. He did not think that the boat was made of wood since wood was absent in this world. The boat had probably been carved from stone.

The fisherman could be of stone, too. He certainly had not moved any more than a granite statue would. If that were so, then the monk's cloak and hood on him were of stone, too.

Doc had to keep moving the instrument slowly because the boat, like the river, was moving sluggishly. Then he started, and he lost the boat for a moment. The fisherman had shifted. By the time that he was in the screen again, he was on his feet and holding the pole with both hands. The line from the pole was too thin for Doc's instrument to reflect, but Doc knew that there was a line. Proof of its existence was climbing out of the river on the line.

The thing ascending the line hand over hand had a ghostly-white face with enormous eyes. A snub human nose. Thick pale lips. A rounded chin. Under which hung a loose bladder of skin. The thing had a high and bulging forehead. If it had a head of hair, it was not visible. It had no ears or ear openings that Doc could see. The neck was fat, and the body was a baby's, the arms and legs very short. It stood swaying, its nonhuman round feet with long webbed toes spread out on the stone bottom of the boat. The fingers were also long and webbed.

Doc widened the field of vision. The fisherman was three times as tall as the catch. If the former was six feet high, then the catch was two feet tall.

Doc's muscles tightened, and the back of his neck chilled. The fisherman had turned so that Doc could see the profile under the hood. It was human and familiar. The big hooked nose could be Dante Alighieri's.

Stop thinking like this, Doc told himself. That is not the centuries-dead Florentine poet. He—or it—is probably, no, certainly, not even human. Free's initial claim that the dead were reincarnated here was ridiculous.

Now the fisherman had put the pole down in the boat. Now he was picking up the large but slim fishhook at the end of the line and was walking carefully—didn't want to rock the boat—toward the creature that looked like a hybrid of baby and frog. Now he had grabbed its neck—the creature was not struggling—and had savagely driven the end of the hook through one side of the bladder below the neck and out through the other side.

Even then the creature was passive. Perhaps it was in shock, though Doc did not think so. Something in its attitude indicated that it was fully cooperating. And now the fisherman had tossed the creature into the water. He walked back to the pole, lifted it, and sat down, becoming again a stone-still Izaak Walton. The pole did not move, which meant that the thing on the hook was not struggling.

What was the prey for which the baby-frog would be bait? Anything big enough to swallow it would be too big for the simple Tom-Sawyer fishing tackle to handle.

Getting answers here is secondary, Doc thought. I shouldn't be wasting time lying here and watching. I must be moving on. Besides, in this place, what I see from a distance, even with the viewer, may be quite different from what I'd see close up.

Nevertheless, he did not get up at once. The fisherman maintained his unhuman lack of movement, no wriggling, no looking around, no scratching of nose or hair. Only the boat and the river moved, and they did so very slowly. Nor had anything else moved except some shadows seen out of the corners of his eyes. When he looked directly at where the shadows had been, he saw only the pale dead-looking light.

Though he kept the viewer on the boat, with occasional sweeps across the floor, he could not help but think of other things. For instance, what was the ecosystem of this place? There had to be some kind of order here despite all the appearances of illogic and chaos. Everything he had seen had to be obeying or acting in accordance with a "law," a "principle." Everything had to be interconnected here as much as everything above it was. The "laws" of entropy, of energy input and output, conception, reproduction, growth, aging, and death had to operate in this deep underground. There had to be a system and an interdependent network.

What?

Doc vowed that, before he left here—if he did leave—he would at least have an inkling of the system. He would have some data on which he could theorize.

Finally he rose. He was ready to go on. But, lacking a parachute or enough rope, he could not get down or along the glass-smooth wall below the ledge. He could go to the right or the left on the ledge. One direction had to lead down to the cave floor. There was traffic from the lower levels to the upper, and, thus, this ledge was the highway. Perhaps both the left and right were used. He could not, however, afford the time to take one and find out that it petered out somewhere on the side of the immense bowl.

Take the left. Why? Because that was the sinister side. It seemed to him that the sinister would always be the right direction in this place. Chuckling feebly at his feeble pun, he began walking faster than caution recommended, his left shoulder brushing against the wall now and then.

After a quarter of a mile, the ledge began sloping gently downward. In an hour, he was halfway to the floor and above a roughly three-cornered opening in the wall into which the dark river flowed. By then the fisherman had inserted his pole into a socket in the corner of the boat and was rowing back up the river. Were his oars also made of stone?

The ledge took Caliban to the other side of the cavern before it reached the floor. He stood there for a while and listened to the total silence, which was a ringing in his ears. The fear bell ringing, he thought. Someone is at the front door and pressing on the button.

Though he had no reason to think so, he felt that he was getting close to his goal. Which perhaps explained why his fear had come back and was moving closer to that sheer hysterical horror he had suffered during an incident in his first venture into the cave so many years ago.

Caliban, your hindbrain is trying to take over, he told himself. Use your forebrain. Don't use it to rationalize and justify what your hindbrain is telling you. Don't turn and run away. Don't walk away, either. Push on ahead. If you flee now when you are so close, after you've gone through so much, you'll despise yourself forever afterwards. You might as well kill yourself. In which case, if you're going to die if you run away or die if you go ahead, you might as well, no, it'll be much better, if you die because you went ahead.

Despite this, the fire of panic was burning away his reason and courage. It might have caught hold of him and turned him around. He would never know because the vision of The Other sprang into light in some place in his mind. And, as fire lights fire, a cliché but sometimes true, the vision swept away the fear.

The Other was standing at the entrance to a cave. He was smiling and holding up one huge bronze-skinned hand, two fingers forming a V. Then the scene widened, and Doc saw that The Other was about three hundred feet from a great circle of stone symbols brightly lit by burning gas jets at their bases. There were nine: a Greek cross, a hexagon, a crescent, a five-pointed star, a triangle with an eye at its top, a Celtic cross, an O with an X inside it, a snake with its tail in its mouth, and a winged horseshoe. They enclosed a shallow bowl-shaped depression in the rock about three hundred feet in diameter. In the center was another circle of stone symbols, smaller than those that formed the outer circle and unfamiliar to Caliban. Inside the smaller circle was a platform shaped like an 8 on its side. The upper side of the 8 had holes which projected to the far ceiling bright violet-colored rays.

Where the two O's that formed the 8 met, a strip of stone about ten feet wide, was a highbacked chair cut from a bloodred stone. The chair was not empty.

Caliban felt as if every cell in his body had turned over.

The being on the chair, surely Shrassk, She-Who-Eats-Her-Young, was not at all whom or what he had expected.

The fear surged back in; the vision dimmed. But he forced himself to push it back down, though it was like pressing down on a lid over a kettle of cockroaches breeding so furiously that the lid kept rising. For a moment, the vision became brighter and clearer. Doc saw that his Other was making signs using dactylology, indicating that his *Other*, Caliban, must hasten to aid him. Alone, each would go down quickly. Together, they might have a chance.

Caliban began running in a land where it was not good to run.

Lacewing "saw," as the other bronze man—Caliban—ran through the three-cornered opening in granite wall and from there along a ledge that bordered the dark underground river.

The fisherman, in the stone boat, seemed to pace Caliban, though this didn't seem possible, as the path along the river was wide enough, and there was enough of the gray-green luminescence, that the bronze man was able to run at something approaching his top speed. And an impressive speed this was, for Caliban's athleticism surpassed that of the top Olympians. In fact, he had foregone any participation in worldwide sporting events so as not to direct attention toward himself, for he would have easily broken world records in track and field, gymnastics, weightlifting, and swimming, to name a few.

Nonetheless, the sinister fisherman, in a boat of stone that by all rights should have immediately sunk to the bottom of the underground waterway, kept up and even seemed to gain on Caliban as the latter sprinted through the dark passageway.

Caliban plucked a grenade from his belt, set the timer, pulled the pin, and tossed the metal egg in the boat.

He switched direction and sprinted back the way he had come, betting that, although the normal laws of physics seemed not to apply to the sinking of stone in water, perhaps at least the heavy boat's momentum would continue to propel it forward while he reversed course.

His gamble appeared to pay off as the distance between him and the fast-moving boat increased. He dove into the water with perfect timing; the grenade exploded just as his body fully submerged, the water shielding him from the blast and rocky shrapnel.

He emerged in time to see the last of the boat, and the bizarrely unmoving fisherman, sinking beneath the dark mirror of the water's surface.

Caliban pulled himself from the river and trudged along the ledge for another hour. He pushed down the growing dread, and the confusion, at what he had seen sitting upon the throne of Shrassk, when he had seen through The Other's eyes.

The tunnel through which Caliban trekked split, with the underground river spilling into a downsloping channel to the right, and the pathway upon which he walked veering to the left, finally opening into a huge cavern with a sheer drop of two hundred feet or more, and the ceiling of which was punctuated by stalactites from which cool water fell at a steady drip.

The whole space, larger than three football fields, and at least twenty stories tall, glowed in a variety of purplish tones. Caliban noted again that the luminescence had no discernible source.

Ensuring his shoulder-mounted lamps were lit, and flame-gun at the ready (though holstered), he secured one end of a safety rope to a protruding rock and looped the other around his waist. He skillfully rapelled down the cliff face and paused at an outcropping about twenty-five feet from the bottom. He scanned the whole area to get his bearings. The precipice rounded to the right, and he had a sense that just around this curvature, and out of his sight, was his destination, the chamber which he sought.

He turned to the ground below him and there bloomed, in his mind, a vision of The Other, once again waving at him, and pointing in the direction off to the right, to the chamber which Caliban could not quite yet see, but which he knew was there, the chamber containing the circle of stone symbols, and the bloodred chair, the throne, resting upon the figure eight.

And Caliban could see, in his mind's eye, The Other looking at *him* perched on the narrow projection on the cliff face.

If they were not careful, they would sink into an endless vortex of each seeing the other, seeing the other, seeing the other, in their minds, as if looking deep into an infinite funhouse mirror. He wondered if they could press forth in this manner without going insane.

The Other smiled slightly, as if sharing this thought, then gave a small salute and marched out of Caliban's sight, heading toward the throne chamber.

Caliban kicked off from the narrow ledge and rapelled to the bottom.

Caliban rounded the bend in the rock wall, unconsciously holding his breath.

Within the nine stone symbols, at the bases of which burned gas jets, was enclosed a bowl-shaped theater in the round. In the center of this was the smaller circle of unrecognizable stone symbols, which in turn surrounded the throne of bloodred stone. Sitting upon that highbacked chair was a being.

Goosebumps rose all over Caliban's body. His bowels twisted. His skin felt like it was on fire, and cold streams of sweat burst forth from his forehead and trickled down the small of his back.

Shrassk.

The figure was dressed in black—black top hat, Victorian topcoat, vest, gloves. The face was shadowed but the eyes blazed insanely, as if they were spotlit from offstage. In the man's right hand, a silver blade glinted in the same bright spotlight.

Jack the Ripper leaned forward into the light. He had Doc Caliban's face.

"Hello, Son!"

This was the place, the throne chamber of Shrassk, that had been called by Scott Free an asymptotic space between, and bridging, two universes.

According to Free, the monster was held, contained, partly in Caliban's world, and partly in another, and was suspended between the two universes, acting as a threshold, a door-opener, between both, but itself unable to fully emerge into one or the other.

And the monster, Shrassk, was . . . Jack the Ripper? Doc's father, whose countenance so greatly resembled Doc's facial features and those of his half-brother, Grandrith.

The images, the feelings, all of the visions and dreams that Doc had had since Shrassk began touching his mind flooded over him at once, pounding at his brain, stripping away the hard protective shell he maintained around his emotions.

Shrassk "touched" Caliban's mind.

Doc, as a youth, undergoing the weird mental and physical training mandated by his father, two hours a day, at a minimum. The strange mental calculations and physical fitness regimen, the odd tutors, the strange lack of women in his and his father's everyday life. And then, eventually embracing the curriculum with the same zeal and obsession as that exhibited by his father—perhaps even more so, for he desperately wanted his father's approval.

Caliban, never one for deep self-reflection, was forced to face the question: would he have had any success in his father's program, passed any of the tests and trials, if he had not been, as he learned much later, the biological grandson of an Old Stone Age man whose bones were much thicker and had more surface area for muscle attachment and development than those of modern humans?

If he had not been the grandson of XauXaz, if he was just a "normal" man, would he have faired so well?

Then there was the bizarre mission which his father set for him, a single-minded program to eradicate evil in all its forms, all over the world. And yet he had enlisted in the Nine, unwittingly joining the very people his father had trained him to battle, and in doing so had sold his soul—for the greater good, he told himself, because as an immortal his war against evildoers could continue until he succeeded in wiping them all out.

Caliban had killed. In the Great War, and World War Two. But also, he had killed others accidentally in his own endeavors, and purposefully when acting on behalf of the Nine. These killings were a necessary trade-off, he had told himself, in pursuit of the larger goal, his life's mission, his life's obsession.

Plus, he liked it.

Shit.

He liked it.

Doc's father, James Cloamby, had been Jack the Ripper, and, after the madness induced by the Nine's immortality elixir had passed, had fled England and taken on a new identity, James Caliban, Sr. The father had devoted his son's life to righting his, the father's, wrongs, as if life debits and credits could be paid off this way. His father's obsession was the cause of Doc's own obsession with fighting crime and punishing evildoers, since his father had focused every aspect of Doc's upbringing on this task.

But the father had passed on something else to the son.

The love of the knife. Doc's repressed—and sometimes not so repressed—love of violence and killing, which also manifested in sexual repression. For the two, as he had learned when the Nine had manipulated him into the great battle against his half-brother, Grandrith, were intimately related.

To what did Caliban truly aspire? Did he really need to transform himself into a complete pacifist in order to finally overcome his repressed obsessions?

Could he continue to keep each foot in two worlds, the world of fighting and death, and the world of peace?

What must he confront in order to move forward?

Shrassk, dwelling at the threshold, had accumulated and filled the labyrinthine caverns with small and corrupt lives. Some of these were the monster's own children (not Children), the Ssk'eth. There were other souls as well, and perhaps the collecting of these, the life-forces of those aboveground dwellers who peddled in lies and hypocrisy for power and profit, and those who blindly followed the hypocrites to their ultimate demise . . . perhaps all these powered Shrassk's spontaneous reproduction.

Shrassk touched Caliban more deeply, and he now "saw" The Other facing Shrassk in his own cavernous throne room. Caliban speculated at length about himself and The Other. They each appeared to be inhabiting alternate or parallel dimensions occupying the same space, but vibrating at different wavelengths, sitting at "right angles" to each other. But he sensed it was more than that, and he also sensed that The Other was having the same sorts of thoughts.

Doc felt that he and The Other were aspects of the same being, reflections or aspects of some primary reality. This thought gave him the chills. Was he not real? Was his universe not real?

As he pondered this, the aspect Shrassk presented cycled, and Saucy Jacky bade Caliban farewell, at least for the moment.

In Jack's place sat a woman, a Russian countess he had once known.

The woman's arm extended unnaturally, as if she were elastic, and the elongated fingers reached out like little writhing snakes. She shimmered on the throne, and then was back, but Caliban knew that she was slightly different—a Russian woman known to his counterpart, Lacewing.

He saw the past through The Other's eyes, The Other's memories.

The Other battled the prison camp commandant, the self-styled baron who was rarely seen without his ridiculous monocle and the huge cigar like a submarine wrapped in tobacco leaves, and his mistress, the Russian countess. Her hair was ash-blonde, her figure splendid, her skin as white and pure and unblemished as that of a baby. Her tresses fell in waves around large, deep blue eyes with thick, dark lashes, and lips of brilliant red which held the improbably long cigarette holder. Unusually long-fingered hands were encased in black elbow-length gloves, and his imagined removal of those gloves, the slow revealing of the soft flesh and scarlet tipped fingers beneath, held a promise of sensual delight. This was an experience at which the young Lacewing could only guess—until it became all too real, and the countess seduced him, apparently with the baron's blessing.

Lacewing had succumbed to the temptation.

Later, he had learned just how vile the countess, Lili, was, how she reveled in the suffering of others, when the brother of a peasant she had tortured tossed acid in her face, badly burning her. And then her back had been broken in the course of his escape from the German camp. The woman to whom he had made love (which he had later bitterly regretted), and who had tried to kill him, had been paralyzed from the waist down in the massive train wreck.

The Other, Lacewing, felt Shrassk touch his mind with another vision.

Lili stretched her limbs in unnatural contortions, grinning horribly, the right side of her face horribly scarred, revealed when her wavy ash-blonde hair flew in the wind.

Lacewing realized, in that moment, that she had not been paralyzed, and that the vision of her and the baron he had thought he saw, all those years ago on the medical campus of Johns Hopkins, had been no illusion. It had been real. They had both survived the chaos of the events when he and his comrades had escaped from the German camp.

And Lacewing knew that the only explanation for the healed broken back was that Lili could not be quite human. The stories the wailing man had told Lacewing about the shapeshifting Ssk'eth . . . Lili was one of them, or a human-Ssk'eth hybrid who had some shape-altering abilities, abilities that had enabled her to survive the crashing train wreck, the crushing steel, and to heal her broken back. The dream vision progressed, and Lacewing saw this was true: Lili gave birth to their son, and then over time slowly healed her broken back, followed later by the final healing of her facial scars. If she had been, genetically, fully Ssk'eth, these changes and healings could have been accomplished in weeks or months. As a half-human, it took decades for her to master her abilities and make the transitions.

Shrassk tapped into the depths of Lacewing's mind and brought to the forefront what he had always suspected. His greatest enemy, the one he fought repeatedly in the '30s, was his own not-quite-human son. The slippery baron was there as well, overseeing his grandson's efforts.

Grandson! Lacewing was sickened at the revelation. Lili had not been the baron's mistress; she was his daughter!

The dreamlike vision shifted and now Caliban saw his own past, rather than Lacewing's. A tiny portion of his brain screamed, "Alert! Alert!" with alarm at what might be happening while he and Lacewing were in the throes of the visions. But he, and presumably Lacewing, seemed to be helpless to do anything but let the images and memories wash over him.

Caliban saw *his* Lili, the woman who had hated him, the one he had known when he was a prisoner in the German camp. She did not become pregnant by Caliban; his pathologically repressive attitude toward sex prevented that. Shrassk's revelation for Caliban was this: his own great nemesis, the only super villain to battle him twice in the 1930s, was Lili herself. Or rather, *himself*, for after healing her broken back, she had slowly morphed herself into a man, and come after the one who had spurned and defeated her.

The fool Caliban hadn't even realized he had already faced her-him back in 1918.

Caliban was beaten down by the shocking discoveries—including the confirmation that the baron The Other had known appeared to be the spitting image of a young XauXaz. How could that be and what in hell was happening?

Shrassk was not done.

The image of the creature perched on Shrassk's throne wavered again, and in Lili's place sat Big-Eyes Llewellyn in her dressing gown, legs casually crossed, smiling crookedly at him. Poor, dead Big-Eyes, who had wronged him, certainly abused him. But who perhaps did not deserve the death penalty he had meted out in return, did not deserve to have her neck snapped like a chicken's, did not deserve to have her blood-soaked corpse tossed aside like so much refuse.

Caliban was more tainted. He had more for which to atone. He had succumbed to the temptation of killing and to the Nine's offer of immortality, selling himself to them. He thought he had killed Lili at the German camp (and really, when it came down to it, he had meant to), he had killed Big-Eyes in an insane rage, and following this had joined the Nine in exchange for the immortality elixir, even though he had just put himself through a year of spiritual healing in which he had vowed to not kill again in the pursuit of his goals and mission.

Wildman—for this was Lacewing's real name—had less penance to pay. He had yielded to the temptation of sex with her. But otherwise he had escaped from Lili. Later, he had gone a bit mad in the wake of his father's murder, and the subsequent murder of a beloved professor who was like an uncle or father figure to him, and as a result had killed his enemies with abandon on several missions with his five aides. He had come to his senses and reinstated the no-killing mandate which his father had instilled in him during the long years of training.

Importantly, Wildman had not sacrificed his soul to the Nine, and had never entered into a devil's bargain with them in exchange for immortality.

Caliban sat hard on the ground, mentally and physically exhausted. He was overcome and distraught at the grueling review of his life and actions. Shrassk had stripped away the layers, right down to the bone. She had done the same to The Other, Wildman.

Caliban raised his head. Big-Eyes—Shrassk—still sat on the throne, silent, smiling quizzically at him.

A great mist seemed to have settled on the chamber, and the nine gas-fueled torches glowed like gas lamps in a London fog. But the haze was not water vapor; it felt to Caliban as if reality itself was somehow thinner, and a great gauze had been pulled down over it to patch and hold it together.

The angles at which the universes were positioned in relation to each other now overlapped. The nine esoteric symbols cut into the stone pillars, lit by the gaslight, wavered and duplicated. Caliban's vision was doubled.

The borders had been weakened by Shrassk, by the psychological ordeal through which she had put the two bronze men, the tapping into their shared experiences. Was this her plan? Was this the monster's way out of the asymptotic nether space that held her at bay?

Was there more mental torture, more replay of all the errors of their lives, to come?

Through the mist, beyond the weakened and blurred border between the universes, Caliban saw The Other, sitting cross-legged, facing him.

The Other withdrew from a large pocket a sealed plastic bag, and from this removed a long root, reddish-brown in color, and appearing in shape somewhat like a foot, part human and part cloven hoof.

Caliban brought forth a similar plant. Both men, using their knives, shaved flakes of the plants into two small piles in front of them.

On the bloodred throne, Big-Eyes' orbs grew even larger as each of the men struck the flints on their lighters and applied the flames to the root shavings. Was that alarm on her face? Was an entity such as Shrassk even capable of apprehension, or other base emotions?

The plants caught the sparks and burned in small but steady blazes. The two bronze men fanned each pile, encouraging the flames to completely devour the plant matter. These burned warm and orange, and gave forth noxious smoke and fumes, black and pungent.

The two men breathed this in deeply.

Their eyes rolled up in their heads, golden-flecked irises whirling like little pools. Their lips moved with weird mutterings, just under their breaths. Their limbs convulsed involuntarily, and muscles twitched. Sinewy fingers trembled and dropped the lighters. The two men, both still seated cross-legged, moved back and forth in rhythm with each other, swaying in time to the pipes of music only they could hear.

The smoke swirled gently about them and settled, cloaking them in a black-gray pall.

Their minds swam together in an infinite black sea, and their thoughts merged.

They opened the way, widening their perceptions. Every person's brain could access the perceptions with stimulus—magical rituals, incantations, electricity.

The stimulus showed the truth, revealed the horrors all around them.

Many who had opened the way did not understand at all, but

the two bronze men did, for they had each studied, in their own ways, before undertaking their secret journeys: Caliban, the works of Le Garrault; Lacewing, the occult studies he had dismissed, in another life, as irrational.

Caliban recalled his initial speculation that Shrassk's "touching" was what caused Lovecraft to document the so-called Cthulhu Mythos in the form of fictional tales. The two men, thinking as one, now saw that the Mythos was indeed true—but was only one reality.

There were many realities, all coexisting at right angles, occasionally touching.

Contradictorily, there was one basic reality with many interpretations.

Both, and neither, were true—and false.

They could now "see" Shrassk as she really was, the monstrous dweller at the threshold not just of two universes, but of the pluriverse itself. The thing bubbled and gurgled, a monster of fire, and of ice. Tentacles thrashed, unblinking eyes gazed, and teeth gnashed—but of course the tentacles and orbs and teeth were only human interpretations of what the monster looked like.

Shrassk was the all-and-one, the one-and-all, not subject to the laws of time and space, being coexistent with all time and coterminous with all space. Shrassk saw all, knew all. Time was meaningless. She had been trapped, held suspended, in the nether space between universes for infinity, or attoseconds.

Mere words would never adequately describe the monstrosity.

It didn't matter.

The two men saw the idea of the perception of time as limited. Once matter was transcended, one could see everything, everywhere, simultaneously, and could see that the end was sure and horrible, though a long way off.

They both thought of Blake's quote: "Time is the mercy of Eternity."

The two Docs, thinking in tandem, went deeper. The monster on hold reproduced asexually, always generating twins: one an unutterably monstrous and dangerous Child, and one a vaguely humanoid bloblike thing that could take on many shapes.

Shrassk, in order to enter a physical universe, required an

invocation or invitation. Willingness, acquiescence, on the part of the aspirant, was key. Many had begun, but not completed, invocations to Shrassk to enter their worlds—although these aborted invocations had created small rips between the nether space and the universes. In her rage at her entrapment, Shrassk had devoured most of the relatively slow-witted unutterably monstrous Children, while many of the quicker-witted blob-humanoid tentacled twins had escaped the nether space via the tiny tears into adjacent dimensions.

While Shrassk hung in limbo at the gateway to the multitudes of worlds, many of her bloblike twins, the Ssk'eth, remained confined to the caverns. These were, in a sense, as Scott Free had said, lost and corrupted souls who had escaped one trap, the nether space, only to find themselves caught and condemned to a new version of Hell. Others, like Free, had escaped the caves and made it all the way to the Earth's surface. From there, over the countless eons, even more had fled to other star systems. All of these had caused, at one time or another, varying degrees of chaos, both on Earth and elsewhere.

The two Docs realized that the men they had each encountered back in '48, and again recently, who had confessed to being Ssk'eth shapeshifters—Caliban's Mr. Free, and Lacewing's Mr. Cri—had each left out a key piece of information: they were also children of Shrassk.

Then they had an unsettling thought. What if only Shrassk's nether space was "real," and all others were some sort of simulation? What if they only thought they were real, but in truth they and their worlds were manifestations of Shassk's nightmares?

Doc and The Other, Lacewing, continued to think as one. Logically, why would Shrassk be trying to escape from the nether space if their universes were not real? Why would Shrassk want to escape into her own nightmare? The Docs played devil's advocate: what if their worlds were indeed simulated, but were not Shrassk's nightmares, but dreams, dreams of planes that were far more palatable than the one to which she was confined?

Caliban and Wildman wondered if there were others like Shrassk. Were they competitive, like any other sentient beings, seeking power, leaving the others out in the cold? If Shrassk was confined to the nether nexus of the universes, had others already escaped to other realms? Had they originated with the formation of the universes? Or were they perhaps the survivors from an earlier universe, biding their time, waiting, to grow, to expand, to overcome?

If there were others like Shrassk, competing with each other in factions, surely they and their enemies were insane because they could see all time, knew what was coming, and couldn't stop it. Determinism with a vengeance was certain to drive anyone, or anything, mad.

And yet they, and the two bronze men, whose minds were being blasted with this forbidden noesis, had some hope to break the chains of determinism, the only thing that kept them going.

They knew the worst part of facing Shrassk, worse even than nothingness, would be to be absorbed by her, become truly evil, an evil beyond which any humans knew—even as, paradoxically, they knew that Shrassk and others like her (if there were such) did not operate within human conceptions of Good and Evil. But the evil beyond which any humans knew was just the reverse of what mystics described when good people became absorbed, became one with the Good and knew ecstasy indescribable even if they lost their individuality. Those absorbed by Shrassk became Evil and suffered anguish and despair to a degree unknown before.

The two bronze men fell through themselves, and their private terrors, and humiliations, downward to their own naked egos, seared by the fires of psychic hell, and then to the terrors beyond themselves. Into the nonhuman, the beyond- or above-human, and the beasts who were infrahuman. They were tempted by the visions of the naked women they'd avoided in their celibate lives, and these were countered by hopeful visions of married life, children, the real meaning of humanity. Caliban saw Trish. Lacewing saw his wife and daughter.

They were thrust deeper into a place where they saw the emptiness, the disappointments, the frustrations, irritations, and the uselessness of all of these.

The uselessness of life itself.

Then true nothingness, beyond the physical presence in the Earth's bowels of the entity, She-Who-Eats-Her-Young.

They had pierced the veil, transcended their universes into the nether space.

The two Docs, fresh in their knowledge of the pluriverse, and in their lack of knowledge, wondered if they were unique, or if there were other iterations, other versions of them in different planes of existence.

But the two Docs, of one mind, also could not shake the notion that they were more than simply alternate universe versions of each other, but rather they were somehow different manifestations of the same being.

The two Docs had coalesced, merged, into one, each superimposed over the other, slightly out of phase, but acting as a monoentity, the Doc unity. They were, essentially, the same person. Their different dimensional origins, family backgrounds, life histories, were irrelevant.

The noxious smoke slowly settled to the ground and dissipated, leaving the two Docs with nausea and pounding headaches. But they were otherwise clearheaded. Surrounding the entire chamber in which the Doc unity stood, the great ring of stone symbols lit by gas jets, encircling the bowl in which was another loop of stone symbols, in the center of which was the bloodred throne sitting upon the platform shaped like an 8 on its side, was a sphere of shimmering mist. The Doc unity knew that this was a veil, enshrouding the nether space in which Shrassk hung, and in which they were now encased.

The borders between all were thin, wispy.

Another man stood with them in the circular stone chamber.

He was a large man, with heavy brows, hazel eyes that seemed protean in the cavern's purple glow, and a Roman nose. His neck and arms had cords of muscle. His hair was dark, his skin bronzed. He exuded an air of power and presence similar to that given off by the Doc unity.

The part of the Doc unity that accessed Lacewing's memories gave an uncharacteristic cry: "You! The baron!"

The other part that was still Caliban said, "XauXaz!"

The Old Man, XauXaz, twenty-five thousand or thirty thousand years old, but looking to be perhaps in his late thirties or early forties, was swathed in all white robes.

He grinned. He called out, tauntingly, "Tekeli-li! Tekeli-li!"

Then he shed the white robes, underneath which he wore tough khaki pants and a short-sleeved shirt, and brown climbing boots. He stared at the Doc unity curiously.

"What happened to you two? You look like you're . . . overlapping one another."

Ignoring the question, the Doc unity said, "You are dead."

"Obviously," XauXaz replied with a slight smile, "I am not dead. One version of me is dead in your world, Caliban. I am Wildman's XauXaz."

"But," the Doc unity replied, "Wildman and his partner eliminated the Nine—the Nine in their universe—twelve years ago."

The Old Man shrugged. "You missed me."

"Caliban is baffled," the Doc unity said. "Wildman recognizes you as the commandant of the German prison camp he was interned at. Caliban's commandant, Colonel Arnold Etzel von Bissell, was very different."

"Oh, it was me." The reply was offhand. "I've followed you both around for years. Sometimes you recognized me, sensed I was there. Other times I presented a very different aspect."

"Are you a shapeshifter as well?" the Doc unity asked.

"Ha! No. Just a—" XauXaz waved and wiggled his fingers dramatically "—master of disguise."

The Doc unity said, "Wildman recognized you, or sensed you, on occasion. Now that you're here in front of Caliban, he also realizes you—XauXaz—were near a few times. You were—"

"Don't be tiresome. And stop calling me XauXaz. I'm going by Arnie at the moment. Now, listen. Shrassk is getting impatient."

Indeed, as the conversation ensued, the being occupying the blooded throne continued to rotate through the three aspects, like a projector advancing photographic slides on a regular cadence: the scowling Ripper, grinning Lili, and Big-Eyes with her perpetual expression of death-shock.

"Wait, we're not done," the Doc unity said. "If you were the commandant at Caliban's prison camp, then where was *his* XauXaz? How do you present the appearance of relative youth, when by taking the Nine's elixir you should look about a hundred years old? And if you're Wildman's XauXaz, how did you get into Caliban's universe?"

"Too many questions, too many questions!"

The Doc unity was adamant. "Is Shrassk getting impatient with *us*, or with *you*? Answer us."

Arnie sighed. "Very well. I learned about the other universe and my counterpart in 1720. Caliban's Nine were very naughty, trying to invoke Shrassk then, and when they aborted their plans, Shrassk tapped on my shoulder. But the tapping was an itch I couldn't scratch, for hundreds of years—until I picked up some extraterrestrial technology. Thank you, spawn of Ssk'eth, ha, ha! Oh, it needed some tweaking, it made this god-awful clanging, but I took care of that. It only worked in conjunction with the dimensional flaws caused by Shrassk, so I was the only one who could traverse the universes, and the time streams. As Wildman and his friend were working to wipe out my immortal colleagues in the Nine, I hopped universes and time, found myself in 1720—get it, *found myself*—and killed him off. There can be only one.

"I went back and forth between the universes for years, playing both XauXazs. What fun!

"And I got a new elixir, one that worked better than the Nine's." Arnie looked slyly at the Doc unity and winked broadly. "But you know all about that, don't you?"

He drew a Zeppelin-like cigar from a vest pocket, bit and spit out the tip, and flicked a disposable lighter.

The Doc unity stepped forward and knocked the cigar out of Arnie's mouth. It landed near one of the stone pillars. "We know all about your cigars. Keep talking."

Arnie sighed and looked hurt. "Soon I was traveling everywhere, even to the pinnacle of a series of worlds where laws of physics were very different from our own. What a trip!"

"So, there *are* multiple worlds beyond the two we know?" the Doc unity asked.

"Of course!" Arnie said. "Think of the pluriverse, or the multiverse, as a conglomeration of infinite layers all of which are unique and stand on their own, following their own timelines as events unfold and diverge, though some can intersect each other for brief periods when the angles shift, or flaws between them weaken. Some dimensions even have differing laws of physics and scientific principles—and some of these are 'artificial,' in the sense that beings greater than yourselves created them.

"And guess who I ran into on one of these pocket worlds . . . a young Anana, of all people! Although she didn't know me. Those who made the pocket worlds were a lot like me, they liked to joke around and play tricks on each other, so I convinced one of them to shunt the little girl back in time and dump her on prehistoric Earth about 30,000 years ago. Ha, ha! Left her naked and alone with only her scientific knowledge and her will to survive . . . which I knew she would. Poof, here we are!"

"You are a sick man," the Doc unity said.

"Yes! But listen," Arnie said. "The two universes from which you each come have a different quality; they are tied together in a way others are not. They used to be one universe.

"That world split when someone—I won't say who—decided to unwisely dabble in time travel. His or her interference caused the split. I and a few other of the Nine were born before the split, though at the time it occurred we didn't know it. So, we were duplicated. When I learned of the split, I decided, as I said, to do away with my counterpart. Too much of a good thing."

"That's nonsense," the Doc unity said. "Current thinking regarding quantum universes proposes that every action taken at every possible moment causes split streams and different universes. That this occurred only with two universes, yours and mine, is ridiculous."

"Both can be true," Arnie countered. "The two universes were split unnaturally, and it may never be possible for them to come together again. Nonetheless, they remained tied together, one to the other, in some unknowable way, whereas other universes, when split by divergent events, went their own completely different ways with no regard to how other universes progressed. These two worlds are different, mutations if you will, that are inextricably linked together by fraying stitches. While other quantum split universes go their separate ways, diverging infinitely over the eons, these two worlds have remained joined at the hip, so to speak. Different, and yet so similar in many inexplicable ways. Think of it as a room full of mirrors, each mirror a different universe. One mirror is broken, cracked down the middle, the two split pieces still being held tightly together by the frame which encases it. The mirror cannot be repaired, but it still reflects, in many aspects, the same images."

"If someone caused the divergence," the Doc unity said, "which one is the prime world?"

"Non-sequitur," Arnie said. "Both are prime, and neither are prime. You must know," Arnie added, "that I am grandfather to both of you. It was I, Caliban, who was the old Norwegian, Bileyg, who impregnated your grandmother—not *your* XauXaz, he was dead by then." He smiled wolfishly. "And of course, I am also your grandfather, Wildman. You're inter-dimensional first cousins!" Arnie laughed.

On the high-backed chair, Shrassk's rotating aspects flipped back to Lili.

Arnie jerked a thumb in "her" direction and chided the Doc unity. "You thought she was my mistress. Really disappointed you chaps didn't figure out the Lilis were my daughters. I even named the prison camps after her . . . how many clues did you need?"

The Doc unity, rarely visibly provoked, looked angered.

"Now," Arnie said, "let's get down to business."

"Yes, let's," the Doc unity replied. "What's your game? How did you get here?"

"The same way I get anywhere," Arnie replied. He pulled an oversized nineteenth-century pocket watch from a vest pocket and dangled it by the chain. The pearlescent lid fluctuated in the gaslight as if it were the boiling surface of some brew being stirred by three witches. On it was embossed the charioteer constellation, Auriga, surrounding a tiny blue sapphire indicating Capella.

"Bless alien technology—though of course these extraterrestrials, ultimately, owed their existence to Shrassk, sprang from her seed. I got the schematics from a sea captain, a mathematical genius, really, and then secured an actual device and reverse engineered it. Once Shrassk 'touched' me and I learned of the other universes and of my doppelgänger, I realized the device already exists in multiple places and times simultaneously, and therefore is a sender and also a receiver—if one uses it in conjunction with Shrassk's 'touchings' and the flaws between universes she created."

"Did you also use drugs?" The Doc unity pointed at the cigar laying on the ground.

Arnie laughed. "The Nine are *always* using drugs. There are certain substances, as you have found, which help one access corridors of communication. Among other things."

"Do you suppose," the Doc unity asked, "that using this extra-terrestrial technology, and constantly imbibing the smoke of the devil's foot root, and traversing the dimensional doorways enabled by Shrassk, has driven you a bit mad?"

Arnie peered at the Doc unity, curiously. "You, Caliban, are you in there? Did you like it when the *f'dalydn'dadyedar* grabbed and almost tore off your penis? You, Wildman, did you have to eat any of the brown gunk that stank like rotting onions, in order to survive on the trek down here? You were right, you know, the stuff, *pr'rohag'assl*, is excrement. Shit. It all seeps through the cracks in the ground and the walls, leaking from and escaping the underground sewage system. Did you eat it? Did you eat shit?"

Arnie took a breath, then smiled in anticipation. "Now. No more stalling, no more questions. Shrassk and her Children have awakened. She-Who-Eats-Her-Children 'touched' you, tapped into your dreams and gave you visions, in order to draw you here. You're going to help release them."

The Doc unity said, "Caliban realizes you pointed him in the right direction to eliminate Tilatoc. That was where Shrassk first started tapping into his dreams and presenting him with visions that bordered dream and reality."

"Gods," Arnie said, "I know your skulls are thick, but Jesus!" He laughed. "Or rather, Yeshua! I set up the whole thing. Wildman and his pal's defeat of their Nine. Caliban and Grandrith's rebellion against their Nine . . . and by the way what's taking you so long to wipe them out?

"So, here we all are, and here's what you're going to do. What did Cri and Free tell each of you about how Shrassk can escape?"

"'Shrassk is imprisoned by geometry,'" the Doc unity said, "'but if it escapes, will do so by algebra.'"

"Right," Arnie said. "Shrassk is trapped by the geometry of the multiverse. She is the end toward which the beginning aims. Shrassk is held in abeyance, in the nether or non-space, by the configuration of the universes. Like the geometric center of a vast, faceted jewel."

"And Shrassk will be freed by algebra—the mathematics of substitution," the Doc unity said.

"By George! He's got it!" Arnie said. "For Shrassk to emerge, someone else needs to take its place in exchange. One of you will do that."

"Neither of us will do that," the Doc unity said. "Why don't you do it?" the unity added dryly.

"Oh no, not me!" Arnie said. "One of you needs to do it. If I'm the one to release Shrassk, I'd be the one substituted and would be trapped in the nether space."

"Why don't we all skip it," the Doc unity said, "and go home."

"No, no, no. Shrassk is going to enter the physical universe—or universes. That's all there is to it. You need to play your part."

"Pass."

"Look, Shrassk plans to subject you two to mental dream-torture until one of you agrees."

On the highbacked throne, the Jack the Ripper aspect of Shrassk nodded vigorously with an evil grin.

"One of you," Arnie said, "will invariably take a sacrificial attitude to save the other man, and will swap places with her. We know how this ends. Let's skip the torture and cut to the chase."

The Doc unity pondered this, and nodded slowly. "The psychic torture is not necessary. There does not appear to be a way out of the quandary you describe. Just please explain the process."

"Shrassk will substitute with and inhabit either you, Wildman, or you, Caliban, in the physical universe. It doesn't matter which. Once Shrassk is here, she will kill the other of you remaining here. Sorry!"

"And how," the Doc unity asked, "do you plan to control Shrassk, in its physical body, and her monstrous Children?"

"Ah, once Shrassk is released, the possibilities are endless, literally endless. Dreams. Mastery of space and time because Shrassk is space and time. Merging of worlds, of the pluriverse. The list goes on.

"Now. Enough. Perform the substitution. Do it now, or Shrassk will blast your minds with visions that will reduce you to gibbering idiots—and then you'll still do it."

The Doc unity nodded slowly and removed a waterproof pouch from an outer pocket. From this was withdrawn an ancient and yellowed parchment. The document felt evil and cold.

Arnie drew in a sharp breath and whispered, "The Gaw'frugh fragment. I knew you could locate it."

The Gaw'frugh fragment was a surviving piece of an even older writing, supposedly lost, the original Gaw'froozh or Gaw'frugh Manuscript. The Doc unity carefully spread out the yellowed parchment material to reveal the arcane writings in a syllabary indecipherable by all but a few scholars and linguistic experts, among whom were Caliban and Wildman. This was in an esoteric script, related to a pre-Basque language.

The parchment, the Gaw'frugh fragment, was a "bad writing," in the vocabulary of eighth-century Arabic. It contained the ritual for summoning Shrassk, to invoke and invite it, to expose it, to make her reveal herself.

The Doc unity read the invocation aloud, reciting the passages, over and over, in a low, droning voice that gradually, repetitively, increased in pitch and volume, until, with the ninth repetition, the Doc unity was practically screaming the terrible words into the void.

The Doc unity, the twin Docs, dreamed at each other.

The barriers between their two universes and the nether dimension weakened and broke down.

The Doc unity, the two Doc doppelgängers, two consciousnesses operating as one, both *substituted* at the exact same time.

The math didn't work.

Shrassk, now invoked, now released, rejected the Doc unity. She went for the only being with whom the math would work.

Arnie—XauXaz—was *substituted* for Shrassk.

Shrassk, the infinite, the ending and the beginning, inhabited XauXaz's immortal body.

Was she present on both Earths? Not quite, the Doc unity realized. Shrassk was free in the cavern which was currently the intersection of the nether space and the two Earths.

But it would not be long until the substitution was hardened.

The Doc unity brought forth the other object Lacewing had brought.

XauXaz's body trembled and quaked, as if with a palsy. The protean eyes, sometimes blue, sometimes green, rolled up in his skull. Froth bubbled from between his lips.

Lacewing held up the other occult artifact he had secured, evil and cold like the Gaw'frugh fragment.

Perhaps the two objects, the two evils, had been lying around for a long time, perhaps a million or more years, made by a great enemy of Shrassk.

This second object, the nine-sided green stone which was flat on both sides, was the Sigil of Dembron. The Sigil—or the "Harri," as Lacewing called it, a Basque word meaning "the stone"—was brought up by fishermen in the eleventh century from a place that, in the Ice Age, had been buried deep beneath the ice. It gave the impression of shifting, of something not quite right, something below its surface. It emanated cold, which was psychic, not physical. The Sigil, according to Lacewing's esoteric studies, acted in many ways as a direct connection to Shrassk. It strained out any psychic or psychological influences. The item was a two-edged weapon, likely to recoil on the user if not handled properly. Instead of keeping out psychic influences, it could let them all in and tear the brains of the user apart.

The name of the sigil, Dembron, came from a thirteenth-century wizard of France who had perished under mysterious circumstances. The sigil had appeared at various times since the eleventh century, but its location had not been known since 1683.

The Gaw'frugh fragment provided guidance on how to properly use the sigil, the Harri, or perhaps more accurately how to avoid misuse and backfire. Dembron's sigil was a six-sided plaque, one and a quarter of an inch long and wide, bearing an eye and tooth and tentacle forming a triskelion of a sort, all carved from the smooth, nine-sided poison-green stone.

The other side of the Harri contained one word in an unknown writing, of six letters. The word was in the same alphabet as that in the Gaw'frugh fragment.

XauXaz's body, inhabited by Shrassk, continued to thrash about on the ground. The *substitution* was not quite complete. The Doc unity knew that Shrassk didn't care whom she inhabited, but XauXaz cared. They were battling, internally, for control of the body.

XauXaz, of course, was losing. Shrassk was solidifying her residence, and would soon use the body as a vessel to penetrate the universes.

The Doc unity once again read, from the Gaw'frugh parchment, the evil language, the invocation, the summoning, repeating the wicked phrases again and again, but this time coupling the reading with the use of the Harri and the forbidden word inscribed on the Sigil of Dembron. The twin Docs gambled that the two evils would cancel each other rather than reflecting back on the user of the sigil.

The nexus gate opened once more, swirling yellow-brown clouds like the L.A. smog. The monstrous Children of Shrassk breached the gate and sprang forth.

The things were massive and shot out of the gate at great speed, trailing hot white flames in their wake, forcing the Doc unity to dive aside out of their path.

The Doc unity, still in a transcendental state and tapped into Shrassk, saw that the Children were furious and terrible because Shrassk, in her rage, had devoured others of their kind in the nether space, where they could not fight back, while their smaller, bloblike shapeshifter twins had escaped.

But here, in a physical universe, with Shrassk dwelling in a physical body . . .

The Children raced toward Shrassk-XauXaz, eyeballs and teeth forming and rippling across gelatinous surfaces which waxed and waned like the tide of some infinite sea. They numbered perhaps three, though the constantly shifting and morphing made it difficult for the Doc unity to tell, with any certainty, one creature from the next. They acted in congress, white knife-edged, flaming tentacles slashing and burning deep cuts in XauXaz's body.

The Doc unity watched the slaughter unfold from behind one of the tall pillars, and held tight to the stone, the one marked with an O encircling an X, as Shrassk-XauXaz was whipped around in the chamber by the furious winds and vortex forces of the gate connected to Shrassk's nether space.

Other tentacles of the Children reached and plucked Shrassk-XauXaz from the air as he was sucked toward the maelstrom. White tentacles sprouted needlelike prongs that whirled at blinding speed like the steel blades of a blender, shredding XauXaz's body into an unrecognizable pile of meat and blood and bone that splattered and landed heavily and wetly on the cavern floor.

The Children descended upon the heap of flesh and devoured it in a tornado of mouths and teeth, from which flew XauXaz's head, rolling like a bowling ball and coming to rest against the side of the stone pillar opposite the Doc unity. As the Children fed, they uttered horrible cries, *"Tekeli-li! Tekeli-li!"*

The physical body of XauXaz slaughtered, Shrassk evacuated the dead mound of flesh. The Children blasted the non-corporeal Shrassk with fire, psychic fire, the light of which showed the Doc unity what was happening, and in some way cleansed the Doc unity as it burned Shrassk.

And Shrassk, the key to holding open the gate between her non-space universe and the physical universes, and no longer able to inhabit a physical dimension, was sucked, along with the Children, back into their nether space prison.

The vortex gate shrank, and infinite whiteness exploded and suffused the whole chamber, blinding the Doc unity amid the screams of the Children: *"Tekeli-li! Tekeli-li!"*

The gate contracted and popped closed with a last great jet of white flame that collapsed to a pinpoint of blazing light and then blankness.

Shrassk and the Children were gone.

Had Shrassk been killed by the Children, or had they all been sucked back into the nether space and the juncture of the pluriverse before she was slain? Could she even be killed, since she was contemporaneous with all time and coterminous with all space?

The Doc unity decided that, in the end, for now at least, it didn't matter. Shrassk was back where she belonged, trapped.

From the darkness high above in the cave came a terrific shriek, and two ravens dived downward, separating from the blackness, and circled the stone pillar against which XauXaz's skull rested, giving a hue and cry that sounded to the Doc unity like nothing so much as anguish and grief.

The two ravens swooped down upon XauXaz's disembodied head. One of the two dipped a beak and plucked out the right eyeball, leaving the left staring unseeingly into space. The raven popped the fleshy orb down its gullet.

The two birds spun and flapped silently back into the Stygian depths.

The part of the Doc unity that was Caliban recalled the ancestral saying: "The old man would sit again on the High Chair at Castle Grandrith when the two ravens returned." His half-brother, Grandrith, had thought years ago that XauXaz was dead and that the old man would never sit; now that XauXaz was, truly and finally, dead, the two ravens would not return.

The sphere of mist surrounding the throne chamber now rapidly contracted, shrinking in upon itself.

The Doc unity felt regret, regret at the lack of time to learn from each other, to explore their lives, so similar, and yet with significant distinctions.

The two Docs, mirror images superimposed over each other, floating, began to drift apart.

Curiosity, the endless need to seek knowledge, was their over-whelming emotion.

Caliban was disappointed he had not questioned XauXaz about the elaborate funeral that had been held for him at Stonehenge, and his true connection to that sacred place. He wondered if he had missed an opportunity to interrogate the immortal about Clio's whereabouts. Was she really being held in the caves of the Nine, or had that been a false vision?

Wildman knew that this variant of XauXaz had not limited his torments to only him, but had targeted other members of his extended family over the centuries. He wished he had had the chance to confirm if XauXaz had, in fact, been some of these tormentors, in disguise.

Both men wanted more time together as the Doc unity to ruminate over the similarities and dissimilarities of their lives. Both shared an equal amusement that their exploits had been recounted in the pages of pulp fiction magazines.

Both bronze men regretted not pressing XauXaz on Lili's fate—both of their Lilis. Were they dead? Alive?

The two men continued to glide away from each other, arms extended. They appeared to hold hands, though this was an optical illusion, for their hands were in transitorily connected dimensions which were sealing back off from each other. The shrinking sphere of mist split in two, now surrounding each of their bodies. Each man smiled wistfully at the other, and both raised their huge bronze-skinned hands in farewell, holding up two fingers forming a V.

Wildman disappeared as his encircling sphere contracted to a dot and vanished.

Caliban sank to his knees, alone in the dark at the base of the bloodred throne, the gas lights extinguished. He wept.

Days later, when he emerged from the caverns, and was greeted by his friends, Pauncho and Barney and Trish, he hugged them all for a long, long time.

AFTER THE FIRE

1993

Caliban sat in the hut, eyes closed, a solitary figure, meditating and journeying.

Outside, the wind howled and tore through the jagged mountain peaks.

Caliban heard, or thought he heard, something outside. No one but a fool would climb these mountains at this time of year, in this storm, to seek him out.

Caliban arose from the lotus position. He wore only shorts. His corded and cabled muscles rippled magnificently under his bronzed skin.

He opened the door and the wind rushed in, whipping snow and hard ice flakes against his exposed skin.

He didn't feel it.

Caliban squinted, scanned left, right, above. Even with his magnificent vision, his gold-flecked eyes could detect nothing in the raging blizzard.

He closed the wood door, and resumed the lotus position on the wicker mat, in front of which a flame burned in a small brazier. This was certainly not enough to heat the hut, but was sufficient for Caliban's purpose, steadying and focusing his mind in pursuit of more transcendental studies and insights . . .

His experiences in the deep caverns had left him transmogrified.

There was much of Wildman in him, and he knew much of him, Caliban, in Wildman.

He soared, seeking.

A faint hissing noise came from in front of Caliban, between him and the door.

He opened his eyes. A small circle, bordered in silver and translucent in the center, hovered in the air. The circle enlarged and irised open from the center.

A man stepped through this, and Caliban could see, behind the man and within the circumference of the circle, what appeared to be highly sophisticated technical equipment against the backdrop of a green sky.

The man was about six feet and one inch tall, and looked to weigh about one hundred and ninety pounds. His shoulders were broad, and his waist was lean. His hair was reddish-bronze, much like Caliban's own, and shoulder-length. He had a craggy brow, long upper lip, and deeply cleft chin. His eyes were leaf green.

In one hand the man carried a dark leather satchel that resembled a case for some sort of a musical instrument.

He was naked except for a loincloth.

The man said in a midwestern American accent, "I'm looking for Anana."

BONUS MATERIAL

THE WILD HUNTSMAN

WIN SCOTT ECKERT

The Greystokes, like the present Queen of England, can trace their ancestry through Egbert, king of Wessex, to the great god Woden in Denmark of the third century A.D . . . *The founders of the Greystoke line were secret worshippers of Woden long after their neighbors had converted to Christianity . . .*

Thus, Tarzan has as ancestor Woden. It would be difficult to find a more highly placed forefather than the All-Father.

Perhaps the great god of the North is not dead but is in hiding. It pleased the Wild Huntsman to direct the falling star of Wold Newton near the two coaches. Thus, in a manner of speaking, he fathered the children of the occupants. The mutated and recessive genes would be reinforced, kept from being lost, by the frequent marriages among the descendants of the irradiated parents.

—Philip José Farmer, *Tarzan Alive: A Definitive Biography of Lord Greystoke*

Africa, remote mountains near Uganda, 1720

The Old Man sat quietly in his secluded cavern. His one good eye was closed and he appeared to be meditating. His other eye was covered by a black patch.

The Old Man was a giant. Or rather, although he was a large man, there was a strength about him that gave the impression he was a giant.

171

His white beard fell to his waist. His hazel eye was strong, and protean, shifting color in the flickering candlelight.

He wore a double-headed raven headpiece. The headpiece looked heavy for a man of his age—he appeared to be ninety, or perhaps even older. Despite the deep lines, like tiny crevasses crisscrossing his face, his neck was thick and strong, and cords of muscle banded his arms and legs.

He had been known by countless names, many of which even he had forgotten through the ages, and he had inspired legends, folktales, and myths. In these were varying degrees of truth.

For he truly deserved the appellation "Old Man." He had been born in the Old Stone Age, and was at least twenty-five thousand, and perhaps thirty thousand years old.

The candles wavered in a slight breeze and one extinguished.

There should have been no breeze here, twenty caverns deep in the labyrinth of the Nine.

The Old Man opened his eye and looked into the mirror directly across from him.

The cavern had had no mirror when he had closed his eye in meditation.

The Old Man and the reflection, the Other in the mirror, watched each other for a long, long time. It was an admirable exercise in motionlessness.

Then the Old Man extended a finger and tapped his own eye patch pointedly. The Other's eye patch was on the opposite side of the Old Man's, rather than on the same as in a true mirror image.

In the mirror, the Other Old Man grinned ruefully and gave a slight shrug of the shoulders, as if to say, Good one. You got me!

Then the Other in the mirror swiftly reached into the folds of his ancient robes, withdrew a horn-handled dagger, and launched it at the Old Man.

The wickedly sharp blade flew through the mirror, causing a slight ripple like that of a pebble tossed in a pond. It slipped between the Old Man's ribs and penetrated his heart, causing instantaneous death.

Death. Thirty thousand years of breathing, fighting, lovemaking, scheming, thinking, killing, dreaming . . . snuffed out, with the flick of a wrist.

The Old Man slumped to the cavern's dirt floor. His one eye, no longer protean, stared at the ceiling.

The Other Old Man stepped gingerly through the mirror and bent down over his counterpart. He lifted his own eye patch, revealing a perfectly good hazel eye, in which gold flecks seemed to swirl and eddy. Singing quietly to himself—"You are him as I am him like we are me, no more of thee and me"—he closed the Old Man's unseeing eye and winked at the corpse.

A gentle knock came at the heavy wooden door separating the Old Man's private chambers from the rest of those of the Nine. It was the Speaker for the Nine, summoning him to the annual ceremonies.

He told the Speaker to return in five minutes. Then he hefted the corpse with the ease of lifting an infant, hopped through the mirror, and landed in a substantially identical cavern. He concealed the body under a pile of furs and blankets, to be disposed of later.

He retrieved a pocket mirror—a real mirror—from a small wooden box carved with crawling and twisted serpents, and adjusted the eye patch and the double-headed raven headpiece. He touched up his makeup, ensuring it exactly duplicated the crags and valleys on his late counterpart's face.

Satisfied, he again bounded through the mirror that was not a mirror. He pulled an oversized nineteenth-century pocket watch from deep within the folds of his robes. The pearlescent lid was as protean as his eyes, the embossed constellation of Auriga—the charioteer—shifting around a tiny blue sapphire representing the brightest star, Capella.

He worked at the watch and the mirror-gate closed in upon itself, just as the Speaker called him once more.

"XauXaz, Old Father, it is time."

Blakeney Hall, East Riding of Yorkshire, near the village of Wold Newton
11 December 1795

Shortly after the nine terrible and shattering clangings came again, John Gribardsun found the dead man hanging in the library.

To those the clangings summoned, the tolling was as loud as if it had been made while they were standing under the bourdon bell of the cathedral at Notre Dame de Paris. The unexplained, horrific clamor brought the men running from all over Sir Percy's estate.

Sir Percy Blakeney, General Sir Hezekiah Fogg, and Dr. Siger

Holmes arrived first, followed by some of Sir Percy's other guests: Colonel Bozzo-Corona (accompanied, as always, by his man, Lecoq), Sir Hugh Drummond, and Honoré Delagardie, whom Sir Percy had saved from Madame la Guillotine.

The men stood in silence for a moment, watching the swaying corpse hanging from a stout rope which in turn was fastened to the high ceiling by the chandelier.

Sir Percy turned to Holmes. "Get a knife," but before the latter could act Gribardsun, who was known to them as Sir John Gribson, had leapt like a jungle cat upon a side table and was already cutting down the unfortunate deceased. He passed the corpse down to the others and regained the floor with ease.

Sir Percy turned the body over to get a good look at his face. "Iain Bond, aide-de-camp to de Winter, the King's representative at our little congregation . . ."

The men gathered around while Holmes made a quick examination. The hawk-nosed doctor, lean and wiry, looked up after a cursory survey. "Strangled, just as one would expect with hanging."

"The second murder in as many days," Fogg said.

"But each one different," Bozzo-Corona noted.

"Both heralded by that demmed bell ringing," Sir Percy countered.

"Indeed, but each carried out by different methods," Drummond said. "Gerolstein was found with a knife in his heart."

"Perhaps no great loss," Delagardie added.

"Now, now, my boy," Sir Percy said, "the last thing you want to do now is cast suspicion on yourself, eh?"

"But Percy, he insulted Philippa with his base attentions!"

"My sister as well as your wife," Drummond reminded Delagardie, "but Gerolstein's insults are not worth the gallows. And his brother may arrive at any moment; the last thing needed at the moment is a challenge to a duel."

"Right now suspicion is cast on everyone," Colonel Bozzo-Corona said. He pointed to Gribardsun. "This one is clearly strong enough to have committed both murders."

Gribardsun shrugged. "Just about anyone is."

"I am not," the Colonel said with a sardonic smile. "I am but a frail, old man."

"Demme me, sir! We're not going to find the killer slinging accusations at each other," Sir Percy said. "Call some footmen and we'll store the body with Gerolstein's. And someone fetch de Winter; as His Majesty's representative, at least he can assist in dealing with the parish constabulary."

Gribardsun padded around the estate, weaving through hidden garden paths and hedges. His passing was utterly silent, as befitted his jungle upbringing and years of experience as a woodsman, although of course he could do little to prevent his scent from being detected downwind.

He thought about the terrible din that portended the two murders. He had heard a similar clangor several other times in the past 150 years, and while he hadn't discovered the source, it always seemed to accompany some misfortune or unfortunate occurrence.

In his long life, Gribardsun had generally taken pains—with a few exceptions—to avoid involvement in key historical events, not always with success. Besides, as scientists he had worked with reasoned, who was to say that his involvement was not part of the natural flow of history? That the unnatural pealing of unseen bells had come to this place, at this time, reinforced his decision to attend Sir Percy's conclave. If he didn't solve the mystery of the clanging here and now, it seemed likely he'd have more opportunities in the years to come.

He stopped.

He scented a vaguely familiar smell, one that tickled the edges of his memory. He had an extraordinary sense of smell, almost equal to that of the higher primates among whom he had been raised. Some few who knew the particulars of Gribardsun's background—the real story, not the fictionalized and romanticized tales written for popular magazines—speculated that these were an unknown line of australopithecines; others postulated they were Bili apes, a species of large chimpanzee first identified some one hundred years after his birth.

He tracked the scent, circumnavigating the estate once on the ground, and again after taking to the trees.

Gribardsun stopped, turned, scented the air once more, and gave up. The trail had gone cold. He dropped easily from the high branches of a large beech tree, retrieved his boots, and made for the house.

As he passed through a small terraced garden, he heard the low strain of several voices in deep conversation. The exchange came from the drawing room, on the other side of high windows which had been closed against the December chill.

He leapt to a balcony, from it caught a tangle of vinery, and stealthily scrambled to a short overhanging roof. He flipped over the roof ledge with ease and silently scuttled over to a window. He clung upside down and dipped his head just past the top of the window, and peered into the room.

Gribardsun's hearing was almost as uncanny as his sense of smell, and he hung there, at ease, listening to the men inside. Sir Percy Blakeney. Fitzwilliam Darcy. Sir Hezekiah Fogg. George Edward Rutherford, the 11th Baron Tennington. Dr. Siger Holmes. William de Winter. John Clayton, the 3rd Duke of Greystoke.

With the exception of Fogg and Holmes and de Winter, all the men in the room were his great-great grandfathers. Siger Holmes' granddaughter was, or would be, his great aunt.

Coming to Blakeney Hall was a great risk.

But he couldn't leave.

He eavesdropped.

"This was supposed to be a gathering of the best minds, the most politically astute. Men of power, those who could influence statesmen." Sir Percy tossed his snuff box down in disgust. "Demme me! Things are going to hell on the Continent. The Revolution's excesses in the Reign of Terror, the Thermidorian Reaction, and the White Terror in response. And the Red Reign of Terror. I brought the best and brightest here to strategize—how to end the violence, the endless cycles of revenge?

"Instead," Sir Percy concluded, "it's a farce. More violence, more death."

"Someone seeks to sabotage your assembly before it starts," Lord Tennington said.

"And who would do that?" Lord Greystoke asked.

"Who has the most to gain?" de Winter countered.

"Colonel Bozzo-Corona, perhaps," Holmes said.

"With what motive?" Darcy asked.

"Unknown," Holmes said. "But I witnessed the Colonel's man Lecoq meet with Countess Carody in Paris last month."

"Interesting, yes, my dear Holmes," Sir Percy said. "But that doesn't necessarily implicate the Colonel in any wrongdoing."

"Their meeting was illicit," Holmes replied, "conducted at the Calyx Bar."

"Perhaps Lecoq and the Countess . . ." Sir Hezekiah said.

"I'm afraid not, Fogg," Sir Percy said. "I think the Countess does not prefer such company."

"Certainly she is a noble and he a commoner, and yet it is not unheard of—"

"I mean, Fogg, that Countess Nadine Carody does not prefer *any* such company."

Darcy flushed with embarrassment at the turn the conversation had taken. "Surely such speculation . . ."

"Marguerite and Alice have assured me that it is so," Sir Percy said.

"All the more reason to assume Lecoq met the Countess on behalf of the Colonel," Holmes said. "No other conclusion fits the facts at hand."

"If you are correct," de Winter said, "then, as Darcy pointed out, we still have no idea why."

"As I said," Tennington interjected, "sabotage the meeting."

"But to what purpose?" Darcy asked.

"Perhaps Colonel Bozzo-Corona doesn't share Sir Percy's vision of peace on the Continent," Greystoke said.

"And yet," Sir Percy replied, "we seem to be aligned. The Colonel and his Brothers of Mercy gave Marguerite and Alice the Heart of Ahriman to help us defeat Baron de Musard."

"I still say that lot—the Colonel, Kramm, Carody, Gerolstein— bear further watching," Tennington said.

"But Gerolstein's own brother was murdered!" Sir Hezekiah said.

"What better way to cast suspicion away from themselves than to sacrifice one of their useless pawns?" de Winter asked. "I agree with Tennington, beware of them."

Sir Percy nodded in reluctant agreement. "I'll tell Sir Hugh and Delagardie and Gribson—he's a distant relative of yours, eh what, Greystoke?—to keep their eyes open as well."

He took a pinch of snuff, and sneezed. "To think Marguerite gave up wintering at the Crescent for this . . ."

Gribardsun left his perch and crept along the rooftop to the other side of the estate. The tinkling of a piano drew him to the music room, where another gathering and opportunity to listen in seemed likely.

He found a toehold, lowered his head to peer into the frosted windows, and saw a large group of the estate's female guests—many of them his ancestresses, and many of them currently in the common state of pregnancy. Alice Clarke Raffles played the piano, while Lady Blakeney and Elizabeth Darcy watched her play.

Two small groups held quiet conversations. In one corner Countess Carody, Miss Caroline Bingley, and Philippa Delagardie, née Drummond, were sitting with Alicia, Lady Greystoke. Lady Tennington, Violet Clarke Holmes, and Elizabeth de Winter formed another small group, while Lady Drummond sat by herself, reading.

There was no one thread of conversation to follow, but he did pick up several interesting pieces of information.

Several of the ladies were put out by the short notice of the invitation to Blakeney Hall; such affairs usually called for months of preparation.

Caroline Bingley, in particular, seemed intent on complaining that the quickly arranged gathering was in poor taste, to which her sister-in-law, Elizabeth Bennet, replied with a rebuke, at once gentle and sharp, that it was a shame there weren't nearly as many unattached nobles in attendance as Miss Bingley might have hoped.

Lady Blakeney laughed it off, blaming Sir Percy for the timing. Alice supported her, and spoke of men's affairs waiting for no one.

Gribardsun supposed that not all the women had been brought into confidence regarding the true nature of the gathering, and Sir Percy's plans to end the Continental strife once and for all.

He also sensed a tension in the air, which was perfectly natural, given the two unexplained killings. Most of the ladies had no prior acquaintance with danger. And many of them were pregnant, and understandably apprehensive that something dreadful might happen to them and their unborn children.

Some few of the women had encountered danger and adventure,

however, and appeared more at ease, if not sanguine, in the wake of the terrible events. Gribardsun focused his attention on them.

Two of these were Lady Marguerite Blakeney and Alice Clarke Raffles, whom Gribardsun gathered had shared an exploit last month in France, battling a baron called de Musard. Gribardsun had also confronted a Baron de Musard once, killed him in fact, in the late 1500s in France. He resolved to learn more about this if he could.

Elizabeth de Winter also seemed less affected by the past days' events, although this was perhaps natural given her husband's high position in the government.

Countess Nadine Carody appeared outright indifferent to the murders, and Gribardsun noted that she had also not been offended in the least by the expedient invitation to England. In fact she had seemed glad to come on short notice.

Many roads appeared to lead to the Countess. She had conducted a strange meeting with Lecoq in Paris last month, and apparently was in league with Colonel Bozzo-Corona in some way.

Gribardsun focused on her. She watched Lady Blakeney the way a lioness regarded her next meal.

He recalled that she smelled . . . strange. Almost like a corpse, but he could smell the lifeblood pumping through her veins.

Countess Carody was mysterious. But was she the key to the mystery at hand?

It warranted further investigation.

Nighttime, and a new moon.

And what was the Continental contingent doing wandering the grounds, taking advantage of the pitch-black night?

Nothing good, Gribardsun decided. He swung from his perch to a lower branch, still out of sight of those he spied upon, and settled in to listen.

"I must have satisfaction!" Gerolstein cried.

"Meaning what?" Gustavas Kramm asked.

"Delagardie must pay."

"We have no proof Honoré Delagardie killed your brother," Kramm replied. "And why would he also kill Bond?"

"To cover his tracks, throw us off his scent," Gerolstein said.

"Nonsense. You give the boy too much credit," the Colonel said. "Have a care. We must tread lightly here."

"But—"

"Enough!" the Colonel said. "Kramm, take him to his rooms and keep him there. We cannot afford a misstep now."

Gribardsun watched Kramm march off with the reluctant Gerolstein in tow. He elected to stay with Bozzo-Corona, Lecoq, and Countess Carody, and his decision was rewarded a moment later.

"Do you suppose Sir Percy and the others suspect us of these murders, my father?" Lecoq asked.

Gribardsun watched carefully as the supposedly feeble old man, the patriarch of the Brothers of Mercy, answered: "They'd be fools not to, my son."

"Perhaps," Countess Carody said, "they are dimly beginning to realize that you were behind Baron de Musard all along."

"And that through setting Blakeney and de Musard against each other," the Colonel said, "I manipulated Blakeney into convening this so-called 'conclave' of his? As I said, Sir Percy is no fool, but I doubt he is that perceptive."

"Perhaps not, my father, but if you'll forgive me, his friend Holmes may be," Lecoq said. "And Blakeney's friend, Fogg. There is something . . . something not quite right about him. I beg you leave to spy upon them further."

The sinister old man regarded his lieutenant, then said: "Very well, my son, you may go. But remember your longer-term mission. Ingratiate yourself to Delagardie. He will need another coachman once Lupin moves on. You will be our man inside once Sir Percy's conclave disbands—if we can manage this unforeseen situation of murder and death, and can all part as trusted allies."

"Or at least part leaving them thinking we are all trusted allies," Countess Carody amended.

Lecoq nodded his thanks to the Colonel and returned to the house, followed by the silent Gribardsun, who took a circuitous route through the shadows and yet kept his quarry in sight.

Lecoq soon discovered, however, that his targets had retired for the evening, and took himself to his own quarters.

And Gribardsun . . . John Gribardsun kept the silent night watch over Blakeney Hall.

THE WILD HUNTSMAN

Blakeney Hall, East Riding of Yorkshire, near the village of Wold Newton
12 December 1795

The dreadful clangings, and death, summoned them the next morning. Sir Percy, Siger Holmes, and Gribardsun arrived first.

Miss Caroline Bingley lay in her bed, blue of face, limbs bloated and distended. The body had been discovered by her chambermaid.

Holmes examined her fingernails, peeled back her eyelids, and sniffed at the corpse's face. He pulled a sheet up over the gruesome discovery. "A fast acting poison. Body's still warm. I'd say she's been dead ten minutes, maybe fifteen."

"Which coincides with those demmed bells," Sir Percy said. He turned to the others. "Did anyone see anything? You, Sir John—" he gestured to Gribardsun "—you were up, prowling these halls early this morning. Did you notice anything?"

Gribardsun shook his head, expressionless. Inside, he burned. Another killing, and he had failed to prevent it. Each slaying heralded by the ominous tolling, as of funeral bells, but funeral bells which pierced the brain as if one were standing directly under them.

And that maddeningly familiar scent . . .

"Miss Caroline Bingley," Sir Percy said, bringing Gribardsun's attention back to the cadaver. "Demmed wretched woman. Darcy will have a deuced time composing a letter of condolence to her brother."

"And I'm having a deuced time explaining all this and keeping the local constabulary at bay," William de Winter declared as he entered the death chamber. "I saw the value of this assembly of yours when you first described it to me, Sir Percy, but I declare that any benefit which may result from this meeting is being quickly diminished by these abominable murders."

"I agree, de Winter—"

"I've already lost my best man, Iain Bond," de Winter continued, "and His Majesty is rapidly losing patience with this conclave. We must have results, and soon, or I'll order this assembly adjourned." He turned to the two footmen who stood quietly in the hallway. "Meantime, store this body with the others. I'll be in my rooms, concocting some story or other about Miss Bingley's untimely demise. Apoplexy, or some such, I suppose." He stalked out.

The sun sank toward the horizon, washing Blakeney Hall in a blazing orange-red burn, as Gribardsun stalked the grounds searching for a clue, for the slightest scrap or hint of information. It could not be said that he stalked his prey, for he couldn't even scent his target.

That morning, in Miss Bingley's chambers, he had caught that scent again. He sifted through millennia of memories both ancient and recent, and still could not place it.

He had left the estate and spent the day patrolling the outskirts, haunting the surrounding woods and gardens, hoping to pick up the spoor again.

It was all to no avail, but his head was clear and he felt energized by the outdoor air. He thought of ages past and the unspoiled, savage world he had sought out, found, and which he was slowly losing once again. Civilization was slowly, but inexorably, closing in upon him as the centuries passed.

The day had seen the denizens of Blakeney Hall keep to their rooms, a growing sense of dread and anxiety hanging over the entire estate. Very few felt safe enough to venture out, and the pregnant women—a few of them, at least—fretted over themselves and their unborn. Some of the others, Gribardsun knew, such as Lady Blakeney and her friend Alice, were not given to fretting under any circumstances.

The sun disappeared and twilight encroached, bringing the first hint of starlight. The waxing crescent moon, soon to rise, would provide little light, which suited him, for he intended to resume his watch over Colonel Bozzo-Corona's man Albert Lecoq this night.

Gribardsun found the supposed coachman with one of his peers at the stables. Swinging to the roof, nimbly and silently, he crept in an upper window, and swung between the rafters until he reached a spot where he could observe and listen to the two men, Lecoq and Louis Lupin, ostensibly coachmen to Honoré Delagardie. Of the other coachmen, Arthur Blake and Etienne Austin—Sir Percy had rescued the latter from Madame la Guillotine several years ago—there was no sign.

Lecoq and Lupin sat on short wooden stools, a dark lantern on a barrel casting a sliver of luminescence as they played *vingt-et-un* and spoke in harsh whispers.

"So they suspect the Colonel set up Sir Percy in that de Musard matter, only to then come to the heroic rescue by supplying the Heart of Ahriman?" Lupin asked.

"We don't believe so, not yet anyway," came Lecoq's reply. "Dr. Holmes may be perceptive enough to land on the truth, but I've been keeping my ears open, and they don't seem to have put it together yet.

"But we do believe they suspect us in these bizarre murders," Lecoq continued. "Sir Percy, and Greystoke, and the rest have become singularly closed-mouthed in our presence. As a result, the talks have stalled. The Colonel grows impatient, and speaks of departing within the next few days."

"Then is all lost?" Lupin implored. "Will we not all agree to give Napoleon the signal, and put an end to this madness in France?"

"Your half-brother has been perfectly positioned, and the time is ripe, it is true, for action," Lecoq replied. "He can impose stability in France, and on the Continent. The Colonel and the Brothers of Mercy had hoped to protect their flanks by bringing the British in on the plan, and indeed, making them think it was their own idea. But these inexplicable killings . . ."

"And if the Colonel decides that we are to leave, that the British will not join us?" Lupin asked.

"I imagine he will act anyway, giving your sibling the go ahead," Lecoq said. "But it would be better to have the British on our side."

Gribardsun heard a scrape, so slight that the two Frenchmen would not have been able to detect it. He shifted stealthily in the rafters and identified the source: Arthur Blake, covertly observing Lupin and Lecoq from the main entrance to the stables, and not realizing that he, in turn, was being observed.

This was getting interesting. Gribardsun was sure that Blake had only just arrived; otherwise, he would have detected the coachman earlier.

"Then perhaps we should try to solve the mystery of these 'ringing bell murders' ourselves," Lupin said, "and put a stop to them before any more damage is done."

"And just how do you propose to do that?" Lecoq asked, skepticism painting his rough features.

"Well . . ." Lupin revealed his cards.

"*Vingt-et-un*," Lecoq declared, revealing his cards with a triumphant grin.

Arthur Blake left his place of concealment at the main stable door and made for the estate.

Gribardsun decided there was more profit in hearing what the coachman would report to his master. He decamped from the stable rafters, as soundlessly as he had entered, leapt to the ground with the sleek grace of a black panther, and trailed Blake at a discreet distance.

The coachman entered the main house, and Gribardsun took a chance that Blake would seek out Sir Percy in his private study. He scaled the stone walls and once again traversed the roof as easily as if it were the upper levels of the jungle forest he knew so well.

He came to the spot above Blakeney's private chambers, found a grip, and as he had several other times in the past few days, hung upside down from the gable, with his ear close to the study windows.

Gribardsun's gamble paid off. He heard Blake knock and his master bid him enter.

As the latter did so, however, it was not Sir Percy who spoke first but Sir Hezekiah Fogg. "Well, Blake, what is your report?"

There was a long pause, and Sir Hezekiah spoke again. "Go ahead, we've swept the room for listening devices."

"Very well, Sir Hezekiah, I've just come from the stables," Blake replied.

"Ah, and what do our French 'coachmen' have to say for themselves, cousin?" Sir Percy drawled. Gribardsun heard Blakeney take a snort of snuff.

"Well, as you say, Sir Percy, they're no more coachmen than I am. But as to what I heard, they're of a mind to solve these murders themselves. They seem to think if they can do so, it will mitigate some damage, although I missed the beginnings of their conversation and can't tell exactly what they meant by that."

"If these Frenchies start meddling," Sir Hezekiah interjected, "it could ruin everything."

"Well," Sir Percy replied, "at least we can be pretty well assured they're not Capelleans. They don't seem to recognize that the clangings are caused by a distorter."

"Or distorters," Blake said.

"But they wouldn't admit knowing the sounds if they did," Sir Hezekiah said.

"True, sir," Blake said, "but Lecoq and Lupin didn't know they were being observed, and spoke as if they didn't know what the tolling was. My opinion is they're not Capellean."

"Well," Sir Percy said, "*somebody* around here is a Capellean. I've never seen or held an actual distorter, but I know the meaning of these clamorous sounds."

"Aye," Sir Hezekiah said. "Someone must know you are an Eridanean agent, and that I am an Old Eridanean. For whatever reason, they mean to disrupt the assembly you've brought together here."

"Is it really in the Capelleans' interest to foment further discord, or rather prevent us from quelling the discord, in France?" Sir Percy asked. "I'm not so sure."

"What else could it be?" Sir Hezekiah said. "We have the tolling which signals the use of a distorter; murders in which no sign of the culprit can be found, and thus which can only be explained by someone transmitting in and out using a distorter; and consequent disruption of your secret meeting. The Eridaneans prefer that your conclave succeed. The only logical conclusion is Capellean sabotage."

"Yes, it makes sense when you put it that way . . ." Sir Percy said. "Y'know, Fogg, you could give Dr. Holmes some lessons in logic."

"A brilliant man," Sir Hezekiah conceded. "Perhaps we should recruit him to the Eridanean cause."

"Perhaps, someday," Sir Percy said. "Here and now, we need to prepare for tomorrow. A murder a day. We have to suppose there'll be another, or at least an attempt, tomorrow."

"What do you have in mind, Sir Percy?" Blake asked.

"We need to keep everyone together, for the whole day. Everyone within view of everyone else. No demmed transmitting in and out, sight unseen."

"And . . . ?" Sir Hezekiah asked.

Gribardsun listened to Sir Percy take another snort of snuff.

"I think," the man who had also been known as the Scarlet Pimpernel said, "that we should get away from Blakeney Hall for a bit. I do believe a carriage ride is in order."

Gribardsun's ebony hair hung in his face, covering his piercing gray eyes, as he sat alone in his room, staring at the floor, brooding.

He reflected back on the other occasions he'd heard the strange clanging, and went over again in his head the conversation he'd just heard. The information he'd gleaned from Blakeney, Fogg, and Blake—these "Eridaneans"—answered many questions and raised as many new ones.

Eridaneans and Capelleans. Some sort of competing secret societies, so-called because their membership, rituals, and purpose were clandestine?

Perhaps related to the Illuminati? The Rosicrucians? These groups were supposedly interested in gathering secret knowledge from all over the world. Listening devices (unknown in 1795) and "distorters" which "transmitted" people or things (unknown even in his own time—although he supposed that his ship, the *H. G. Wells I*, was, after all, a sort of teleportation device) certainly could be characterized as "secret knowledge."

He had also heard rumblings, through the ages, whispered in the darkness when the fire fell to crackling embers, of a society, truly secret, in that no one, or almost no one, knew of its very existence. The Nine.

The nine bell tolls that signaled each murder.

His brain raced now, unbidden, and another part of his mind, compartmentalized, knew he was making stream-of-consciousness connections, stitching seemingly unrelated items together into a grand tapestry.

He thought of the importance of the number nine in Khokarsan culture, and of the nine-sided temple of Kho. The Door of the Nine, which gave unto the temple. And the nine primary aspects of Kho.

Gribardsun blinked, shook his head, coming out of his fugue.

He almost had it. Not quite, but it was almost there.

Khokarsa. Africa. Thirteen thousand years ago. And the tickling, niggling scent that accompanied each slaying.

He put it aside, not forcing it, and came back to the Eridaneans and Capelleans. Were they secret societies? What other explanation was there? Teleportation technology was extremely advanced. Too advanced, in fact, to reasonably have been developed in this time and place, even by progressive intellectuals operating surreptitiously. The scientific and technological infrastructure just wouldn't support it.

Extraterrestrials?

Could celestial races be interfering in human affairs? It certainly would not surprise him, given his prior experiences in Africa of exotic plants and the massive crystalline root system—both clearly of alien origin—which had infested large swaths of the continent, leading to the great calamity and the end of the Khokarsan civilization.

But were they extraterrestrials? Blakeney, Fogg, and Blake—the Eridaneans, as they called themselves—seemed fully human and appeared to be on the side of right. And Blakeney was his great-great-grandfather.

Gribardsun decided he'd reserve complete judgment for the future, but would still investigate the ungodly clangings which signaled teleportation—"transmission"—if he came through this tomorrow, and if he heard them again in the future. And he'd put a stop to the strange rivalry between the Capelleans and Eridaneans if he could.

Gribardsun thought about tomorrow, the momentous day. Blakeney had proposed a carriage ride; certainly no one bent on sabotage would propose that.

But if sabotage was the murderer's object, sabotage of *what*, precisely?

Sabotage of Sir Percy's conclave, of his attempt to quell the raging fires in France and prevent them from spreading to the rest of Europe?

Or sabotage of . . . tomorrow itself?

East Riding of Yorkshire, near the village of Wold Newton
13 December 1795, 2:00 P.M.

True to his word, Sir Percy Blakeney had rousted the inhabitants and guests for a day away from the grim pall that overhung Blakeney Hall.

Two huge carriages leisurely passed through the village of Thwing and turned onto Rainsburgh Lane.

The first was occupied by Greystoke, Tennington, Honoré Delagardie, Fitzwilliam Darcy, and their wives. It was driven by Delagardie's two coachmen, Lecoq and Lupin.

The second held Sir Percy, Lady Blakeney, and Alice Clarke Raffles, as well as Alice's sister Violet and Violet's husband, Dr. Holmes. Rounding out the passengers were Sir Hugh Drummond and his wife, Lady Georgia Dewhurst Drummond. Driving the coach were Albert Blake and Etienne Austin.

Gribardsun—Sir John Gribson, to the carriage party—rode alongside on horseback, as did a physician friend of Holmes, Sebastian Noel. Noel had arrived in the area yesterday and was staying at an inn in the nearby village of Wold Newton, toward which they were now circling back. At the party's restful pace, the village was perhaps half an hour or slightly more away.

Colonel Bozzo-Corona, Kramm, and Gerolstein had not elected to join the party. The wizened old Colonel had seen Sir Percy and the others off, and before they departed, Gribardsun had overheard them speaking frankly about the situation they faced. The upshot had been that if there was no progress on the negotiations and plans within the next two days, the Colonel and his party would take their leave of Blakeney Hall.

Shortly thereafter, Gribardsun observed Sir Percy speaking quietly to Fogg and de Winter; as the latter two had not joined the carriage party, Gribardsun assumed they had agreed to keep an eye on the Colonel and his associates and ensure no mischief ensued back at Blakeney Hall while the others were absent.

Countess Carody also begged off, to the chagrin of Marguerite and Alice and Lizzie Darcy, claiming too much sun would be unfavorable to her complexion—this despite the enclosed carriages.

At 2:25 P.M., a light cloud cover hovered in the distance. There was a crisp and refreshing chill in the air as the party traversed the gently rolling farmland. Gribardsun rode alongside Sir Percy's carriage and listened as the baronet pointed out Major Edward Topham's Wold Cottage in the distance on the left, and regaled his fellow passengers with slightly risqué accounts of the unmarried Topham, the actress Mrs. Mary Wells, and their three surviving daughters, to the accompaniment of many chuckles and some outright laughter. Sir Percy was quick to note the loveliness of Major Topham's three children, Juliet, Harriet, and Maria.

Blakeney's tale-telling was affectionate. It was clear he held his friend Topham, as well as his amorous exploits, in high regard. This came as no surprise to the other carriage passengers, who well knew that his lady loves, Lady Blakeney and Alice, were both among the foremost actresses of their day.

At 2:30, nine ominous clangings rang out across the countryside.

The two carriages stopped amidst the uneasy chatter of the occupants, as they attempted to hone in on the source.

After a brief pause, the nine bells tolled again, seemingly coming from everywhere and nowhere.

While the party, nerves on edge, debated the meaning of the earsplitting clangor and the wisdom of further investigation, particularly given the presence of the many gravid ladies, John Gribardsun galloped away, leaving the others far behind.

The bells pealed again, and the cycle of nine clangings repeated on a regular cadence as he rode hard down Rainsburgh Lane and turned into the short drive leading to Wold Cottage.

How could anyone, other than himself, know about today? And were they—whoever they were—here to sabotage?

Gribardsun urged his horse on past Topham's abode. He had come to observe the momentous event of December 13, and now it seemed that someone—whoever was associated with, or causing, the clangings and the murders—might succeed in stopping what history said had happened. Gribardsun had been stalking his prey, getting closer and closer, trying to ensure that each incident, each death, did not result in an alteration in the streams of Time—and now it seemed that catastrophe loomed over him.

What would happen if he failed? Would he just . . . wink out of existence?

The scientists who had worked on Project Chronos said no, that whatever he or other time travelers did in the past would be a natural part of the fabric of history. Dr. Jacob Moishe, the scientist leading the project team that had invented the time machine later utilized by Gribardsun's expedition, had demonstrated that if time travel were going to change history, it had already done so.

Moishe, however, had not taken an immortal, now some fourteen-thousand years old, into account in his calculations. With that in mind, Gribardsun had tried to keep a low profile throughout history, but on the other hand had been unable to resist selectively intervening—a push here, a tug there—in some key events. Particularly key events that pertained to his own history.

The regular clanging became louder and louder as he closed in on it, heading in the direction of a field past Major Topham's cottage. He calculated that it was 2:40. Sir Percy's party—the carriages and the horses—were not close to the impact site. Not close enough, anyway.

If they were not there at three o'clock, all was lost.

Gribardsun came over a low rise, making for the field which was empty save for some scattered farmhands. In four years, the field would not be quite so empty; the site would be marked by an obelisk erected by Topham commemorating the event. Gribardsun had visited the site several times, the last in the 2060s.

Then Gribardsun saw *Him.* Smelled *Him.* The scent clicked, and he remembered. *He* looked now the same age as *He* had then, so long ago.

Thirteen thousand years ago.

10,814 B.C. (786 A.T.)

John Gribardsun couldn't believe his nose.

The way other men relied primarily on their sense of sight, and yet often couldn't believe their eyes, despite the evidence in front of them, he could not believe his nose.

Gribardsun picked up the man's spoor before he saw him. No two men, or women, had the exact same scent. Each was unique, among billions, and Gribardsun could recognize the distinctive scent signature of a specific human as easily as a normal man would recognize someone he knew and had seen before.

But this scent defied belief. It was impossible. From his personal perspective, it had been over one thousand years since he had encountered the human being with that scent signature. Perhaps his memory was faulty.

And yet he must trust the evidence before his nose.

Gribardsun had come to this area, a jungle thick with vegetation thousands of miles south of Khokarsa, on the unexplored shores of the inland sea, to investigate the uncanny root system which seemed to be infesting much of this part of Africa. He suspected it might now be extending from Khokarsa to these lands, and he had set a tribe of Gokako—a squat and hairy slant-browed group of Neanderthals, very rare in these far southern lands—at excavating key areas in his search for the root system.

Gribardsun knew of the devastation which could and would be caused in Khokarsa by the alien organism—for alien it was—and hoped to prevent the destruction from reaching these lands. He had had direct experience with similar patterns of annihilation caused by the crystalline roots, having lived through a series of shattering earthquakes in central Africa in 1918. The city which would arise here, which would be founded by Lupoeth, a priestess of Kho, was, and would be, very important to him. He hoped to prevent the spread of ruin, the great cataclysm which was inevitable elsewhere, to these lush lands.

A push here, a nudge there.

The wind shifted, and Gribardsun picked up the scent again, the scent which he could not believe. He whirled.

"You cannot be here," he said in Khokarsan. He was too surprised to consider any alternative languages, but in any event Khokarsan was a probable choice for this time and place—even if the man he spoke to could not be of this time and place.

"Why not?" the other replied, in the same language. Then: "Do you know me?"

Gribardsun did know the man. How come the knowledge was not reciprocal?

The last time Gribardsun had seen the man, in Africa, in 1912, the man had looked like a native witch doctor. Gribardsun, a young man of twenty-three, had saved the witch doctor from a lion. In gratitude, the witch doctor had offered him everlasting life.

Gribardsun had laughed, but said why not. He didn't believe the man, but if there were any truth to the claims, he'd have been a fool to decline the offer.

After a procedure which lasted a month, and greatly sickened him, he'd wondered if he had been a fool to accept. The process involved multiple blood transfusions from the witch doctor and continuous imbibing of a concoction brewed from rare herbs.

But, as he had learned over decades, centuries, and finally millennia, it had worked.

Gribardsun thought about the man's question, "Do you know me?" The man smelled exactly like the witch doctor, but looked nothing like him, which he didn't understand. When Gribardsun had met the man in 1912, the man must have been very, very old. This made sense, if he thought about it. The man was an immortal, and had passed the secret of immortality on to Gribardsun.

The man before him was the younger version, although he could not explain the difference in appearance. This man was Caucasoid, a large man, with hazel eyes, heavy brows, and a Roman nose. His hair was dark, his skin bronzed, and he looked to be in his late thirties or perhaps early forties. Like Gribardsun, he wore clothing appropriate for the jungle, which is to say, very little: a loincloth of antelope hide, a leather pouch, and tough moccasins.

Gribardsun responded to the man's question: "Perhaps."

"I don't know you," the man replied. "Or rather, I should say, I have never met you. But I know who you are. I've been looking for you, Sahhindar."

Gribardsun shrugged. "Some call me that."

"Sahhindar, the Gray-Eyed Archer God," the man continued, and he smiled broadly. "Also the god of plants, of bronze, and of Time. As I've listened to the legends and stories about you over the centuries, it's become clear to me that you are a fellow immortal. I confess that I did not connect the dots, however, until this very minute, that you are also a time traveler. I had never assumed that 'the god of Time' was a literal appellation. That was my mistake."

"What do you want?"

"Perfect." The man grinned at him again. "Straight to the point. I sought you out to discover your source of youth."

Gribardsun's mind raced. "Why?"

"Because it may be more effective than my own."

"Meaning?"

The man smiled his infernal smile.

Gribardsun put his hand on the hilt of the big steel hunting knife which hung in a sheath on his belt and said, "Tell me, or I will remove that smile and replace it with a red one."

"Now *that* would be a grievous mistake, and I think you know it," the man said. "But, I will tell you. There is no point in not being forthright, for once, because this *must* happen.

"If I am correct," the man continued, "you do not age at all. I do age, albeit extraordinarily slowly, and barring accident or murder, someday my body will be very, very old, and it will die. This day may come after millennia, or tens of millennia, but it will come. I would prefer that it didn't."

"And why would I help you with anything, assuming I'm in a position to do so?" Gribardsun asked, his gray eyes piercing the other man's.

"I think," the man replied, "you are beginning to suspect that you have no choice. *If,* that is, you would like me to reciprocate in the future. That's the crux of it, isn't it?"

"If you are correct," Gribardsun said, "how were you—will you—be able to appear to me in the guise of a native African witch doctor?"

"I have no idea," the man grinned, "but now that you've told me that's what I need to do, it appears I'll have plenty of time to figure it out."

"You never told me the precise herbs needed, the exact recipe." Gribardsun said.

"Aha! *Herbs.* The god of plants. Well?" the man prodded.

"I am observant. And an expert botanist. But my knowledge of the herbs used is nonetheless imperfect, and is based on best guesses at the plants and herbs which were growing nearby when I received the treatment."

"But these plants and herbs do exist in this time as well?"

"Yes, or at least some that are very closely related."

"Tell me, show me, and I will be on my way."

"It won't be that simple," Gribardsun said. "The herbal mixture is a vile brew, and I look forward to forcing it down your throat, but it is useless without the other component of the treatment."

"Which is?"

Gribardsun's eyes were hooded. The other man may have had him over the proverbial barrel, but likewise he too had the man over a barrel. He was in control now.

Gribardsun patted the hilt of his steel knife again. "A blood transfusion. From me to you."

The man's perpetual grin faded a few degrees.

"Whatever it takes," he said. "I've endured far worse."

"I cannot guarantee the treatment will work as perfectly on you as it has seemed to work on me," Gribardsun warned. "There *are* slight differences in the plants and herbs, as I mentioned."

"I'll take the risk," the man said dryly. "Can we get on with it?"

"What is your name?" Gribardsun asked.

A sly look came over the man's face and his eyes seemed to shift color, taking on a faint yellowish tint. "I've many names, just as you seem to have, Sahhindar. But you can call me Kethnu. It's as good a name as any other right now."

"*Kethnu.* 'Head man.' High opinion of yourself."

Kethnu shrugged, and his infernal grin broadened again.

"Kethnu, sit down," Gribardsun ordered. "I hope you don't have anyone who will miss you for the next month or so."

He smiled and drew his blade.

East Riding of Yorkshire, near the village of Wold Newton
13 December 1795, 2:40 P.M.

The man Gribardsun had known as Kethnu stood alone in the middle of the field. He was a large man, although perhaps not quite as tall as Gribardsun, and exuded an air of power in the same way Gribardsun did. He still looked to be in his late thirties, and wore his sideburns long. A bushy mustache perched under a Roman nose.

He wore riding dress, similar to Gribardsun's, appropriate for the cold December day and weather: a white, high-collared double-breasted waistcoat, and snug leather riding breeches reaching almost to the tops of his boots.

Unlike Gribardsun, who was no dandy, Kethnu wore around his neck a sterling silver quizzing glass attached to a long black ribbon. The quizzing glass' handle was six-sided and crafted from a pearlescent blue material which Gribardsun couldn't identify.

In his right hand, Kethnu held a large pocket watch attached to a silver chain which disappeared into a pouch on his waistcoat. The pocket watch's lid was of the same pearlescent material as the quizzing glass' handle, and was embossed with an elaborate pattern highlighted by a brilliant blue star sapphire. The blue sapphire reminded Gribardsun of the *nethkarna*, the seed of the Tree of Kho, which the Khokarsan oracles had planted beneath their temples to tap into the root system across Africa, thus gaining their oracular powers.

It was from this watch that the terrible clangings emanated.

"It's been a long time," the other immortal greeted Gribardsun, in between cycles of the riotous nine clangs. There was no trace of irony in the comment. His gray eyes, touched with green, glinted.

"It has," the Englishman acknowledged. "I don't suppose you call yourself 'Kethnu' any longer."

"No indeed," the other man replied. "So much time, and so many names. One which I keep coming back to of late—*of late* being relative, of course—is XauXaz."

"From 'head man' to 'high one.'"

"You are a linguist, my friend. You know your Proto-Germanic."

"The millennia have not taught you humility," Gribardsun said.

"You expected otherwise?" XauXaz asked. Chuckling, he sketched a bow and gestured theatrically to the pocket watch. "Now I am also a time traveler."

"I don't believe you," Gribardsun replied. "It is not possible for anyone else to travel to any time during my lifetime—which is to say, all the way back to 12,000 B.C."

"It is only prevented for *you*," XauXaz answered. "This time distorter works on different principles. It opens gates, and allows one to pass through them, rather than simply shifting stationary masses in time."

Gribardsun gestured to the distorter. "Turn it off."

XauXaz smiled and shook his head slowly.

Gribardsun turned and looked in the distance. Even with his excellent eyesight, he could barely make out the carriage party, still out on Rainsburgh Lane. The horrendous tolling, symbol of murder and death to those carriage passengers, was a deterrent. There was no doubt they would avoid this place, from which the din originated, in an effort to keep the ladies and their unborn children safe.

It was 2:43 P.M.

At three o'clock it would be too late.

Gribardsun attacked.

XauXaz parried, and the two men gripped each other's hands, boots digging into the earth as they thrust against each other.

They pressed back and forth, each struggling for an advantage, and Gribardsun was inwardly surprised to discover the other man seemed to nearly match him in strength.

As if reading his mind, XauXaz grunted, "My bones are thicker than any modern man's, with greater surface area for muscle attachment. Remember, I am a Cro-Magnon."

Gribardsun thrust his right arm downward, caught XauXaz's lower thigh in a crushing grip in his strong fingers, and hoisted the other man above his head as if lifting a barbell. He spun around a few times to disrupt XauXaz's equilibrium and catapulted him headfirst to the ground.

No follower of gentlemen's rules of civilized fighting, Gribardsun followed up with a sharp kick to the abdomen, causing XauXaz to expel a great rush of air, and another kick to the face.

XauXaz rolled away and came back up on his feet, blood streaming from his mouth. "Of course, your bones are much thicker as well." He grinned. "I've been visiting the Ladies Greystoke in their bedchambers for quite some time now. I am your grandfather several times over. How does that make you feel, my boy?"

Gribardsun dived at the other man and took his feet out from under him. XauXaz fell on top of him and they tangled and rolled. The jungle man thrust powerful legs and flipped his opponent over his head, but XauXaz landed deftly on his feet.

The Englishman came back to his feet as well but the other man was at him, and he took a solid one-two punch to the kidneys.

He barely twitched at the pain, side-stepped a third punch, and jackhammered his foot into XauXaz's jaw.

XauXaz was momentarily stunned and the other man pressed the advantage, slamming his opponent's face down in the dirt. He put an elbow firmly in the back of the Old Stone Age man's neck, and wrenched his arm behind his back at an increasingly unnatural angle.

Gribardsun tugged at the twisted arm and simultaneously pressed down with his elbow, eliciting a grunt. He reached under XauXaz's torso, felt for the silver chain, and pulled the outsized pocket watch from underneath the other man's body. Still holding XauXaz immobile, he worked the clasp, popped the watch lid, and started to fumble at the buttons inside.

"I wouldn't," XauXaz said. His voice was low and firm, belying his current position.

"Then you do it," Gribardsun said. "Turn it off, or I'll snap your arm, followed by your neck." He placed the watch on the ground next to the hand that was not attached to XauXaz's twisted arm.

XauXaz worked at the mechanism with his free hand, and the clangings stopped.

Still holding the Cro-Magnon's left arm firmly behind him, Gribardsun grabbed him by the nape of his neck with his right hand and lifted him bodily to his feet. He threw his right arm around the other man's neck and exerted pressure on his throat with the crook of his elbow.

He peered into the distance. The carriage riders had halted at the intersection of Rainsburgh Lane and the short drive leading to Wold Cottage.

"They've stopped to discuss it," XauXaz said. His voice remained calm. "They were following the bells to their source, to investigate, but now the bells have stopped. They've stopped also, to discuss and debate it."

Gribardsun watched, saying nothing.

"Are you here to observe, or stop it from happening?" XauXaz asked.

Gribardsun considered the wisdom of being drawn into conversation with this man. He continued to watch the carriage party, which remained stalled at the distant, too distant, driveway.

"I was here to observe," Gribardsun finally replied. "Now I'm here to ensure it happens."

"Then let me go and restart the distorter." XauXaz's voice was mild.

Gribardsun tightened his arm around the other's neck.

"I estimate it is now 2:48 P.M.," XauXaz said. Was that the tiniest note of desperation creeping into his voice? "Time is running out. Quite literally running out."

Still, Gribardsun said nothing.

"See the small rise behind us?" XauXaz asked.

"What of it?" Gribardsun's voice was as immovable as the steel-corded muscles holding XauXaz fast.

"At least let us climb up there and conceal ourselves—in case Blakeney and the rest do head this way," XauXaz said.

Gribardsun considered this. Then he bent down, grabbed the distorter, threw XauXaz to the ground and dragged him up the hillock.

Reaching the top, Gribardsun took XauXaz in a firm hand-grip about the throat and forced him to crouch down. Gribardsun knelt beside him. His strong fingers remained tight around XauXaz's windpipe.

XauXaz gestured to speak and Gribardsun loosened his clutch slightly.

"You don't trust me," XauXaz croaked, mock reproach in his voice.

"Say something worth saying," Gribardsun said.

"Well, you're right not to trust me, of course. Except now. It's ten minutes to three o'clock. Do you see those farmhands approaching from a nearby field?"

Gribardsun gave a curt nod.

"Their names are John Shipley and Kevin Cook," XauXaz said. "If you know your history, you know they witnessed it too. The moment is approaching.

"Now," XauXaz, continued, "look at the two carriages. They're still at the driveway into Wold Cottage—about ten minutes away."

Gribardsun was silent. The wind gusted and coal-black hair whipped in his face.

XauXaz pressed his point. "They're too far away. They're not going to make it. Give me back the distorter."

Gribardsun watched. The carriages sat idle while the men, tiny stick figures in the distance, appeared to confer.

"You came here to watch it happen. Instead, you're stopping it from happening," XauXaz said. "Why would I have given you the elixir in 1912, if I intended to go about mucking about with the timeline?"

Gribardsun still watched. A man remounted his horse—Sebastian Noel. The coachmen clambered back onto their perches atop the carriages.

The vehicles turned, pointing away from Wold Cottage and oriented back toward the village of Wold Newton.

"*Give it to me.*"

Gribardsun handed over the distorter.

XauXaz worked at it and a riotous clanging ensued, reverberating in the air and shaking them to the bone.

They watched as, in the distance, the carriage riders spurred into action. The coachman turned the carriages back toward Wold Cottage and drove at high speed, seeking the source of the noise which had, to them, signaled death over the past three days.

From the other direction, the farmhands also came their way, seeking the cause of the din.

John Gribardsun and XauXaz crouched down at the top of the rise, out of sight, to observe.

The distorter's awful pealing continued for several more minutes. The carriages came carefully down a dirt trail—it could hardly be called a road—and pulled up below the rise where XauXaz and Gribardsun were hidden.

XauXaz worked at the distorter's controls and the din ceased. The two men out of time watched as Sir Percy ordered the carriages to a halt in the middle of the field.

The carriage party hardly had time to gather their wits when from the air all around came a series of loud claps, like pistol reports. A light like burning phosphorous blazed and streaked across the sky, hissing through the air, leaving what looked like sparks trailing behind it.

The leading edge of the burning light struck the ground near the carriages, spewing dirt and mud and earth everywhere. The blazing light and the sizzling noise caused the horses to panic, and the passengers cried out in alarm as the carriages were pulled and tugged, but the coachmen swiftly brought the terrified beasts under control.

The passengers were still shaken, but quickly came out of their shock. Gribardsun and XauXaz watched silently as Sir Percy, Greystoke, Holmes, Darcy, and the other men alighted and followed the burrowed trail in the ground to the end of its trajectory. They saw Topham's shepherd, as well the farmhands, John Shipley and Kevin Cook, come alongside. The group cautiously began digging. Eventually, as nothing untoward transpired, the women also descended and came to watch as a large stone, smoking and smelling of sulfur, was dug out from where it had buried itself almost two feet deep in the earth.

Atop their perch, still crouching down out of site, Gribardsun looked at XauXaz. "Why?"

XauXaz grinned at him. He lifted the quizzing glass to a yellow-tinted eye and arched a thick dark brow, giving him a superior air. "Why what?" he queried.

"What is your motivation? Why lead them all to the meteor crash site? Why do you care?"

XauXaz shrugged. "A lot happens in thirty thousand years—give or take. A man makes friends, and enemies. Enemies who become friends and allies. Friends and allies who become enemies. Perhaps one of their descendants—" he gestured to the crowd below, gathered around the smoking meteor "—will be in a position to assist me one day."

"Their children, and grandchildren, and great-grandchildren," Gribardsun replied, "will all be born as history recorded, whether or not these people witnessed the meteor today."

"Not necessarily," XauXaz said. "You know as well as I that these people are now special. Their children will have special abilities, abilities they may need just to survive. Who is to say you would have survived your jungle upbringing if your great-great grandfathers were not here today, close to the meteor, being exposed to its heat and energy?"

"You seem to know much about me and my upbringing. But never mind that," Gribardsun said. "You can't count on help from one of their descendants—"

"You helped me by sharing the elixir of your blood, so many millennia ago."

"I had no choice. If I hadn't, then you would not have been alive to share the elixir with me in 1912."

"Perhaps someone else, someday, will also have no choice, and will help me," XauXaz said.

"No, there is more to it than that. What is the real reason behind your intervention here today?"

XauXaz smiled again. He pulled a mother-of-pearl and silver snuff box from a vest pocket. It was inlaid with symbols similar to those on the pocket watch distorter. He took a pinch, snorted, and wiped his nose with a silk handkerchief. He looked at Gribardsun, as if calculating.

Then he spoke.

"The elixir I received from you was much better than that which my friends who are also my enemies had given me. It conferred eternal youth. With the other elixir, I aged, but very, very slowly. And I needed repeated doses of the other elixir. Not so with yours.

"But even your elixir, I have found, was imperfect. Or it worked imperfectly on me."

"I did warn you that might be the case," Gribardsun said. "The differences in the plants and herbs thirteen thousand years ago."

"Indeed, you did warn me," XauXaz agreed mildly. "And I have had little reason to complain, at least to this point. Your elixir kept me young, while my friends who are also my enemies, with their lesser elixir, continued to age. I would be quite elderly now, had I only taken their lesser elixir. In fact, if you believe in the theory of divergent timelines, then I have—or is it had?—a parallel universe counterpart who indeed continued to age in the very way I describe.

"As it was, I had to pretend to age alongside my friends who are also my enemies, as I should have done if I were using their elixir.

"However, as I said, your elixir has started to fail me. About one hundred years ago—one hundred from my perspective—I came to realize this. I was, at the time, playing the part of a seal-hunting schooner captain named Larsen. I started experiencing blinding, debilitating headaches. Eventually, they proved my undoing and those who served under me revolted." XauXaz laughed. "You might say the headaches were the 'death' of me. It was time to move on and create a new identity anyway. But I instinctively understood that the elixir was failing me."

"So you thought to find me here?" Gribardsun asked. "You thought to earn my good graces by luring Sir Percy and his guests to the meteor site, in the hopes that I would return the favor and give you another dose? If so, you are sadly misguided."

XauXaz shook his head and laughed softly. "No, no. I know you have no reason to help me. And no reason to have any love for me—although you should. As I mentioned, I am your grandfather, many times over, and you owe me a genetic debt. But no, I know you will not."

"You are right," Gribardsun said simply. "You murdered unnecessarily to create this scenario."

"What—you, purveyor of the law of the jungle, of kill or be killed? You are judging me for this, of all things?"

"I kill when attacked, to defend myself. And I kill for food, as Nature dictates."

"You kill to live, which is nothing more than I have done. Those small people who died, you will find if you dig deep into the historical records, actually did die at this time. Although the records were altered by de Winter and his cronies as to the place of death. I have altered nothing; Time unfolded as intended."

"You are a murderer," Gribardsun repeated.

"They were *dead already*, you fool." XauXaz was no longer grinning. "What are their small, piggish lives compared to those who travel in time as we do? Everyone you meet is already dead."

"Everyone I meet is vibrantly alive."

"Then why not share your blood elixir with all of them? Make them all immortal?"

Gribardsun stared at him.

"I'll tell you why," XauXaz said. "Because you want to *live*. You *can't* share the elixir with many others, because you *didn't*. You weren't born in, didn't grow up in, a world where the elixir was commonplace. Therefore you didn't share it around during the long, long life you've lived from 12,000 B.C. until now. Who can say why you didn't share it? I think it's because you want to live, and too many other immortals running around could jeopardize that.

"But for whatever reason, whether I'm right or wrong about the reasons, the fact remains that you didn't share it, and you're stuck with that.

"And of course," XauXaz concluded, "I agree with your decision. The elixir should not be shared lightly."

"Then you know that I will not share the elixir with you again," Gribardsun said. "I'm glad that it's failing you now."

"Perhaps it's unnecessary to share it with me again," XauXaz said. "Perhaps it was your genetic legacy, the altered genes you carry as a result of your great-great-grandfathers being exposed to the meteor, which makes the elixir work so perfectly in you."

A shrewd look swept across his face. "And now I have been exposed to the meteor's effects as well. Perhaps that alone will have a positive effect on the elixir's efficacy. Perhaps that's all I needed."

"But if not, then you will die," Gribardsun said flatly.

"If not," said XauXaz, "then perchance a descendant, or descendants, of those down there digging up that celestial stone will provide what I need to unlock the secret of the perfect elixir. Their genes themselves may help me derive, or distill, the formula.

"They'll be brilliant, of course. The geniuses flourishing from the event we just witnessed will be unmatched in the annals of history. Perhaps one of them will beat me to creating the perfect elixir. Many of them have tried—or will try. Most of their elixirs are imperfect to one degree or another, but intriguing nonetheless.

"For instance, the Royal Jelly treatment requires several elements which were difficult to obtain—including a shard of the very meteor we just watched plummet from the sky."

Gribardsun tensed and XauXaz laughed. "Not to worry. I'd be pleased to grab a piece of it now, but history says I didn't. So I won't try. I did try once, however, and ended up jousting with Sherlock Holmes over it in 1917, and again a few years later when he caught up with me.

"Then, of course, there's the nefarious Mastermind from the Far East—the grandson of the 3rd Duke of Greystoke, there—who's reputed to have an 'Oil of Life.' A very dangerous man, and he has a large organization at his command. I've skirmished with him once or twice, and may yet take him on directly." XauXaz smiled wistfully. "It might almost be a fair fight.

"But it's another of these geniuses—I think you know him, my own grandson, James Clarke Wildman—in whom I place the most hope. In fact, it was in my guise as a German baron that I clashed with him, near the end of the Great War, and opened his mind to the possibility of an elixir—among other things. Wildman and his wife have not been seen publicly for many years, but I have reason to believe he may be as young as he ever was."

Gribardsun's gray eyes had narrowed during this recitation. XauXaz was oversharing. Why? Perhaps the fellow immortal was lonely, and this had been the first chance in millennia to unburden himself.

More likely he was simply a sociopath.

XauXaz's next words bore this out. "If one of them succeeds in developing the elixir before I do, I'll crush them and take it, of course.

"You know," XauXaz's voice lowered to a mock-confidential whisper, as if sharing secrets among treasured friends, "it's not only time travel that makes everyone dead to people like you and me. It's the elixir. Once you're immortal, you're walking among the dead. Kill them as they clutch and scrabble for their piggish lives. Love them, hurt them, do whatever you want to them. It just doesn't matter if you help them along to *Niflheimr*, because sooner or later—mostly sooner—they die anyway and there you are still breathing. And you are consequently more alive than they ever can be."

"Enough," Gribardsun said. "You've done what you came here to do, and your incessant talk is tiresome."

"Yes, I did what needed to be done. Did you know, John," XauXaz said slyly, "that *you* needed to be here, at Wold Newton, as well as I did? Even when you were young, very young, you had special qualities. Your own British Secret Service was quite interested in you. You exhibited instances of what their scientists called the 'human magnetic moment.'"

XauXaz went silent and stared at Gribardsun, a trace of mockery in his protean eyes.

"Say what you have to say or begone," Gribardsun said. "I have no more patience for your serpentine gamesmanship."

XauXaz continued to regard him, as a scientist would regard an interesting specimen. Then he shrugged, as if in acquiescence.

"What an amazing chain of events we've witnessed here today," he said. "Do you suppose the meteor would have fallen, *right here in this particular spot*, if you hadn't been *right here* as well to guide it?"

Then—XauXaz was gone, the only sign of his passing an inrush of air filling the vacuum of space he had occupied.

Gribardsun peered over the ridge, and watched the men and women below, watched his own past and future being made, watched as the history of all humanity took a great leap forward.

1972

XauXaz was tired.

He didn't tire easily, but time travel tended to take it out of him. Much as modern humans who flitted over time zones in a matter of hours suffered from jet-lag, he suffered from distorter-lag.

He had discovered the Capellean distorter in the 1930s. The following decade, he had modified it to suppress the telltale "clangings," if and when he so desired. He recalled with fondness how his impossible comings and goings had baffled the Gray Man of Ice during their clashes.

Just this year, prompted by rumors of similar advances with other distorters, he had succeeded in improving the device to also serve as a time distorter.

And thus he was finally able to scratch the itch that had been festering at him for over 250 years, since it had first begun plaguing him in 1720.

XauXaz had become aware of the existence of the parallel universe in 1720 when the Shrassk entity tapped into his mind. He had learned that the other world had been created tens of thousands of years ago when one universe had split into two, as a cell divides.

Since he had been alive when the universe divided, he, and everyone else living at the time, was also divided. The only others from that time still alive now were his allies-enemies in the Nine, Anana and Iwaldi, and so they too existed in both universes—though of course his own Nine had been wiped out by Wildman and the Englishman earlier this year, and Iwaldi in the other universe had been killed just a few years ago.

Since 1720, he had known that he had a living counterpart, an exact twin in another world.

This he could not bear.

It drove him mad, madder than even twenty thousand, or twenty-five thousand, or more, years of life had driven him.

He had to kill his Other.

For XauXaz, a decision made was a decision implemented, a fait accompli, *even 252 years after making that decision. He could afford to take the long view.*

With the distorter—now a time distorter—he traveled back to 1720, the earliest time he could access the other world. The Shrassk entity, which had been invoked by the Nine of that other world in 1720, had been brought forth to their world from its nether-space, acted in concert with his distorter to create a dimensional gate, a gate only he could access.

Thus he crossed the boundary, killing his counterpart.

This done, he was greatly relieved.

Of course, the Nine in this parallel universe could be as dangerous to him—perhaps even more dangerous—than his own Nine. It would pay to keep tabs on them.

Living as two people in two different worlds for the past year had been complicated, but had been worth the risk, doubling his chances of finding a more permanent elixir.

He thought of the other two with whom he had comprised the Germanic trinity, his brothers Ebnaz XauXaz and Thrithjaz. They were still alive at the time of the universe's division, and thus also existed in both worlds. It was fortunate for him they had died before the advent of Shrassk. The Other Ebnaz XauXaz and Other Thrithjaz might have seen through his deception. On his own world, he had simply kept Sahhindar's elixir from his brothers; he had pretended to age alongside them, as if he were using their elixir, and watched them die of old age.

Nonetheless, it had been exhausting, traveling to the other world day after day for the past 248 days, while 248 yearly ceremonies passed deep in the Nine's caverns below central Africa.

When the Nine of that other world finally became suspicious, in 1968, he had been forced to give up his imposture and fake the Other XauXaz's death. Still, he was proud of what he had accomplished in that world, in so short a time.

He was particularly pleased that he had injected himself (he laughed to himself, silently amused at his own pun) into the bloodline of John Cloamby, Lord Grandrith and Cloamby's half-brother, Doctor James Caliban, with midnight visits—in the guise of the elderly and charismatic Mister Bileyg—to their more-than-willing grandmother, and then set the brothers against each other so that they had, in turn, both revolted against the Nine.

Once he found the more permanent elixir, he'd need to ensure the Nine on that other world were eliminated. This was a good first step. He couldn't wait to see how it turned out.

Once more, he lived the life of just one XauXaz.

The one and only.

And now, he had done what needed to be done in 1795, and could rest before the next phase.

He put down the newspaper. The story of the supposed deaths of Doctor James Clarke Wildman and his wife in their private plane far above the Arctic Circle was a fascinating ruse, but much too coincidental given the alleged deaths of Greystoke and his wife Jane just a few months before.

He thought of his prior engagements with his grandson, who had known him as Baron von Hessel.

If Wildman was on to him, aware of his existence and the threat he posed, then it was time to go after Wildman, before Wildman found him first . . .

A private clinic in upstate New York was Wildman's last known location. Perhaps there were clues to be found there. There was a daughter, Patricia Wildman. His own great-granddaughter.

She could be made to talk.

A candle flickered with a soft movement of air. There should have been no air movement here.

XauXaz heard a soft scuff behind him.

He turned.

John Gribardsun stepped out of the shadows.

SCANS OF NOTES AND LETTERS FROM FARMER'S FILES

What follows are examples of the some of the materials found in Philip José Farmer's "Magic Filing Cabinet" that contributed to the creation of this book. Whenever possible Farmer's ideas, notes, and prose have been woven into the novel. These consist of some typed and some handwritten notes, and even a letter by Farmer that readers should find of particular interest.

STORY IDEA:

The govt agent investigating Caliban's upstate college — on the trail — (the 9 are using C's college to turn out super-criminals now ?—

Lord Clanbrastil, 3rd creation, a character for

THE UNSPEAKABLE DWELLER? see Burkes Extinct Peerage

[handwritten note:] for convenience sake —

portmanteau title
of Graymesse
of ERB, Watson, & Holms
Greystoke / Graymunster / Holdernesse

check — Sphinx of Ice — (Verne)
narrator — Johnny's
grandfather?

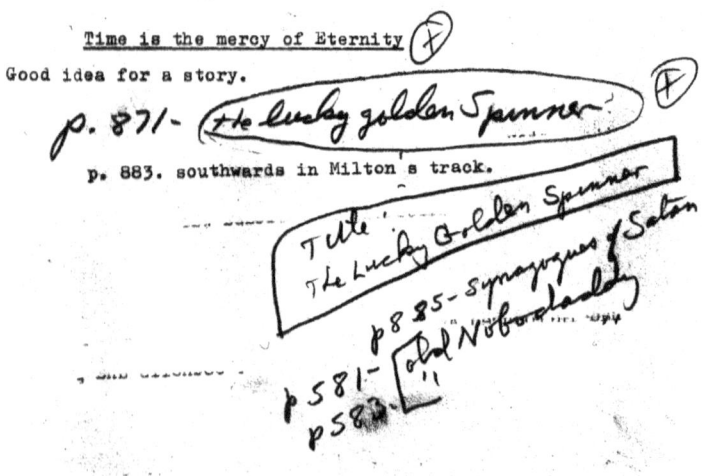

Blake's Works, Modern Library, page 867:

Time is the mercy of Eternity ⓧ
Good idea for a story.

p. 871 — the lucky golden Spinner ⓕ
p. 883. southwards in Milton's track.

Title:
The Lucky Golden Spinner
p 825 — Synagogues of Satan
p 581 — old Nobodaddy
p 58

savage/farmer

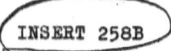

INSERT 258B

A third member of the family might have volunteered
for the expedition if Doc could have located him. This was
Jongor (John Gordon). His father was Captain Robert Gordon,
an ex-naval aviator for the United States. ~~~~~~~~~~~~~~~~~
Robert Gordon was descended on his mother's side from the
ancient Welsh families of Moore and Gronow and on his father's
side from the ~~~~~~~~~~~~~~ Scots Gordons. One of his
ancestors was a Macgregor, the infamous Highlands outlaw,
Rob Roy. (Sir Richard Francis Burton was also descended from
him.) Robert Gordon was a member of a branch of the house of
Earlston, sprung from Alexander, the second son of William
de Gordoune, the sixth ~~~~ Lord of Lochinvar. Through
this line Robert Gordon was a descendant also of the youth
immortalized by Sir Walter Scott. He was related to George Gordon,
Lord Byron, through Byron's mother, a daughter of George Gordon
of Gight, ~~~~~~ county Aberdeen. and also through ~~~~~~
~~~~~~ the Reverend Richard Byron, the poet's great-uncle,
who married a Mary Farmer.

Jongor's mother, Elizabeth Rivers, was the daughter of
Patrick Rivers and Nyad Drummond. Nyad was the daughter of
John Drummond and Bread Butler. (See adendum 2 of Tarzan
Alive for their genealogy.) Patrick Rivers was the uncle
of Patricia Rivers, who married a Sir Hector Brandon of
Brandon Abbas, Devonshire. Grey eyes seemed to have run in
this family, if P.C. Wren's Beau Geste is to be trusted.
Sir Hector was a rotter but of the landed gentry and was
a scion of a family ~~ whose head was Sir Charles Brandon
~~~~~~

Philip José Farmer

Aug. 30, 1988

Philip José Farmer
5911 N. Isabell Ave.
Peoria IL 61614

Lou Aronica
Bantam Doubleday Dell Pub. Gr.
666 Fifth Ave.
NY NY 10103

Dear Lou:

Thanks for your letter of Aug. 24 replying to my latest
inquiry. Apparently, my original letters didn't get through.
I'm writing a new letter based on the previous.

To begin with: My DOC SAVAGE: HIS APOCALYPTIC LIFE, a biography
and study of Doc and his adventures, was published in hc by Doubleday in 1973 and then by Bantam in sc in 1975. In the book I suggested
I'd like to write a Doc Savage novel titled ESCAPE FROM LOKI.
This would be about Doc's early adventures in World War I when
he flew for the Americans. He was only sixteen then but lied about
his age. He is shot down and captured by the Germans. He makes
a number of escapes but is caught. Finally, he's shipped to Loki,
a prisoner of war camp high in the mountains. Loki is supposedly
escape-proof and the most incorrigible prisoners are sent there.

Doc meets, for the first time, those men who will be his
future aides: Monk, Ham, Renny, Johnny, and Long Tom. Doc is, in
some ways, a callow youth but one who knows more than most youths
his age. Though he is only a lieutenant, he becomes the leader of
a group of older men who outrank him.

Despite the almost fiendish obstacles that the prison commandant, Colonel Baron Arnold Etzel von Bissell, has built around the
camp, part of which is a cave in the Bavarian Alps, Doc and crew
manage to escape. This is done very ingeniously and partly through
the help of some gadgets the young Savage builds from materials
at hand.

After a hard journey, Doc and men reach Switzerland and then
manage to get out of the country to rejoin their outfits. But they
agree to meet after the war is over and start their campaign against
evil.

But the fanatical baron is still after them, and there is
a denouement in which the baron is killed.

That's a very brief outline. If, say, in a year's time,
the end of the current series of Savage novels is near, I'd like
to have a contract to write ESCAPE FROM LOKI. This will be based
on a detailed outline of the projected novel.

I think it would be better if the book were published under
my own name. That way, we can get the Savage fans and my own reader-
ship, which sometimes overlap, anyway.

After years of trying to get the rights back to the Savage
biography, I finally got them from Doubleday. I'd like to revise
the DOC SAVAGE: HIS APOCALYPTIC LIFE, bring it up to date, correct
any errors, do some rewriting. But that will be some time in the
future, at least a year and a half from now. Please keep it in
mind if you're interested.

Best,

Phil

Philip Jose Farmer

Copy to Ted Chichak, Scott Meredith Literary Agency.

Excerpt of letter by Farmer printed in *Moebius Trip* #18, October 1973.

put them in a binder with a labeled cover, but I don't have time or patience for this. I hope that you keep this format up and that all fanzines follow your pioneering example.

Though the contents are all interesting, I don't have time to loc them all. So I'll confine myself to two items close to home, that is, to me and mine.

I liked Don Ayres' review of The Other Log of Phileas Fogg, of course. However, I must defend myself against his speculation that using a noted literary character in a novel of your own might not be entirely proper.

This ploy is an ancient and honorable tradition. It is, in fact, the highest form of compliment to the author who originated the character. As far as I know, it was Jules Verne himself who first did it. He admired E. A. Poe's The Narrative of Arthur Gordon Pym and was distressed that Poe hadn't written a sequel. So he wrote it -- The Sphinx of Ice. This, to his satisfaction, anyway, cleared up the mystery left unsolved at the end of Poe's story.

Also, Verne wrote two sequels to Wyss's The Swiss Family Robinson which have appeared in English translation. These were Their Island Home and The Castaways of the Flag. He also wrote two other sequels which, if they've appeared in English, I've not seen.

I doubt that Verne, if he were

alive today, would object to Fogg being written into a science-fictional tale by another author. Certainly, he'd have no ethical grounds on which to stand. I hope some day to run across Verne on the banks of The River and tell him about Fogg's other log.

Note that Lovecraft continued this tradition when he wrote At The Mountains of Madness, a sequel to Verne's The Sphinx of Ice. Note also that I'm thinking about writing a sequel to Lovecraft's tale. In this, Doc Caliban (my pastiche of Doc Savage) meets the Cthulhu Mythos.

It's a long yellow brick road from Poe's 1838 tale to Verne's to Lovecraft's to Farmer's 1974 tale, and I suppose some will say that it illustrates progressive degeneration, devolution rather than evolution. But you can't keep a good writer down or even a bad one.

Then there are, of course, the many Sherlock Holmes sequels or pastiches written by people who love the Holmes stories and can't stand the idea of there being no more. Many of these are of cases which Watson referred to but did not detail. So we have the Giant Rat of Sumatra and other cases which would be entirely unexplained if some Sherlockian had not felt impelled to write a version.

Tarzan has similarly given rise to many pastiches. In these he ap-

14

15

//the end towards which the beginning aims--
//--the two evils cancel each other?
--the sigil gives impression of shifting, not quite right, something
below its syrface--emanates cold, which is psychic, not physical--
the Harri, basque word meaning the stone or a stone--brought
up by fishermen in eleventh century from a place once below
the above the surface in Ice Age--
// the goal or end: achieved, the dstruction of The Nameless One--
with an atom bomb--has to be set to go off after he gets out
of the cave--if leasee, then he must return the two objects to
whom?--to the chief of chiefs, whowants to use it, not realizing
its evil--or rather, the chief wants to sell it again--not
realizing what its possession can do to him--
//--sees very bad things, the unconscious repressed things--
boiling out of him--one, raised in the religion, rejected it,
but the child's beliefs still in him--if he can get out of this
alive, might be purged--
//it's fire that sores the things--because its fire--psychic fire--
that must cleanse a man--the light of the fire shows him these
things--the flame, the heat, burns them out, or he himself is
burned--
//--

213

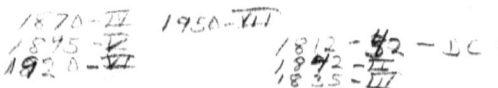

1870-II 1950-VII
1845-III
1920-VII
1812-92 - LC !
1892-IV
1835-III

// = two items: ~~which~~ which do what?--one strains out any psychic
or psychological influence-- the other -- a ritual from the
Necronomicon.?   a xerox from Miskatonic U.? or one of the
original pages, supposedly lost, in Arabic, a bad writing, use
Burton's term--Lacewing, of course, knows Arabic--something
about al-Hazrred, ~~al-~~ hazred not the normal name for mad--
a non-Arabic ~~word~~ still in the vocabulary of 8th century Arabic,
lost since-- adopted by the pre-Moslem Arabs of Arabia from
an early tribe, perhaps that of Ad-- hazr-ad; adbecoming ed later,
influenced by the a in hazr- Arabic syllabification making the
word haz-red--

. //----the ritual to summon Yug-Sothoth, in this case, to expose
him, make him reveal himself itself make it reveal itself--
no sex, so it

//--OR, a pre al-Hazred fragment, from the legendary Gaw'fr~~ugh~~   ooz??
manuscript--which al-Hazred probably read-- a pre-Basque language,
spoken by people whose living descendants, mixed with others,
still resemble somewhat the Neanderthal man.

--the psych item is a two-edged weapon, likely to recoil on
the user--if not handled properly, instead of keeping out
psychic influences, lets them all in and tears the brain of
the user apart--

// what is it called? the sigil of Dembron--a thirteenth-century
wizard of France, who perished under mysterious circumstances--
sigil appeared at various times but ~~not heard~~ its location not
known since 1683--   *Le Harre*

//Dembron probably misused it or failed--but the Gaw'frugh fragment
tells how to use it or a similar sigil--Dembrons sigil is
a six-sided plaque- one and 1/4th inch long and wide--bearing
an eye and a tooth and tentacle forming a triskelion of a sort--
carved from a smooth poison-green stone-- the other side
contains one word in an unknown writing--six letters--
//--brot up by fishermen from a place that had once been above
water, at the end of the Ice Age--

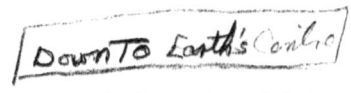

Towards the Center of Earth

5Hg8

or   THE CONTRACT

1. the monster who dwells at the center of Earth--a fire monster--
not necessarily--

2. the Cthulhu lords may be competetive, like any other sentient
beings--and Shge Shgrraunidd may be planning to take over, leaving
the others out in the cold or as Its subordinates--

3. ref. to those who've been its subordiantes, the Nine--

4. Lacewing (pseudonym) is on a contract--which he likes because
he's been rather financially constricted for some years--
NO, wouldnt be, tho ostensibly retired, still knows how to
invest his money--BUT perhaps this enemies have made sure
that he's short of money--and two because he's wanted to
invade the cave but has been afraid. Could it be hell? Something
else? The imps--Mr Wail--lying to him about its true nature?--

5. Lacewing is 77 years old but you'd never know it to see
him at rest or in action, looks like he's 33, a young 33--

6. essential point: who's the Cthulhu thing, what's he doing, and
what effect does he have on Lacewing, and how does L. get him,
carry out the contract?

7. why should the C. things Worry about Earth? simply, power--
the force that drives all sentients--

8. an extrapolation about the origin of the C. things--
why would they be involved in this? originated with the formation
of the universe? or perhaps survivors from an earlier universe?--
willing to bide their time, their conception and experience of
time different from humans?--which gives humans an advantage.
since they can move much faster-- like insects but different from,
being sentient, like the Old Ones--

9. perhaps it turns out that there are no Good Old Ones, the
Ancients, all have been corrupted--

10. but how interpret the trees, boulders, the thing that attacked
Doc Savage. ??--the belief of Mr Wail that they're all humans
doomed to hell?--

11. better title: Towards the Center of Things?????

12. the story is as much about Docas (lacwing's) discovery of himself
as about the discovery and conquest of Shgrraunidd.

13. Shgrraunidd's own thoughts--his weariness with eternity--
Time s Mercy--it's the C. things' own perceptivity of time--
their sluggishness, that allows man to win--in this case, anyway--

Down to earths center??

The Ice Djinn or the Ice Genius

bronze, code name, Lacewing (an insect with golden eyes);

story takes place elsewhere than in the Maine cavern but ref.

made to it; following Mr. Wail after catching a glimpse of him;
30 years since the adventure in the Maine cavern; Lacewing
doesnt look as if he were 76(?) years old--a big man, doesnt look
tho like he did in public life, had always disguised his features,
since 1919, wounded in the war--

//--seen two men capture Wail (now under name of Mr. Cri)--
followed them, they drive to the Canadian glacier.

//but The Ice Genius--whats and whos that?--the die genius is
one of Cthulhus boys--?-if so, any mention of him in the pantheon?--
dont remember--any--make up own name--Sh'enkmrz?--biding his
time, waiting, to grow, expand, and now going to do so--
the new ice age coming up--

//but the ice genius?--sounds like a man who does something awful
with ice to the world.--but a genius is also a tutelary spirit--
and there are bad geniuses--

//--

1978
1901

1934 -

33 in FC

The things with the
Unpronounceable Names.

Caliban   LaCenak
~~Sketre~~   La Banac
LaBance

Cthulhu story:

a contract is put out on Yug-Shagoth or Whomever

... ... Y-S killed? how could it be done? how was
Y-S recognized in the first place? what menace or danger
is he that he has to wasted?

(the wasting of Wegg-Shigoog?)

a human mechanic or an unhuman one?

a doc caliban story, short?

could a nuclear explosion kill one of the Old Ones?

A CONTRACT ON THE ODD ONE

but the employer doesnt tell the killer what the price is--

that is, what price the killer must pay for a successful mission--
what is't? the killer becomes an Old One, because the Old Ones
cannot die--

use Ouspensky's idea of perception of time as being
limited--once matter is transcended--the human can see things
everywhere, simultaneously, and he sees that the end is
sure and horrible though a long way off--

vonnegut's tramalfadorians see things as ouspansky postulates--
this for the paper--presented to Extrapolation later--

write wymer, ask him if paper OK--

//--the Old Ones and their enemies are insane because they
can see all time, know whats coming, cant stop it--
determinism with a vengeance--

but some hope to break the chains of determinism, the only
thing that keeps them going--but they too are mad, though
their insanity is of a different kind from their enemies--

The killer becomes an Old One

The Contract--the one man who can fight Cthulhu

Doc Caliban? or hes called by his contract code name--

yellow eyes ▆▆▆▆ by a chemical--a big man--but his features
not the true ones--

//who'd give him the contract--how did the person or group
know about The Old Ones--why did they think Cthulhu could be
fought?--what gate of entry used--what weapons?--uses eletrical
probes at different places in brain to open the gates of perception--
carries the probes attached to battery, under a metal skullcap
or wig--?

//--his buddies, Pauncho and Kpakchop with him or alone--
goes down into the depths--of Up from Earths Center--

//-- The Skirmish Before Armageddon, Patrol Action Before
Armageddon--

//--The cave near Miskatonic U.-- ~~Ask Jack bring it along~~

//--The door opened with a bang, closed with a whimper.
The door banged, then whimpered.

//--DOWN TO THE CENTER

//--Story says cave in Maine but this was because the writer
changed its true location. it was Rhode Island.

NO

SKIRMISH BEFORE ARMAGEDDON

// Code name: Brass, Doc, Cal? Bronze

The door banged, then whimpered.

The man with the code name of Bronze ....

Doc Bronze) has been hired by a group of people at Miskatonic
U. Theyre believers in the supposedly fictional Cthulhu Mythos--
strange activities near the cave in Maine(just call it NEngland)--
(No one has seen his true features since he was twelve--
a remarkable man--the ~~only man who could possibly handle this--~~
~~or, at least, one of only~~ four men, ~~and the~~ others were too
aged now. Outfits himself with electronic probes and weapons--
enters alone, the loneliest job in the world, unique.
But if he fails, might stir the forces of hell itself--no
hyperbole here--   provoke

-2-

the armageddon threatening is not the one described in the bible--
tho that might be an allegory, no, not allegory, a symbolic
account--its time to attack before it gets too late--

//bronze is scared but brave--goes down the hole, remembers
certain things--it should get hotter below a certain level
but the walls of the caves, tunnels, lined with something which
keeps the heat out--check strata and temps in geograph geological
texts--

//people thatve sent him have also sent a ship out to locate
the sunken island in the Pacific. want to arrange somehow to
drop an atomic bomb--because the thingthere is vulnerable to
physical effects--as proved by story of a Norwegian, Johansen--
but who's in the cave? minions of K'rresh-Angill; and K-2 itself,
perhaps--

//--the danger is not so much physical as psychic--and Bronze
encounters terrors drawn from his own mind but also knows there are
objective terrors there--the solution is to separate which is
which--his electronic stimulation-inhibition device to help him,
but he has to act swiftly and make no errors of judgement--

//--Bronze is, later, if he survives, to help steal an atomic
bomb, or make one himself--and drop it--but activity around
the cave (none on Pacific-makes this a priority assignment--

//--one of group says, This is a man bound triple bound in brass--
and so he gets code name of Brass--or is Bronze better--

//--he doesnt see any of the ghost-people he saw in 1948--

check chronology-- 1977-1948 saw 29 years ago--now its fears
and humiliations and lost loves, and also evocations of the
deepest creatures from the abyss of the human unconscious--
sees things peculiar to himself and those who belong to every
human being--plus the knowledge that the universe is
basically meaningless, death is forever, and everything is
futile--

//--but could he also be shown people hed known, people who claim
there is a hell and theyre in it--and its up to him to rescue
them?

//sees mother, father, his old aides--appealing--

the abyss opens before his feet, nothing, the face of nothingness--
which no man has ever seen before--true abysmal terror--

what does nothing look like? not black, no color or absence of
it--is black absence of color?

//-- downward, the consciousness of hundreds of miles of rock
above him, the overbearing consciousness of all this weight--
alone as no man before him, since even the astronauts have
each others company and communication with Earth and can see

the Earth and stars--

Philip José Farmer

-3-

thinks of tales of the Old Ones--how no man has ever conquered or
escaped them--and the First Race, the Elder Gods, Nodens Itself,
doesnt concern itself with those besieged by the

the worst thing will be to be absorbed by one of The Old Ones--
become a part of it, become truly evil, an evil beyond any which
humans know--just the reverse of the mystics who say that
the good people become absorbed, become one with the Good and
know ecstasy undescribable even if they lose their individuality--
those absorbed by the Old Ones become evil and suffer anguish
and depair to a degree unknown before--that is the worst part
of facing them--worse even than nothingness--which all, The
Elders and The Ancient Ones, will eventually know, God himself
will become nothingness, become what he was before He somehow
constructed this great illusion--

//--travels thru the circle of himself and his private terrors,
humiliations, etc.,to those which exist beyond himself--

//   the real--

//but downwards to his own naked ego--seared by the fires of
psychic hell--

then into the nonhuman, the beyond or above-human, beasts being
infrahuman or below human--

//--during the trip, tempted by visions of naked women he'd
avoided in his celibate life--then visions of married life, children,
the real meaning of humanity--(Pat (Trish?)

//then into a place where he sees the emptiness, the disappointments,
the frustrations, irritations, and uselessnesses of these--

//--then the uselessness of life itself--

//then true nothingness, beyond the physical presence and
entity of The Thing With No Name--

//sees also his homosexual elements--

//--the thing with no name--others, Cthulhu, Nyarlathotep,
etc. have names, but this thing in earths bowels has no name--

//--finds that God himself is imprisoned here and releases him,
or decides to let him stay here--

//God, by contact with humanity, has become corrupted--

//--end, comes out, hikers tell him theres no cave there/
what is he talking about?

//--

220

God, by contact, with humanity, has become corrupted, this is the greatest peril of all and the greatest, the supreme, illusion, he's almost convinced--

//--does he run across himself? or at last moment a man appears with a document from the backers, authorizing him to accompany ronze? who is this person?

//--The Thing With No Name--The Nameless One--which is itself a name--mankind unable to tag, label, categorize everything-- even a unique thing, entity, has a name if no category, but categorylessness is itself a category--

//--

THE LEASOR OF TWO EVILS

//--the contractor(contractee?) finds out that there is only

way he can kill Yug-Sothoth-so he goes to the little shop

on Bleek Street, by a warehouse--and buys two objets d'art--

but has to talk the contractor into putting out the money for them--

then???--

//-- why wld the contractor want to knock off

Yug-Sothoth--?? why would he pick out the Mechanic for this

particular job?--who is the mehcanic?--does he have any idea of

what he's doing//**

//--   perhaps the two objets have been lying around

for a long time, like a million years--made by the great

enemy of Yug-Sothoth--lost--ending up in this little street-shop--

with nobody having the slightest idea what theyre about--

and our hero comes along and gets them by chance--he's a collector--

once he has the objets--the two evils, he's sucked into the

underground battle between humans and the forces of cosmic evil--

//--

CTHULHU STORY
NOTES

for Chtulhu or Robeson story: The Unevadable Hound; the
uncatchable Fox--w which

//Cth. story--a man's brain is experimented with, drugs?
opens his perceptions, andhe sees something no other person ever
has, and lived--see unstendily widening of perceptions--
Yug Unsoth--and this opening does what the former magicl
"magical" rituals did, as explained the Nec.--opens the way--
hes possessed--but for good or evil? and what are the consequences?--science, accidentally, takes the place of the
ancient rituals--
//

//--not necessarily a drug--electrical exp. with probes--
every person's brain has the perceptions but need stimulus--
and the Mag. incantations privided these--but other things, too--
open this with the hero rising from sleep, going to the
beathroom, opening the door on way back, and finding
himself in an endless e series of rooms, some of the doors of
which hes afraid to popen--
the stimulus shows him The Truth--the Horrors around us--
which religions are devised to prevent us from seeing--
religions dont open the way to teurth and the real--shut
the doors, blinders, dark glasses, etc.

//--the people whove opened the way dont understand at all,
butthe hero dos, because hes read the Cthulhu mythos, which he
thought was a fictional construct by HPL, but understads now that
its true--but only one reality--what about William Blake s--
or was Blakes a vision misinterpreted by him, he made up
fictional names for HPL's things--or is it that there are
many realities--all coexisting at right angles, occaisonally
touching--the, Universe is a Horror to Homo sapiens?--
Arthur Machen s interpretation?--

//THE INTERPRETATION a title?--one basic reality with many
interpretations?--

//--ends with Cthulhu or one of the vil or good monsters on
Hollywood and Vine, tenttalaes thrashing, but of course the
tentafaes are only the humans interpretations of what
the monster looks like--

//--Ultimate Reality-- we are playthings, cattle to provide meat--
or just the opposite--the monsters are afraid of us--

//--the monsters are afraid of us--a big fraud to scare us,
blind us-- *inthe Wizard of Oz situation* --

Philip José Farmer's
Original Prose and Outline

Philip José Farmer

In the 1983 World Fantasy Convention Program there appeared a tantalizing excerpt called *The Monster on Hold*, a chapter from a proposed novel in the Lord Grandrith/Doc Caliban series by Philip José Farmer.

What follows are three chapters from an earlier version of a Doc sequel, fantastic, thought-provoking stuff, from a folder in the "Magic Filing Cabinet" in Farmer's basement suitably labeled "Cthulhu Story." These chapters likely date to the mid-to-late 1970s.

In order to avoid confusion with *Monster* we've chosen to call this excerpt by one of Farmer's earlier titles, "Down to Earth's Centre." There are several similarities and many differences between the two manuscripts. However, both involve Doc descending deep into a subterranean complex to confront an unspeakable evil. Both are meant to serve as an unofficial sequel to the final Doc Savage novel published during the original pulp run, *Up from Earth's Center*, written by Lester Dent. In fact, some of Phil's notes indicated he was toying with writing about Savage, or Caliban, or "Doc Bronze," or "Doc Brass." The notes also debate the use of Pat Savage (from the Doc Savage novels) vs. Trish Wilde (from the Doc Caliban stories). The protagonist in "Down to Earth's Centre" is referred to only by a code-name. Given the parallel universe aspect Farmer later introduced in the 1983 *Monster on Hold* Doc Caliban chapter, it makes sense that this earlier excerpt features a different version of Doc, one who, like Caliban, experienced some very odd events in a New England cavern system in 1948.

DOWN TO EARTH'S CENTRE

1.

T he door opened with a bang and closed with a whimper.
       The man with the code name of Lacewing was startled,
though he expected the unexpected. So, the nightmare was beginning.
His descent into this cave had been the prelude to the nightmare. It
aroused vivid memories of the last time he'd been here, November
1948. Twenty-nine years ago almost to the day.

Lights from the top of his beryllium-alloy helmet and from atop
each shoulder showed him the narrow gap and the cavern beyond.
When he'd been here before, there had been no door. And now, when
the lights were off, he could see by a faint grisly, purplish glow which
the walls seemed to exude.

His body was covered with a pale yellow suit of flexible metallic
material. The face was hidden by a gas mask. A holster in a belt
carried a .55-caliber automatic with a ten-round clip of explosive
bullets. Attached to the belt were ten hand grenades. A metal cylinder
was attached to the back of one shoulder. From it ran a metal hose,
its other end held by a clip on the belt. A cylinder on the back of the
other shoulder held water and food.

If the gun, grenades and flame-thrower were not enough, and he
thought they wouldn't be, he carried in a large pocket on his chest
two items which he hoped would be more than enough.

Somewhere in the darkness ahead and below, something tittered.
Did they know he was here? Or was that sound just one of the many
that had echoed for God knew how many centuries, or millennia, in
this underground complex?

He sighed, and he edged sidewise along the stone narrowness
and then emerged into the great cave. His lights struck something
that ran behind a stalagmite. It was so fast that he saw only a blur of
a naked body that resembled a human being. But its skin was gray,
its head was misshapen, its arms and legs very long, the hands and
feet enormous. Was it his imagination or had the overlong fingers
and toes seemed webbed?

It was too early to start using his weapons. He had a long way to
go on his journey down towards earth's centre. He was alone because
the men he could trust were dead or too old.

He bent his head back and played the helmet's beam on the roof. Gray stone oozed water and a light like that at the bottom of a shallow sea. Something clung to one of the many stalactites hanging down from the ceiling, like teeth in a giant's mouth. When the light struck it, it moved quickly around to the other side. It wasn't a bat, since there were none here. But it had batlike wings.

The man now calling himself Lacewing, after the insect with golden eyes, moved forward. He bent his head down so the light would play on a large round instrument banded to the wrist of his left hand. Its face was covered with tiny dials. The humidity was 86; the temperature, 73 F. He expected these to remain about the same, though he could not be sure. Long ago he'd figured out that the labyrinthine passages downward were covered by something which insulated them against the rising heat of the earth's depths.

The floor sloped at a more-or-less sixty degrees to the horizontal. Once, he halted. By the base of a stalagmite lay a body, face downward. It was a woman with a hairless head, her skin bone-gray. He approached her carefully and prodded her with the toe of his boot. She did not react. He turned her over, fully expecting her to explode into a screaming harpy.

But she remained inert, the eyes glazed, the mouth hanging open. The dead playing dead.

Lacewing wore gloves as thin as a surgeon's but more durable. He removed a cigarette lighter from a pocket and rotated its flint. He held the flame an inch from the open eyes, and the thing shrieked and rose up and fled, wailing.

He said, "God!" and he hoped that that spirit was with him. But here was a place in which He possibly did not venture. It was territory staked out by another.

What especially shook him was that the thing had the face of a woman who'd hated him, had tried to kill him, and had instead died herself, though he had not been directly responsible for her demise.

He resumed walking. The slope steepened, then eased again. The chronometer showed that two hours had passed. The temperature had not changed, but the humidity was steadily decreasing. Now and then he turned to look behind him. The lights never struck any moving beings, but always there were shadows that suggested these.

He was sure he was being followed, and every half mile meant more dogging him.

There was a sonic amplifier inserted in one ear. He turned up its power and heard shufflings, as of dragging feet, twitterings, and once a voice mutter something in an unknown language. He kept glancing at the chronometer to reassure himself that time still existed. In this dark place, buried under millions of tons of rock, it was difficult to believe that time had not stopped forever. In a sense it had ceased. Those creatures gathering behind him, and perhaps ahead of him, existed outside of time as known on the surface.

At the end of three hours he had to fight the impulse to turn and throw a grenade. Its blast, the fire within the sound and the smoke, would dispel the horde. But they would come back, and he would have one less weapon.

Finally, after four hours, he stopped behind a grotesquely shaped stalagmite. After urinating, he unstrapped the container on his left shoulder, drank, and ate some of the pemmican he had prepared himself. The shadows grew thicker behind the formations rising from the floor. Once, just for a second, the silhouette of something monstrous, a snouted head with a tall crest rising from the skull, flashed and was gone.

He estimated that he was at least four miles beneath the surface. The air should have been thick and unbearably hot. But a slight breeze moved, bringing a hint of water. It also carried the stench of rotten flesh.

His ears sang with the music of utter silence.

And then a screech filled the cavern, a high-pitched yell from hundreds of throats, some of them surely not human. Out into the lights ran, bounded, and rolled hundreds of things, the eyes of some flashing red.

2.

Six weeks before, a man had entered a shop on Hollywood Boulevard a few blocks from Vine. The man was close to seven feet tall, white-haired, white-bearded, and wrinkle-faced. His eyes were blue, but someone standing close beside him might have noticed that he wore contact lenses. The man looked around the large store, which dealt mainly in comic books and science-fiction. He walked over to a counter behind which sat an enormously fat man with spectacles so thick they looked like the bottoms of Coca-Cola bottles.

"Lacewing," the old man said softly.

The fat man rubbed his unshaven jowls. "Follow me."

He rose ponderously from his chair and went through a door. When the big old man had entered, the fat man closed and locked the door. He waddled down a short hall and into a slovenly bedroom, the door of which he locked also. He sat down by a table. The other accepted his curt invitation to take a chair opposite him. He refused the offer of a cigar and a beer.

The fat man drank, then said, "This place isn't bugged. I made sure of that."

The old man pointed at a small steel safe, covered with dust, in a corner. "They're in there?"

"Maybe. First I got to make sure who you are. *They* told me to take all precautions. You know what happens if you don't obey *their* orders."

"I'm not under *their* orders," Lacewing said. "They did a job for me, for which *they* were well paid. But, very well."

He removed the contact lenses. The fat man looked closely into his eyes. "Yeah. O.K. I wondered why you were using the name of Lacewing. Sounds like some fairy. So I looked it up in the dictionary. A lacewing's an insect with golden eyes."

The fat man shook his head, his jowls swinging like half-reefed sails in a breeze, water bags on the side of a walking camel. He put a pudgy paw on the old man's arm, caught a fold of skin in his fingers, and pulled. The big veined pale wrinkled material tore loose, revealing smooth deeply-tanned skin beneath. Lacewing's hand came down and squeezed on the offending arm. The fat man's face twisted, and he turned white. Lacewing released the arm. The fat man groaned and held his arm. "You must have bent them together. Jesus! Man! I didn't mean nothing!"

Lacewing said, "Now you know." He patted the pseudoskin down flat. "Get them out of the safe."

The fat man got up unsteadily, his right arm dangling, and went to the safe. His body blocked the view of Lacewing, who, purposefully, showed no interest in the combination numbers.

The fat man brought over a small steel box in one hand, put it on the table, and unlocked it. He opened the lid and said, "I was told you was to check them out. Don't worry, I wouldn't cross *them* . . . or you either."

Lacewing chose the larger object to unwrap first. The cords and paper off, a transparent plastic envelope containing a roughly rectangular and ragged-edged sheet of some yellowed parchment material was revealed. The side to the fat man was blank. Lacewing looked at the writing, which was of an alphabet only a few scholars could read. And they wouldn't admit it.

He rewrapped it, and untied the cords of the second package and removed the paper. He held in his hands a nine-sided greenish stone, flat on both sides, a word in the same alphabet or syllabary incised on one side. A hole had been drilled at one end, ostensibly for a cord to be worn around the neck.

The fat man leaned over the table to look closely at it. But he straightened up and backed away. "There's something coming from it! It's . . . cold . . . evil!"

Lacewing could feel the emanations too, but he said nothing. After rewrapping it, he put both objects in the box, locked it, and slipped the box into a capacious pocket inside his huge overcoat.

The fat man asked, "They're O.K.?"

Lacewing nodded.

The fat man said, "What are . . . ?"

Lacewing raised a hand and said, "Don't ask." He rose, and a minute later walked out of the store. He wondered what the fat man was thinking; he could guess what questions burned in the fat man as the stone did in his pocket. He would have liked to ask him what he'd been doing since he disappeared in 1949. Here was a very rich man, a surgeon, an inventor, a philanthropist, a crime-fighter. One of New York's biggest newspapers had called him "a combination of Leonardo da Vinci, Sherlock Holmes, Croesus, and Tarzan. The last of the Renaissance men." And suddenly he'd dropped out of sight. Lacewing knew about the rumors because he'd heard them while in hiding. The one which everybody knew was that the Mafia had finally disposed of him. But the tales told in certain criminal circles was that he'd been engaged, in partnership with a certain Englishman, in fighting an underground battle against the nine persons who secretly ruled the world. The criminals in the know, very few, actually, had word that he was to be killed on sight and a tremendous sum would be paid to the person who would bring his hands and head as proof that the deed had been done.

Then, all of a sudden, the word was that the Nine had been wiped out, but the two nemeses had been killed in the final conflict. The first part of this was true. The second was based on information which Lacewing and his partner had released. Organized crime and many high governmental officials throughout the world had rejoiced. They would not have to share their spoils any longer with the nine controllers.

And then a rumor had followed this. The two had discovered that the Nine had been themselves controlled by even more powerful things. Not persons but things.

That had been scoffed at as sheer fantasy. The cognoscenti were aware that they had been governed by some shadowy and all-powerful organization. That control was gone overnight. But that there were beings, not even human, who had dictated to the Nine, that was unbelievable.

The few very well-informed among the criminal world had their doubts about the falseness of this report. But they kept their silence. There was no way of proving their suspicions. Besides, since the overrulers were gone, and no one had replaced them, why worry about it?

The man now calling himself Lacewing had heard other rumors, however. There was a story that he had been to Antarctica to investigate the story of a long-dead aide about a hidden city there. And there was the tale that he had encountered some terrifying things deep in a cave in New England. Both, as he knew, were essentially true, though the details of the bruited-about stories were mostly incorrect.

He'd heard variations of the these tales in Manhattan, Brooklyn, Chicago, Los Angeles, Bristol, Marseilles, Athens, Budapest, Tel Aviv, Istanbul, Saigon, Lhasa, New Delhi, Brisbane, Tokyo, Hawaii, Buenos Aires, Nairobi, Johannesburg, Cairo, a village in New Guinea, Easter Island, and Guatemala. They were told in soft voices in circles high and low. Nor did the tellers know whom they were talking to.

Lacewing had always been a rationalist, a skeptic, a scientist. But in 1948, when he had trailed a man, or what he believed to be a man, into a subterranean complex, he had found things that he couldn't explain. He could have stumbled into the inferno described by Dante, but he refused to believe that. The weird forms of life could not be the souls of the dead. There was no such thing as Hell, not, at least, that which some Christians postulated.

After his terrifying experiences there, he had blocked up the entrance. Not to keep the things from getting out, since that seemed impossible, but to keep humans from going into it. For the first time in his life he'd encountered beings whom he dared not combat.

However, though he intended to leave them alone, they, whoever they were, would not let him go his own way. After a series of "accidents" and attacks, in which twice he was badly injured, he decided to go underground. Knowing that if he tried to run his financial empire from a secret HQ, he could be traced, he withdrew a large amount of money, hid portions here and there, and just dropped out of sight. It hurt him not to let the men closest to him, his best friends and aides, privy to his plan. But they could be seized and information wrested from them. He heard through various sources that they had looked for him for a long while. Failing, they had retired, since they were getting into late middle age and he was the one who'd held them together. He'd sent them notes then, telling them that he was still alive but couldn't reveal his whereabouts. If he succeeded some day, perhaps, he would re-emerge, and they would hold a reunion. He imagined that they had been deeply hurt, but he had to stay away from them for their sake and his.

As it was, he was being shadowed and a number of times barely escaped being killed. He kept moving on until he had felt he had shaken his pursuers. During his travels, he did considerable research into a field which he would once have dismissed as being too irrational to deserve more than a surface study: the occult.

Twenty-five and a half years later, he had determined what he needed to reopen the war. But he had to have a large organization to look for, locate, and get the two items he needed. His own worldwide agency had been dissolved shortly after his disappearance. So he had made contact with the chiefs of an organization that had once been his bitterest enemy. They were evil, but they were human. Moreover, he was sure that they were not under the control of the forces that were after him.

The meetings had taken some delicate arrangements. The chiefs were surprised that he was still alive. Naturally, they were suspicious. Was he setting a trap for them? But finally the conferences were held under circumstances which ensured that neither he nor they could harm the other.

It had been difficult for him to convince them that he was not insane. But he had done so, and they, who had committed the most horrifying of crimes in cold blood, were horrified and their blood frozen. They were also frightened. But he did not ask them to get involved. He only required that they obtain for him the two items he desired.

The chief of chiefs, the *capo di capi*, had said yes. They would attempt to get the items, provided, of course, that he pay the price. Business as usual, even if Armageddon threatened. In 1977 he got the word to go to the store in Hollywood. During the two years of waiting, he had planned the attack. Then he'd gotten the two items, and he'd taken six months experimenting with them. He'd also pursued researches ranging from geological through psychic. And he'd resisted the temptation, most often occurring late at night, to call in his former aides to help him.

Much of his life, he'd been alone but not lonely. Now, however, as he considered what he hoped to do, he felt a loneliness that sometimes made him throw himself on the floor and beat his fists against it while he wept. Until a few years ago he had not believed in a soul, since there was no scientific evidence for its existence. Now he knew that when he went down into the depths, he was placing his soul in jeopardy. Using the two items, pitting evil against evil, he was in direst peril. Even if they were weapons for good, they would not thereby be changed in nature. And, unless handled with a steady mastery, they would be as dangerous as the foe against which they would be opposed.

3.

The things rushed forward into the three lights. There were hundreds of them, closely packed, of many strange shapes. But whatever they looked like, they seemed to him to have been human once. He already had taken the cigarette lighter out, and when the nearest, a creature that looked more like a kangaroo with an elephantine trunk than a man, was about forty feet away, he rolled the flint. The flame was feeble, but the kangaroo-thing screamed and bounded to one side and was lost in the shadows. Those just behind it yelled also; some fell; others piled up on it; for a moment, there was before him a mass from which thrashing legs and arms and eyes big with horror protruded. Then the creatures had disentangled themselves and run, leaped, and rolled after their fellows.

Lacewing stood unmoving, holding the lighter above his head. The echoing screams had died out; the thud of splayed feet had vanished. The only noise was the nonsound of silence hissing in his ears.

He turned off the lighter and wheeled and strode down the slope. After an hour he came through an arch beyond which was a cavern as wide as ten Grand Central Stations side by side and as high as ten and as long as twenty. It too held stalagmites and stalactites and had many openings off the floor and in the walls. From these faces stuck out, some of them more gargoylish than human.

He walked on, though he had to turn every twenty yards or so. The shadows were gathering behind him again, and now he could hear, when he stood still, a breathing. It was the collective breath of hundreds amplified by the acoustic properties of this vast hollow. Now and then twittering flitted through the air. He looked up but could see no flying creatures.

What were these things following him? Long ago, when he had followed the trail of the strange man who'd led him here, and had caught him, the man had told him that this was Hell and the things were the souls of the dead. He hadn't believed that. But the man claimed to have died centuries ago, to have been a doomed soul who had managed to escape from Hell. Lacewing had disbelieved this, too. Nevertheless, the weird little fellow had vanished from a room in which Lacewing had locked him and which was watched by a policeman.

But the man was no wraith. He was solid and warm to the touch, and these things here were solid, though cold. And they breathed. Which meant they had blood, or something like blood, and, therefore, could be killed. But what did they eat? Was their source of food further down? If they ate, and they must, why, since hundreds of them resided here, had he seen no excreta?

He had a queasy feeling that they ate it. But if that were so, they were not human. They'd be poisoned by their own waste matter.

To get answers, one must submit questions. And the thing at the end of the trail—if indeed it was there—was not noted for giving answers.

Thirteen hours had passed. He had eaten and drunk three times. Then he came to another one more in a series of caves, great and small. This was the largest, and its stones were many-colored, throwing jewels of light back in the beams. There were strange formations scattered everywhere, more like massive branches of coral than anything. Their upper extremities seemed to sway slightly, though it could be imagination deceiving him. Once he thought he saw a boulder, which looked like a scarlet-and-green-streaked giant human brain, move a few inches.

He came to a river, a dark sullen stream sliding slowly along. It was about half a mile wide here, and on the other side a smooth wall of stone, spotted with patches of green-blue, like lichen, or a leprosy of mineral, prevented any passage in that direction.

The surface of the water was smooth except for an occasional large bubble or swirling, as if its depths concealed living creatures.

Suddenly, a great scream arose, and hundreds of feet slapped against the smooth stone floor behind. He whirled, bringing out the lighter at the same time. Its flame guttered up, but by the lights of his beams shining from his helmet and suit he saw that the things had their eyes closed. They were shutting out the flame, their hands or semblances thereof outstretched, blindly charging. They hoped to sweep him into the river by their sheer mass. Or perhaps they thought he would not dare to leap into the cold dark stream, and they would seize him and tear him apart.

His left hand grabbed a small metal ring on the left side of his suit. He yanked, a cord came out, and the suit around his chest and back, under his arms, swelled. He could not hear the hissing of air inflating the section, but he didn't need that for verification. He released the thumb activating the lighter but still held it up above him. He turned and leaped out into the water. For a moment his face was below the surface, but the suit was waterproof. Nevertheless he felt the cold penetrate it; it was like the chill of approaching death.

The sluggish current bore him slowly away. He had expected, for no good reason, that the things would not follow him. Perhaps he was attributing his dread of the river to them. But they spilled into the stream, and they began swimming towards him.

He ignited the lighter again. They screamed when the fire flared in their eyes, but then they closed their eyes and thrashed sightlessly towards him.

THE MONSTER ON HOLD

Farmer's introductory remarks appear at the beginning of this book, "What Has Gone Before." Here are the remainder of his remarks from the 1983 World Fantasy Convention Program outlining outlining the novel, followed by a chapter of the proposed novel.

The events of *The Monster on Hold* begin in the late 1970s when Doc Caliban penetrates Tilatoc's supposedly impregnable fortress hideout in northern Canada. I won't describe the result because I don't want to reveal too much about the novel. But Caliban goes into hiding again. He hears that Anana has decreed that whoever kills Grandrith and Caliban will become Council members even if they are not candidates. (Caliban almost loses his life when he gains this piece of information.) When the second section of the novel begins (in 1984), Caliban is in Los Angeles and disguised as an old wino. Tired of running, he's decided to attack, but, first, he needs a lead. One night, a juvenile gang jumps him, thinking he's easy prey. He disposes of them quite bloodily, but he spots a man observing the fight. Later, he sees the man shadowing him. After trapping him, Caliban questions him, using a truth drug he invented in the 1930s. As Caliban suspects, the man is an agent of the Nine. Caliban allows him to escape and then trails him. This leads to a series of adventures I'll omit in this outline.

During these, Caliban begins to suffer from a recurring nightmare and has dreams alternating with these in which he sees himself or somebody like himself. However, this man, whom he calls The Other, also at times in Caliban's dreams seems to be dreaming of Caliban.

Caliban thinks he has shaken himself loose of the Nine's agents, but then another appears. Caliban catches him and then recognizes him as a man he last saw in 1948.

He's shaken. The man, now calling himself Scott Free, figured prominently in an adventure which Caliban recalls with horror and much puzzlement. That is, when he does think about it, which is as seldom as he can help.

Caliban and his aides and some others had ventured deep into a labyrinthine cavern complex in New England. There they had encountered things which Mr. Free (one of the party) had said were the metamorphosed spirits of the dead. "Devils." Free claimed to be a lower-echelon devil who had escaped from Hades. Caliban, a rationalist and agnostic, did not believe Free's explanation. Yet, some of the events had no acceptable explanations. Whatever the truth, Caliban had escaped something very horrible. He had had no desire to explore the caverns again. At the same time his scientific curiosity about them had tormented him from time to time.

The adventure had been thirty-six years ago, and here is Mr. Free looking as young as then and trying to make him his prisoner. By whose orders?

That of the thing which Free had implied was Satan? That of the Nine? Or was he trying to get Caliban on his own?

Doc gets into contact with his two aides, "Pauncho" van Veelar and Barney Banks. They're living under assumed names in upper New York but come at once when Doc summons them.

The truth drug fails to work on Free, but Caliban forces a story out of him which seems to be true. At least, the instruments that Doc used indicate this. Free confesses that the story about the cavern being Hades and its inhabitants being doomed souls is false. But he was born in the middle of the eighteenth century, and he had worked for the Nine. Too ambitious, he doublecrossed the Nine to gain a vast fortune. Caught, he expected to be tortured and killed. Instead he was condemned to be one of the guards in the cavern complex in New England.

There he discovered that he was to help guard some thing that he could only describe as "the monster in abeyance" or "the monster on hold." But it did have a name, Shrassk, meaning "She-Who-Eats-Her-Children." Free has never seen the monster. He says that in the eighteenth century the Nine were faced with a situation similar to that of Grandrith's and Caliban's revolt. Then, three candidates had tried to over throw the Nine. They had so disrupted the organization, slain so many agents and candidates, come so close to killing some of the Nine, that the Council, in desperation, had summoned a thing from another dimension or perhaps from a parallel universe.

(Not too parallel, Free says. Caliban says that things are either parallel or they're not. Free says that the other universe is, then, asymptotic. Which explains why the area in which the monster is contained in the cave is partly in this world, partly out of it. Or, from what he's heard, it may be suspended between two universes, acting as a sort of bridge.)

Shrassk, Free says, has the power, perhaps uncontrolled by it, a wild talent, to touch the subconscious of some sensitive human receptors and cause nightmares. God only knows what else.

Its touching may have been what caused Lovecraft to form his Cthulhu mythos, a dimly perceived and mostly fictional concept but based on the real horror.

In any event, Shrassk was not to be released directly upon the world in an effort to get the three rebels of the eighteenth century. While Shrassk was held in abeyance, it would reproduce after some mysterious mating and conception, and its "children" would be loosed to seek out and destroy the three without fail. Some children, that is.

Before that happened, the three rebels were caught, tortured, and then fed to Shrassk. It would not, however, go back to where it had come from. The Nine had to maintain the guards for the children and the forces that held it back from entering this world. Meanwhile, Shrassk was breeding, though very slowly, more of the children. Free says that Shrassk is imprisoned by geometry but, if it escapes, will do so by algebra. He is unable to clarify this enigmatic remark.

In 1948, Free had escaped from the cavern but had been forced to re-enter the cavern by Caliban and his aides. After they had gotten out of the cave, Free had teleported himself from jail. But teleportation is a power not always on tap. After a few "discharges," as Free puts it, the user has to recharge his battery.

Doc doesn't believe the story about TP. He thinks Free is lying and that he's just a superb escape artist.

Now, Free says, the Nine are so desperate that they are considering letting loose a "child" to destroy Grandrith, Caliban, Caliban's cousin, Pat Wilde, and van Veelar and Banks. If that "child" doesn't succeed, another will be released.

Doc wonders if the truth drug isn't ineffective on Free and if Free hasn't been planted by the Nine to allure Caliban to go back to the cave. Nevertheless, he decides that he will attack. He gets into contact with van Veelar and Banks and, after some difficulty, with his cousin, Pat. After taking the small stone fortress at the opening of the cave, the four descend into the many-leveled subterranean complex. This time, they penetrate much deeper than in 1948. They encounter a greater variety of denizens than the first time, including one which Doc thinks for a while is Shrassk. Doc becomes separated from his companions and has to go on alone.

The following is the first draft of a chapter of the proposed novel.

Free had said that the "children" were born out of flame by Shrassk.

Why then, as Caliban had proved so many times in the past twelve hours, were they terrified by fire? Was it fire itself, the reality, or the idea of fire that panicked them? Or both? Or something else?

He crouched behind the seven-foot-high cone of dark brown stuff oozing from the wide crack in the rock floor. Its rotten-onion stink and his knowledge of its origin sickened him. That the cone was building up at the rate of a quart every five minutes meant that monsters like the one he had just killed were in the neighborhood. Unless, that is, the dead thing was excreting after death and its wastes were flowing through the undersurface fissure complex. No. This cone was too far from the carcass.

Others of its kind must be nearby.

Soft noises came from the other side of the cone. Whisperings, chitterings. Nonhuman. He moved slowly along the edge of the cone. The gray-green light seemed to be dimming somewhat. Was the chocolate-brown goo absorbing the light? Nonsense. Or was it? He could not know here what was or was not nonsense. Anyway, calling something nonsense meant only that you did not understand it.

He looked around the cone. In the half-light he could see the rear of a creature he had not encountered so far. It had a tail two feet long, about an inch in diameter, hairless, studded with dark warts, and exuding slime. The tail was switching back and forth much like that of a cat thinking whatever sphinxlike thoughts a cat thought.

He moved slowly further around the edge of the cone, prepared to duck back if the thing should turn its eyes—if it had any—toward him. Then he saw that he had been wrong in assuming that the creature had a posterior part. It was two feet in diameter and a foot high. There was no head, hence, no rear, just an armored dome from which four tails—some kind of flexible members, anyway—extended. If the tail he had first seen came from the south of the round body, the others extended from the north, west, and east. The end of the west tail was stuck into the brown cone and was, since it was twice as large in diameter as the others, swollen with the sucking-in of the excrement.

Because the thing seemed to be eyeless, Caliban stepped forward two paces. Beyond the creature were four others, all feeding with the tail-like "west" organs.

Beyond them, its back to him—he supposed it was the back—was a bipedal creature. It was almost as tall as he and was unclothed. Though human in form, its skin was a dull blue. Black ridges ran both vertically and horizontally over its legs and body and hairless head. The ridges formed squares in the center of which was a livid red circle the size of a silver dollar. One hand, quite human, held a shepherd's staff.

The whisperings and chitterings came from the "shepherd."

The creature began to turn around. Caliban backed away around the cone. He looked around. No living thing in sight—as far as he knew. Here, he could not be sure what was or was not living. The rock floor slanted upwards at a ten-degree angle to the horizontal. At least, what he thought was the horizontal. The only relief to the smoothness and emptiness were some tall rock spirals, huge boulders, and brown cones here and there. The warm thick air passed slowly over his sweating skin.

He walked in the opposite direction so that he could watch the shepherd while it was facing the other way. And then the flickerings began again—flickerings he knew now were not phenomena outside him—and he saw The Other, his near-double.

For a moment he was frightened. Shrassk was touching his mind again. But, he reassured himself, that did not mean that Shrassk knew where he was. On the other hand . . .

He slid that possibility into a drawer in his mind and watched the vision with inner eyes while the outer watched the cone. If that shepherd strolled around the cone, it would have him at a disadvantage. He should go ahead with his plan. But he could not move.

The man who looked so much like him was walking through a rock tunnel filled with the same light as this cavern, the gray-green of an old bone spotted with lichen. He, too, wore a backpack and a harness to which was attached many containers for instruments and weapons. Suddenly, The Other stopped. His expression shifted from intense wariness to fright. That quickly passed and he stared straight ahead as if he were seeing something puzzling.

Caliban relaxed a trifle. The other man was probably also touched by Shrassk. He was seeing Caliban as Caliban was seeing him.

Caliban anticipated that they might soon do more than just see one another. It seemed to him that The Other was not perhaps in the same universe as Caliban's. Not yet. Perhaps never. But Shrassk was in the third universe which was a bridge between Caliban's and The Other's. A crossroads. And Caliban and The Other could leave their two worlds to meet in the third, Shrassk's.

This anticipation was based on Free's explanation, which meant that neither was grounded in reality.

Doc forced himself to move. With the first step, the little glowing stage and its single performer vanished. It was as if his connection with the vision had been switched off by muscular action. By the time that he came to the other side of the cone, he was running and his mind was completely wrapped around his intent. A big knife was in one hand and the gas-powered pistol was in the other.

The shepherd has his back to him. It was turning one of the round things with its staff so that the tail on the south side could be inserted into the cone. Caliban slowed down just a little because he was astonished. The crook at the end of the shepherd's staff was straight now. Its end had split into two, and these were clamped around the lower edge of the dome-shaped cone-eater. Using these, the shepherd was turning the thing so that it could insert another tail into the goo.

The checkerboard-skinned thing must have heard him or have felt the vibrations of Caliban's boots through the rock floor and its bare soles. It yanked the staff from the edge of the round tailed thing and whirled. The ends of the staff merged together.

Caliban noted this and also the sex of the shepherd. It had no testicles, but a thin orange-prepuced penis reached to its knees.

The shepherd grinned, exposing four beaverlike teeth. Its face was human except for the black squares and red spots. It raised the staff as if it were going to throw it at Doc. The end nearest Doc swelled, the shaft shrinking in length and diameter as substance flowed into the end, and the end became a thin pointed two-edged blade.

Doc raised the gas-pistol and squeezed the trigger. There was a hiss. The projectile appeared, its needle point buried in the blue chest. The thing staggered back two steps. It should have been unconscious in four seconds, but, screaming, it ran at Doc, the staff held as if it were a spear. Which it now was. The thing's arm came down; the spear flashed at Doc. He ducked. The spear missed, but the lower back end sagged, became supple, and whipped around Doc's arm.

Still holding the pistol, Doc sawed with his knife at the creature squeezing on his arm. Its body seemed to be as hard as hickory though it was as flexible as rubber.

By then the shepherd was upon him. Doc brought the knife up from the snake-shaft and down into the shepherd's thigh. The blade sank halfway into the flesh, but Doc was knocked down by the impact of its body. He rolled away and started to get up. The snake-shaft coiled the rest of its body around Doc's neck. He fell on his back, dropped the knife and pistol, and, while the thing cut his breath off, got his fingers between it and his neck, though not without cutting his skin with his fingernails, and, with a mighty yank, uncoiled it and cast it away.

Few men would have had the power to do that, but Doc had

no time to congratulate himself on that. The shaft was writhing on the floor in an effort to reach him. Lacking the belly plates of the true snake, it was making little progress. The shepherd, however, screaming, blood gushing from its wound, was hobbling towards him. Doc rolled away until his right hand was within reach of the snake-shaft. His fingers closed around it just back of the head, which was swelling—toward what shape?—and he rose to his feet and threw the thing at the shepherd in one fluid movement. He had taken the chance that the staff might be so quick that it would whip itself around his wrist or even, perhaps, around his neck again. But, cracking it like a whip, he had avoided that. Now the shaft fell around the shepherd's head, chittered something, and the shaft fell off it.

Doc had hurled himself against the shepherd then, and he had knocked it down. It started to get up, but Doc's boot caught it under its rounded and cleft chin. It fell back, unconscious.

Panting, Doc bent over the shepherd. Since he wanted no witness left behind, no one to tell—whom?—that he had been this way, he intended to drag the shepherd to a nearby deep fissure and drop it in. He screamed and straightened up and grabbed at his crotch. Something had wrapped itself around his penis and was squeezing it. For a few seconds, he was so taken by shock and surprise that he did not recognize what it was that had seized him. Now he saw that the proboscislike sex organ of the shepherd—if it was a sex organ—had coiled itself around his penis. It was yanking at it as if it was trying to tear his organ off. Fortunately, the cloth of Doc's pants was interfering with the effort.

The shepherd seemed to be still knocked out. The drug from the hypodermic and its wound had surely done their work. But they should also have made its sex organ, or whatever it was, flaccid. Knocked it out, too. Unless it was partially independent of the blood supply of the main body.

No time to think. Gritting his teeth, Doc backed away, the shepherd's body dragging behind, pulled by the proboscis attached to Doc's penis. The pain became worse. He had a vision of his organ being torn out by the roots, but he kept backing until he was by the knife. He fell to his knees, grabbed it, and sliced away the blue length and orange prepuce with one motion. Blood, almost black in the dim light, geysered out from the shepherd.

"God Almighty!"

Doc staggered to the gas gun, picked it up, sheathed it and the knife, and ran. The pain faded away but not the memory. After a few yards, he slowed to a walk. A glance showed him the shepherd's still body, the shaft writhing, and the five round things. What next? When he reached the far wall of the cavern, he went along it for perhaps a quarter of a mile and found in the shadows the entrance of a smooth downslanting tunnel. With both arms outspread, he could touch its walls. The top was a foot higher than his six feet and seven inches.

The tunnel, after a half a mile, ended with a flaring out as if it were a trumpet. Before him was silence and the biggest cavern yet. The walls opposite him were draped in blackness which, for a second, he thought moved. The ceiling soared into darkness. The floor, far below, was bathed in a brighter light than that which he had gone through and was now green-yellow. Its source, however, was still unknown.

A ledge extended from the tunnel exit. Two feet wide, it ran more or less horizontally from both sides of the tunnel mouth as far as he could see. The straight drop from the ledge to the floor was, he estimated, about a mile. From here, the floor seemed to be smooth among the ridges, hillocks, and curious shapes, some of which looked human. Vaguely. They could not be, however. For one thing, they did not move. For another, they would have to be far larger than elephants for him to make out their shapes at this distance and in this twilight.

For the first time, he saw water in large quantity. A river wound through a rock channel, its surface dark, smooth, and oily. Perhaps it wasn't water.

Something darker than the river and the stone banks moved slowly on the surface. Doc removed his backpack and took out the night-vision subsonic-transmitter. He lay down on the ledge, his elbows propped near the edge, put the viewscreen to his eyes, swept the area that had attracted his attention, adjusted the dials, moved the instrument back and forth, and held it steady.

The slowly floating mass was a rowboat with an unmoving figure seated in it. The figure seemed to have its back to him. But something extended from its front out over the water. A fishing rod? What kind of creatures could live in the barren river? There was no food for them. Unless . . . there were cracks in the riverbottom and the chocolately onion-stinking stuff oozed up from them. Maybe the "fish" ate that stuff.

Doc moved the line of sight over the boat. It was white, though that may not have been its color. Objects on which the instrument focused looked white; objects near the edge of the screen and in the background were dark. He did not think that the boat was made of wood since wood was absent in this world. The boat had probably been carved from stone.

The fisherman could be of stone, too. He certainly had not moved any more than a granite statue would. If that were so, then the monk's cloak and hood on him were of stone, too.

Doc had to keep moving the instrument slowly because the boat, like the river, was moving sluggishly. Then he started, and he lost the boat for a moment. The fisherman had shifted. By the time that he was in the screen again, he was on his feet and holding the pole with both hands. The line from the pole was too thin for Doc's instrument to reflect, but Doc knew that there was a line. Proof of its existence was climbing out of the river on the line.

The thing ascending the line hand over hand had a ghostly-white face with enormous eyes. A snub human nose. Thick pale lips. A rounded chin. Under which hung a loose bladder of skin. The thing had a high and bulging forehead. If it had a head of hair, it was not visible. It had no ears or ear openings that Doc could see. The neck was fat, and the body was a baby's, the arms and legs very short. It stood swaying, its nonhuman round feet with long webbed toes spread out on the stone bottom of the boat. The fingers were also long and webbed.

Doc widened the field of vision. The fisherman was three times as tall as the catch. If the former was six feet high, then the catch was two feet tall.

Doc's muscles tightened, and the back of his neck chilled. The fisherman had turned so that Doc could see the profile under the hood. It was human and familiar. The big hooked nose could be Dante Alighieri's.

Stop thinking like this, Doc told himself. That is not the centuries-dead Florentine poet. He—or it—is probably, no, certainly, not even human. Free's claim that the dead were reincarnated here was ridiculous.

Now the fisherman had put the pole down in the boat. Now he was picking up the large but slim fishhook at the end of the line and was walking carefully—didn't want to rock the boat—toward the creature that looked like a hybrid of baby and frog. Now he had grabbed its neck—the creature was not struggling—and had savagely driven the end of the hook through one side of the bladder below the neck and out through the other side.

Even then the creature was passive. Perhaps it was in shock, though Doc did not think so. Something in its attitude indicated that it was fully cooperating. And now the fisherman had tossed the creature into the water. He walked back to the pole, lifted it, and sat down, becoming again a stone-still Izaak Walton. The pole did not move, which meant that the thing on the hook was not struggling.

What was the prey for which the baby-frog would be bait? Anything big enough to swallow it would be too big for the simple Tom-Sawyer fishing tackle to handle.

Getting answers here is secondary, Doc thought. I shouldn't be wasting time lying here and watching. I must be moving on. Besides, in this place, what I see from a distance, even with the viewer, may be quite different from what I'd see close up.

Nevertheless, he did not get up at once. The fisherman maintained his unhuman lack of movement, no wriggling, no looking around, no scratching of nose or hair. Only the boat and the river moved, and they did so very slowly. Nor had anything else moved except some shadows seen out of the corners of his eyes. When he looked directly at where the shadows had been, he saw only the pale dead-looking light.

Though he kept the viewer on the boat, with occasional sweeps across the floor, he could not help but think of other things. For instance, what was the ecosystem of this place? There had to be some kind of order here despite all the appearances of illogic and chaos. Everything he had seen had to be obeying or acting in accordance with a "law," a "principle." Everything had to be interconnected here as much as everything above it was. The "laws" of entropy, of energy input and output, conception, reproduction, growth, aging, and death had to operate in this deep underground. There had to be a system and an interdependent network.

What?

Doc vowed that, before he left here—if he did leave—he would at least have an inkling of the system. He would have some data on which he could theorize.

Finally he rose. He was ready to go on. But, lacking a parachute or enough rope, he could not get down or along the glass-smooth wall below the ledge. He could go to the right or the left on the ledge. One direction had to lead down to the cave floor. There was traffic from the lower levels to the upper, and, thus, this ledge was the highway. Perhaps both the left and right were used. He could not, however, afford the time to take one and find out that it petered out somewhere on the side of the immense bowl.

Take the left. Why? Because that was the sinister side. It seemed to him that the sinister would always be the right direction in this place. Chuckling feebly at his feeble pun, he began walking faster than caution recommended, his left shoulder brushing against the wall now and then.

After a quarter of a mile, the ledge began sloping gently downward. In an hour, he was halfway to the floor and above a roughly three-cornered opening in the wall into which the dark river flowed. By then the fisherman had inserted his pole into a socket in the corner of the boat and was rowing back up the river. Were his oars also made of stone?

The ledge took Caliban to the other side of the cavern before it reached the floor. He stood there for a while and listened to the total silence, which was a ringing in his ears. The fear bell ringing, he thought. Someone is at the front door and pressing on the button.

Though he had no reason to think so, he felt that he was getting close to his goal. Which perhaps explained why his fear had come back and was moving closer to that sheer hysterical horror he had suffered during an incident in his first venture into the cave so many years ago.

Caliban, your hindbrain is trying to take over, he told himself. Use your forebrain. Don't use it to rationalize and justify what your hindbrain is telling you. Don't turn and run away. Don't walk away, either. Push on ahead. If you flee now when you are so close, after you've gone through so much, you'll despise yourself forever afterwards. You might as well kill yourself. In which case, if you're going to die if you run away or die if you go ahead, you might as well, no, it'll be much better, if you die because you went ahead.

Despite this, the fire of panic was burning away his reason and courage. It might have caught hold of him and turned him around. He would never know because the vision of The Other sprang into light in some place in his mind. And, as fire lights fire, a cliché but sometimes true, the vision swept away the fear.

The Other was standing at the entrance to a cave. He was smiling and holding up one huge bronze-skinned hand, two fingers forming a V. Then the scene widened, and Doc saw that The Other was about three hundred feet from a great circle of stone symbols brightly lit by burning gas jets at their bases. There were nine: a Greek cross, a hexagon, a crescent, a five-pointed star, a triangle with an eye at its top, a Celtic cross, an O with an X inside it, a snake with its tail in its mouth, and a winged horseshoe. They enclosed a shallow bowl-shaped depression in the rock about three hundred feet in diameter. In the center was another circle of stone symbols, smaller than those that formed the outer circle and unfamiliar to Caliban. Inside the smaller circle was a platform shaped like an 8 on its side. The upper side of the 8 had holes which projected to the far ceiling bright violet-colored rays.

Where the two O's that formed the 8 met, a strip of stone about ten feet wide, was a highbacked chair cut from a bloodred stone. The chair was not empty.

Caliban felt as if every cell in his body had turned over.

The being on the chair, surely Shrassk, She-Who-Eats-Her-Young, was not at all whom or what he had expected.

The fear surged back in; the vision dimmed. But he forced himself to push it back down, though it was like pressing down on a lid over a kettle of cockroaches breeding so furiously that the lid kept rising. For a moment, the vision became brighter and clearer. Doc saw that his Other was making signs using dactylology, indicating that his *Other*, Caliban, must hasten to aid him. Alone, each would go down quickly. Together, they might have a chance.

Caliban began running in a land where it was not good to run.

Thus ends this chapter. Will Caliban and The Other kill Shrassk?

Or will they be lucky to get away with life and limb? Will both survive? Will Doc Caliban ever analyze the ecosystem of what might or might not be Hell?

You will find out when *The Monster on Hold* is published.

A Tale of Two Universes

Win Scott Eckert

Philip José Farmer's Secrets of the Nine series, *A Feast Unknown* (1969), *Lord of the Trees* (1970), and *The Mad Goblin* (1970), recount the ongoing battle of the ape-man Lord Grandrith and the man of bronze Doc Caliban against the Nine, a secret cabal of immortals bent on amassing power and manipulating the course of world events. These novels present an interesting conundrum for followers of Farmer's Wold Newton mythos.

Farmer wrote two biographies which kicked off the Wold Newton Family in earnest after he wrote the Nine novels: *Tarzan Alive: A Definitive Biography of Lord Greystoke* (1972) and *Doc Savage: His Apocalyptic Life* (1973; revised 1975; revised 2013). In these biographies, he uncovered the true identities of the men whose adventures had been presented to the world in the guise of popular fiction under the fabricated names "Lord Greystoke" and "Doc Savage."

And the true identities Farmer revealed were *not* John Cloamby, Lord Grandrith, and Doctor James Caliban, despite having written the Nine novels just a few years earlier, sourced directly from Grandrith's and Caliban's memoirs.

Instead, "Lord Greystoke's" real name remains undisclosed (although there are many hints in the strands and threads presented in *Tarzan Alive*), while "Doc Savage's" real name is Doctor James Clarke Wildman, Jr.

Furthermore, the backgrounds of Greystoke and Grandrith, and of Wildman and Caliban, are bursting with significant similarities and noteworthy differences.

Greystoke and Grandrith are both feral men. Both were born after their parents were shipwrecked off the coast of Gabon, were raised by sub-humans or "great apes," and went on to become "Wild Men of the Jungle," discover secret sources of gold, and have many wondrous adventures. Both men have similar Apollo-like physiques, are about six-foot-three inches tall, and have coal black hair and gray eyes.

Both jungle lords have "biographers," the term Grandrith uses when referring to the man who wrote a series of highly fictionalized novels and stories about him for popular consumption. Grandrith then goes his biographer one better, writing his own autobiographical memoirs, of which *A Feast Unknown* is Volume IX and *Lord of the Trees* is Volume X.

As for Greystoke, Philip José Farmer followed in the footsteps of the jungle lord's original biographer with a more realistic biographical overview of his adventures, *Tarzan Alive*, as well as two novels presented as fiction, *The Adventure of the Peerless Peer* and *Tarzan and the Dark Heart of Time.*

Greystoke was born on November 22, 1888, a few minutes after midnight. Grandrith was born on November 21, 1888, at 11:45 P.M. Both are immortal.

Greystoke's immortality was conferred by a grateful witch doctor. The month-long process involved a vile brew of herbs and a blood transfusion. The one-time procedure resulted in eternal youth.

Grandrith's immortality came from annual visits to the secret caverns of the Nine, somewhere in Africa, where "candidates" participated in a ceremony requiring the painful removal and consumption of certain parts of flesh. The Nine's elixir caused the regrowth of any lost organs and tissue. The immortality elixir could extend life to as much as 30,000 years before death due to old age.

Unlike the two jungle lords, Wildman and Caliban are "Men of the Metropolis," of science and technology. They are champions of justice. Both have bronzed skin and hair, and are about six-foot-seven inches tall. They were each raised by their fathers, in a bizarre training program, to the height of physical and mental perfection, with the goal of fighting evildoers all over the world. Both men are geniuses, surgeons at the top of their field, and world-class experts in a variety of disciplines and sciences, including biology, engineering, physics, archaeology, chemistry, law, and more. Both are responsible for inventions and scientific breakthroughs far beyond their time.

Wildman and Caliban each battled criminals with the aid of a band of five adventurers, beginning in the 1930s. Both men had cousins named Patricia. James Wildman's cousin was Pat "Savage" (or really, "Wildman," as Farmer discovered), while James Caliban's cousin was Trish Wilde.

Both men, of course, are nicknamed "Doc."

As with Greystoke and Grandrith, Wildman's and Caliban's adventures were fictionalized in pulp magazine stories. There was no mention of sex in these, but *A Feast Unknown* reveals that Doc Caliban had an ongoing (if repressed) sexual relationship with his cousin Trish Wilde. Farmer speculates on Doc Wildman's sexuality in *Doc Savage: His Apocalyptic Life*, but firm information comes from his novel *The Evil in Pemberley House* (coauthored with Win Scott Eckert) wherein we discover that he has a daughter, Patricia Wildman, born in 1950, who takes after her father in many respects.

James Clarke Wildman, Jr., was born on November 12, 1901. James Caliban was born in 1903 (*A Feast Unknown*) or 1901 (*The Mad Goblin*). The 1901 date makes more sense, as Grandrith mentions in *Lord of the Trees* that Caliban fought in the Great War: ". . . he served with distinction as a commissioned officer in the U.S. Army in 1918." And in *The Mad Goblin*, it's noted that, "When Doc was only seventeen and a lieutenant in World War I, he had captured two German soldiers at the same time that he had been cut off by the advance of the enemy."

In *A Feast Unknown*, Grandrith spied upon Caliban's elderly aides, the dapper Mr. Rivers and the apish Mr. Simmons, and learned from them the 1903 date. We can assume they misspoke, or he misheard them.

Of course, seventeen is underage, but many who fought had enlisted before the age of eighteen. Doc Wildman certainly did, entering the Great War as a combat pilot at the age of sixteen, as outlined in Farmer's *Escape from Loki: Doc Savage's First Adventure*.

Farmer speculated that Doc Wildman had access to an immortality elixir in the form of Kavuru pills discovered by his relative, Greystoke. Doc Caliban was also a candidate of the Nine and beholden to that secret organization in exchange for the same immortality elixir as Grandrith used.

The source of Grandrith's and Caliban's strength, intelligence, physical perfection, and extraordinary abilities differs from that of Greystoke and Wildman. The latter two are inheritors of the Wold Newton gene, reinforced in them by generations of intermarriage.

As for half-brothers Lord Grandrith and Doc Caliban, their amazing capabilities and talents derive from their grandfather, the immortal member of the Nine called XauXaz, inserting himself into the family line many times over. Since Grandrith and Caliban are the grandsons of a Cro-Magnon man, their bones are much larger and have a much greater surface area for muscle attachment.

Grandrith also believes that XauXaz's brothers, Ebn XauXaz and Thrithjaz, contributed to the Grandrith family line in a similar fashion, and that Castle Grandrith may have been used by the Nine, or some members of the Nine, as a breeding farm. It is strongly implied that the Grandrith lineage is the result of an elaborate eugenics program, carried out by the Nine over the millennia.

Grandrith's and Caliban's genealogies also differ from those of Greystoke and Wildman.

Lord Grandrith's father is actually the man known to the world as his uncle: John Cloamby. His legal father, James Cloamby, Viscount Grandrith, is actually his uncle, although the Viscount was married to Grandrith's mother, Alexandra Applethwaite. John Cloamby, in the madness brought on by the Nine's elixir, raped his sister-in-law Alexandra, resulting in pregnancy and the birth of Lord Grandrith, the jungle lord. The mad John Cloamby also became the serial killer known as Jack the Ripper.

Later, the madness subsided and John Cloamby escaped to America, changed his surname to Caliban, became a doctor, and fathered James Caliban.

The real father of John and James Cloamby, and their brother Patrick Cloamby, was XauXaz of the Nine. Patrick Cloamby was the father of Trish Wilde; he preceded his brother John to America after assaulting and almost killing a teacher (presumably under the influence of the elixir), also became a doctor, and changed his surname to Wilde in order to escape his past. Trish Wilde was born in 1911.

We know much more about Greystoke's and Wildman's genealogies, which have been extensively traced by Philip José Farmer and documented as the Wold Newton Family in two essays: "A Case of a Case of Identity Recased, or, *The Grey Eyes Have It*" (published as an addendum to *Tarzan Alive*) and "The Fabulous Family Tree of Doc Savage (Another Excursion into Creative Mythography)" (published as an addendum to the biography *Doc Savage: His Apocalyptic Life*).

The Wold Newton Family genealogy is far too extensive and tangled to cover in depth here, but from these tracts we know that Greystoke and Wildman are kin (they are cousins, sharing the same great-grandfather, among other relations), and are also closely related to many other crimefighters, adventurers, geniuses, and criminal masterminds. These extraordinary people all share the Wold Newton gene, which is reinforced to different degrees based on the amount of intermarriage in their backgrounds.

The Wold Newton mutation occurred when the Wold Cottage meteor struck on December 13, 1795, exposing seven couples and their coachmen to the ionized radiation of the meteor. They "were riding in two coaches past Wold Newton, Yorkshire . . . A meteorite struck only twenty yards from the two coaches . . . The bright light and heat and thunderous roar of the meteorite blinded and terrorized the passengers, coachmen, and horses . . . They never guessed, being ignorant of ionization, that the fallen star had affected them and their unborn." (*Tarzan Alive*, Addendum 2, pp. 247-248.) This was "the single cause of this nova of genetic splendor, this outburst of great detectives, scientists, and explorers of exotic worlds, this last efflorescence of true heroes in an otherwise degenerate age." (*Tarzan Alive*, Addendum 2, pp. 230-231.)

Farmer discovered that many other well-known people are part of the Wold Newton Family. A short list includes: Solomon Kane (a pre-meteor strike ancestor); The Scarlet Pimpernel (present at the meteor strike); Fitzwilliam Darcy and his wife, Elizabeth Bennet (present at the meteor strike); Sherlock Holmes and his foe Professor

Moriarty (aka Captain Nemo); Phileas Fogg; A.J. Raffles; the evil Fu Manchu and his archrival, Sir Denis Nayland Smith; Sir Richard Hannay; Lord Peter Wimsey; The Shadow; Sam Spade; Doc Savage's friend and associate Monk Mayfair, his cousin Pat Savage, and his daughter Patricia Wildman; The Spider; Nero Wolfe (the son of Sherlock Holmes); The Avenger; Philip Marlowe; James Bond; Travis McGee; and many others.

As I noted in the afterword to Farmer's *The Other Log of Phileas Fogg* (reissued by Titan Books, 2012), his researches are extremely well-sourced, including a personal interview with the jungle lord and countless hours spent poring over Burke's *Peerage*. Following the Greystoke and Wildman biographies, Farmer related adventures of the Wold Newton Family in the guise of fiction, similarly sourced from newly-discovered, or unpublished, manuscripts and diaries.

Which brings us to the conundrum I previously noted.

The prior publication of the Nine novels *A Feast Unknown, Lord of the Trees*, and *The Mad Goblin* have created the idea in some readers that the Wold Newton biographies, novels, and stories are all works of fiction. After all, the first two novels are also sourced, from the memoirs of Lord Grandrith, and edited for publication by Farmer. *The Mad Goblin* was written by Doc Caliban in the third person singular, though again it is autobiographical and Farmer edited it for publication.

Farmer claims, in essence, that both the Wold Newton stories and the Nine novels are true. They are all—or almost all—based on the accounts of the men and women who experienced the adventures and survived to tell the tales. Or they are sourced from manuscripts, memoirs, and diaries left behind by those who lived through amazing exploits.

However, some readers have concluded that it all must be fiction—make-believe, the result of Farmer's overactive imagination—because the Wold Newton tales and the Nine novels appear to be mutually exclusive, based on the differing accounts and histories as outlined above.

There are several potential explanations for the apparent discrepancies. Perhaps the Nine novels are somewhat fictionalized adventures of the real Greystoke and Savage. Farmer published the books and then went on to reveal perhaps truer backgrounds of these men in *Tarzan Alive* and *Doc Savage: His Apocalyptic Life*, followed by Wold Newton novels such as *The Other Log of Phileas Fogg*, *Time's Last Gift*, *The Adventure of the Peerless Peer*, the Khokarsa series (*Hadon of Ancient Opar*, *Flight to Opar*, and *The Song of Kwasin*), *Ironcastle*, *Escape from Loki*, *Tarzan and the Dark Heart of Time*, and *The Evil in Pemberley House*. But even all of these have analogical and coded information in them, and don't reveal the whole truth. This scenario is convincingly described in Christopher Paul Carey's persuasive essay, "Tarzan Through a Glass Darkly, in *The Man Who Met Tarzan*, Meteor House, 2021.

In this set-up, Farmer's initial meeting with "James Claymore" (the putative John Cloamby) at the home of a mutual friend in Kansas City, Missouri, as recounted by Farmer in his "Editor's Note" to *A Feast Unknown*, might be a falsehood created by Farmer to lend legitimacy to his manuscript. Perhaps Farmer had stumbled upon rumors and half-truths regarding the events of *A Feast Unknown*, *Lord of the Trees*, and *The Mad Goblin*, and had crafted these into a rousing adventure trilogy. If so, Farmer may have been embarrassed when he actually met the real Greystoke a few years later, although it's not clear from their interview that the two men discussed the incident.[1]

Alternatively, Lord Grandrith's and Doc Caliban's escapades could have occurred much as Farmer documented them, based on these supermen's memoirs. In this scenario, the two heroes coexist in-universe alongside their more famous analogues in the Wold Newton Universe. Farmer scholar Dennis E. Power is a proponent of this theory, and has outlined his thoughts in an intricate series of interconnected articles on his website, *The Wold Newton Universe: A Secret History* (pjfarmer.com/secret/index.htm). Briefly, Power suggests that Grandrith and Caliban are the result of an elaborate plan by the Nine to create doppelgängers of Greystoke and Wildman.

Power, discussing Grandrith and Caliban vis-à-vis the Wold

---

[1] "An Exclusive Interview with Lord Greystoke." Originally published as "Tarzan Lives" in *Esquire*, April 1972; reprinted in Farmer's *Tarzan Alive: A Definitive Biography of Lord Greystoke*, University of Nebraska Press Bison Books, 2006; reprinted in *The Man Who Met Tarzan*, Paul Spiteri, ed., Meteor House, 2021.

Newton Family, suggests that, "Although the characters of Doc Caliban and Lord Grandrith can be placed in the Wold Newton Universe, we must ask if they were members of the Wold Newton Family. I would doubt that they were immediately related to the Wold Newton line, but a relationship possibly exists. Farmer claimed that [Greystoke] was descended from Odin. In all three of the Doc Caliban/Lord Grandrith novels, the claim is made that XauXaz was Odin. If not all of XauXaz's families and progeny were designated for the Nine's breeding programs, then it is a possibility that he was a distant ancestor to Greystoke and [Doc Wildman]."

Under this scenario, Farmer met Cloamby (as "James Claymore") much as described in *A Feast Unknown*, and was later put in touch with Caliban, serving as the editor of their manuscripts. A few years later he met and interviewed Greystoke.

A third explanation is that Lord Grandrith and Doc Caliban exist in a universe which is parallel, but very similar, to the Wold Newton Universe. This alternate universe may share a common past with the Wold Newton Universe, but perhaps diverged from it at some point in the distant millennia. Or perhaps the two universes have always been parallel and coexistent.

The parallel universe theory is supported by the outline and prose chapter Farmer wrote for the fourth Nine novel, *The Monster on Hold*. The fragment was introduced by Farmer at the 1983 World Fantasy Convention, and was published in the convention program. During a series of adventures in which Doc Caliban continues to battle the forces of the Nine, he "begins to suffer from a recurring nightmare and has dreams alternating with these in which he sees himself or somebody like himself. However, this man, whom he calls The Other, also at times in Caliban's dreams seems to be dreaming of Caliban."

Later, when Caliban has descended below the surface into a labyrinthine series of miles-deep caverns, in search of the extra-dimensional entity known as Shrassk, a being which had been invoked and then imprisoned by the Nine in the eighteenth century, Caliban has another vision of The Other: "The Other was standing at the entrance to a cave. He was smiling and holding up one huge bronze-skinned hand, two fingers forming a V."

A Tale of Two Universes

"One huge bronze-skinned hand."
The Other is Doc Wildman, communicating to Caliban across the dimensional void.

Dennis Power takes a different view: "In this fragment, Farmer seemed to indicate that Doc Caliban and the Nine lived in an alternate universe from [Doc Wildman]. While Shrassk, the . . . monster, was most likely extra-dimensional, Doc Caliban of course was not, although he may have become trapped in other-dimensional space by the machinations of the Nine. I think that Farmer may have made the assertion that Doc Caliban, Grandrith, etc., resided in a different universe for a few reasons. First of all was the safety of his family. Having learned that the Nine were not entirely wiped out, he wanted to demonstrate that he was not a threat to them. By placing them in another universe, it is as if he was saying that not only were they fictional, but also that no true life counterparts ever existed in the real world. Also, he may have been trying to forever end the controversial theory that Grandrith and Caliban were [Greystoke] and [Doc Wildman]. This theory still raises the hackles today among casual readers of Farmer's works who have only read *A Feast Unknown, Lord of the Trees,* or *The Mad Goblin,* and not his biographies or authorized novels about the real [Greystoke] and Doc."

Nonetheless, if one disagrees with Power, the parallel universe explanation begs the question how Farmer came into possession of Grandrith's memoirs.

Could Farmer have received Grandrith's and Caliban's manuscripts from an alternate universe? Assuming that Farmer's recounting of meeting Grandrith in Kansas City is accurate—at least from Farmer's perspective—how might this have occurred? And how did Grandrith subsequently deliver Volume X of his memoirs (which became *Lord of the Trees*) to Farmer? How did Farmer receive Doc Caliban's manuscript for *The Mad Goblin*?

Perhaps Grandrith learned how to cross the dimensional gate and delivered his manuscripts and that of Caliban to a noted writer of science-fiction in an alternate universe who would understand it? Probably not, as Doc Caliban does not seem to have any knowledge of the parallel universe in 1977 and 1984 (the dates of the two known fragments by Farmer, "Down to Earth's Centre" and *The*

Monster on Hold); presumably, if Grandrith had learned to traverse the dimensions in the late 1960s, he would have informed his half-brother Caliban.

Could someone else have passed through the dimensional gate and given the manuscript to Farmer? It would not have been hard for someone else to pose as John Cloamby, Lord Grandrith (or rather, "James Claymore") at the home of a mutual friend in Kansas City, Missouri, as recounted by Farmer in his "Editor's Note" to *A Feast Unknown*, since Farmer had never met him, and indeed had never heard of him. But Farmer, with his fascination with Edgar Rice Burroughs' tales of a jungle lord raised by "apes," would have been instantly hooked by the story of a real-life feral man brought up under such unusual circumstances, and it would not have been hard to convince him that Grandrith was the real-life inspiration for Burroughs' tales—which, in fact, was largely true, as there likely was a Burroughs in each universe who wrote tales about their respective jungle lords.

Much later, when Farmer learned of the events of *The Monster on Hold*—perhaps Caliban discovered how to transmit information though the dimensional veil? or Farmer himself has a doppelgänger in Caliban's universe and transmitted the information to his duplicate in dreams or visions?—Farmer realized he had been duped back in the late 1960s. Or at least partially duped. For the man, "James Claymore," who had delivered the manuscripts to him had not been Lord Grandrith, but someone who had had other reasons for making the manuscripts public in Farmer's universe.

Information Farmer received also strongly indicated that there also existed a secret organization of the Nine in Wildman and Greystoke's dimension, known colloquially as the Wold Newton Universe. Depending on whether the two universes diverged at some common point in the distant past, or whether they have always been coexistent, the Nine in each universe might conceivably have had some members in common, immortal members who were alive when the universes divided.

Or, the makeup of the Nine could have been completely different in each universe.

Either way, if one of the Nine learned how to cross the dimensions, he may have posed as Lord Grandrith ("James Claymore") and delivered the manuscript for *A Feast Unknown* to Farmer with the intent of causing much disruption and consternation among the members of the Nine in the Wold Newton Universe. These members of the Nine, upon reading *A Feast Unknown* (for surely the book would be quickly brought to their attention and they would intently analyze it) would recognize much of themselves, and would also see a great many differences, but the overriding questions posed among them would be *how?* and *why?*

It would take someone of a Trickster's mentality to conceive of such a stunt. Someone with a long reputation for causing chaos, someone who is capricious and cunning, someone who changes his shape—or changes identities—as easily as others change their clothing.

As Christopher Paul Carey pointed out, when discussing *Escape from Loki: Doc Savage's First Adventure* in his "The Green Eyes Have It—Or Are They Blue? Or, Another Case of Identity Recased,[2] "One thing is for certain, and that is that [Baron] von Hessel presented himself to Doc in the role of the Norse All-father god Odin to Doc's Siegfried. Odin is the cynical god who gave up his left eye for a look at the future."

One member of the immortal Nine fits this description, and in fact is understood to be the person who was the historical basis for Odin: XauXaz.

Of course, as the 1968 events of *A Feast Unknown* unfold, XauXaz is recently deceased.

Deceased in the Nine's Universe, at any rate.

Win Scott Eckert
Denver, Colorado
July 2012 (Revised 2021)

---

[2] *Myths for the Modern Age: Philip José Farmer's Wold Newton Universe*, Win Scott Eckert, ed., MonkeyBrain Books, 2005; revised in Christopher Paul Carey's *The Grandest Adventure: Writings on Philip José Farmer*, Leaky Boot Press, 2018.

A Feast Revealed

A Chronology of Major Events Pertinent to the Secrets of the Nine Series

With selected entries from Philip José Farmer's *Tarzan Alive: A Definitive Biography of Lord Greystoke*, *Doc Savage: His Apocalyptic Life*, and other sources

Win Scott Eckert

In "A Tale of Two Universes," I made the case that Farmer's Nine novels, featuring the ape-man Lord Grandrith and his half-brother Doc Caliban, the man of bronze, take place in a parallel universe to the Wold Newton Universe.[1] I also suggested that "Depending on whether the two universes diverged at some common point in the distant past, or whether they have always been coexistent, the Nine in each universe might conceivably have had some members in common, immortal members who were alive when the universes divided."

Keeping these points in mind, what follows is a timeline of the Nine Universe of Lord Grandrith and Doc Caliban. Relevant

---

[1] Philip José Farmer's Wold Newton Universe novels and biographies are: *Tarzan Alive: A Definitive Biography of Lord Greystoke*, *Doc Savage: His Apocalyptic Life*, *The Other Log of Phileas Fogg*, *Time's Last Gift*, *The Adventure of the Peerless Peer*, the Khokarsa series (*Hadon of Ancient Opar*, *Flight to Opar*, and *The Song of Kwasin* [with Christopher Paul Carey]), *Ironcastle*, *Escape from Loki: Doc Savage's First Adventure*, *Tarzan and the Dark Heart of Time*, and *The Evil in Pemberley House* (with Win Scott Eckert).

information from *Tarzan Alive* and other sources is included, as well as a few speculative additions.

Some of the entries below take place in the Wold Newton Universe, but have direct bearing on the continuity of the universe of Lord Grandrith and Doc Caliban.

Due to the influence of time travel and dimensional breaches on the Grandrith/Caliban continuity, the Chronology is presented in causal order rather than strict chronological order.

PRE-DIVERGENCE EVENTS

The following events take place before a quantum event causes the universe to divide into two parallel universes, which then diverge somewhat over the millennia.

Thus, the events described here are part of a shared common past of the two parallel universes.

Approx. 40,000 B.C.E.
An Old Stone Age people discover an elixir giving them an extremely extended youth, as well as immunity to any disease and to breakdown of their cells. They do age, but so slowly that someone taking the elixir at age twenty-five looks only fifty after 15,000 years, or one hundred after 30,000 years. (*Lord of the Trees*)

Approx. 40,000 B.C.E.
Birth of XauXaz's father. (*The Mad Goblin*)

Approx. 30,000 B.C.E.
Birth of Anana, chieftainess of the Nine. (*A Feast Unknown*)

Approx. 30,000 B.C.E.
Birth of XauXaz and his brothers, Ebn XauXaz and Thrithjaz. (*A Feast Unknown*)

Approx. 26,000 B.C.E.
A quantum event causes the universe to split into two

parallel universes; the continuities of these universes diverge as the millennia pass, creating two parallel timelines.

EVENTS IN THE WOLD NEWTON UNIVERSE

The post-divergence entries described here take place in the continuity known as the WOLD NEWTON UNIVERSE.

Mid 1600s
> Two rival extraterrestrial races, the Eridaneans and the Capelleans, arrive on Earth and are stranded. Over the centuries, the warring alien races, which are very long-lived, are forced to adopt human guise; they covertly continue their rivalry while living amongst humans. The two races use "distorters," very powerful personal teleporters, in furtherance of their conflict. As the aliens die off, many humans are secretly inducted into the ranks of both the Eridaneans and the Capelleans, in furtherance of the conflict. These humans are given an elixir allowing them to live at least one thousand years, barring accidental death. (*The Other Log of Phileas Fogg*)

Early 1700s
> The use of distorters by the Eridaneans and the Capelleans in the Wold Newton Universe creates tiny tears in the pluriverse, weakening the dimensional barrier between the Wold Newton Universe and the Grandrith/Caliban Universe. ("The Wild Huntsman")

1720
> The Nine in the Wold Newton Universe become aware of the Shrassk entity (which was invoked by their counterparts in the Grandrith/Caliban Universe) and place guards around the deep caves in Maine where it's located to prevent her and her Children from escaping into their world.

November 22, 1888, a few minutes after midnight
> John Clayton III (the future eighth duke of Greystoke) is

born on the coast of French Equatorial Africa (Gabon). He becomes the eponymous hero of *Tarzan Alive* and is a member of the Wold Newton Family. (*Tarzan Alive*)

November 12, 1901
James Clarke "Doc" Wildman, Jr., a Wold Newton Family member, is born on the schooner *Orion* in a cove off the northern tip of Andros Island, Bahamas. His parents are James Clarke Wildman, Sr. and Arronaxe Larsen. (*Doc Savage: His Apocalyptic Life*)

He later acquires the nickname "Doc." Doc's maternal grandparents are the notorious Wolf Larsen (from Jack London's *The Sea Wolf*) and Arronaxe Land, who is the daughter of Ned Land (from Jules Verne's *20,000 Leagues under the Sea*).

Hubert Robertson and Ned Land are also present. It is possible that they, along with Wildman, Sr., have gathered to discuss their plans against the Nine.

(See Christopher Paul Carey's essay "The Green Eyes Have It—Or Are They Blue? or Another Case of Identity Recased," in his *The Grandest Adventure: Writings on Philip José Farmer*, Leaky Boot Press, 2018, wherein he proposes that Wolf Larsen and Baron von Hessel [from Farmer's *Escape from Loki*], among others, are all the same man, and indeed may also be the historical Woden [Odin], the immortal member of the Nine known as XauXaz.)

March 31–July 1918
Sixteen-year-old James Clarke Wildman is captured during the Great War and sent to prison camp Loki where he battles Baron von Hessel and meets future colleagues in his forthcoming battle against evil. (*Escape from Loki: Doc Savage's First Adventure*)

Unknown to Wildman, Baron von Hessel is Wildman's grandfather and an immortal member of the Nine. (Carey's "The Green Eyes Have It"; Eckert's "The Wild Huntsman")

1925

James Clarke Wildman joins an Antarctic expedition as meteorologist and second-in-command ("a bronze giant of a man"). (*Who Goes There?* revised as *Frozen Hell*; *The Monster on Hold*)

1926

Wildman, Jr., takes his M.D. at Johns Hopkins.

1929

The leader of the Miskatonic University expedition to Antarctica, "Professor Dyer," is really Professor Littlejohn, one of Doc Wildman's five assistants. (*At the Mountains of Madness*; *Doc Savage: His Apocalyptic Life*)

Early 1930s

Doc Wildman begins conducting brain operations on criminals in an effort to cure them of criminality.

November 1948

Doc Wildman descends into the depths of New England caverns and has a terrifying adventure which cannot be explained by rational means. (*Up from Earth's Center*, a Doc Savage novel by Lester Dent)

Late 1949

Doc Wildman "retires" from public view.

February 1950

Marriage of Doctor James Clarke Wildman, Jr., and Adélaïde Johnston Lupin.

November 12, 1950

Birth of Patricia Clarke Lupin Wildman.

1972

Lord Greystoke ("the Englishman") and Doc Wildman

defeat the Nine in the Wold Newton Universe; unbeknownst to them, the Wold Newton Universe version of XauXaz survives.

Wildman and Greystoke spread stories and rumors that they were also killed in the battle that wiped out the Nine. (*The Monster on Hold*)

Greystoke, his wife Jane, and various family members fake their deaths and take new identities in order to avoid unwanted questions. (*Tarzan Alive*)

Wildman fully retires and devotes himself to scientific research. A short time later, Wildman and his wife Adélaïde Lupin Wildman fake their deaths in a plane crash, somewhere in the Arctic, possibly to evade . . . something. Shortly thereafter, their daughter, Patricia, becomes heir to a great legacy upon the deaths of John Clayton III and his wife Jane. (*The Evil in Pemberley House*; "The Wild Huntsman")

The near-simultaneous demises of these accomplished men, Wildman and Clayton, are not noted by the public as generally remarkable . . . although perhaps they should be.

1977 / 1984 / 1993

The events of *The Monster on Hold*.

In 1984, in the caverns beneath Maine, which he last visited in 1948, Doc Wildman sees a man who looks remarkably like him from across the dimensional void. The other man is Doc Caliban. (*The Monster on Hold*)

2070–12,000 B.C.E.

The jungle lord, John Clayton III, now calling himself John Gribardsun, is part of the expedition of the time vessel *H. G. Wells I* which travels back in time from 2070 to 12,000 B.C.E. (*Time's Last Gift*)

Gribardsun lives 14,000 years without aging, as noted in the canonical books about the jungle lord and by Gribardsun himself: "As you know now, I was fortunate enough to be given an elixir by a witch doctor who was the last man of his tribe. He belonged to a family the original head of which, some generations before, had discovered how to make the elixir, a vile-tasting devil's brew, from certain African herbs, blood, and several other constituents I will not even hint at. He had a high regard for me because I saved his life and also because he thought I was some sort of a demigod. He knew of my rather peculiar upbringing." (*Time's Last Gift*)

It is important to note that this elixir differs from that of the Nine in that it bestows true eternal youth as well as immortality. Imbibers of the Nine's elixir age about one hundred biological years over 20,000 to 30,000 years.

(See "Gribardsun through the Ages: A Chronology of Major Events Pertinent to *Time's Last Gift*" by Win Scott Eckert and Dennis E. Power in the Titan Books edition of *Time's Last Gift* for complete information on this time-traveling immortal jungle lord.)

10,814 B.C.E.

Gribardsun encounters Nine member XauXaz (who calls himself Kethnu at this point in time) near Khokarsa in ancient Africa; Kethnu acquires Gribardsun's immortality elixir. Gribardsun's elixir prevents any aging whatsoever, whereas with the Nine's elixir, the user's body will age perhaps one hundred years over tens of thousands of years, and the user will still eventually die. Kethnu/XauXaz does not share this improved elixir with his fellow Nine members. ("The Wild Huntsman")

December 13, 1795

The immortal John Gribardsun, still living forward through time from 12,000 B.C.E., comes to witness the Wold Newton meteor strike, which imbued his ancestors with, and passed on to him, the qualities of supermen. He is an invitee at the Conclave called by Sir Percy Blakeney, and held in Wold Newton, in December 1795.

XauXaz is also present, having time-traveled to the event from the year 1972.

(See Eckert's short stories "Is He in Hell?" [*The Worlds*

of Philip José Farmer 1: Protean Dimensions, Meteor House,
2010] and "The Wild Huntsman")

2070

The *H. G. Wells I* time-travel expedition occurs again,
attempting to reach a point 14,000 years in the past:

"When the *H. G. Wells I* voyaged into time (again),
he felt sorry for John II, Rachel, Drummond, and Robert.
This trip would not take them to the France of 12,000 B.C.
Somewhere along the transit, the vessel and its passengers
would disappear. He did not know how or to where. But the
same time barrier that had existed from 1872 to 2070 would
prevent the vessel from existing in 12,000 B.C.

It was supposed to appear the same day that he, John
I, had appeared. His cells had not replaced themselves yet,
which meant that the ship and its passengers would go elsewhere.

He liked to think that Rachel and the others had not
just disintegrated. ***Perhaps they were shunted off into a
parallel world.***

The temporal obstacle was removed the moment the
vessel was launched. There would be no more John II's, John
III's, John IV's, and so on. Ad infinitum.

If it were not for the time barrier, John II would also
have lived 14,000 years or so and have waited in the wings
while John III prepared to board the vessel. And then John
IV and then John V. Until the world was crowded with
them.

The circuit of time was broken now. No need to worry
about those others."

(*Time's Last Gift*, emphasis added)

26,000 B.C.E.

Owing to the impossibility of arriving in 12,000 B.C.E. (see
prior entry), John Gribardsun and the expedition in the
time vessel *H. G. Wells I* are "bounced" an additional 14,000
years into the past, arriving in 26,000 B.C.E.

(See the short story "Into Time's Abyss" by John Allen

Small in *The Worlds of Philip José Farmer 2: Of Dust and Soul*, Meteor House, 2011)

The time travelers' arrival in a different time period causes a quantum division and creates two parallel universes, which diverge over time.

The Nine organization already exists at the time of the quantum split, and the group's membership includes the Nine's leader Anana; XauXaz; and XauXaz's brothers, Ebn XauXaz and Thrithjaz.

Since these Nine members are already alive and immortal at the time of the quantum split, these doppelgängers live on through the millennia in parallel universes: the Wold Newton Universe and the universe of Lord Grandrith and Doc Caliban.

Through the ages, the two universes diverge somewhat, and the membership of the Nine in each universe mirrors that divergence. By 1720, both XauXazs are still alive in each universe; XauXaz's brothers in the Grandrith/Caliban Universe are deceased (their status in the Wold Newton Universe is unknown, but it is likely they are deceased); and Anana is still alive in the Grandrith/Caliban Universe (it is unknown if she is still alive in the Wold Newton Universe).

Events in the Grandrith/Caliban Universe

The post-divergence entries described here take place in the continuity known as the GRANDRITH/CALIBAN UNIVERSE unless otherwise indicated.

Approx. 10,000 B.C.E.
Birth of Iwaldi. (*The Mad Goblin*)

1900 BCE–1600 B.C.E.
Stonehenge is built in three phases by the Wessex People, supervised by XauXaz. (*Lord of the Trees*, *The Mad Goblin*)
(Presumably the XauXaz counterpart in the Wold Newton Universe also plays a part in the building of Stonehenge in that universe.)

1241

Iwaldi's castle is built in Gramzdorf, Germany, upon an even more ancient keep and series of caves. (*The Mad Goblin*)

1641

Birth of Barbara Villiers, 1st Duchess of Cleveland, Countess Castlemaine. (*The Mad Goblin*)

Early 1700s

The use of distorters by the Eridaneans and the Capelleans in the Wold Newton Universe creates tiny tears in the pluriverse, weakening the dimensional barrier between the Wold Newton Universe and the Grandrith/Caliban Universe. ("The Wild Huntsman")

1709

Barbara Villiers, a candidate of the Nine, fakes her death. (*The Mad Goblin*)

(Barbara Villiers also has a counterpart in the Wold Newton Universe with the same name and titles, but it is unknown if the doppelgänger was also recruited by the Nine in that dimension.)

1720

The Nine in the Grandrith/Caliban Universe become aware of Shrassk, a multidimensional entity, and invoke the creature to quell a rebellion among three candidates of the Nine. Shrassk has the power, perhaps uncontrolled by it, a wild talent, to touch the subconscious of some sensitive human receptors and cause nightmares. After the rebellion, recognizing the danger posed by the entity, the Nine imprison Shrassk. Shrassk and her Children are suspended in a nether space, with the potential to act as a sort of bridge between the Grandrith/Caliban Universe and the Wold Newton Universe. The Nine place guards around the deep caves in Maine where Shrassk is located to prevent her and her Children from escaping into their world. (*The Monster on Hold*)

1720

Wold Newton Universe

The Nine in the Wold Newton Universe become aware of the Shrassk entity (which was invoked by their counterparts in the Grandrith/Caliban Universe) and place guards around the deep caves in Maine where it's located to prevent her and her Children from escaping into their world.

1720–1968

Wold Newton Universe and Grandrith/Caliban Universe

XauXaz from the Wold Newton Universe discovers and utilizes the "bridge" created by Shrassk to travel back and forth between the universes; he accesses the bridge using a Capellean distorter (there are no distorters in the Grandrith/Caliban Universe because the Eridanean/Capellean conflict on Earth has not happened there). Shrassk taps XauXaz's subconscious, but XauXaz is the only human to overcome Shrassk's influence and thus use Shrassk's dimension bridge for his own purposes.

XauXaz is the counterpart, but much younger appearing, of the XauXaz from the Grandrith/Caliban Universe; unlike XauXaz or any member of the Nine in either universe, the Wold Newton Universe's XauXaz had not aged one hundred years over tens of thousands of years. This is because he has, or at least once had, access to an elixir like John Gribardsun's, which functions differently than the Nine's elixir.

The Wold Newton Universe's XauXaz crosses over to the Grandrith/Caliban Universe and murders his counterpart—the Grandrith/Caliban Universe's XauXaz. Between 1720 and 1968, he travels back and forth between the dimensions, playing the part of XauXaz in both universes, with both groups of the Nine. ("The Wild Huntsman")

Late 1850s–Early 1860s

XauXaz, during his many crossover trips from the Wold Newton Universe ("The Wild Huntsman"), takes the guise of elderly Swedish gentlemen "Mister Bileyg" and over the course of a few years pays several midnight visits to Catstarn Hall on the Grandrith Estate, and to the woman who will become the mother of three brothers: James, John, and Patrick Cloamby. (*A Feast Unknown*)

The woman's sterile husband, Viscount Grandrith, who is fifty-five but looks thirty, commits suicide after his wife takes her own life. He suspected that her own suicide was brought on by a guilty conscience due to her infidelity. (*A Feast Unknown*)

Thus, the XauXaz of the Wold Newton Universe is the grandfather of the Grandrith/Caliban Universe's John Cloamby, aka Lord Grandrith; James "Doc" Caliban; and Trish Wilde. (*A Feast Unknown*; "The Wild Huntsman")

He is also the grandfather of the Wold Newton Universe's James Clarke "Doc" Wildman (Carey's "The Green Eyes Have It") and the ancestor many times over of Greystoke the jungle lord and other members of the Wold Newton Family. ("The Wild Huntsman")

1881

James Murtagh is born in Meiringen, Switzerland, and is raised from the age of eight in Wales. Like his notorious father, he goes on to become an extremely talented mathematician, a genius, who teaches higher mathematics at Oxford and the University of Talinn. He is also a candidate of the Nine. (*The Mad Goblin*)

March 21, 1888

Alexandra Applethwaite's brother-in-law, John Cloamby, rapes her in the streets of Whitechapel while suffering insanity under the influence of the Nine's elixir. She becomes pregnant. (*A Feast Unknown*)

John Cloamby goes on to commit more murders, and is

known as Jack the Ripper. Finally, the insanity subsides and, remorse-stricken, he changes his surname to Caliban and disappears to America, eventually fathering James "Doc" Caliban. (*A Feast Unknown*)

May or June, 1888

James Cloamby, Viscount Grandrith, and wife Alexandra Applethwaite sail for West Africa, where James is assigned to conduct a secret investigation for the Colonial Office. They are later marooned on the coast of French Equatorial Africa. (*A Feast Unknown*)

November 21, 1888 at 11:45 P.M.

John Cloamby (the future Lord Grandrith) is born prematurely on the coast of French Equatorial Africa (Gabon). He becomes the lord of the trees. (*A Feast Unknown*)

1889

Deaths of James Cloamby and Alexandra Applethwaite; John Cloamby is adopted and raised by The Folk. (*A Feast Unknown*)

1898

John Cloamby discovers his mother and legal father/uncle's (James Cloamby) cabin along with books and tools. (*Lord of the Trees*)

1901

Birth of James Caliban, later known as "Doc" Caliban. He is the half-brother of John Cloamby, Lord Grandrith. (*The Mad Goblin*)

A Feast Unknown gives Caliban's birth year as 1903. The 1901 date from *The Mad Goblin* makes more sense, as Grandrith mentions in *Lord of the Trees* that Caliban fought in the Great War: ". . . he served with distinction as a commissioned officer in the U.S. Army in 1918." And in *The Mad Goblin*, it's noted that, "When Doc was only

seventeen and a lieutenant in World War I, he had captured
two German soldiers at the same time that he had been cut
off by the advance of the enemy."

In *A Feast Unknown*, Grandrith spied upon Caliban's
elderly aides, Rivers and Simmons, and learned the 1903
date. Either they misspoke, or Grandrith misheard them.

1908

John Cloamby first lays eyes on Clio Jeanne de Carriol.
(*Lord of the Trees*)

1911

Birth of Patricia "Trish" Wilde, cousin of James "Doc" Caliban and John Cloamby, Lord Grandrith. (*The Mad Goblin*)

Trish's father is Patrick Cloamby, who traveled to
Canada at a very young age, after assaulting and nearly
killing a teacher; this presumably occurred sometime before
1888. Patrick Cloamby changed his surname to Wilde and
became a doctor. (*A Feast Unknown*)

Lord Grandrith discovers a hidden valley containing a
ruined city in Africa; the gold he uncovers at the site, which
he names Ophir, becomes the source of his immense wealth.
(*A Feast Unknown*)

November 21, 1913

Marriage of John Cloamby and Clio Jeanne de Carriol. (*A
Feast Unknown*)

December 1913

An agent of the Nine approaches John Cloamby and his
wife Clio. (*Lord of the Trees*)

At this point, the Nine consist of Anana, a thirty-
millennia-old Caucasian woman; XauXaz; Ing, a Nordic;
Iwaldi, a dwarf; Yeshua, a Hebrew born about 3 B.C.E.;
Mubaniga, an ancient proto-Bantu; two proto-Mongolians,
Jiizfan and Shaumbim; and Tilatoc, an Amerindian from
Central America or perhaps North America. (*Lord of the Trees*)

1918

The underage James Caliban serves as a Lieutenant during the Great War. (*Lord of the Trees, The Mad Goblin*)

1920

Lord Grandrith and his wife Clio are formally inducted into the Nine as "candidates" and they begin attending the annual ceremonies to receive the elixir. (*A Feast Unknown*)

According to Grandrith, the "candidates of the Nine" number five hundred or more, and are the elite of the organization with whom the elixir is shared. A lower echelon, the "servants of the Nine," number perhaps half a million and are not aware of the elixir. (*Lord of the Trees*)

1921

James Murtagh is inducted as a candidate of the Nine. (*Lord of the Trees*)

1925

James Caliban joins an Antarctic expedition as meteor-ol-ogist and second-in-command ("a bronze giant of a man"). (*Who Goes There?* revised as *Frozen Hell; The Monster on Hold*)

1926

Doc Caliban completes his medical internship. He already has several Ph.Ds. in a variety of disciplines, and a law degree from Harvard. (*The Mad Goblin*)

1927

Caliban takes his M.D. at Johns Hopkins.

The Nine make first contact with Caliban. (*The Mad Goblin*)

1928

Doc Caliban is formally invited to join the Nine. (*The Mad Goblin*)

Doc Caliban kills a gangster's moll, Big-Eyes Llewellyn, while breaking up a drug-smuggling ring in Los Angeles. His remorse over this act sends him into a suicidal depression. He withdraws from society for almost a year, retreating to a hideaway in the Arctic Circle. (*A Feast Unknown*; *The Monster on Hold*)

1929

Doc Caliban, upon returning to civilization, meets his cousin Trish Wilde for the first time. (*A Feast Unknown*)

Caliban (and presumably also Trish Wilde) undergoes the first of the terrible annual ceremonies in order to receive the Nine's elixir. (*The Mad Goblin*)

Caliban secretly accompanies the Miskatonic University expedition to Antarctica; the group's leader, "Professor Dyer," is really Professor Williams, one of Caliban's five assistants. (*At the Mountains of Madness*; *The Monster on Hold*)

1932

Births of William Grier "Pauncho" van Veelar (son of "Jocko" Simmons) and Barney Albany Banks (son of "Porky" Rivers). (*Lord of the Trees*)

Simmons and Rivers are two of Doc Caliban's five adventurous aides, the other three being Williams, Shorthans, and Kidfast. (*The Mad Goblin*)

Early 1930s

Doc Caliban begins conducting brain operations on criminals in an effort to cure them of criminality.

Late 1930s

Doc Caliban secretly begins researches into independently creating the Nine's elixir—or an elixir superior to that of the Nine. (*A Feast Unknown*)

1943

Grandrith loses his right leg below the knee after the RAF

bomber he's piloting crashes after a mission over Hamburg. The leg regrows in six months due to the Nine's elixir. (*A Feast Unknown*)

1944

Grandrith's boat is sunk in the Indian Ocean, giving him his first experience fighting sharks. (*Lord of the Trees*)

1945

The Nine hold a highly important meeting, presumably regarding World War II. (*A Feast Unknown*)

The result of this meeting may have been a mission assigned to Lord Grandrith:

"My own philosophy is simple and practical and not at all based on the idea that life is sacred. If a man is out to kill you, you kill him first. This has nothing to do with the rules of warfare as conducted by nations. When I was a member of the British forces in World War II, I observed the Geneva rules. That is, I did except in two cases, where I had orders from the Nine, and their orders superseded anybody's. In return for giving me a very extended youth, they demanded a high price sometimes. But I had had no qualms about killing the men the Nine wanted out of the way, especially since they were the enemy. If I were to tell you that several of them were the highest and most famous of our enemy, you might find it difficult to believe. Especially since the world believes that they committed suicide to keep from falling into the hands of the Russians." (*Lord of the Trees*)

Farmer and pulp expert Rick Lai reasons that "the highest and most famous of our enemy" were Adolph Hitler and Joseph Goebbels: "Grandrith says that both high-ranking Axis officials supposedly committed suicide because they were afraid of being captured by the Russians. This fits Hitler and Goebbels. Goering and Himmler committed suicide in American custody, and are ruled out. Grandrith also says both leaders were men. Therefore, Eva Braun and Mrs. Magda Goebbels aren't being directly referenced.

Japanese leaders like Sugiyama knew that the USA, not the USSR, would judge them. The only possible exceptions might be Japanese officials in Manchuria which the Russians invaded after the Nazis surrendered. It isn't difficult to reconcile the 'suicide pact' deaths of Goebbels's wife and children with Grandrith's statement. Magda Goebbels could have gone crazy after seeing Grandrith kill her husband, and then killed her children and then herself. All Grandrith then had to do was make it look like Joseph Goebbels was part of Magda's suicide pact. Whether the Eva Braun of the Grandrith/Caliban universe killed herself or was executed by Grandrith is debatable."

1946

Doc Caliban issues a report to the Nine regarding mankind's eventual destruction of the earth through pollution and mass starvation. (*The Mad Goblin*)

1947

Lord Grandrith once again visits his parents' cabin on the coast of Gabon. (*Lord of the Trees*)

1948

Up until this point in time, Doc Caliban believes that Lord Grandrith is a fictional character in a series of fantastic novels. In this year, Caliban also begins brain transplant experiments. (*A Feast Unknown*)

Lord Grandrith decides to secretly begin writing his memoirs, knowing they are unpublishable due to his membership in the Nine. (*Lord of the Trees*)

An agent of the Nine discovers an orphaned baby of The Folk; the Nine order the baby to be raised with the children of two Kenyan agents of the Nine. (*Lord of the Trees*)

November 1948

Doc Caliban descends into the deep New England caverns and battles terrifying shapeless creatures and tentacled beings. (*The Monster on Hold*)

Early 1950s

Pauncho van Veelar and Barney Banks serve in the same Marine outfit during the Korean War. (*Lord of the Trees*)

1958

Lord Grandrith first sees James Murtagh during the Nine's grisly annual rites, held in the caves deep in east central Africa. (*Lord of the Trees*)

1966

Doc Caliban cuts off some of his fingers in an effort to isolate elements of the elixir. The fingers regrow, of course. (*A Feast Unknown*)

March 21–April 1968

Events of *A Feast Unknown.*

Death of one member of the Nine, XauXaz, due to extreme old age. He is the first member of the Nine to die in about two thousand years. The last member was XauXaz's brother Thrithjaz, and the "preseating" ceremony which Grandrith, Caliban, and seven other candidates attend is the first to be held since then. (*A Feast Unknown*)

Grandrith and Caliban discover they are half-brothers, and after overcoming the madness brought on by the Nine's elixir, they turn against the Nine. (*A Feast Unknown*)

In "The Wild Huntsman," it is revealed that the XauXaz who appeared to die in 1968 in *A Feast Unknown* was actually murdered by his counterpart from the Wold Newton Universe about 250 years earlier, and the parallel universe counterpart had been impersonating him ever since. With the Nine in Grandrith's universe starting to become suspicious of him, the doppelgänger faked his death in 1968, thus setting off the chain of events in the Secrets of the Nine series.

May 1968

In Los Angeles, Lord Grandrith mails the manuscript for

Volume IX of his memoirs (published as *A Feast Unknown*) to a man he believes to be his editor. (*Lord of the Trees*)

In reality, the man is XauXaz from the parallel dimension known as the Wold Newton Universe.

XauXaz travels back to the Wold Newton dimension and, pretending to be a man calling himself "James Claymore," mails the manuscript from Western Samoa (see *A Feast Unknown*) to science-fiction author Philip José Farmer for publication.

Mid 1968

Pauncho van Veelar and Barney Banks, who have not seen their "uncle" Doc Caliban since 1963, are shocked to see that he has still not aged. Caliban recruits them into the fight against the Nine. (*The Mad Goblin*)

1968–1969

Lord Grandrith and Clio circle the globe twice in an effort to shake the Nine from their trail, while Doc Caliban, Trish Wilde, Pauncho, and Barney lie in wait, planning their next move.

Eventually, Doc and company get a line on the location of one of the Nine, Iwaldi, and prepare to go after him. (*The Mad Goblin*)

Meanwhile, Grandrith leaves Clio safely ensconced in a London hideaway (or so he thinks) and heads to Africa to scout out the caves of the Nine. (*Lord of the Trees*)

1969

Events of the intertwined sequels to *A Feast Unknown*: *Lord of the Trees*/ *The Mad Goblin*.

Lord Grandrith kills a member of the Nine, Mubaniga, and another, Jiizfan, dies in the battle at Stonehenge. (*Lord of the Trees*)

Another member, Iwaldi, is killed by James Murtagh during the Stonehenge battle. Murtagh also dies. (*The Mad Goblin*)

With the deaths of XauXaz, Mubaniga, Jiizfan, and Iwaldi, the Nine are left with four empty spots to fill. Surviving members of the Nine are Anana, Ing, Yeshua, Shaumbim, and Tilatoc.

There are ambiguous and sometimes contradictory references to the amount of time that has passed since the events of *A Feast Unknown*—understandable, given that the follow-up manuscripts were separately written by Grandrith (*Lord of the Trees*) and Caliban (*The Mad Goblin*).

Some descriptions in *Lord of the Trees* of the amount of time passed since *A Feast Unknown* indicate that it is still 1968 and that only two months, or eight months, have passed, but other references in both *Lord of the Trees* and *The Mad Goblin* indicate a year has passed, pointing to a 1969 date. There is a reference to "spring" in *The Mad Goblin*, but also two references to the "winter solstice." The conflicting time references—surely purposeful on the part of Grandrith, Caliban, and their editor, Farmer—have resulted in a general 1969 date for these adventures in this Chronology.

1977 / 1984 / 1993

The events of *The Monster on Hold*.

In 1984, in the caverns beneath Maine, which he last visited in 1948, Doc Caliban sees a man who looks remarkably like him from across the dimensional void. The other man is Doc Wildman. (*The Monster on Hold*)

A Brief Sketch of the Wold Newton Universe's XauXaz

Mythological/Religious
Woden/Wotan/Odin.

10,814 B.C.E.

Kethnu. "The Wild Huntsman." Wants Gribardsun's "witch doctor" elixir (it's better than the Nine's elixir; in fact, it's the most effective immortality elixir in two universes).

1720

XauXaz from 1972 (using time distorter based on Eridanean teleportation distorter) travels to the Grandrith/Caliban Universe, kills that universe's XauXaz, and takes his place from 1720 to 1968.

13 December 1795

XauXaz. "The Wild Huntsman." Present at Wold Newton meteor strike (via time travel from 1972); battles Gribardsun; manipulates events to ensure Wold Newton Family comes into existence, knowing he may need their scientific genius in the future.

c. 1810s

Lars Ulf Larsson (in the Grandrith/Caliban Universe). *Image of the Beast*. Norwegian sailor involved with Dolores del Osorojo.

c. 1880s

Wolf Larsen. *The Sea-Wolf*. Marries and abandons Doc Wildman's grandmother.

1912

"Witch doctor." *Tarzan and the Foreign Legion*. Gives Greystoke (later known as Gribardsun) the elixir with blood sharing, so that his younger self can get it back in 10,814 B.C.E.

1917

Baron Ulf von Waldman. "The Adventure of the Fallen Stone." Gribardsun's "witch doctor" elixir doesn't work quite as well on him as it does/did on Gribardsun/Greystoke, and it's starting to wear off; he's seeking help in recreating the elixir.

Undocumented time period

Karl Woldheim. "The Adventure of the Fallen Stone."

Undocumented time period
Carl Waldhaus. "The Adventure of the Fallen Stone."

1918

Baron von Hessel. *Escape from Loki*. Trying to recruit his grandson Wildman to help recreate the "witch doctor" elixir, among other things.

1929–1930
Larsen, the sailor. *At the Mountains of Madness*. Just tagging along . . .

1930s

Acquires an Eridanean distorter.

1937

Baron Karl. *Fortress of Solitude*. Keeping tabs on his grandson (the son of Lili Bugov) battling Wildman in the Wold Newton Universe, as well as his daughter/son (aka Lili Bugov) battling Caliban in the Grandrith/Caliban Universe.

1939

Captain Larsen of the transport ship *Saigon*. *Tarzan and the Castaways*. Probably trying to capture Greystoke to get another blood sample.

1939

Baron Orrest Karl Lestzky. *The Golden Man*. Noted brain surgeon rivaling Doc Wildman.

1944–1946
Dr. Karl Walden. *Hunt the Avenger*. Trying to recruit and strongarm The Avenger into helping recreate the "witch doctor" elixir. The Countess Lilya Zarov, aka Lili Bugov, also is involved.

1948

Dr. Karl Linningen ("Dr. Karl"). *Up from Earth's Center*.

Manipulating Doc Wildman into penetrating the cavernous depths which lead to Shrassk; he also traveled to the Grandrith/Caliban Universe and similarly manipulated Doc Caliban (as "Dr. Carlos").

1967

Dr. Karl Stipier. *Honey West and T.H.E. Cat: A Girl and Her Cat.* Sidelining in selling bioweapons and advanced technology to the highest bidders.

1968

Masquerading as the XauXaz of the Grandrith/Caliban Universe, he fakes his death as that version of XauXaz (XauXaz's death noted in *A Feast Unknown*).

1972

Succeeds in modifying Eridanean teleportation distorter to function as a time distorter ("The Wild Huntsman"). Makes many trips to Grandrith/Caliban universe (each year, 1720–1968), as well as other time periods in the Wold Newton Universe (see prior entries, such as 13 December 1795), and even other "pocket universes" within the pluriverse.

1974

Behind some of the events of *The Scarlet Jaguar.*

1984

Arnie/XauXaz. *The Monster on Hold.*

A Note from the Coauthor

I would be more than remiss if I failed to acknowledge and pay tribute to the extraordinary speculative essays and other works which informed some aspects of *The Monster on Hold*, as well as "The Wild Huntsman."

First and foremost among these is Christopher Paul Carey's "The Green Eyes Have It—Or Are They Blue? or Another Case of Identity Recased" in my *Myths for the Modern Age: Philip José Farmer's Wold Newton Universe* (MonkeyBrain Books, 2005) and revised in Carey's own *The Grandest Adventure: Writings on Philip José Farmer* (Leaky Boot Press, 2018). The latter volume also contains Carey's indispensable "Farmer's *Escape from Loki*: A Closer Look." These works, not incidentally, also inspired the appearance of a certain Trickster, in various guises, in some of my other tales. I am immensely grateful for Carey's work and owe a large debt to it, and to him.

Particularly for "The Wild Huntsman," (which previously appeared in *The Worlds of Philip José Farmer 3: Portraits of a Trickster* [Meteor House, 2012] and *Tales of the Wold Newton Universe* [Titan Books, 2013]), the creatively mythological essays from which I drew, are: Dennis E. Power's "The Royal Jelly Problem," "Triple Tarzan Tangle," and "The Root of the Wold Newton Family Tree" (all available at Power's *The Wold Newton Universe: A Secret History*, www.pjfarmer.com/secret/index.htm); and Jean-Marc Lofficier's "Will There Be Light Tomorrow?" (*Shadowmen: Heroes and Villains of French Pulp Fiction*, Black Coat Press, 2003). Minor, but important, elements were taken from Cheryl L. Huttner's "Name of a Thousand Blue Demons" and Rick Lai's "The Secret History of Captain Nemo" (both in *Myths for the Modern Age*).

It's important to note that while I incorporated many of the speculations presented in the essays noted above, I just as often deviated from them to follow my own path. None of the articles listed above were adopted wholesale.

I also owe a debt to my fellow "fiction" scribes. The notion that an Eridanean (or Capellean) teleportation distorter could be modified into a time distorter comes from Paul Spiteri's "Time Distorter" tales in *Farmerphile* no. 15 and *The Worlds of Philip José Farmer 1: Protean Dimensions* (Meteor House, 2010), although the time distorter herein works differently. "The Wild Huntsman" also has ties to John Allen Small's "Into Time's Abyss" (*The Worlds of Philip José Farmer 2: Of Dust and Soul*, Meteor House, 2011) and Christopher Paul Carey's novella *Exiles of Kho* (Meteor House, 2012) which I'll let readers suss out for themselves.

Readers of *Myths for the Modern Age* may note that "The Wild Huntsman" contradicts my own "Who's Going to Take Over the World When I'm Gone? (A Look at the Genealogies of Wold Newton Family Super-Villains and Their Nemeses)" in its treatment of Baron von Hessel. My only defense in this regard is that someone, somewhere along the way, must have been lying.

It does happen.

Which brings us to *The Monster on Hold*. If you've read both *Monster* and "Huntsman," and didn't first skip ahead to read this volume's back matter, you know that I incorporated elements of the latter into the former. And though I maintain that the latter is true in spirit to the themes and myths found in Farmer's work, it is wholly my own extrapolation. Which is why, for the posthumously collaborative *Monster*, and for the reader's benefit, we have also included in this volume as much of Farmer's original notes and prose as possible.

Unlike the situation with *The Evil in Pemberley House*, I did not have the opportunity to discuss *Monster* with Phil and Bette. No one, save Phil himself, could have finished *Monster* the way he would have. But I did my utmost to follow the directions in which his notes, outline, and prose pointed, and to complete the manuscript in a manner faithful to the themes and mythologies which run throughout his work.

And I can never express enough gratitude to Phil, for I do believe his notes and outline did indeed point the way. I wish he had completed the book, and am honored that his estate allowed me to do so.

I've been asked if one must read (or reread) the first three novels in the Secrets of the Nine series in order to understand and enjoy *Monster*. My response to this, firstly, is, presumably speaking to a Farmer fan, "Why wouldn't you want to?" followed by, "It is the fourth in a series, after all . . ." Nonetheless, I did my best to recap prior events so that *Monster* can be read and understood as a stand-alone. I reiterate, however, that readers' enjoyment of the book and understanding of certain references may be enhanced with the three prior books, *A Feast Unknown*, *Lord of the Trees*, and *The Mad Goblin*, fresh in their minds.

Lastly, because everything is connected, I recommend other Farmer books and stories which may shed light on this or that aspect of the novel: *Tarzan Alive: A Definitive Biography of Lord Greystoke*, *Doc Savage: His Apocalyptic Life*, *Image of the Beast*, *Blown*, *Love Song*, *Time's Last Gift*, *The Other Log of Phileas Fogg*, *The Adventure of the Peerless Peer*, "The Problem of the Sore Bridge—Among Others," *Gods of Opar: Tales of Lost Khokarsa* (*Hadon of Ancient Opar*, *Flight to Opar*, and *The Song of Kwasin*), *Ironcastle*, *Escape from Loki: Doc Savage's First Adventure*, *Tarzan and the Dark Heart of Time*, *The Evil in Pemberley House*, *Up from the Bottomless Pit*, and the World of Tiers series.

Win Scott Eckert
Somewhere in the wilds of Colorado
September 2021

About the Authors

Philip José Farmer was born on January 26, 1918 in North Terre Haute, Indiana. He grew up in Peoria, Illinois where he spent much of his childhood reading everything from the Bible and books on mythology to the classics by Baum, Carroll, Cervantes, Defoe, Dickens, Homer, London, Swift, and Twain to popular works by Burroughs, Doyle, Haggard, Verne, and Wells.

He sold his first story, a mainstream tale titled "O'Brien and Obrenov," to *Adventure* in 1946 before he decided to try his hand at science fiction. His next published story, "The Lovers," appeared in the August 1952 issue of *Startling Stories*, and is noted for breaking the taboo on sex in science fiction, as well as for earning Farmer a Hugo Award for "Most Promising New Talent."

Married and with two children, he soon quit his job to become a full-time writer, but after selling several more stories to the science fiction pulps, his career hit a stumbling block when he "won" the Shasta Prize Novel Contest. The grand prize was four thousand dollars (a lot of money in 1953), but he never received his winnings. Instead, the publisher asked Farmer for rewrites while the prize money was invested in another book, which bombed. By the time the truth came out, Farmer had lost his house and was forced to take up full time employment.

Farmer left Peoria with his family in 1956 and moved around the country working as a technical writer for the space-defense industry, eventually ending up in Beverly Hills, California in 1965. All the while he continued to write and sell science fiction short stories and novels, launching his popular World of Tiers series and even winning a second Hugo Award for the novella "Riders of the Purple Wage." Then, just before the moon landing in 1969, he was laid off from his technical writing job, so he decided to write fiction full time once again. This time it stuck.

In 1970, Farmer moved back to Peoria with his family and again his career began to take off, this time with a third Hugo Award win, for *To Your Scattered Bodies Go*, the opening novel in his bestselling Riverworld series. For the next few years Farmer sought inspiration from the popular literature he so loved, writing novels such as *The Mad Goblin* (a Doc Savage pastiche), *Lord of the Trees* and *Lord Tyger* (both Tarzan pastiches), *The Wind Whales of Ishmael* (a science fiction sequel to *Moby Dick*), *The Other Log of Phileas Fogg* (the "true" story behind Jules Verne's *Around the World in Eighty Days*), and *Venus on the Half-Shell* (written as if by Kilgore Trout, a character from the works of Kurt Vonnegut). He also wrote two "biographies" during this period: *Tarzan Alive: A Definitive Biography of Lord Greystoke* and *Doc Savage: His Apocalyptic Life*.

The next two decades saw the publication of the Dayworld trilogy, as well as further installments in the Riverworld and World of Tiers series. Farmer also fulfilled his lifelong ambition to write an Oz novel, and authorized Doc Savage and Tarzan novels, with the publication of *A Barnstormer in Oz*, *Escape from Loki*, and *Tarzan and the Dark Heart of Time*. Late in his career, Farmer tried his hand at a different genre with *Nothing Burns in Hell*, a detective novel set in his hometown of Peoria.

After Farmer retired from writing in 1999, new collections such as *Pearls from Peoria* and *Venus on the Half-Shell and Others* continued to appear, as did new collaborative works such as *The Evil in Pemberley House* (with Win Scott Eckert), *The Song of Kwasin* (with Christopher Paul Carey), and *Dayworld: A Hole in Wednesday* (with Danny Adams).

Farmer passed on February 25, 2009, but his fan base is as ardent as ever, still gathering at annual FarmerCons.

Win Scott Eckert is a novelist, editor, essayist, and writer of short fiction. He is steeped in the works of famed science fiction writer Philip José Farmer, particularly Farmer's shared universe literary-crossover Wold Newton cycle and the Lord Grandrith/Doc Caliban series. He has a deep interest in studying fictional biographies, creating detailed chronologies of fictional characters and universes, and exploring the metafictional connections between seemingly unrelated works, which resulted in *Myths for the Modern Age: Philip José Farmer's Wold Newton Universe* (MonkeyBrain Books), a 2007 Locus Awards finalist, and the critically acclaimed, encyclopedic *Crossovers: A Secret Chronology of the World 1 & 2* (Black Coat Press, 2010).

Eckert has also chronicled the exploits of popular characters, including Zorro, Sexton Blake, the Phantom, Honey West, the Scarlet Pimpernel, the Domino Lady, and the Green Hornet, all of which can be found in the pages of anthologies from Moonstone Books, Meteor House (*The Worlds of Philip José Farmer*), Black Coat Press (*Tales of the Shadowmen*), and Titan Books (*Tales of the Wold Newton Universe*).

He contributed a new foreword to the 2006 edition of Farmer's well-known fictional biography, *Tarzan Alive: A Definitive Biography of Lord Greystoke* (University of Nebraska/Bison Books), as well as several forewords and afterwords to Titan Books' reissues of Farmer's novels. He played a key role in reissuing Meteor House's definitive editions of Farmer's fictional biography *Doc Savage: His Apocalyptic Life* (2013), and Farmer's authorized Burroughs novel, *Tarzan and the Dark Heart of Time* (2018).

Eckert is the authorized legacy author of Farmer's Patricia Wildman series (*The Evil in Pemberley House*, *The Scarlet Jaguar*). His latest releases are an authorized Avenger book from Moonstone, *Hunt the Avenger* (2019), and an authorized novel in the new Edgar Rice Burroughs Universe, *Tarzan: Battle for Pellucidar* (2020).

Find him online at www.winscotteckert.com and @woldnewton (Twitter).

METEOR HOUSE TITLES

THE WORLDS OF PHILIP JOSÉ FARMER
Anthology Series edited by Michael Croteau
Volume 1: Protean Dimensions
Volume 2: Of Dust and Soul
Volume 3: Portraits of a Trickster
Volume 4: Voyages to Strange Days

The Man Who Met Tarzan by Philip José Farmer
A Rough Knight for the Queen by Philip José Farmer
The Best of Farmerphile edited by Michael Croteau
The Philip José Farmer Centennial Collection edited by Michael Croteau
Greatheart Silver and Other Pulp Heroes by Philip José Farmer
Up from the Bottomless Pit by Philip José Farmer

SECRETS OF THE NINE SERIES
The Monster on Hold by Win Scott Eckert
It's Always Darkest by Frank Schildiner

WOLD NEWTON SERIES
Doc Savage: His Apocalyptic Life by Philip José Farmer
Tarzan and the Dark Heart of Time by Philip José Farmer

THE KHOKARSA SERIES
Exiles of Kho by Christopher Paul Carey
Flight to Opar (Restored Edition) by Philip José Farmer
The Song of Kwasin by Philip José Farmer and Christopher Paul Carey
Hadon, King of Opar by Christopher Paul Carey
Blood of Ancient Opar by Christopher Paul Carey

THE PAT WILDMAN SERIES
The Evil in Pemberley House by Philip José Farmer and Win Scott Eckert
The Scarlet Jaguar by Win Scott Eckert

THE PHILEAS FOGG SERIES
Phileas Fogg and the War of Shadows by Josh Reynolds
Phileas Fogg and the Heart of Osra by Josh Reynolds